MORE THAN DEAD

MORE THAN DEAD

Luke Hudson Mystery 1

Shannon, enjoy the ride!
S Resler Nelson

S Resler Nelson

ISBN: 1512159778
ISBN 13: 9781512159776

DEDICATION

With love and remembrance of my parents
Eugene Everett Resler, Sr.
Harriett Louise Resler

ACKNOWLEDGEMENTS

I would like to give special thanks the following people for their contributions to this novel: Marion Hansen, Ned Welker, Linda Smith, Dr. Kay Wood, Dr. Bryan Nolte DVM, former Police Chief Mark Moline, Officer Lenny Bruno, author Deborah Cox, and especially my husband, Paul.

PART I – A LONG SHOT

"A difference of opinion is what makes horse racing and missionaries."

–Will Rogers

CHAPTER 1

Sunrise hovered in the East, two hours away, as Kayla Owens drove in darkness to the Long Meadows Racetrack. After the turmoil last night, she questioned her decision to arrive before anyone else in her barn, but curiosity and impatience overruled caution. Kayla slowed and stopped her old Honda Accord at the security gate. She anticipated the night guard wouldn't recognize her so she flashed her credentials. He glanced at the pass and waved her through. Her exercise rider's license allowed her on the track's backside, which was closed to the general public. But along with that privilege, all employees were monitored.

Kayla parked behind Shed Row D, where the trainer she worked for stalled his horses. She locked her car and carried her Styrofoam cup of coffee and half eaten breakfast sandwich. A chill March wind cut through her thin jacket and she shivered. Bits of sawdust and an unclaimed betting ticket blew across her path.

Inside the shed row, concrete block walls barred most of the wind. Few lights shone overhead, just enough to see, so horses could rest without the glare. She placed her coffee and sandwich on an upended bucket and approached a stall with the stable sign Dark Saint on the door. Scheduled

3

to ride the colt in less than two hours, she wondered how the impetuous three-year-old would perform.

Stepping closer, she peered through the open top-half of the stall door. The colt had paced for some time judging by his deep, irregular oval path carved in the sawdust. Kayla puzzled why he still wore his halter and a lead rope that dragged on the ground and could tangle in his legs.

The horse stopped at the far left corner and eyed her with suspicion. He was as dark as the night except for a small star on his forehead. When the colt tossed his head and moved again, Kayla's eyes followed his trembling body as he rounded the front right corner.

Shocked, she gasped and covered her mouth to suppress a scream. Her boss lay in a fetal position in the sawdust, his back protecting his body from the horse. He faced the front wall, his neck twisted and head upturned, staring at her with glassy blue eyes.

She stumbled backwards in disbelief and then stepped forward to gaze into the stall again. Fighting for composure, she pulled her cell phone from her pocket and punched in 911. A female dispatcher came on the line, and Kayla gushed, "I'm at the Long Meadows Racetrack, and I...I just discovered my boss, Jack Monroe. He's in a stall with a horse and he's lying on the ground. I think he's dead."

The dispatcher asked, "Are you in any danger?"

"I don't know." She wandered to the shed row's main light switches. "I just turned on all the lights and I don't see anyone around."

"Do you want to remain on the line until the police arrive?"

"No, I think I'll be okay." She gave her name and described her location, then was told first responders would arrive soon.

"Please tell them no sirens. That will spook the horse even more."

The dispatcher left her with one demand. "In the meantime, do not go in the stall or disturb anything around the area. Leave that to the professionals. Okay?"

"Okay," she promised and ended the call.

Kayla turned away from the stalls and fixated on the shadowy night, avoiding the thought of her prone boss, but she couldn't erase the image of his lifeless face. Still shaking, she diverted her eyes back to the shed row and all the empty stalls.

During the past year, she had watched Monroe's position as a top trainer decline. She exercised his horses to gain enough experience for a jockey's license. What would happen to her now? In her twenty-two years, Kayla had lived on the fringe of poverty with a hard working mother, a deadbeat father, and no siblings. Medium height, slim, and muscular, she was built for riding sport horses. Her path to success would be through the track, if she didn't get injured or killed first. Racing was a dangerous business.

Kayla meandered back to Dark Saint, and looked in as he continued pacing clockwise past Monroe. The colt stopped at the bunched body, lowered his head, sniffed, and snorted a long, soft sigh. He sensed death.

A PHONE CALL AROUSED DETECTIVE LUKE HUDSON from a deep sleep. Reluctant to answer, he fumbled in the dark and picked up on the fifth ring. He glanced at the digital clock on his dresser, five forty-five Sunday morning.

"Hudson? Sergeant Ross here," his boss grumbled. "We have a situation at the racetrack. A trainer at Long Meadows was found on the ground in a horse's stall about fifteen minutes ago. They think he's dead."

"What the hell?" Luke doubted, still half asleep.

"First responders are standing around waiting for someone with horse sense to show up. I figure that's you. Consider this a Code 3 and go to Shed Row D."

The Sergeant didn't sound in a good mood.

Hudson rolled out of bed and dressed, splashed cologne on his face, ran a comb through his unruly hair, and grabbed a tie he'd put on later. He scooped up his wallet, keys, badge, and belt, and strapped on his gun. Most off-duty calls were emergencies, and he had encountered this routine often in his twenty-four years of law enforcement. Until five years ago, his wife slept in the bed beside him. He remembered how much she hated those calls. She often turned in silence to face the wall and go back to sleep, but he'd hear about it later in some subtle way.

He rushed from his duplex and backed his unmarked, black SUV out of the garage. Clearing the driveway, he turned into the quiet tree-lined street. Pre-dawn on a Sunday, the traffic was light, so he made good time without sirens and flashing lights. Bidwell city buildings faded to suburban homes, then country properties and open fields, before he curved onto Long Meadows Road that led to the track.

Hudson followed California racing and had for years, not to gamble, but to reconnect with horses and his past. He knew horses died on the track and so did jockeys. But a trainer killed at a racetrack was about as rare as a snowstorm in Death Valley.

Arriving at Long Meadows, he drove to the backside security gate, flashed his badge, and a guard signaled him through.

Almost a thousand race horses stabled in some forty shed rows on the backside that sprawled left of the main track and towering grandstands. The structures hid in dark silhouettes, except for Shed Row D, flooded with lights.

Hudson reached the barn and found two cop cars, an ambulance, and the EMT van, all with lights flashing. He pulled in behind the van and stopped.

Emerging from the warmth of his Tahoe, he stepped into the frigid predawn air. His partner, Jimmy Kidder, was there to greet him. They looked enough alike to be father and son—both tall, dark haired, and blue eyed.

More wide-eyed than usual, Kidder shook his buzz-cut head and ventured, "Man, this is something else. I rode out with a patrol and we've all been waiting for you."

Luke had never encountered a scene like this one. An enormous black horse occupied the stall with the downed victim. Distressed and high-strung, the horse bounced around, tossing his head from side to side, as he snorted and pawed the ground. Responders stood frozen, power-less to act.

Immediately, Hudson ordered the responders to cut their emergency lights, keep their voices low, and stand back to give the horse some room. Then he asked Kidder if the 911 caller was present. He said that would be Kayla Owens and pointed to her. Jimmy added that she discovered the victim, who was her boss. Luke surmised that if she worked for the trainer, she'd know how to handle the rowdy Thoroughbred.

When the two approached her, Owens stiffened, sizing up Hudson—another detective, no doubt. He wore a dark blue suit, no tie, and walked with a distinguished air despite his slight limp. Kidder, whom she had met, followed alongside. Bidwell Police Department badges hung around their necks on lanyards like masculine necklaces.

"Are you Kayla Owens?" Hudson asked.

"Yes," she answered, and with hesitation shook his outstretched hand.

"I'm Detective Luke Hudson, Bidwell Police," he announced.

Owens held back, ill at ease. He guessed she was younger than twenty five, but then the older he got the harder it was to discern age. In the March cold, she wore a baggy coat and jeans on her petite, lean body. Short, dark hair framed an attractive, fine featured face.

She pointed to the right. "My boss, uh…Mr. Monroe, is in the front corner of the stall, with the horse."

"Don't go anywhere," he ordered her.

He and Kidder turned and walked to an EMT in charge. Hudson noticed the horse had stopped to grab a bite of hay and carried it in his mouth as he pranced around, a sign the colt had focused for a moment on something more than the crowd of spectators.

Luke told the EMT, "When the horse calms down a little more, we can get him out of the stall so you can assess the victim."

"Good, cause the damned horse has put everything on hold."

"I know," said Hudson, remaining calm. "I'm working on it."

CHAPTER 2

Alone, Luke advanced to the stall, speaking to the nervous horse in a soft voice, careful not to rile him further. He stared over the top door at the trainer curled on the ground. A rugged looking man, he was middle aged with graying hair and strong features. Lying on his side, his upturned face stared at the overhead beams. Hudson motioned for a photographer to join him and take photos while the horse remained in the stall with the victim. He cautioned, "No sudden moves and no more photographs than necessary. The flashes will get this horse going again."

The tech was quiet as he took several photos, trying to get quick shots while the horse stomped around the stall. Dark Saint bared his teeth and charged the young man, forcing him to dodge the assaults. The colt was making a game of going after the photographer, so Luke was relieved when the tech finished, lowered his camera, and stepped back.

"I didn't touch anything," Kayla offered from afar. "I was told not to disturb things."

"That's good," Hudson countered, "but we need to move the horse so we can process the scene. Can you do that?"

"I think I can handle him," Kayla said with measured assurance, as she approached the stall.

"Is this the position you found him in?" Hudson gestured at the victim.

She nodded yes and stood still, studying Dark Saint's mood. He seemed to have settled some, no longer vocalizing and leaping around.

In a resolute move, she opened the stall door and closed it behind her, as Hudson bolted it shut. She focused her eyes on the horse and avoided looking at the body in the corner.

"Easy, Saint," she said several times, trying to calm him. When the horse stepped on his trailing lead rope, she grabbed it. Once she had a solid hold on him, the edgy colt became more controllable. Whispering to him, she rubbed and scratched his neck until he relaxed enough to lower his head.

Kayla raised her voice to those outside the stall and warned, "You'd better all stand back. He may come blasting out the door."

Everyone backed away, giving her room to bring Dark Saint out. In spite of her strong grip on the lead rope, the colt bolted through the door and whirled, yanking her with him. He reared his head and snorted the loud, air-filled blast horses spew when confronting danger. On-lookers fanned out, giving her an even wider berth.

Detective Hudson stared in awe as she led the dancing horse to an adjoining stall. He knew race horses and this one was magnificent. A tall seventeen hands high, the horse exuded class, and his black coat shimmered under the lights.

"Close the door behind me," she said to no one in particular. Hudson latched it, and stood at the stall. When she unclipped the rope from the halter and stepped back towards the door, he reopened it.

"Well done," he told her, and turned to the medical team and first responders. "Now we can get to work." Within seconds, the paramedics were with the victim. Several crime scene technicians crowded in the twelve by twelve stall. In turn, they photographed the body, took measurements, made diagrams of the victim's location, and began searching for evidence, collecting and labeling anything of interest. They all wore sterile latex gloves.

Luke saw that the medical examiner, Ned Jackson, and his team had arrived, so he and Jimmy joined them. The foregone conclusion must be that the victim was dead.

"Holy shit," Ned grimaced as he addressed Hudson. "Have you ever seen anything like this?"

"Can't say that I have," Luke frowned. "It's one for the books."

Ned was eager for his turn to investigate the scene. Medium statured and wiry, Jackson lacked little patience when a corpse demanded his observant and methodical attention. As soon as the EMTs and CSI techs vacated the stall, Ned and his team moved in.

Hudson and Kidder chose to stay out of the way for the moment. Luke spotted Kayla Owens and kept an eye on her, telling Jimmy to do the same. "We don't want her ducking out."

He walked to an officer who was ready to put up yellow crime scene tape, and together they decided how much of the shed row should be cordoned off. The two secured the tape, wrapping it around the overhang posts, to keep people away from the stalls and breezeway. A few racetrack employees, grooms, and trainers had gathered, and the officer asked them to step back. With the area cordoned off, another officer began signing in those responders who crossed the tape line. Luke told Jimmy to have Kayla Owens sign in and keep her close to him. Those inside the crime scene area could be asked to sign statements and appear in court regarding the case.

Then Hudson returned to the victim's stall, now less crowded.

"We found this in the sawdust, under his body," Ned remarked to Luke, holding up a syringe with a bent needle intact, now enclosed in a plastic evidence bag. "It looks like there's enough of the contents left to test the composition."

"Good. What's your initial assessment of the vic?" he asked Ned. "Can you tell if he was injured by the horse?"

Ned shoved his wire-rimmed glasses back up the bridge of his nose and continued exploring the body while he talked, unbuttoning and opening Monroe's shirt. "That will have to be determined when I get him on the table. There's no blood or obvious broken bones, but he does have a puncture wound in his right hand. He appears to have been dead for close to three hours, but again, we need tests to substantiate time and cause of death. Soon as we can get him out of here, we will."

Luke understood the broad use of drugs around race-tracks. He beckoned to his partner, who was standing near the open stall door, seeming a bit lost or else deep in thought. "Jimmy, they found a syringe in the stall, so we need a track vet out here to draw blood on the horse and check for any drugs. It's possible that the trainer gave the horse a shot. Also, have a technician assist the vet in checking the horse's hooves, looking for traces of the victim's blood, body tissue, hair, and fibers, anything that might indicate the horse came in contact with the deceased."

A track security guard was now on the scene and Jimmy sought his aid in calling a veterinarian.

Hudson turned his attention back to Jackson and said, "According to the 911 caller, the victim is a horse trainer by the name of Jack Monroe. He has a son who works as his assistant trainer. That's all we know about him for now."

He stayed with Ned, observing and asking questions, jotting down bits of information. Before the team brought in a stretcher and body bag, the victim's hands were bagged to protect any stray tissue under the nails or contamination of the puncture mark. When Monroe was removed, the technicians moved in to further collect specimens from the concrete block walls and examine the ground he had occupied.

Luke was surprised to see Police Chief Tom Walker eyeing the body, now covered and on a gurney, being carried from the stall. He knew Walker's presence meant the Chief would micromanage the case.

The rank and file often referred to Walker as a hard ass. He had served in the military and then law enforcement in Chicago, the murder capital of the country. Walker left his post as a Chicago PD captain about six years ago to become Bidwell's police chief, but the small California town atmosphere failed to relax his leadership style. He remained strict, adhered to a firm militaristic chain of command, and lacked the slightest sense of humor.

Walker looked at Hudson and motioned to him. Luke nodded as he approached the Chief, who stood outside the crime scene perimeter.

"Hudson, what do we have so far?" Walker asked, while he diverted glances to the overall action.

"Sir, the victim was dead upon our arrival," he began, and brought Walker up to speed. "As for the deceased, Jack Monroe was a prominent trainer, one of the bigger names at Long Meadows."

The Chief grimaced, not pleased with the revelation that Monroe was a high profile trainer.

Hudson continued, "I want to question Monroe's employees as soon as possible this morning. So far, we have a pretty short list—just Owens, who discovered the body; the assistant trainer Shawn Monroe, who was his son; and a groom, Carlos Montoya."

The Chief interjected, "It's my understanding that the son has been notified and is on his way to the track. The deceased was divorced and had no other children. It's just as well that the body's been removed. It's never easy dealing with next of kin."

Walker's voice trailed then came back strong to the issue at hand. "Hudson, I want your full attention on this case. Wrap up the initial investigation here and then go to headquarters. If this guy is well-known, his death is going to get a lot of publicity, so we have to handle it with care."

The Chief was stocky and pudgy, his belt disappearing under his overlapping belly. An abrupt, private man, he had grown more aloof in the last year or so, further distancing himself from his officers. Without another word, the Chief walked away and wandered over to talk to Homicide Sergeant Robert Ross, Luke's superior.

Hudson discounted the Chief's attitude and returned to the unfinished task of securing the area and leaving an officer on duty to continue surveillance. All curiosity seekers would be questioned because sometimes a perpetrator returns to the scene as an onlooker, while seeking the thrill of reliving the crime. He had seen numerous deaths as he worked his way up to Detective Level III in the LAPD, and they were all different. The slightest observation or tiniest shred of evidence might unravel a crime.

He glanced at his watch. Six-thirty and the sun still hid below the mountains in the East, casting a thin blue line along the horizon. The backside stirred with grooms, trainers, exercise riders, hot walkers, and jockeys. Most of them attended horses and ignored the turmoil at Shed Row

D. Hudson wondered where the trainer's other employees were, while nearby, Kidder talked to the veterinarian.

Kayla appeared alone in spite of all the commotion around her, so Luke ambled over to her.

"How are you holding up?" he asked.

"Not well. Can I leave now? I have a dog at home I need to go feed, and I can't take much more of this," she said, looking around in dismay, fighting back tears.

The dog feeding comment struck him as odd.

"Don't you feed your dog before you come to work?"

She objected to his question. "Not always. I think I forgot this morning. None of this is the way it was supposed to be."

"And what were you expecting?"

"I was supposed to ride Dark Saint in a timed workout this morning. Now who knows what will happen," she said as a statement not a question.

"Do you usually arrive before anyone else from your barn?" he pressed her.

Again, his probing annoyed her. "No, but I thought I'd get here early today since I was riding Saint. I was going to eat, clean and check tack, and be ready. Besides, we had a sick horse yesterday evening so I thought I could check on him."

"Why was the horse sick?"

"Shawn Monroe knows the details," she answered, dodging specifics.

"Do you feel safe coming in ahead of others and being pretty much alone here?"

"Yes," she answered. "There're usually a few people around. Anyways, I'm here at feeding time, which starts around six. Things are running late today."

"Is there anyone else who should be here by now?" He kept the conversation going. She relaxed more with questions not concerning her.

"Well, Mr. Monroe was often here even a bit before six, and his son, too. And then the groom, Carlos Montoya, gets here around six and so do I."

Hudson prepped her for a trip to headquarters. "Well, we need to get a statement from you at the police station."

Her eyes flashed fear. "Am I a suspect or something?"

"No, but since you were first to find the vic..., uh, your boss, we need to ask you some routine questions and this is not a good place to talk."

He observed Kayla's bloodshot eyes, either from crying or sleep deprivation, and added, "You don't look like you're in shape to be behind the wheel. Detective Kidder and I will drive you in. It won't take that long, and then we'll bring you back to your car. Okay?"

Kayla looked at the bucket where she'd left her coffee and sandwich. A barn cat had helped itself to the unfinished food and overturned the latte. In his new stall, Dark Saint huddled in a corner, with his rump to the door and his head down, blocking it all out.

Owens waved at a striking young man walking towards her. He was tall, about Kidder's age, frowning and glancing about, upset by the disorder in the barn.

"That's Shawn, my boss's son," she explained to the detectives, relieved to see him.

"Stay put," Hudson told her, and ducked under the tape, making his way to the son. He wanted to take him aside and ease the shock of his father's death. This was the hardest part of his job and one he seldom dealt with in such a direct manner.

They met beyond the crime scene activity and Luke held out his hand. "Detective Luke Hudson, Bidwell Police. I gather you're Shawn Monroe?"

He nodded and they shook hands. Luke continued, "I'm in charge of your dad's case. Sorry about what happened. It's a damn shame."

Young Monroe asked, "Is my dad still here?"

"The ambulance took his body about five minutes ago."

"I wanted to come here and take care of the horses first. It's what Dad would have wanted me to do."

"Sure," Luke said. "Understandable."

Shawn looked around. "What's Kayla doing here?"

"She made the 911 call around 5:30 this morning. She discovered your dad in Dark Saint's stall. What is her exact connection with your stable?"

"She's licensed as both an exercise rider and a groom, so she works in both capacities. She usually rides claimers and allowance horses, but she was stepping up to work a horse of Dark Saint's caliber. I imagine she's pretty disappointed."

He paused and his eyes searched again for Kayla beyond the tape. "Well, since she's here, I'll put her to work feeding the horses."

Hudson interrupted that thought. "Actually, we're planning to take her to headquarters for questioning. And when you're free, we'd like to talk to you, too. Get some feedback from you and fill you in on what's going on."

The son was uneasy. "That will work, I guess. We have a groom, Carlos Montoya, who should be here any minute now. He can feed and take care of things while I'm gone. I just need to check on Saint, and look in on a horse that was sick yesterday."

Luke asked, "When did Montoya leave last evening?"

"Oh, he and Kayla were here until about seven, since they were caring for a horse with a drug reaction. I'll explain that later."

The son hesitated, "As soon as I can leave, I guess I should go see Dad at the morgue, but I want to remember him the way he was." Fidgeting, head lowered, he struggled with the finality of his dad's death. Hudson was uncomfortable, too. No words soothed a moment like this.

Then the young trainer stared the detective straight in the eye, "I have to ask. Did it look like Dad was killed by the horse?"

"That hasn't been determined yet. The autopsy will be the definitive word."

Shawn mumbled. "Dad loved horses, so I wouldn't want him to go that way."

Hudson avoided mention of the hypodermic needle found under his dad, keeping that for later. While they talked, the son slipped quick glances at Kayla, often enough that Hudson thought it worth noting.

He told Shawn to finish his chores here, go see his dad at the morgue, then come to the police headquarters.

Shawn asked, "When is Kayla going in for Q and A?"

"As soon as possible," Luke assured him.

Carlos Montoya arrived in the shed row and walked up to Shawn. The groom was short in stature but sturdy, with dark hair and eyes, Hispanic, and fortyish.

"What's goin' on, boss? Is someone hurt?" he asked, nonplussed and confused.

Shawn Monroe deferred to Hudson, who told Carlos what had happened. Dismayed, Carlos shook his head.

Luke asked Carlos what time he left last night and Carlos reaffirmed his departure.

"I go around seven. That when Mr. Monroe and Shawn go, too."

Hudson asked, "What about Kayla?"

"She offer to watch the horse a leetle longer. Said she no mind."

"And why was the horse sick?" Luke inquired of Carlos.

Before he could answer, Shawn interrupted. "It's a long story. I said I'll explain later."

Luke ignored the son and persisted with Carlos, "Then give me the short version."

"Go Laddie Go, he sick on Lasix. He breathe too hard and that dangerous. So Doc come and we stay round 'til Laddie better."

Carlos's English was a little rough and he started to apologize, but Luke waved his hand and said, "*No hay problema.* That's about all I know in Spanish," he grinned and Carlos relaxed.

Hudson continued with Carlos. "Where did you go when you left the track?"

Comfortable with the questions, Carlos replied, "I go home and eat. My wife have neighbors over and they stay 'til...umm, ten. Then I go to bed. I give you names and you talk to my wife."

Luke got contact information and said he would do a routine follow-up.

"When you left last night, did you notice anything unusual, other than the horse's problem?"

Carlos answered, "Mr. Monroe mad about sick horse. He say he might be back. I offer to come back, but he say it his problem."

"We were all concerned," Shawn interjected.

"And where were you last night?" Hudson asked the son to get a reaction.

"I'm surprised you'd even ask," he huffed, "but Dad and I went home together, ate dinner, and went to bed. We live in the same house, but I didn't hear him leave and go back to the track."

Luke considered Shawn's demeanor too composed. He was either in shock or indifferent.

CHAPTER 3

On the drive back to headquarters, the sun peered over the purple snow-capped mountains. Everyone was silent. Luke drove, with Jimmy in the passenger seat, staring out the side window, and Kayla in back. There was nothing like the sudden death of a good person to make one reflective.

As the miles rolled by, Luke pondered his own life, something he hadn't done in a while. He was 49 and divorced, with no kids. Sometimes he missed not having children, but Jimmy Kidder was like a son to him. In fact, he called him Kid some of the time, except around Chief Walker, who would consider that unprofessional. Kidder didn't mind. They began working together soon after Luke was hired by the Bidwell Police Department. Jimmy was raised by an aunt, so Luke figured the kid could use a father figure. In their off time, they went fishing or to the track.

Luke's wife, Sally, left him five years ago when he worked for the LAPD as a detective, and a top one at that. She complained he was married to his job, which was true, and that when he left for work, she never knew if she'd see him alive again, which was also true. She moved out before he was shot in the line of duty, but she visited him in the hospital, even helped him when he first went home. The divorce was amicable and they still talked on the phone from time to time, friendship rather than children bonding them together. Neither remarried.

The shooting incident happened after his divorce. He was in pursuit of an armed robber, running after him though a vacant lot. The punk panicked, spun around, and pulled off several shots. One hit Luke in the right thigh and brought him to the ground. The shooter was never caught, at least not for that crime. Luke couldn't even make a credible ID of him, since he wore a hoody that hid his face. He looked like hundreds of LA kids.

Luke's femur was shattered, necessitating reconstructive surgery, plates and screws, and insertion of a titanium rod. It left him with a long recovery, rehab, and a slight limp. After a leave of absence from the LAPD, he decided not to stay in Los Angeles County and moved to Northern California. Bidwell was a small town of about 50,000, the largest municipality in Park County, and the county seat. Luke welcomed the quieter pace. Maybe Sally wouldn't have left if he'd been a cop here.

Bidwell nestled near the foothills of the Sierras, and a tributary of the Sacramento River meandered along the city's edge. In earlier days, Bidwell was a small farming community, but city expansion and tourism encroached on the pastoral setting. In recent years, farming dwindled, as drought and population growth in the West claimed more water. Only the rugged mountains to the east remained remote.

Luke's mind shifted to the present, and he looked in the rearview mirror at Kayla, who was nodding off, and then at Kidder, who broke the silence.

"How about stopping for a take-out breakfast?" Jimmy proposed. "I'm starved."

They were coming to a fast-food row on the way to the station, so Hudson pulled into the drive-through at McDonald's. Jimmy put in the order: One latte and an egg-and-ham McMuffin for Kayla, plus black coffees and two breakfast burritos, the standard for Luke and himself. Jimmy passed Kayla's food back to her and she thanked him. He and Luke sipped coffee and would wait until they got to headquarters to eat.

At the station, Luke asked Kayla to wait in the reception area while he and Jimmy went into Luke's office to talk and eat their burritos.

They briefly discussed strategy and Hudson explained. "We'll question her in here. It's too intimidating in the interrogation room. I'm hoping she'll relax and open up a little."

Jimmy nodded and stood to bring in Kayla. No sooner had he left the room than the phone rang and Lieutenant Arnold Dodd was on the line.

"Damage control, Luke," Dodd said. "The press is already hounding us about the trainer's death at the track. I told them we have no specifics, that next of kin has been notified, and that we will keep them informed as things unfold. You know nothing."

"That's pretty much the truth," Hudson quipped.

"Anything we feed the press will come from my office."

"Suits me," Hudson agreed, and said he had to go, as Kayla and Kidder entered the room.

Luke pointed her to a seat across the desk from him and told her to make herself comfortable, so she removed her coat and draped it over the back of her chair. Kidder took a seat near Luke, also facing her. Kayla crossed her legs, and Hudson noticed how tired and stressed she looked.

"First of all," Luke started, "we're just trying to piece together what happened last night. You're not a suspect. You are here because you discovered the body of Jack Monroe. As I ask questions, Detective Kidder will take notes. I'd like to record this conversation, with your approval." Technically, he had to get her permission because she hadn't been arrested.

She balked at that. "Why do you have to record it?"

"I don't have to. It's up to you, but recording does help keep an accurate record of what's said."

"Okay, I guess," she said. "I'm ready."

He turned on the recorder.

"Good. I'll start with a question we've asked everyone else connected with your barn. When did you leave the track last night?"

"I was there late. We had a horse, Go Laddie Go, in the last race of the day that reacted to Lasix. Mr. Monroe didn't like using Lasix, but it's something everyone does. I guess it gives a race horse a more competitive edge. It keeps them from bleeding from the lungs."

Luke was interested, "Who is the horse's owner?"

"Mr. Bergman."

"Does he own other horses in training with Monroe?"

She hesitated. "He owns Dark Saint, too."

Jimmy noted that, she observed. "Anyways, the Lasix shot depleted Laddie's body fluids. So after the race he got the thumps and the vet had to give him a lot of electrolytes to counteract the shot. Then me and Carlos had to walk him around the shed row and watch that he didn't have some other side effects. So we stayed until after seven."

"Who was the vet?" Luke asked.

"Doc Riley."

Hudson made a mental note to talk to the vet. "How exactly did the horse act?"

"His sides were heaving with a thumping motion. His heart was beating irregularly, I guess, or too hard, so his breathing was labored. It's not serious if it's treated right away, but a horse can die with it, too, I've heard."

"It sounds like you know something about veterinary medicine," Luke added.

"It's just stuff you pick up."

He saw an opening. "Have you ever given shots to a horse?"

"Heavens, no! Only vets do that." Kayla was emphatic. "It's illegal for trainers and other track personnel to be in possession of syringes and medications."

At this point, Kayla squirmed and Hudson changed the subject. "So how old are you?"

"I'm twenty-two."

"Did you start with Monroe?"

"No, I rode for several trainers before Mr. Monroe hired me last year to work just for him. Unless you have a bunch of horses in training, you can't justify a full time exercise rider, and he had about twenty horses then."

"But you did other odd jobs for him, right?"

"Yes, especially after Mr. Bergman started pulling his horses from the stable."

"Why was Bergman leaving Monroe's barn?"

"You'll have to ask him," she replied, unruffled.

Luke had heard enough about horses. "So you still haven't told us what time you left last evening."

"Oh, I think everyone at our barn left around seven except me. I told Mr. Monroe I would stick around and check in later on Laddie."

"So when did you wrap it up?" he persisted.

"I don't know."

"You don't know?"

"No, I wasn't wearing a watch and I went back to my car to eat a sandwich from my cooler, drink a Coke, and relax. You know, listen to music. I must have dozed off. It was later when I woke up. I checked on the horse one last time and headed home."

He distrusted her ambiguous answers. "So if you don't know what time you left the track, what time did you get home? Surely you noticed then."

"Well, I didn't. What's the big deal?"

Luke was getting irritated. "The big deal is that we know when your boss died, and we'd like to know who was around then, and what they might have seen. Does that make sense?"

"Yes," she muttered, contrite. "I'm just tired. I told you I didn't see anything and if I did, I'd tell you."

Hudson wasn't done. "How well did you get along with Jack Monroe?"

"We got along good. I was grateful for the breaks he gave me. He was a nice man." She offered no other specifics.

Luke wanted a reaction. "How about your relationship with his son?"

"What do you mean," she flashed.

"How well do you get along with him?"

"Fine, but Mr. Monroe called the shots. He ran a tight ship."

Luke suspected the last comment wasn't her words, but something she'd heard. "And by a 'tight ship' you mean..."

"Shawn ran the daily barn stuff, but Mr. Monroe ran the horses."

"In other words, Shawn didn't share in the training," he paraphrased.

"I didn't say that."

"You implied it," he countered. "So when you exercised horses, Jack Monroe gave the orders?"

"Yes. After all, it was his stable," she said, backing off. "Shawn was just the assistant."

"How well did the two of them get along? In your opinion."

"How am I supposed to know all this inside stuff?"

Luke tired of her playing him. "For someone who rides horses for a living, I would expect you to be observant. Now, please answer the question."

"They got along good. Shawn respected his dad and was trying to learn all he could. That's what I *observed*," she replied, with sarcasm.

She was either cocky by nature, tired and crabby, or not being upfront. Luke settled on his last impression and changed directions. "What was Jack Monroe's mood last night?"

"How would I know?" she scowled, still defiant and surly.

"Well, let's put it another way. Did Monroe blame anyone for the sick horse or did he take responsibility, since he called all the shots?"

"I haven't the faintest idea," she lied, and Luke knew it. He would deal with her later, after they talked with Monroe's son.

Hudson rose and said, "Thanks, I think we're done. Please wait outside my office and we'll join you in a minute."

She picked up her coat and purse and started to leave without looking back.

"One last thing." Luke's remark stopped her. "There was an empty syringe with hypodermic needle found in Dark Saint's stall."

She looked back at him, perturbed. "So that's what your questioning was about. Let me tell you something. It doesn't surprise me at all. There are enough drugs going around the track that anyone could have chucked it in the stall. It's happened before." With that, she walked out and closed the door.

Jimmy hung back to talk with Luke.

"Why was she so combative? Do you think she's hiding something?" Jimmy posed.

"She had a quick comeback for the shot, and by her own admission she was at the track late. I'd like to know how late. Officer Tate said the security guard doesn't recall what time Kayla left, but admitted he doesn't pay much attention to people leaving, just coming in."

"Well, she wasn't much help," Jimmy noted, "and her behavior was suspicious, if you ask me."

"I'm with you." Luke said. "It'll be interesting to see how Shawn reacts to questioning. I also want to know more about Bergman. Jack Monroe was one of the best known trainers at Long Meadows, so if Bergman was pulling horses away, maybe there was an owner-trainer rift."

Luke paused, then proposed, "I'll call Shawn Monroe now. If he's at the track, we'll both take Kayla back and talk to him there, alone. We don't want those two talking to each other before we do."

Jimmy left to watch Kayla while she wrote up her statement, and Luke rang the son. Shawn Monroe said he was just leaving the morgue and could meet them at police headquarters. Hudson explained they were bringing Kayla back to the track and Shawn could meet with him and Kidder at the barn instead, if he preferred. The son grabbed the offer.

When Luke found Kidder, he whispered to Luke, "She's been working on her statement. I've watched her pretty close, so she wouldn't have time to text Monroe. She's almost done."

Kayla joined them and handed Jimmy her statement. Then she excused herself and left for the restroom.

Kidder shrugged and said, "I guess you can't follow her everywhere."

Luke grinned and Jimmy turned serious. "Kayla chatted earlier about her past. She grew up in southern Oregon where she lived with her mom, a nurse's aide. They didn't have money for much of anything, especially a horse. So she found work with a quarter horse trainer, feeding and mucking stalls at his stable. He raced a few horses at Grants Pass Downs in the summer. That's where she began exercise riding, and from there she graduated to Long Meadows. She's had kind of a hard life."

CHAPTER 4

However talkative Kayla had been with Jimmy, she shut down on the drive back to the track and they all rode in silence. She fiddled with her phone, but put it away when Luke glared at her in the rearview mirror.

Hudson relaxed and recalled the history of the track, most of it before his move to Bidwell. It was a multi-million dollar venture, financed by a small group of Las Vegas investors with a company called Trackon Corporation, some fifteen years ago. After eleven years, Long Meadows still struggled to turn a profit. Even so, the track was a huge benefit to the community, employing over three hundred people in concessions, betting windows, restaurants and bars, security, grounds, and maintenance. Private businesses supplied horse feed, bedding, and track footing for over a thousand horses. Each horse daily consumed ten to fifteen gallons of water, twenty-five pounds of hay, and another ten or more pounds of grain. The seasonal workers numbered at least seven hundred—trainers, jockeys, veterinarians, grooms, gate crews, outriders, a bugler, a track announcer, office staff, and a general manager. They needed housing, food, gas, medical care, and life's necessities. A racetrack is big business to a community, but four years ago Trackon closed the facility without prior warning and declared bankruptcy. Insiders suspected foul play, a siphoning of funds, or gross mismanagement, but nothing was ever proven because the closure was never investigated.

When Luke came on board with the BPD, he did a little sleuthing on his own. His theory was mishandling of funds, but he was too new to the scene and lacked any tangible evidence. Still he kept his senses honed to any new clues. It was a case he'd love to break wide open, because he suspected there was a scathing scandal under the surface.

The track lay vacant for a year before a wealthy foreign investor, an Arab from Dubai now residing in the States, purchased the track. Abdul "Abe" Zayet dropped many millions into a full year of reconstruction to revitalize Long Meadows. The facility received a complete makeover, including a green meadow infield with a large fountain in the middle of a sprawling pond, abundant flowers and shrubs, a new winner's circle, turf course, additional shed rows, and improved track footing. Further renovations took place in the restaurants and clubhouse.

Racing from March through October, Long Meadows reopened with a week of ceremonies more than a year ago. Increased purse monies and additional stakes races changed the track from a marginal venue to state-of-the-art, even without the casino advantage some states had. The track ended up filling the void left by the closures of Hollywood Park and Bay Meadows.

During the non-racing months, Long Meadows stayed open with off-track betting, restaurants, gala parties and weddings, art shows, and special events. Zayet knew how to spend money, but he also knew how to make it.

The track upgrades brought in bigger trainers and better horses. Hudson believed that was what attracted a trainer of Jack Monroe's caliber from Kentucky to the facility, and more big names from California were seeking stalls for their strings of horses. Long Meadows had turned this town and county into a destination. No wonder Chief Walker was troubled by Monroe's death.

When they pulled up to the track security gate, Luke showed his badge and drove through, parking at Shed Row D where Kayla had left her car. Jimmy helped her out of Hudson's unmarked car and eyed her as she turned and meandered towards her old gray Honda. Shoulders rounded and head down, she never looked back.

Luke took in the pre-race sights and sounds of the track. Sunday was a race day. Monday and Tuesday were "dark" days—no racing, but training would still go on. Wednesday through Sunday were full card days, meaning eight or so races a day.

Horses strolled on mechanical hot walkers while their stalls were cleaned. Veterinarians checked legs, gave shots, and documented charts. Grooms unblanketed horses and brushed them until their sleek bodies glistened in the morning sun. Still other horses poked their heads over stall doors and watched the action around them as they munched from hay nets hanging by their doors. The backside hummed a steady rhythm.

Shed Row D had twenty stalls and a few tack rooms. An overhang roof covered the breezeway where employees worked, protected from the weather. Luke and Jimmy walked to Monroe's section of the barn. Crime scene tape still cordoned off the stall where Monroe had died. They found the son near Dark Saint's stall, and it struck Luke for the first time how much Shawn resembled his dad with the same dark brown hair, blue eyes, and strong stature.

Shawn was occupied with a veterinarian and he introduced the detectives to Doc Steven Riley. The vet didn't fit Hudson's image of one, wearing worn jeans, a light jacket, and a baseball cap on backwards. But Luke supposed that's the nature of the job, casual and hands-on. Jimmy indicated he was the vet who arrived to draw blood from Dark Saint, so Luke took the opportunity to ask about the report rather than wait.

"Sorry to interrupt," he started, "but do you have any results on Dark Saint's tests?"

"Not yet; I'm here to check on another horse. As soon as I have the findings, I'll contact you and Shawn. I've worked for Jack for over a year and knew about him long before that. Too bad his death involves questions about drug use."

Uneasy, Shawn's jaw flexed and tightened as the vet talked.

Doc Riley ignored him. "Jack was unwavering in opposition to racing drugs and he used only authorized, necessary meds. Dark Saint is a May foal, so he was younger than most two-year-olds, and larger. When he started racing in June, he did well, undefeated in four starts including a graded stakes. But in late September, he showed signs of wear. We X-rayed him and, as we suspected, he had bucked shins in both front legs."

A jockey came by and Shawn Monroe wandered off so the two could talk out of earshot. Doc took advantage of the distraction, and revealed, "Jack was being pressured to medicate Saint to mask any unsoundness."

"Pressured by whom?" Luke probed in a lowered voice.

"Dave Bergman for one, Dark Saint's owner. Bergman wanted to race him in the Breeders' Cup Juvenile last October, which is a two million dollar race. And when Jack said no, that began their conflict. Jack thought the colt was borderline sound and needed rest. Bergman knew it, but he didn't want to listen."

Riley glanced to see Monroe still engaged with the rider, and continued, "Just recently, Bergman talked to me about giving more pain killers and performance enhancers to the colt. He has some hot shot buyer from Santa Anita who is looking to pay upwards of six million for the horse as a Kentucky Derby prospect. Trouble is, since Saint's lay-off, he hasn't produced a good workout. And that's because the horse still hasn't fully recovered. He needs another month or so to be ready for a three-year-old campaign."

Shawn returned and stepped into the conversation, overhearing the last sentence. "Saint is getting there, though, and he's about ready for a Derby campaign."

Riley disagreed, "Jack and I said absolutely not, that Saint should be brought back slowly and then he might be ready for the Preakness in June, which is a shorter race with a smaller field of horses and less demanding. But Bergman wanted none of that and said he was moving his horse to another trainer who, as he put it, would go along with him. Jack said, fine, at least Saint's injuries wouldn't be on his hands."

The son was defensive. "Remember, it's ultimately the owner who calls the shots. He's the one putting up the money. The way it came down, Bergman moved ten of his horses to other trainers."

Luke inquired of Shawn, "When was that done?"

"Several weeks ago, so Dad knew Saint and the few left were here on borrowed time."

"How did you feel about that?"

Shawn shrugged, but didn't reply.

Luke considered whether he should tip his hand about the shot and decided he would, since Kayla would say something to Monroe anyway. At least this way he could assess reactions.

All Hudson said was that a syringe was found in the stall. Riley shook his head, but Shawn was expressionless, without comment.

The vet gave the detectives his card, inviting more discussion. "I'm done here, but give me a call if you have any questions."

"Thanks. Will do," Luke said and caught the son's disapproving look.

As Riley got in his truck and left, Hudson glanced down the shed row. The stalls were more than half empty. Clouds were forming overhead and a chill wind swept through the stable. Carlos, the groom, worked at the far end cleaning tack, and if he heard anything, he pretended to neither care nor eavesdrop.

Luke explained to Shawn they'd like to ask him some routine questions. He obliged and retrieved three folding chairs from the tack room. In the tepid breezeway, they sat while Luke questioned and Jimmy took notes. The routine went much the way it had with Kayla.

Shawn said his dad was well respected and everyone in the barn got along. Kayla must have arrived early because the timed ride was scheduled for six thirty-five.

He explained, "My dad wanted Dark Saint to go first on the track, so the footing would be smooth and easier on the horse. Later in the morning, the track gets pretty chewed up."

Luke wondered, "Why would Kayla ride Saint for such an important workout when she's not that experienced? I mean, wouldn't Bergman want a jockey, considering the high stakes?"

The question surprised Shawn because it revealed how well the detective understood racing.

"It was something they worked out," he answered with care.

"Who is 'they'?" Luke asked.

"Bergman and my dad. It was a short run, four furlongs. I guess they thought she could handle it."

Luke made a mental note of the comment and would take it up with Riley. He sensed the son was either withholding or skirting around pertinent information.

Shawn fumbled with his smart phone, read a text message, and answered it.

"That was Kayla," he said. "She wants a few days off, so I told her fine."

Luke went back to questioning. "So you can think of no one who disagreed with your dad enough to harm him?"

"Nope," he answered without thought. "My understanding is that the cause of death was heart failure, so why are you trying to make something more out of it?"

"It's our job to cover all the bases," Luke replied. "You have to admit the circumstances are unusual."

"Not really. It appears Dad came back to check on the sick horse and while he was here, he went in Saint's stall and had a heart attack. The horse is a handful, so when Dad put the halter on him, maybe he got rambunctious."

"Why would your dad even put a halter on the horse unless he was going to do something with him? You know about the syringe found in the stall."

"Don't you guys ever let up? Dad was anti-drugs, and he wasn't trying to drug a horse in the middle of the night. I'm guessing that syringe was chucked there by someone in passing."

Hudson pointed out, "That's what Kayla said. But why would someone throw a syringe in the stall unless they were setting up your dad?"

"Whoa. There you go again, hunting for conspiracy theories," he bounced back. "You know racetracks. There're plenty of shots given. Even a vet can drop a syringe. So one found in the sawdust is no big mystery."

Luke gave him something to ponder. "Depends on what's in it."

Shawn didn't have a smart comeback for that. He rose from his chair and said, "If you guys are about through, I've got some work to do."

"Just one last question," Luke added, as he and Jimmy stood. "Did it ever bother you that your dad ran the show and you were not an equal player?"

"Who told you that?" he asked, frowning.

"Kayla saw it that way."

"Well, she doesn't know everything. My dad and I worked well together. If he appeared to call the shots, he was supposed to. He was the trainer, and I was his assistant. He was teaching me everything he knew, and I loved him for that. You can put that in your report." he scoffed.

Hudson chose to leave on better terms. "Hey, I know emotions are high and we're all concerned about your dad's death. He was a good man."

A long silence passed between them.

Luke broke the impasse. "We'd like to get a statement from you regarding what happened last night, as you see it."

Jimmy handed Shawn a clipboard with the statement form on it. He took it grudgingly, pulled out a pen, and started writing without looking at either detective.

"If it's okay with you, I'd like to talk to Carlos now," Luke suggested. "It will save us another trip back. It's just routine."

"Sure, have at it," Shawn grumbled.

"Jimmy will be around to answer any questions about the statement process."

Shawn clearly didn't like the idea, but he went through the motions anyway.

Luke left the two and ambled over to Carlos who had been brushing a gray mare, but put her away in anticipation that he'd be next. Carlos echoed what Luke had already heard. The stable got along and nothing stood out as suspicious. Montoya's whereabouts last night had been verified, so there was little to discuss at this point. Luke suspected Carlos would seek employment elsewhere because this barn wouldn't support a full-time groom much longer and Kayla would probably fill in.

He asked Carlos if that was the case and he nodded yes.

"I have family to feed," he said. "Jus' between you and me."

"Of course," Luke promised him. Any break in the case might come from Carlos since he was leaving anyway and had less at stake.

He gave Carlos his card. "If you think of something, we could use your help," he said and shook Carlos's strong, calloused hand.

Luke joined his partner as Shawn Monroe finished his short statement, signed it, and handed it to Jimmy. Then the son stood in front of Dark Saint's stall and cast a cold stare at the detectives as they walked away.

ON THEIR WAY BACK TO THE STATION, Jimmy drove and Luke snoozed. It was afternoon now and a light, gentle spring rain fell. The rhythm of the windshield wipers and the splashing rain mesmerized Jimmy, and he shook his head to stay awake. When he stopped at their favorite coffee house, Luke awoke and stretched.

It was warm and cozy inside. They each picked up a cup of coffee and a cinnamon roll to take to their table while they waited for their sandwiches. The deli was filled with young college students and professionals engrossed in their laptops or smart phones. The two detectives found a small table in a back corner.

Luke said, "Besides the statements, we both need to write up some notes, impressions to this point. We also should schedule this Dave Bergman to come in and talk to us. That could get interesting."

Jimmy put cream and two packets of sugar in his dark brew and stirred it while Luke watched.

"You usually drink your coffee black."

"I know, but I need all the sugar stimulation I can get," Jimmy reasoned, taking a big bite of his cinnamon roll covered with pecans and a caramel glaze.

"You're going to eat your dessert first?" Luke quizzed.

"Sure, ever watch a horse or a dog eat? They always eat the best first. We could learn a lot from the animal kingdom."

They laughed together.

Finishing their late lunch, the two returned to the station, and went to Luke's office to complete some paperwork while the facts were fresh in their minds.

Within minutes, Police Chief Tom Walker poked his head in the door and said he wanted to talk to them. Both detectives were surprised. Rarely was the Chief in on a Sunday.

Walker entered, hands on hips, while Luke and Jimmy rose from their chairs and addressed him.

The Chief began, "I got a call while you were out, from Abe Zayet, the track's owner. He's concerned about bad publicity. As he put it, 'The new racing season was off to a good start, and now this.' He said the horse racing publications are already off and running with the news, pun intended. He believes the incident was accidental because he can't imagine anyone wanting to hurt a guy like Jack Monroe."

Luke stood taller. "Sir, we have some evidence to the contrary. In fact, our number one person of interest might be the owner of the horse that was in the stall where Monroe died. His name is Dave Bergman, and we've requested he come in for questioning."

"Damn it to hell," Walker cursed. "You mean David Bergman? He's the biggest real estate developer in this part of the state."

Walker's face turned red all the way to his receding hairline.

"Be that as it may, he's not looking so good right now," Luke asserted. "He had a lot to gain and little to lose by drugging his horse. And a shot meant for the horse ended up in the trainer."

"This is one hell of a mess," the Chief barked, "and I expect you to fix it."

"What do you mean by that?" Luke asked, his temper rising. "Am I supposed to investigate this case and get to the truth or not?"

"Of course you're supposed to, but just try to keep a lid on it. I don't have to remind a racing buff like you, that this economy doesn't need a track scandal. Long Meadows brings in a lot of revenue. So I want you to tread easy with Bergman until you're sure about any involvement he might have, if *any*."

Luke was incensed. "You know you don't solve cases by treading easy."

"I'm not asking you not to do your job. But you can be heavy handed, and alls I'm saying is we've got a delicate situation all the way around, so handle with care."

"I'll do that," Luke retorted as Chief Walker left the room in a huff.

CHAPTER 5

Monday, day two of the investigation found Luke sleeping in until seven a.m., a rarity. He awoke, threw on his bathrobe, and ambled out the front door of his duplex rental to pick up *The Morning Sun* newspaper. He lived on a quiet, dead-end street, and an elderly woman in her eighties leased the adjoining rental, adding to his peace and solitude. And she probably appreciated the extra protection of an officer in the complex. The front of his place was unadorned, the ground covered with decorative gravel and a few shrubs. A couple of wooden planters near the entry had distressed rose bushes he'd neglected to prune during the winter.

The fenced back yard was a little larger, with a patch of lawn, some landscaping, and a patio with privacy walls. Above the patio, on the second floor, was a small balcony off the larger bedroom that faced some trees and the receding river beyond. The duplex was average, nothing special, two bedrooms and one and a half baths, plus a one-car garage. It was a far cry from the home he and his wife had in the LA area. But it was clean and bright and fit his lifestyle, since he didn't spend much time at home anyway, except in the evenings. Then he'd come home, watch the evening news with a drink in hand, eat a TV dinner, browse the internet, and retire to read himself to sleep. It was a routine he'd fallen into since his divorce.

Luke stepped back inside and glanced at the front page. He couldn't miss the headline—*Prominent Trainer Found Dead at Long Meadows*. The story by Kate Irving included a file photo of Monroe, smiling at the camera and standing beside a gray horse. The report failed to cover anything he didn't already know. Owens, Bergman, and Shawn Monroe all declined comments, citing the on-going investigation. City Police Lieutenant Arnold Dodd said in a telephone interview that they were awaiting the medical examiner's preliminary report, and he promised more information would be forth-coming as the case unfolds.

A native of Kentucky, Jack Monroe was 52 and moved to the metro area when the track reopened. Irving stated, "He leaves behind his son, Shawn Monroe, 28, who served as his assistant trainer."

Lieutenant Dodd managed to release only scant information, designed to dispel rumors and say little, reducing Irving's story to fillers and few facts.

Hudson dropped the paper on the sofa and climbed the stairs to his bathroom. He looked in the mirror at his two-day-old stubble, noticing wrinkles at the outside edges of his eyes and his dark hair turning gray around the temples. The years were slipping away. Jack Monroe wasn't that much older than he and died much too young.

He stripped and showered, then shaved and donned a clean shirt, a striped tie, and a suit he hadn't worn in a couple of days. Grabbing the newspaper on his way out, he left for the station.

At headquarters, Hudson went straight to his office to review phone messages and place some essential calls. He was fortunate to have his own office and had insisted on it as a condition of employment. Kidder was in the central pod, though he sometimes came in Luke's office to work at a table Luke added for him. They both appreciated quiet space. The police department, like most of the city and county agencies, was squeezed by budget constraints, so extras such as office space and upgraded cars were difficult to obtain.

His first priority was to arrange a meeting with David Bergman. He had planned to have Bergman come in to headquarters, but after his altercation with Chief Walker yesterday, he decided to go easy and interview him at Bergman Enterprises. He called and was able to set up a three p.m. appointment.

Medical Examiner Ned Jackson had called to inform Luke that they may have the prelim lab report today. Hudson was pleased because he would like to see the results before talking to Bergman.

Also on his desk was a notice that Chief Walker wanted an update meeting in his office after lunch. Luke went to find Kidder at his desk, mired in paperwork. He asked Jimmy to come in his office when he could break away.

"Morning, Luke," Jimmy chirped, as he entered later. "What's in the cards today, besides the Chief's meeting?"

Luke let him sit before he started. "We should talk some more to Riley, so I have a call in to him. Also, I'm thinking we could go to the track this morning and canvas as many people on the backside as possible. We can split up to cover more territory. Someone might have seen something but is reluctant to come forward."

"Sounds good to me," Kidder returned. "When do we leave?"

Luke admired his young enthusiasm. "We have the meeting at one, and then an appointment with Bergman at three, so we should go to Long Meadows as soon as possible. We'll tell people we are looking for closure to Jack Monroe's death, so we'd welcome talking to anyone who saw or heard something, whether they think it's significant or not, and it can be an anonymous tip. We pass out our calling cards and hope someone comes through. What do you think?"

"I like it," Kidder said, and they agreed to leave in five minutes. But their plans were altered by a return call from Doc Steven Riley.

"Detective Hudson, I have some free time this morning and wondered if you and your partner would like to drop by my office. I have some information that you probably haven't heard."

Luke welcomed the opportunity.

"I'm at the Bidwell Equine Center. Do you know where that is?"

Hudson said yes, and that they'd meet him in about half an hour.

Before they left, Ned Jackson rang and Luke put the phone on speaker for Jimmy's benefit.

"Ned, here," the medical examiner said. "We have some prelim info." Jackson was often short with words and in a hurry on the phone. "Monroe died of coronary artery spasm. His arteries were consistent with a healthy person his age, but a coronary spasm can be caused by stress or a drug, such as cocaine, heroin, morphine, or other opiates. Question is how?"

"I don't follow," Luke said.

"Well, we found a needle puncture wound in his thigh. So we ran a complete blood panel, thinking he might have OD'd on a drug, and that brought on the coronary spasm and heart failure. But we can't identify the substance we found in his blood stream."

"What do you mean?"

"Just what I said. He has something in his blood that we can't trace. First time for me."

Hudson thought for a moment. "What about the contents left in the syringe? Did you analyze that?"

"Of course," Jackson snapped, annoyed. "That's the first thing we did, and we can't break that down, either, though the contents were the same as in his blood. There was no labeling on the syringe."

Hudson speculated, "I doubt the shot was an authorized drug, since it wasn't labeled. It's possible the syringe contained some kind of exotic horse drug."

"What?" Jackson asked, baffled.

"Yeah, I follow horse racing some, and there are all kinds of drugs horses are given. Some are approved, but others are designed to be hidden from track blood tests."

"That's shady as hell," Jackson reacted. "You mean they get away with that?"

"All too often. Let me look into it. You may have to send a blood sample and syringe contents to a sophisticated lab that specializes in this sort of thing."

"Good Lord," Jackson groused. "I didn't even know that sort of stuff goes on."

"From what I've read, that's only the half of it." Luke paused. "Were there traces of the drug on Monroe's hands?"

"Yes, on the right hand, around the puncture wound, and yes, it matched the contents in the syringe."

"What about fingerprints on the syringe?"

Ned sighed, "I was getting to that. The prints were smeared and inconclusive."

Luke asked, "Did you find other needle marks, like maybe he was an addict?"

"No."

"If Monroe gave himself the shot, isn't the leg an unusual point of entry?"

"It depends. Drug users shoot up in the arm if it's a vein shot, but this was a muscle shot, so the butt, leg, or shoulder, any muscle mass, would work."

"If he gave himself the shot, why choose a cold night in a stall with a rambunctious colt?"

Ned took in an audible breath. "Don't ask me. Maybe he just wanted to confuse a couple of detectives."

Jimmy grinned and so did Hudson, who ventured, "The needle was found under the body, so could the horse have hit Monroe, and he fell on it?"

Ned didn't answer, but Luke wouldn't drop it. "Indulge me for a minute. Could he have received the shot by accident?"

"It would be a long shot, but I suppose it could happen. The needle being bent could indicate it went in at an odd angle." Ned stopped. "Damn it, Hudson. You know I don't like guesswork, but you're good at sucking me in. Frankly, I don't know how or why the shot went in. That's your job."

Luke smiled. "Ned, I like working with you, because you're not afraid to speculate and you think outside the box. I like your theories as well as your facts."

"All right, you win. My *theory* is that either someone jabbed him with the needle, or he got banged around while holding the needle and took a wild shot. But don't quote me."

"Thanks, Ned, you're the best."

"And you're the best bull shitter," Ned said with a light chuckle. "I'll call you when more comes in."

They hung up.

Luke turned to Jimmy. "It's too early to rule anything out, but I do know one thing. A horse weighs four or five times more than a man, so however Monroe got the shot, it was an overdose, probably enough to kill him."

Kidder frowned. "So it could be we're looking at a possible suicide, though I think that's unlikely. I'm inclined to consider an accidental death. You saw how wild that colt was. And if it was neither, then we're looking at murder."

"I've got to make a call back to Ned."

Turning to his iPhone, Luke brought up websites pertaining to race horses and drugs that are used to make horses run faster, ones such as anabolic steroids, cocaine, opiates, Viagra, cobra venom, frog juice, cobalt, and other stimulants, even cancer medications. Many of these substances don't show up in local lab tests, but a lab in Denver, Colorado, on the cutting edge of identifying newly concocted drugs, often deciphers them. He dialed Jackson and suggested he check it out.

Before the ME hung up, Hudson wanted his facts straight. "What are you listing as time and cause of death?"

"Our official time is about two a.m. At this point, we're saying heart failure since that's something we can verify. We don't know what role the shot may have played, so we're not going there yet."

"Good," Luke said, preferring drugs not surface without full proof.

HUDSON AND KIDDER TRAVELED beneath scattered clouds that spread across the valley, threatening showers and partial sunshine. They arrived at the Bidwell Equine Center a few minutes late. The Center was the largest in town, with a medical staff of half a dozen veterinarians and equine surgeons. The main building housed a reception area, where the two detectives entered. An office staffer buzzed Riley and before long, he appeared, greeted them, and took pride in guiding them on a brief tour of the facility. They strolled past two examination rooms, an X-ray room, and a large, sophisticated surgical room. The whole facility was bright and airy, with high ceilings, and the permeating scent of antiseptics, iodine, soaps, and medications. An adjoining building contained stalls and outside paddocks where horses were either recovering or awaiting treatment.

Then Riley ushered them back into the main building to his office. His eyes sparkled and he flashed a quick smile. "This is a fairly new clinic and since Long Meadows reopened, we've expanded a lot."

He motioned to a couple of chairs in front of his desk and said, "Please, have a seat."

Any extra space in the room was filled with medical books, veterinarian journals, and filing cabinets. Atop one of them, in a glass jar, was a fetus of a foal suspended in formaldehyde.

The two detectives got comfortable and declined a cup of coffee, though Riley had one on his cluttered desk and took a sip.

Doc Riley was a swarthy, fit looking guy, fiftyish, judging by his weathered face and sprinkling of gray hair. He settled into a solemn mood.

"Jack Monroe was a good friend of mine," he began. "I still can't wrap my mind around the fact that he's gone."

Riley paused, deep in thought. "He was on the quiet side, but if he liked and trusted you, he would open up with the biggest heart. That's how we were. So I've just got some things bugging me that I have to get off my chest. For Jack's sake."

Luke said, "I can tell you, we got little from talking to Kayla and Shawn. Carlos, too."

"That's what I expected," Riley concurred. "There's a lot going on under the surface. I know because Jack confided in me."

He leaned forward, "I have one request, though. I'd like to keep this conversation just between the three of us."

"No problem there," Luke assured him. "No notes and no recordings. My boss doesn't even know I'm here, so what's said in this room, stays here."

Jimmy nodded agreement.

"Good, then I can tell you what I know."

Riley leaned back in his chair and started with a question. "I'm sure you have picked up on the real difference of opinion between Shawn and Jack when it came to training. Their disagreement was over the use of drugs. Jack was from the old school of trainers and he learned under an old master. He disapproved of the current practice of giving Lasix to almost every horse every time it runs, whether it's needed or not. And he detested the free use of pain killing drugs."

Hudson thought about Ned's report, and would wait for the right moment to mention it. Perceptive to that, Jimmy remained silent.

Riley went on, "The split widened when Bergman demanded more use of drugs and Jack wouldn't go along. Shawn pointed out that if *they* didn't appease Bergman, someone else would. Jack said, 'Then let him leave.' His kid wanted to grow the barn at any cost and Jack didn't. So the result was that Bergman began pulling his horses and Shawn became more frustrated."

"Was he angry enough to harm his dad?" Luke asked.

Riley paused, contemplating. "I don't think so, but Shawn is ambitious and hard-headed. They just didn't see eye-to-eye. Jack's solution was to let his son have the business, what was left of it. And Jack planned to go back to Kentucky."

The detectives were surprised. "How soon was that going to take place?" Jimmy asked.

"Soon. Within a few weeks. That's what all the fuss was over. Shawn said he'd like to placate Bergman to keep his horses and Jack wouldn't budge because he had a high regard for Dark Saint and didn't want to screw him up."

They pondered Riley's words.

"Did Jack talk about his future plans for Kentucky?" Luke inquired.

"Oh, yes. He was hired as the head trainer at Four Winds, one of the top Kentucky farms. He was excited about the prospect."

"How did Shawn like the idea of his dad leaving?" Jimmy inquired.

"He was okay with it. Shawn could stay here and rebuild the business and Kayla could work with him. Now there's another angle," Riley said. "You probably didn't know the two are intimate. Jack caught them going at it in the tack room. As Jack put it, 'They were vertical, but I wish I'd had a bucket of cold water to throw on them'."

Riley grinned, remembering his friend. "Jack developed a real distaste for her after that. He thought his son could and should do better."

The detectives looked at each other and Luke said to Riley, "Now we have some information to share with you—information that shouldn't leave this room. For Jack's sake."

Riley's intercom buzzed, and he answered, "Hold all my calls, unless it's an emergency. Okay, tell him I'm with someone and I'll get back to him in ten minutes."

He punched off and explained, "I'm needed at the track, but I want to hear what you've got."

Luke elaborated on the ME's report and the untraceable drug found in Jack's bloodstream.

Visibly bothered, Riley seemed to be talking to himself. "So there's a good chance some illegal, exotic drugs are being used here? I guess I shouldn't be too surprised. It's just that Zayet prides himself on running a clean track. I wonder if it's dermorphin? It's a pain suppressant, some forty times more powerful than morphine. Dozens of horses have tested positive in other states, but here?"

Riley's eyebrows narrowed, and he stared at the two detectives. "I'll tell you one thing. Jack would never take an illegal drug or give one to a horse. To my knowledge, he never took anything stronger than an aspirin or a shot of Jack Daniel's. Someone else was involved."

Hudson asked, "What's the penalty if someone gave such a shot to the horse?"

"He or she would be fined and probably have their license suspended. Jack had no motive and it would go against everything he believed in."

"Then what do you think happened?"

"My best guess is that Jack walked in on someone about to give an illegal shot to Saint. There was an argument, maybe a scuffle, and Jack took the shot instead of the horse. I've heard of it happening—a misguided shot."

Jimmy pondered, "How would someone get ahold of such a drug?"

Riley played with the prospect. "The drug most likely came from an outside source, a dealer." He shook his head in disgust. "I see what you mean about keeping this quiet. If the authorities thought Jack took the shot they'd think it was either suicide or a drug dosing that went wrong."

Luke asked, "Wouldn't Bergman figure into all this? It was his horse."

Riley admitted, "Bergman had a motive. All he need-ed was one good workout from Saint as a three-year-old. Even though the colt was impressive at two, youngsters can lose form between two and three. The buyer wanted some assurance that Saint hadn't regressed. When Jack and I didn't go along with drug enhancements, maybe Bergman acted on his own."

Hudson knew enough about racing to surmise that starting in March for a Kentucky Derby run the first Saturday in May, meant that Dark Saint was already on a tight time table. He countered, "So if Bergman wanted the horse drugged, why not move him to another barn that might be more willing to do it? Nothing was stopping him."

"Maybe he had an accomplice in Shawn or Kayla. Considering the penalties, someone willing to give an illegal shot is hard to find. Saint was scheduled for a timed workout Sunday. So a performance enhancing drug before the work would make him look good, and Saint's last unofficial workout wasn't up to par."

"Well, we have some direction in the case now," Hudson said, as both he and Jimmy rose to leave. "Thanks for your time and insights. If you think of anything else, give us a call. We're on the same page, as far as Jack is concerned."

As they were walking to the door, Luke asked, "What about Carlos?"

"He had no motive. Jack told him he was leaving and Carlos didn't want to stay and work for Shawn."

"Money is a motive," Luke reminded Riley.

"I know, but I'd be surprised if he's in on it," the vet said. "But then there're plenty of surprises surrounding Jack's death, huh?"

CHAPTER 6

Luke and Jimmy left Riley's office and went to the track. Arriving at the backside shed rows, they parked alongside Shed Row D and walked to Monroe's stall area. Most of the horse name tags were removed, leaving the Monroe Stables sign still hanging where five training horses remained—a gray mare, Dark Saint, and the chestnut, Go Laddie Go, plus two bays. Bergman hadn't moved his last two horses out yet. The stall where Monroe had died was unguarded and unchanged, cordoned off with yellow "Police Line: Do Not Enter" tape around it, a constant reminder of Jack Monroe's fate.

Kidder and Hudson found Monroe's son in a stall with the gray mare. He was wrapping her legs, but when he saw the two of them, he finished the leg wrap and stood up.

"Go ahead and finish," Luke offered.

"I need a break anyway," Shawn replied, carrying the wraps with him as he left the stall.

"Why do you wrap their legs?" Kidder asked, always curious.

"I use a liniment and wrap the legs on a horse that has some swelling or soreness. It helps. This mare is eight and showing some signs of wear and tear," he added. "Their legs are everything."

"That's kind of young to be wearing out, isn't it?" Jimmy questioned.

Shawn shrugged, "Not really. The high end race horses usually leave before seven and retire to breeding programs. The low end claiming mares and geldings keep going. It's all about economics."

Luke changed the subject. "What are your plans? It looks like more horses have left."

"Yeah, but I'll rebuild. I plan to stay here." He didn't elaborate.

Jimmy asked, "What are your plans for your dad's funeral?"

"His body will be flown to Kentucky where he'll be buried after a memorial service. The Monroes have a family plot in Lexington, and some of our relatives are making the arrangements. It's where he belongs."

"Absolutely," Luke agreed, then paused. "You know, something's been bothering me. Could we see your dad's vet records on Dark Saint and Go Laddie Go?"

Shawn hesitated, but didn't resist showing them. "Sure, let me find 'em."

Heading for a cement block tack room next to the stalls, Shawn opened the door, turned on an overhead light, and pulled records out of a dusty file cabinet next to the door. Saddles, bridles, blankets, and tack hung on hooks and racks along the walls. A small desk, a lamp, and a swivel desk chair, a couple of folding chairs, and a cot in the corner filled the room. It made Luke's workplace look like the Oval Office. Shawn shuffled through files and found what he needed.

"Here," he showed Luke, who realized he had over-looked the medical records.

Hudson asked, "Could I borrow these to make copies on both the horses?"

The son balked, but thought better of it. "Here, but I'd like to have them back."

"Of course, you'll get them back tomorrow," Luke promised.

On top was Go Laddie Go's last vet's receipt. Hudson glanced at it and asked, "Is this your Dad's notation? 'Owner ordered Lasix and Doc advised history of intolerance'."

Shawn shrugged, and gestured yes. Hudson let the other papers go for now and would read through them later.

They stepped out of the small tack room office and Luke saw Carlos finishing the leg wraps on the gray.

Kidder looked around and asked, "Has Kayla been back to work?"

"No, not since the morning Dad died. That's okay, because we don't have that much work for her around here anyway."

Luke explained they were at the track to canvas for more information. Carlos listened while Shawn appeared detached.

The detectives went through the motion of giving them cards to hand out and asking them to spread the word, but to Luke the whole idea seemed somewhat futile.

Leaving Shawn and Carlos, they started down Shed Row D to talk with other trainers. Suddenly, Luke realized the enormity of the task, with considerable ground to cover. While contemplating that, Carlos drove alongside them in a quiet, battery-operated golf cart. He stopped and got out.

"Des is the car we use here," he remarked. "Mr. Shawn leave, so I lend it to you. It make work easy."

"Thanks," Luke said, "but we don't want to get you in trouble."

"I prob'ly already in trouble," he grinned. "More if you no bring it back."

Luke and Kidder smiled and said they'd have it back before noon. Then they worked all the shed rows, but no one saw anything, though they expressed regrets about Monroe's death.

DRIVING BACK TO HEADQUARTERS, Luke soaked in the warm spring sunshine, noticing some trees were budding, and the sky was a cloudless, soft blue. They stopped at their favorite deli and took out sandwiches to eat at work before meeting with Chief Walker at one. The meeting was uneventful and short, as Luke had expected. Walker's main interest was their appointment with David Bergman. Luke informed him they would meet at Bergman's office, and it would be routine and informal, to fill Bergman in since he'd been out of town when Monroe's death occurred.

They left the Chief's office, revisited their questioning strategy, and headed for the parking lot to meet with the man they considered to be their number one person of interest. In truth, Hudson intended to push Bergman as far as he dared, and he suspected that Walker didn't believe his little spiel about a low-key meeting with the land baron.

The downtown Bergman Enterprises building was tasteful but not overdone. Luke and Jimmy were ushered to Bergman's office on the top floor, and introduced to David Bergman and Richard McCloud, a gray-haired, confident looking man in a designer suit. Bergman was maybe in his mid-forties, quite young for all the wealth he had amassed. He had a charming, polished way about him that reminded Luke of a salesman. He offered them seats in plush leather chairs.

"Good afternoon, detectives," Bergman started. "I hope you don't mind that my friend, Richard, is here. He was helping me with some legal advice so I asked him to sit in."

"So he's your attorney," Kidder said, notepad in hand.

"An extra pair of ears," Bergman offered, and glanced at Luke. "Just as you have. So let's begin."

Luke shifted in his chair, glanced at his notes, and began, "For the record, I know you were out of town when the incident took place, but where were you exactly?"

"I was at a real estate conference in Seattle. In fact, I was one of the speakers. I can give you my flight schedule and the program if you'd like, for the record." There was a touch of sarcasm in Bergman's voice on his last three words.

"Yes, that will be fine. Fax it over to us." Hudson changed gears. "It's pretty well established that you and Monroe had a parting of the ways. Could you tell us when the split started and what precipitated it?"

Bergman looked at his attorney and then answered, "Jack Monroe was a good trainer; don't get me wrong. But I had a dozen horses with him and I decided to diversify, go with a couple of trainers. Some horses do better on another track with a different style of training. Lots of owners do that. It's nothing unusual. If Monroe hadn't died, my switching trainers wouldn't have mattered."

"That's probably true," Luke agreed. "However, under the circumstances it's an issue we have to pursue. Wasn't it a fact that you and Monroe didn't agree on the use of medications? That you wanted Jack Monroe to okay drugs that he refused to use?"

"I don't know where you get your information, Detective, but as an owner I have the right to make decisions about my horses' meds, with or without a trainer's approval, so that's a *non*-issue."

Luke pushed on, "For example, you wanted Go Laddie Go to have Lasix in spite of Monroe's objections and warning that the horse was sensitive to the drug. And the horse had a reaction to it."

Bergman looked bored. "So? I had the horse run on Lasix, like most of the horses in this country do every day. Sometimes there's a side effect. But since you brought it up, it's a perfect example of how Jack failed to use all the tools at his disposal. And, it's why we differed on training techniques. I wanted Dark Saint to be trained more aggressively because I had a prospective buyer for him, but you're probably aware of that. Jack preferred to wait before bringing Saint along as a three-year-old, so that was our most recent disparity. I had planned to move my last two horses out of Jack's barn when I came back from Seattle, but now I'll wait and see."

"Because the son has a different approach?" Luke asked.

"He does, but frankly, I haven't had time to shop around for another trainer, and now would be an awkward time to leave." Bergman sighed, "If you don't have something new to discuss, I need to get back to work."

His lawyer sat back, arms guarding his chest, waiting for the next question.

Luke didn't know if he was just tired, or unprepared, or somehow outgunned, but Bergman's answers sounded rehearsed. The detective realized he wanted this conversation over as much or more than Bergman did. At least Chief Walker would be appeased that questioning Bergman turned into a waste of time.

Glancing at Kidder, he nodded, prepared to wrap it up. He wouldn't mention the empty syringe in Dark Saint's stall and the illegal shot that initiated Monroe's death, as it would only give Bergman more ammunition.

"One last thing," Luke said. "When is Dark Saint scheduled to work again?"

"Why do you want to know?" Bergman countered, surprised.

"I'd like to be there when he does. I gather it will be soon, given the Derby time constraints. If you don't know, I can get the workout schedule from the track."

Bergman remained a stone. "He runs at 6:45 tomorrow morning."

His attorney cut in, "Gentlemen, we appreciate the chat, but I assume we are done." McCloud rose to show them to the door, while Bergman remained behind his desk.

As soon as they left the company and were in the car, Kidder said, "Well, that was short and bitter."

Luke started the engine. "We didn't have a smoking gun and they both knew it."

"I gather we'll leave for the track before six tomorrow morning."

Hudson nodded yes and Jimmy looked back at the building as they pulled away. "Something will break. I can just feel it. Meanwhile, I say we've earned a drink at The Watering Hole."

Luke smiled, but underneath he was impatient. They still had nothing to go on and it was gnawing at him. He reminded himself he'd worked on cases that took months, even years, to solve, and this was only day two. But the first forty-eight to seventy-two hours were often the most crucial in solving a case.

HUDSON ENTERED HIS DUPLEX and noticed the flashing red message light on his phone. He looked at the clock, noting it was a little past seven. Removing his coat and tie, he sat down and put his feet up, then listened to a recording from his ex-wife, asking him to call her.

He dialed her number and her warm voice followed three empty rings. "Luke? Thanks for calling back. I just felt like talking to you."

"Me, too," he said. "It's been awhile. How have you been?"

"I'm okay, but I hear you're embroiled in a heavy case—a racetrack assignment. That must be right up your alley."

"Where did you hear that?"

"From Charlie," Sally answered, and the mention of his mentor's name brought back good memories. Charles Shaw was retired now from the LAPD, but he had been Luke's partner and like a dad to him for years.

"Good old Charlie," Luke said. "I miss him. What's he been up to?"

"His usual, you know Charlie. He hangs out with the guys and can't quite give up being a cop," she replied and Luke could visualize Sally's reflective smile. "He's been following your case, and says it involves a trainer who was murdered at Long Meadows."

"Well, he's dramatized it a bit. We're not sure it's a murder at this point. It's a complicated case with no viable witnesses, so it's frustrating."

"I'll bet," she said. "I know how you hate loose ends and justice not being served."

"Let's talk about you," he countered. "How's school going?"

Sally was a high school English teacher and dedicated to her work, even though each year had seemed more of a struggle.

"I'm being laid off in June," she said, sadness in her voice.

"How can that be, with tenure and all?" His surprise was genuine.

"It's a growing trend. There are fewer funds for public education, so personnel along with a lot of other things are being cut. When the district does rehire, they'll choose young teachers they can pick up for lower pay and fewer benefits."

"I'm so sorry to hear that. I know what teaching means to you," he said, grappling with her news. "What about your retirement?"

"I do have enough time in to get something back, but another five years would have made a big difference."

Luke hesitated. "Have you thought about what you'll do next?"

"I'm not sure. I guess it will be a new adventure, time for a career change maybe."

She sounded down, which was understandable, but out of character.

He had held back too many times with Sally, so he plunged forward. "You might want to think about getting out of L.A. Maybe come up here and check out life in a smaller town." He winced as he said it, wondering if he'd gone too far.

"I've thought about that," she admitted, the words pleasing him. "It couldn't hurt to leave my options open."

Emboldened, Luke decided to take one step further. "Well, if you do come to Bidwell to look around, you're welcome to stay at my place while you explore. No strings, no expectations, just a modest place to crash. I've got an empty bedroom, and as you well know, I'm not home much, so you'd pretty much have the place to yourself. I can stay with Jimmy."

"That's a kind offer," she said. "I'll think about it. I have a lot to consider in the coming months."

"Yes, you do. I don't mean to be pushy, but I want you to know I'm here for you, like you were for me after I was shot."

"I appreciate it, Luke. Really, I do. Take care and say hello to Jimmy for me."

"Sure will, and tell Charlie I said hi."

He hung up with mixed emotions.

CHAPTER 7

Tuesday, day three, Long Meadows was under a high, gray cloud cover, and a chill breeze swept through. This spring had been mixed, one day sunny and inviting, the next reaching back into winter. Luke wore a sweater vest under his suit jacket and Jimmy was bundled in a trench coat. They both warmed their hands on their coffee cups.

They sat in the first row of the bleachers, watching other horses work until Dark Saint was scheduled to go. One horse had shied at a plastic bag that blew across the track, and unseated his jockey, before bolting off and almost colliding with another horse and rider.

A hundred yards or so up the rail from the detectives, David Bergman and Shawn Monroe, stood where the gate opened to the track. Joined by a third man, perhaps the perspective buyer, they talked and pointed as Dark Saint jogged past them to begin his warmup on the mile track. This was an official workout at six furlongs, or three-quarters of a mile. His finishing time would be posted at Long Meadows and on the internet, along with his ranking amongst the other horses that ran six furlongs today.

Luke and Jimmy walked down to the outside rail for closer scrutiny. When Dark Saint pranced past them, he was as magnificent and proud as the first time the detectives had seen him. His black coat glistened, even in the overcast light, and he began to hop sideways in anticipation of running. The rider was not Kayla, but rather a jockey. He loosened his grip on the reins, so the horse could move out at an extended trot, and that helped settle him.

Dark Saint had a smooth way of going and his movements appeared effortless as he went into the first turn at a lope. He broke into a stronger canter along the backstretch and when the rider received the okay for official timing, the colt exploded into a commanding gallop and powered away. Doc Riley joined Luke and Jimmy, acknowledging them with a nod, but he focused on timing the horse. Dark Saint stretched out, covering twenty feet or more with each lengthening stride.

Into the stretch, Riley stared at his stopwatch. "Too fast, dammit," he said, shaking his head. "I told the dumbasses not to run him too fast."

Dark Saint devoured the ground, his hooves pounding and spraying dirt behind him. He thundered through the homestretch, beyond the finish line, and began slowing on the turn, when he faltered, favoring his left front leg. The jockey pulled him to a stop and jumped off, but it was too late. The horse stood on three legs, in obvious pain.

Shawn and Bergman sprinted onto the track, coming to the aid of their horse, while Riley ducked under the railing and ran to offer assistance. An outrider began waving to other riders on the track, warning them to slow or stop because of the injured horse.

A horse ambulance van was now on the track and moving towards the injured colt. When the van stopped near Dark Saint, another vet emerged from the vehicle and began to assess the damage. Bergman made a gesture indicating Doc Riley's help wasn't needed, but Riley waited and watched anyway before walking back towards Luke and Jimmy. When he reached them, he was shaken.

"The bastards just ruined a good horse," he muttered, mostly to himself, and fell silent.

They watched as Dark Saint was sedated and an inflatable cast was fitted to his left front leg. Then Saint hobbled on three legs up the ramp and into the ambulance. When the horse settled, the doors closed and the van inched away, slowly circling the backstretch and exiting to the backside of the track. From the stables, the horse's leg would be X-rayed and if there was a fracture, he would be vanned off to a clinic where further assessment and treatment, even surgery, could be done. Luke watched enough horse racing to know this scenario all too well. It was the dreaded aspect of the sport he loved, the downside to the beauty, the excitement, and dreams that shattered with broken bones.

Jimmy frowned, brooding and glum. Though he knew a lot less about what was going on than Luke or Riley, he didn't ask. As the three leaned against the rail and watched horses begin their workouts again, Riley spoke, "What a damn shame. If Jack still had the horse, things would have been so different. Saint hadn't worked at that distance all this spring. It was too long, too fast, too soon."

Luke asked, "How bad is it?"

"My guess is a fracture. The bone didn't break through the skin, so that keeps the infection rate down. He'll need surgery and screws inserted. Then he'll be rested for six months or more, *if* there are no complications, such as laminitis."

Laminitis, a serious crippler of the hoof, often resulted in death. Doc Riley was contemplative before continuing. "I heard Shawn say the horse ran in 1:07 and change. To put that in perspective, a winning time at that distance is about one minute and ten. World record time is 1:06 and 5. That's how good he was, or how drugged."

Distraught about the breakdown, Riley vowed, "I'm going to insist that Saint have blood drawn and tested at the Colorado lab. They can identify drugs that are too sophisticated for local testing. You could help move that process along by requesting it as part of your investigation. I'm suspecting the horse was on Sublimaze."

"Never heard of it," Luke said. "But I'm all for the test. Who do I contact?"

Riley asserted, "I'll call Zayet right now. If the track demands the test, that's better yet."

Luke said, "Tell me a little more about the drug."

"Sublimaze has been around a long time, going back to the seventies. Bute and Lasix get the blame for breakdowns, but the real culprits are the narcotics. Sublimaze is a rapid working analgesic-narcotic that gives a horse a false sense of well-being, so they run not even knowing they have legs under them."

Jimmy bemoaned, "When does this drugging end?"

"It won't unless the feds get involved, and it will still be hard to enforce. It's a culture. That's why Jack was so adamant about drugs and horses. Once you tell yourself it's okay, it's a slippery slope."

Riley rang Zayet and asked him if he was aware of the breakdown.

"You are? And you've ordered a vet to investigate? Great. Yes, thanks."

Riley cut the cell call and told Luke, "Zayet's already on it. He's getting an impartial vet to draw blood and get the testing done. I'll get a copy of the results."

There was nothing more to say, so the three exchanged goodbyes and parted. Luke had no stomach for staying around, and Jimmy looked a little peaked, so they left for the station.

BACK AT THE OFFICE, THE INTERCOM BUZZED and the reception-ist told Luke "a Carlos" was on the line. Jimmy was there, so Luke did his usual and put the phone on speaker.

"Carlos, what's up?" he asked.

"Mr. Shawn not know I call," he said, guarded, "but I have news."

"That's great. We could use a little good news about now."

Carlos explained, "I'm on the backside with a young Latino. He say he know something about the night Mr. Monroe die, but he no speak English. So I translate for you," Carlos offered.

"Good, good," Luke said, while he motioned to Jimmy and whispered for him to get Maria to translate, too.

Carlos went on, "He no legal, so he don't talk 'til he hear he no have to say his name. That right?"

"Absolutely," Luke answered. "Tell him *gracias* for his help."

Jimmy re-entered the room with Officer Maria Santos in tow. She could substantiate what was being said in Spanish.

Carlos spoke to his informant, explaining they would tell the *policia lo que paso*, what happened. The Latino explained for several minutes and Maria listened, taking notes.

At last, Carlos said in broken English, "He say on the night Mr. Monroe die, he hear voices in Shed Row D so he go there. He see a young *nina* in the stall with Mr. Monroe and a horse. He say the two argue. He no *comprende*, but Mr. Monroe angry. The *nina* was Kayla. He know she ride for Mr. Monroe. My friend no want to get involve so he walk on. *Son las dos*, he say."

Maria fingered two o'clock, and Luke nodded acknowledgement.

"Does he know anything more?" Luke asked.

Carlos and the informer exchanged a few words.

"No, Senor Luke. That all he know."

"Good work, Carlos," Luke said. "What your friend saw was *muy importante. Muchas gracias.*"

Carlos hung up and Maria confirmed the translation was accurate. Luke asked her if she would sign to corroborate the information when it was put in writing. She said yes, as he thanked her and she left.

The two detectives high-fived. After such a downer morning, they were back on top again. Their next move was to bring in Kayla Owens. Luke suggested that Jimmy call her because she was less intimidated by him. He could say there was new information in the case and he'd like to bring her to the station for more questioning.

It took more than an hour to reach her, but as soon as Jimmy could pick her up, he left.

While Luke waited, the medical examiner called.

"This is Ned. I just got the faxed report. I'll send a copy, but here's the gist of it. The substance in the syringe and Monroe's blood is dermorphin. It's a powerful performance-enhancing potion drawn from the backs of a South American frog. Furthermore, dermorphin is often artificially synthesized. Chemists know that because with the amount of dermorphin out there, an awful lot of frogs would have to be squeezed to produce it naturally. So *sub rosa* pharmaceuticals are cranking out the facsimile."

Luke interrupted, "What did it do in Monroe's system?"

"I'm getting to that. Monroe had two puncture wounds—one in the right hand and one in the left thigh. The hand wound was superficial, but the dermorphin that went into his thigh was more significant. More than three-quarters of the shot went into his system. There's a wide range in overdose levels, depending a person's sensitivity, but the report specifies Monroe's dermorphin level was in the lethal range."

Ned paused, "You following me?"

Luke said yes, and Jackson went on. "The compound has a chemical structure similar to endorphins. In race horses, the drug is given to mask pain and encourage horses to run faster. It inhibits neurons from firing, so it halts pain and creates a good feeling. In a human over-dose, you get sleepy and forget to breathe, or put another way, your respiratory drive shuts down, your blood pressure dips significantly, and that causes your heart to fail."

Luke was lost for words, so the ME continued. "I liken it to what may have happened to Philip Seymour Hoffman. You know, the actor. Authorities said he was found dead on his bathroom floor with a heroin needle sticking out of his left arm. Death can happen that fast."

"You still there?" Ned asked.

"Yes, I'm just dumbfounded. I've seen these kinds of cases with heroin addicts, but with a race horse? It's so senseless."

"I'll tell you something more senseless," Ned fired back. "If someone was in the stall with Monroe and saw what happened and had called 911, he might have been saved. Responders would have given him a drug called Narcan, which contains naloxone hydrochloride. Narcan rapidly reverses the effects of heroin and other opiates. It's a wonder drug because it can bring a person back from the brink of death and buys more time to get to a hospital."

Luke cut in, "I know about Narcan. Police departments use it in emergencies. The whole situation leaves me sick in my gut."

"One more thing," Ned interjected. "Vet Steven Riley called with the results regarding the blood work done on Dark Saint. The horse was not drugged and there's no evidence that his hooves came in contact with the victim. Riley said to pass that on to you."

"Thanks, Ned. I needed that information now more than ever."

LUKE WAS ALREADY IN THE INTERROGATION ROOM, sometimes referred to as the box, when Jimmy brought Kayla in around two in the afternoon. He was quite surprised at her appearance—bloodshot eyes with dark circles under them, her hair and clothes disheveled and unwashed. She looked like someone on drugs, but he didn't think so by the way she acted.

She glanced around at the video and recording equipment in the stark room. There were bare walls and few windows, just a small room filled with a table and four hard, wooden chairs. The room smelled stale and once the door was closed, the silence was unsettling.

Luke noted her nervousness. The guilty were braced and non-plussed. She was not someone calloused or hard-edged, and any of her earlier feistiness had vanished.

Jimmy asked her if she wanted coffee. She nod-ded, said she preferred sugar and cream, and then sat down where Luke indicated, across from him. Jimmy returned with her coffee, the way she liked it, and took a seat beside Luke, readying himself to take notes. He was falling over himself being the "good cop" while Luke took a deep breath and knew he would have to play the "bad cop."

Hudson explained that he would like to record the session and that the video camera would be on as well, if she agreed to it.

Kayla sighed an okay and slumped lower in her chair.

With deliberation, Luke stood up tall and walked halfway around the table towards her as she watched him. He stopped and looked down at her.

"You're in a lot of trouble, Kayla," he said. "For openers, we now have a witness that places you in the stall with Monroe around the time that he died. That makes you our prime suspect."

He'd said enough. She broke down sobbing, her shoulders heaving with each moan. She stared into her lap and wouldn't look up at him. Jimmy offered her Kleenex and she took a handful from the box.

Luke returned to his seat and waited for her to gain some composure. "Since you *are* a prime suspect and we may have to detain you, I'm going to read you your Miranda Rights."

This brought a look of terror to her eyes and elicited more tears. He began anyway. "You have the right to remain silent and refuse to answer questions. Anything you say may be used against you in a court of law."

She wept again and he waited, concerned that she wasn't listening. The recorder was going, documenting her sniffles and nose blowing.

"You have the right to an attorney before speaking to the police and to have an attorney present during questioning now or in the future."

"I can't afford an attorney," she wailed.

"If you can't afford an attorney, one will be appointed for you before any questioning if you wish."

She sat a little straighter and took notice.

Finishing, Luke told her the last right. "If you decide to answer questions now, without an attorney present, you still have the right to stop at any time and obtain an attorney before going on. Do you understand everything I've read to you?"

She nodded.

"Can you speak up?" he insisted, for the recording.

"Yes," she said, almost a whisper. Gone was the spark and sassiness he had seen that first day.

"What do you want to do?" he asked.

"I don't know," she murmured. "It's all a bad dream."

"Well, it's for real, trust me. And you have another problem."

She looked at him with silent resignation.

"You lied to us. You never told us you saw Jack Monroe that night."

"I was terrified!" she cried. "It wasn't supposed to be that way. It was supposed to be a simple shot to the horse to make him run faster. That was all. I know that what I did was wrong, but no one was supposed to get hurt."

Luke wouldn't let go. "Lying to the police is an obstruction of justice. That alone is a punishable offence.

Now maybe the best solution for you is to start cooperating. Tell us everything you know."

"I didn't do this alone, you know," she said with bitterness. "But I'll be the one to pay for it."

He saw an opening. "Not if you turn State's witness."

"What's that?"

"You tell us everything you know, no lies, no stonewalling. We in turn, cut you some slack, and go as easy as we can under the circumstances." Now he had her attention.

"Your promises are vague," she complained.

"I know, because we haven't heard your testimony. I'm being honest as I can with you. I won't promise something I can't deliver," he said, "but I assure you, I'll do what I can."

He waited while she mulled over her options. He reminded her of the right to an attorney and to bypass questioning, but she wondered if that would make her appear more suspect in their eyes. She waived the privilege for now and said, "Go on. Let's get this over with."

Luke reiterated, "Just to be clear, you're agreeing to go the route of State's witness and cooperate with us, correct?"

She mumbled yes.

He didn't want any legal snags later. "We can start with your testimony and if at any time you're uncomfortable with the questioning, you can stop us and demand an attorney. It's your call."

With acquiescence in her voice, she sighed, "I'll cooperate and answer your questions."

"That's all we can ask for," Luke said, with softness in his voice for the first time. "Maybe we should get started."

The two detectives had already strategized how the questioning would unfold, and Jimmy got a quick once-over glance at the ME's latest fax. Hudson, all too aware that he dominated interrogations, opened a notepad and nodded to Kidder to take over.

"Who was in possession of the shot in question, you or Jack Monroe?"

"I was." Kayla glanced at them both and with reluctance spewed out a long sentence. "A man called me the Friday before Mr. Monroe's death and said he worked for the owner of Dark Saint, and that the owner wanted his horse to have a shot that would improve his timed workout scheduled for Sunday. I said, 'Why are you telling me? Go get a vet.' He said, 'Well, the shot isn't exactly legal and the owner was hoping you could do it.' I told him I could lose my license over something like that, but he down-played the risk. He said if it was done right, no one would be the wiser and the shot couldn't be traced."

She paused and asked for a drink of water. Luke got up this time and Jimmy withheld further questions until he returned. She thanked him and Jimmy let her continue. "I didn't like the idea and said so. Then the man, who never identified himself, said the owner would make it worth my time. I asked what he meant by that, and he said five hundred dollars for a successful shot, and a promotion to Santa Anita Park racetrack, because the owner has lots of connections there and could get me on as an exercise rider with a big-name trainer. He didn't say who."

"Did you receive any money?" Kidder asked.

"No, not the way things went down," she stammered. "Maybe I wouldn't have anyway. Looking back on it, I was pretty gullible."

She sat silent for a few moments. "They were careful about covering all their tracks. I never knew or saw the man who referred to Mr. Bergman as 'the owner', and then they did a couple more slick things."

"Such as...," Jimmy urged, not letting her testimony lapse.

"I asked how I would know he was legit and really worked for Bergman. He didn't like me referring to the owner's name on the phone, but I didn't care. He said the owner would be at the stalls Friday afternoon and he would be wearing a hat. When he saw me, he would put his hand to the brim and nod to me, like a hello. If I was willing to do the shot, I was to nod back and that would be my consent. If I didn't want to do the shot, I would just turn away."

Luke wasn't surprised at how well Bergman covered his ass. He'd seen him in action.

Kayla dabbed at her tears and blew her nose again. "The other thing they did that left no trace, was that the shot was delivered in a thermos bottle to my car. I was to leave the window rolled down partway on Saturday so the man could drop the bottle in. The shot was wrapped in an insulating material so it would stay a proper temperature. He said the shots were expensive."

Jimmy asked, "Was the shot in your car Saturday?"

"Yes, I was busy working with Go Laddie Go's problem, and when I went to my car later, it was there on the floor," she said and stopped to take a drink of water.

"Laddie gave me an excuse to hang around that evening and plan when and how to give the shot. The man said it should be given around two a.m. so it would be well into his system by the time Dark Saint ran after six in the morning."

Jimmy's questioning had gone as planned, and Luke appreciated his easy, relaxed style. But the senior detective was poised to tackle some sensitive material and the roles reversed.

Hudson stepped in, "So Bergman used Go Laddie Go as a diversion?"

"I suppose so," she uttered, thinking about it.

"Do you have any idea what was in that shot?"

"No," she avoided eye contact.

"It was demorphin, 'frog juice' as it's called around the track. Have you ever heard of that?"

"Yes," she said, "but I didn't know it was here, at this track."

"Tell us the truth now about those hours you stayed at the track, how you took the shot to Saint's stall, and how Jack Monroe got involved."

This was the part she was dreading. Kayla looked down and with a tremble in her voice, said, "I stayed around after everyone left. I did check on Laddie, like I told you, but I didn't go home until after everything happened. I knew if

I drove out and came back later, I would have to show my credentials again, and the night guard might record or remember what time I returned, so I just stayed. The whole plan was screwed. I was so tired by the time I returned Sunday morning that I probably wouldn't have put in a good ride anyhow."

Luke asked, "Did it ever occur to you that Bergman might substitute another rider?"

Her bewildered expression revealed that idea hadn't crossed her mind.

He asserted, "Did you take the thermos to the stall, and do you still have it?"

"No," she said. "I removed the shot and put it in my coat pocket before I left the car. I dumped the thermos later at a dumpster in town because the man told me I should get rid of it, in case of fingerprints."

"Do you remember what dumpster or what part of town?" Luke inquired, thinking they might recover it.

"To tell the truth, I put it in my apartment's dumpster, knowing they pick up on Mondays." She admitted hiding evidence.

He'd add that infraction to the list, but he didn't want to hound her about it now, so he moved on. "What happened at the stall when Monroe appeared on the scene?"

She halted before proceeding. "I went to the stall and put a halter on Saint. I was to give a shot into the muscle. If it had to be in the vein, I couldn't have done it. The needle was attached to the syringe filled with the drug, and they were in a protective plastic case. So I removed the shot from the case and pinched some skin on the neck, where I was going to give the shot. Mr. Monroe might have been watching me, because just then he opened the stall door and said, 'What the hell are you doing?' He was mad, so mad he was red in the face and his veins were popping out on his neck. He scared me."

Kayla stopped, and Luke impatiently grunted, "Go on."

"Mr. Monroe grabbed for the shot, and I tried to keep it from him. I didn't want him taking the shot from me because then he'd know what was in the syringe. We struggled a little and he took hold of the syringe. I think he might have even stuck himself in the hand while we fought. He pulled until he pried it out of my hand. By then Dark Saint was all worked up. He was jumping around and I wasn't holding on to him anymore. He was loose. Saint spun around and smacked into Mr. Monroe, hard enough to knock him around and he hit the wall. I ran out the stall door, closed it, and took off. I knew I was in serious trouble, but I never dreamed Mr. Monroe would die in that stall."

She broke down again with uncontrollable sobbing. When she gained some self-control, she reached for the piled Kleenexes in her lap, dried her eyes and blew her nose until it was red.

Luke now asked the most crucial question, the one that could put her under arrest for negligent homicide. "Was Mr. Monroe in distress or injured when you left the stall?"

"No!" she cried, insistent. "That's why I was shocked when I returned later. I just ran to my car and drove away.

I went home, showered, fed my dog, got dressed for the morning, and started back to the track. I stopped to get something to eat and when I arrived...you know the rest."

Hudson didn't back off. "Tell me again what Monroe's condition was when you left him. Did he cry out? Was he staggering around? Was the horse still a danger to him?"

"No, none of that," Kayla stressed. "When he— Mr. Monroe—whirled around, he was facing the wall. He didn't hit his head that I could see. When I left, he was just standing there, like he was a little stunned. I had no idea that the horse injured him. I thought he just had a little wind knocked out of him. Saint had stopped bouncing around and I thought Mr. Monroe would get it together and leave with the evidence he'd pried from me. If I knew he was hurt, I wouldn't have left him there."

Hudson didn't quite believe her. He looked at Jimmy and could read the same reaction. She left without knowing Monroe's condition, and that was enough to pursue negligent homicide.

She choked up again. "I liked Mr. Monroe. He gave me a break and was putting me on his best horse. What I did was stupid, but I could never hurt him. Please, believe me." The tears flowed, and Kayla dropped her head. Almost whispering, she said, "I can't talk anymore. I'm done."

"Not yet. We have another question or two," he said, not letting her decide when the interrogation was over, especially since she hadn't asked for a lawyer.

She waited as a lull settled in the room.

Luke asked, "What role did Shawn Monroe play in all this?"

"None," she snapped.

"I find that hard to believe. If Jack Monroe was against the shot, someone other than you must have given the go ahead. It sure wasn't Carlos because he doesn't have the authority, either, so it must have been Shawn."

"Well, you're freakin' wrong," she barked. "It was just me and Bergman who knew."

"We know you have an intimate relationship with Shawn Monroe," Luke divulged.

"As far as I know that isn't a crime."

Hudson said nothing and let her come down a level.

"You lied about everything being rosy at the barn. In fact, your whole first statement was pretty much a lie. Why should we believe you now?" he hit back.

"Because Shawn cared about his dad." She continued to defend him.

"According to our evidence, he cared more about his training career and keeping Bergman as a client. I watched Dark Saint break down today, and it wasn't pretty," he told her, and watched her tear up again.

Hudson considered ordering a polygraph test for her, but the reliability of them was debatable, and in her current mental state she could fail it by over reacting, so he dropped the idea for now. Instead, he tried a different tactic, one to shake her confidence and get her thinking outside the rehearsed strategy she and Shawn had devised.

"You think Shawn Monroe cares about you? Why are you the one sitting here in the hot seat, when he was a player all along?"

She started to interrupt, but Luke stopped her.

"Listen to what we think happened, based on our evidence." He stretched the evidence part, but experience steered him close to the truth.

"After his death, we found Jack Monroe's car behind Shed Row C. He parked far enough away so he could show up in your shed row by surprise. That's why you didn't see him when you came to give Dark Saint a shot. He was probably already there, waiting in the shadows. He suspected something was coming down. And he wasn't alone. Shawn was with him. He came along not to look after his dad, but for damage control."

Kayla tried to respond, but he interrupted her.

"A security guard remembered waving Jack's car through that night." That part was true, but the guard didn't recall whether the son was in the car. Luke continued as though he knew Shawn was there.

"When Jack caught you in the stall, preparing to give the shot, he walked in and wrestled it away, much like you described. But Shawn was in the mix, too. When Jack got the shot away from you, Shawn told you to get out of the stall. Right?"

"No, his father was there alone," she insisted, but her eyes betrayed her.

"You both left, and you drove Shawn home. Neither one of you stayed to see if Jack was okay after being knocked around by the horse. You two left Jack in distress and then he died. That's negligent homicide. Or maybe Shawn pushed the plunger."

"You're nuts!" she exclaimed, with contempt. "He didn't do anything."

"So he *was* there?"

"I didn't say that. You're twisting my words."

Luke shook his head. "No, I'm just trying to get at what really happened."

"Well, it happened exactly like I said, and I'm not changing my testimony because of your cockamamie ideas."

He thought she protested too much. Later, a polygraph on both of them would be valuable.

"I'm just trying to get at the truth, and your track record is shaky at best."

"I'm scared," she lamented. "I've never been in any kind of trouble before, and now this?"

"Telling lies will get you in more trouble, because sooner or later it will all come out," he said, hoping for a breakthrough.

Silence settled in around them like a stifling fog, until Kayla broke the calm. "Am I going to be arrested?"

"Probably," he answered calmly. "You're still withholding information, and unless Shawn is implicated, you're the one left holding the bag."

"Okay, there is more," she confessed. "Shawn was there and we did leave together. It was just a simple shot that went wrong. There was never any intention to harm Mr. Monroe, on my part or Shawn's. How did he die, anyway?"

Hudson had wondered when she would ask. "He took the shot meant for the horse."

"Oh, no..." She started crying again, and the detectives waited for her to clear her head.

"So you see what all this is about?"

Kayla nodded yes, but wouldn't look him in the eye.

"Now will you tell us exactly what happened?"

She finally caught the gravity of the situation.

Luke modulated his voice, soft and concerned, sensing she was close to a meltdown. "I know it isn't easy, but what went wrong?"

"Well, at first, I didn't know Shawn was there. He must have been standing in the shadows. When his dad and I got into a fight over the shot, Shawn came into the stall and told me to give him—uh, Shawn—the shot and get out. But I didn't want Shawn to have it."

"Why not?"

"I didn't want those two going at it."

"Had that happened before? Going at it over something?"

"Sometimes, when their tempers were hot. I handed the syringe to Jack and told Shawn, 'Let's get out of here'. I knew Jack would get the contents analyzed and then we'd be in big trouble. I left the stall and the two started arguing. Saint thought they were mad at him so he went nuts, bouncing all over the place."

"Why didn't they step out of the stall to fight about it?"

"The horse was in the front left corner, blocking the doorway with his rear end. Mr. Monroe was trying to get out, but Saint whirled around and knocked him a good one."

He questioned, "Did Jack take the syringe with his right or left hand?"

Kayla tried to picture it in her mind. "The left hand."

So far she was right. He probed, "When you handed the syringe to Jack, how was he holding it."

She thought about it in a long, pregnant pause and answered, "The plunger was at his thumb, like it would be if you were going to give a shot, and the needle end was where it could point into Monroe's body if he wasn't careful."

Luke visualized that when Dark Saint rammed Monroe, his body hit the plunger, thrusting the needle into Jack and emptying the contents. Or else the shot discharged when Jack hit the wall. Either way was plausible, unless Shawn Monroe did something to his father.

"Where was Shawn at this point?"

She searched her memory. "When Saint swung around and hit Mr. Monroe, the door was clear, so Shawn was able to get out."

Kayla shuddered. "His dad might have been a little stunned, but he never fell down, or said anything, and the horse just stood there, shaking. Shawn and I left, thinking that Jack just got bumped around by the horse but he was okay, and he had the evidence he needed. I dropped Shawn off at home and then went to my place."

Jimmy and Luke looked at each other knowing there were a slew of unanswered questions, and the son's interrogation was top priority.

Luke summed it up. "The crime here was that if you two had stayed with Jack and checked his condition, you'd have seen that he took the shot. And if you'd called 911, he'd probably still be alive. By leaving, you both committed negligent homicide."

Grief mixed with fear wrenched her face. "What does that mean?"

Luke replied, "It means, you were in a position to assist and you two didn't, so as a result, Monroe died. It's not as serious as homicide, but it's a significant charge."

She began crying again and dry heaves wracked her body. When she stopped, she turned to Luke. "Am I going to be arrested?"

Staring into her reddened eyes, Luke emphasized, "For now, you're free to go, but don't leave the county or you *will* be arrested. We need some time to consider your testimony."

JIMMY DROVE HER HOME, WHILE LUKE SAT contemplating the facts. It all added up now. According to Kayla's testimony, neither she nor Shawn planned to hurt Monroe. It was an accident. But she confirmed what Luke had suspected all along. Shawn went with his dad to the stables so he could control the outcome. He wasn't seen by Carlos's witness because he waited in the shadows during the early dispute between his dad and Kayla, prepared to step in at the right moment. After Jack was jostled by the horse, if that's what really happened, the two left Jack unattended. But when his dad didn't come home, wouldn't that have sent red flags that something was wrong? Shouldn't Shawn have driven his car back to the barn to check on him? His lack of concern seemed apathetic, if not cold blooded. It explained why Shawn arrived late Sunday morning, so he wouldn't be the first one at the barn. And why he remained composed at the news of his father's death. Why he lied about what happened when he was interviewed by the detectives, and in his statement to the police. Shawn Monroe was clearly culpable.

As for the drugging, Shawn never touched the syringe and let Kayla do his dirty work. The consequences for the players would be minor. David Bergman, with his money and clout, would emerge unscathed. Shawn and Kayla were guilty of attempting to drug a horse but the plan went awry. They were likely to incur reprimands from racing officials and maybe limited suspensions of their licenses. In the end, they all would walk away, except Jack Monroe, who paid the ultimate price, and that's what kept bothering Luke.

He trusted a negligent homicide charge would rectify that. Even if the preliminary hearing judge threw the case out, Shawn and Kayla would be forced to agonize over their irresponsible behaviors. He would push for the indictment because Jack deserved as much. He gathered his notes and Jimmy's and took the recording to Sergeant Ross, who suggested they take it to the Chief.

Walker was sitting at his desk, bogged down in paper work as usual.

"Chief," Luke said, placing the recorder on Walker's desk, "here's Kayla Owens' testimony. Sir, I want you to listen to it, and then maybe we can talk about what's next."

"Okay," Walker agreed and then sized him up. "Hudson, you look like hell."

"So I've been told," he said, with a weak smile.

"Go home and get some rest. You're making this case too personal."

CHAPTER 8

Wednesday, day four started with Luke and Jimmy in Chief Walker's office. The Chief started by saying he and Ross had listened to the recording and had reached the same conclusions. His position was unequivocal. "Jack Monroe was an innocent bystander who intervened to stop the drugging of a horse in his barn, and his actions resulted in his death. There's not enough evidence against David Bergman to charge him with anything. And, as I see it, Kayla Owens was an accomplice in a plot to drug a horse, but messed it up. So what? According to you, Luke, drugging happens all the time."

Both detectives gaped in amazement. Walker was all but saying they should back off the case.

Hudson disagreed, "I think we could build a decent case against Owens and the son for negligent homicide. She admits they were both there when Monroe was knocked around by the horse. By her own testimony he was stunned by a blow from the horse, which is probably when he got stabbed with the needle. And what did they do? They both left without so much as checking on him. According to Jackson, the shot brought on Monroe's coronary spasm resulting in his death. If Owens or Shawn had called 911, Jack Monroe might still be alive. I'd call that negligent homicide."

Walker was not interested in pursuing it. "Yeah, and what judge is going to buy it? Your premise is not defensible."

"We've barely scratched the surface," Luke hammered back. "The son's involvement is new territory. We haven't even interrogated him yet."

"We're not going there," the Chief's jaw tightened and his nostrils flared.

"Give me one reason why not?" Luke said, angered and combative.

"I don't have to," Walker bristled, "but I will. And then I want you to drop it." Tense silence ensued while the Chief prepared his argument.

"Well, we're waiting," Jimmy said to Luke's surprise.

Walker's frustration showed, "The case is weak, and who gives a shit, anyway?"

"What's that supposed to mean?" Luke growled, disgusted by the Chief's attitude.

Leaning forward in his chair, his pudgy face turning red, Walker said, "An illegal horse drugging is not our business. We have more serious crimes to deal with. Let the track settle it."

Luke was fuming inside. He clenched his fists and said, "A good man is dead. Doesn't that count for something?"

"Of course, it does," the Chief snapped, as if it were a no-brainer. "But their argument will be 'It was an accident' and who's going to refute that? No one. If we go after them for negligent homicide and the prelim judge dumps it, you'll be even more upset. So I say drop it."

"I don't work that way," Luke reminded him. "If I'm on a case and can bring some justice, find some closure, I will."

"And who's going to get closure over this? A son who lost his father? His girlfriend who had no criminal intent? You're losing it, Hudson."

Luke was reaching a boiling point but tried to stay civil. "Sir, with all due respect, I'm concerned about this case setting a bad precedence. If we turn our backs on it, we are conveying the message that law enforcement is not interested in the track's criminal activities. That leaves Zayet hanging out there on his own."

Walker started to interrupt, but Hudson pushed through, "Sooner or later, Zayet will be forced to hire more private protection, and that's wrong. The track deserves the same security and law enforcement commitment as any other business. I don't like your hands off approach."

The Chief shrugged and clinched his teeth. The two men were not backing down, and Jimmy was unsure how to diffuse the mounting hostilities. He offered a glum concession. "At least we cleared Monroe of any wrongdoing."

"Exactly," Walker seized the moment. "If we expose how the shot led to his death, there will be all kinds of speculation about what really happened, from murder to suicide, and you know it. The case is dead and that's the end of it."

Hudson bristled and Walker became more adamant. "I just want to keep David Bergman out of it, the way you wanted to keep Jack Monroe's reputation clean. I guess I'm hoping you'd agree that some cases are not meant to be solved."

Now Luke leaned forward, not believing his ears. "What did you just say?"

Walker spoke hesitantly, not really looking Hudson in the eye, staring above him. "It's a case of letting sleeping dogs lie."

"That's a cynical approach," Hudson sneered.

"No, it isn't," Walker argued. "You know as well as I do that justice isn't always served. How many times does a perp get off on a technicality? Or a judge throws a case out because he has his head up his ass? Or you have a good case but the jury doesn't get it? Or the guilty sentence is reduced to a slap on the wrist?"

A caustic silence filled the room and hung like a shroud.

At last, Luke breathed deep and cut through the tension with a compromise of sorts. "We could go to the track officials with the dermorphin shot violation, and ask them to cite the three people involved—Kayla, Shawn, and Bergman."

Walker tensed at Bergman's name. "What would that entail?" he inquired, considering an option he didn't know existed until now.

Luke explained, "The penalties could be anything from warnings to fines and suspensions. Depends on how serious the racing commission is about the offences. The outcome will be down played because no track wants that information out to the public."

The Chief, seeking conciliation, conceded, "Owens and the son should face some consequences for their actions, but not the negligent homicide charges you had in mind. That's what I object to."

He neglected mentioning Bergman, but before Walker could rethink it, Jimmy added, "It's important that Sergeant Ross comes along, because he'll give more weight to the claims."

Chief Walker was amenable and made the call, arranging an eleven-thirty meeting at Long Meadows with Abdul Zayet, the owner. A cold chill hung in the room as Hudson and Kidder left.

WHEN SERGEANT ROSS AND THE TWO DETECTIVES ARRIVED at Long Meadows, the sun was high and a slight, warming breeze filled the air. The track was being furrowed in preparation for afternoon racing. They found Zayet's office on the third level near the clubhouse, and a security guard was waiting to escort them inside. When they entered, Zayet was a little apprehensive about their visit when he offered his hand and they exchanged pleasantries.

The track owner had a coppery complexion, black hair, expressive brown eyes, and a reserved smile. He wore an expensive three-piece suit, and carried himself with a dignified air, as he took smooth, deliberate strides and stepped behind his desk.

"Please call me Abe," Zayet said, "and make yourselves comfortable." He motioned to the designer chairs. "Can we bring you anything?"

The three of them declined but thanked him, and sat down. Zayet took a seat, too.

"What can I do for you? Have you new information in your case?"

Sergeant Ross explained the drug facts, minus the "fatal shot" to Monroe, while Zayet's untroubled demeanor transformed into genuine concern. Then Ross looked to Hudson for support.

Luke began, "Since there are no civil criminal charges to bring forth, we think justice would best be served under the racetrack's jurisdiction. We believe there should be some hefty consequences for Shawn Monroe, Kayla Owens, and Mr. Bergman for their attempt to illegally drug a horse, and we'd like your cooperation in seeing that happens."

Considering the ramifications, Zayet posed, "I am most troubled by the use of demorphin at Long Meadows. I doubt that it is sold here, but I will look into that possibility. No matter, it was used here, and its purchase or possession is a grave offense."

Zayet rose from his desk and paced in front of the windows that faced the track. He was short, but stately, born in the United Arab Emirates.

"Where I come from," he started, turning to face the three men, "drugs are illegal in racing. And we are not allowed on-track betting. Our citizens go to the races because of their sheer love of horses. That bond between man and horse goes back hundreds of years, when Arabian horses were used in war and also welcomed into their owners' tents.

"When we take our horses to Europe to race them, drugs are severely restricted there as well. But in the United States, almost every horse that runs gets a shot or two. Something is terribly wrong with that."

Zayet looked out at the track, then back at them. "I want this track to set an example, to be a family destination, a place where I can bring my children with pride. I am dedicated to prohibiting any illegal activities here. So you have my word, I will ask for stiff penalties before the California racing commission. A copy of your findings would be helpful, so I can present accurate facts to them."

Sergeant Ross spoke, "Of course, we will provide you with all the information you need. We appreciate your cooperation on this."

"I would hope," Zayet went on, "that this incident can stay out of the press as much as possible. We are only in our second year of racing, and we are struggling to turn a profit. Bad publicity could hurt us."

"We will be sensitive to that," the Sergeant promised.

"I must warn you," Zayet added a caveat. "There are no uniform national drug laws in this country. And while drug use is a growing problem, the industry spends about what it did twenty years ago on drug testing. Most racetracks act as their own little kingdoms, doing whatever they please. If they ban Mr. Bergman's horses from racing here, and Mr. Shawn Monroe from training here, they can take their horses and business to another jurisdiction. For Miss Owens it will be more difficult. If she is suspended here, the word will get out, and she may have fewer opportunities to ride elsewhere. Just so you know there are no guarantees of justice being served as you might like."

"Do what you can, and what you think is right, and we will be satisfied with that," Ross said, and rose from his seat, sensing that they had reached a conclusion. Jimmy and Luke followed suit.

Escorting them to the door, Mr. Zayet offered, "Perhaps you gentlemen would like to have lunch in the clubhouse, my compliments. I want you to leave with positive thoughts about racing," he smiled.

Since it was after twelve, and the races would begin in twenty minutes, they thanked their host and stayed for lunch and the first race.

Luke approved of how Ross had handled the meeting. He and the Sergeant were about the same age and both had big city detective backgrounds in common. Ross was an experienced homicide detective in Phoenix, Arizona, before coming to Bidwell to escape the heat. After his lateral move seven years ago, he was promoted to sergeant about the same time Luke was hired.

As they were eating lunch, Ross commented, "I haven't been to Long Meadows since opening ceremonies. I used to frequent Turf Paradise in Phoenix, and you probably did, too, huh, Luke?"

Hudson grinned, remembering outings there with his folks. "Yeah, once in a while."

Ross sighed, "Now I guess work gets in the way, but I'm beginning to appreciate why you two come here for a little R and R."

As Zayet had intended, they left the track in an upbeat mood.

THURSDAY, DOC RILEY PHONED LUKE. "Detective Hudson, I want to update you on the drug test done on Dark Saint after his timed workout Tuesday. A track official ordered the test and Mr. Bergman objected, but there was nothing he could do about it. The Colorado lab tests were 'inconclusive' for illegal drugs, meaning they couldn't identify all the chemicals in the horse's system. But the horse was full of permissible ones, so I doubt that he felt much."

"How did he get the other shots? I thought you were his vet," Luke said, astonished.

"I thought so, too, but when I was willing to give only Lasix and nothing more on Tuesday, Bergman and Shawn found another vet who would give the additional shots. I've been replaced and their new vet is Tony Arroyo."

"Crap," Luke said, as he mulled it over. "What else do you know?"

Riley sighed, "I know I'm getting out of Dodge. I need a break. I'm flying out Friday to Louisville, Kentucky, so I can attend Jack's memorial service and burial Sunday.

Thanks for keeping Jack's reputation above the fray. He deserved that much."

"That's the least we could do," Luke said. "Too bad we couldn't have brought a stronger case against Kayla and Bergman, but the evidence wasn't there. We have met with Zayet and he will try to bring about some justice through the racing commission."

"Don't hold your breath. The penalties won't amount to much," the vet predicted. "But don't let all this turn you against racing. There are a lot of good, hard-working people at the track. It's like any other profession. There are always some spoilers."

CHAPTER 9

Like it or not, Chief Walker closed the Long Meadows case. Luke was convinced that given enough time, the case could have reached a more just conclusion, but it was out of his control. And things out of his control didn't sit well with him.

Walker didn't understand that drugs at the track were no less important than drugs on the street. In some ways, racing drugs were even more insidious. A junkie made a conscious decision to use drugs, but horses were victims. They had no choice, and people who illegally medicated horses were not just cheats, they were criminals. Yet their crimes had few consequences. As Luke saw it, drugging horses was as sinister as child abuse. In both cases, the sufferers were helpless. But he was obviously the minority report on the issue, so he tried to put it out of his mind—for now.

Weeks went by as Luke and Jimmy took on a case involving a home invasion. The media forgot about Long Meadows and covered the newest crime unfolding, which was much more troubling to the public. Four houses had been burglarized when no one was home. However, in the fifth robbery, an elderly couple was targeted. The gang of four youths broke into their home, knowing they were home, and the couple was taunted before they were critically beaten.

The victimized wife was able to identify one of the kids involved and the police department, with Luke and Jimmy's assistance, rounded them up. Ranging from thirteen to sixteen years old, they were students at Mountain Valley Middle School and Roosevelt High.

Lieutenant Dodd remarked in *The Morning Sun*, "Half of the violent crimes in the United States are gang related. We will not tolerate gangs here." The truth of the matter was that gangs were already here. As Hudson read the story, he mused that a typical, all-American town like Bidwell could mirror all the problems he dealt with in Los Angeles, only on a small scale.

LUKE SAT IN HIS OFFICE on a Friday afternoon in late May, plowing through paperwork on the home invasion case, when the phone rang. He answered and Abe Zayet spoke. "Detective Hudson, I want you to know first the outcome of the racing commission's hearing, which was just handed down. Kayla Owens has had her license suspended for the remainder of the year, for the possession of dermorphin and injection paraphernalia. I recommended no fines be levied against her because of her limited financial resources, and they honored that request." The owner paused, "Shawn Monroe was cleared of any wrongdoing since the commission could not verify who ordered the shot—Shawn or Jack."

Zayet paused and took a deep breath. "You won't be happy with this outcome, either. I proposed a suspension of David Bergman's owner's license for a full year and a $5,000 fine. I was asking for more than I thought would be charged, in case they chose to go easier on him. The commission threw out his case entirely, saying that there wasn't sufficient evidence that he purchased the drug or ordered it used. I am sorry about the ruling."

Luke was disappointed, but not surprised. "Well, you did what you could. It's out of our hands now."

"It's not entirely out of mine, though," Zayet confided. "I told Bergman and Monroe's son they would be closely scrutinized if they continue racing here. Bergman got the message and moved out his last horse, a claimer that he gave to our relocation program. I hear the horse is going to the Sheriff's mounted patrol. As for Dark Saint, I guess Bergman left him in recovery somewhere with Shawn Monroe."

"So Shawn is still at Long Meadows?" Luke asked.

"He's here, but he's being monitored by our security. Kayla Owens is working for him off track, but I have no control over that. And I'm still looking into how much illegal drug use is going on at the track. I want it stopped."

"Well, I admire you for that," Luke said in earnest. "Thanks for letting me know about the rulings."

The flow of information should have gone the other direction, to Sergeant Ross and then down to Luke. But he guessed Zayet called him first because he was more aware of how the track justice system worked.

Hudson ended the call and strolled in to Ross's office to relay the content of Zayet's call. The Sergeant sat at his desk and behind him were windows, with venetian blinds half closed to the street. Soft slants of late afternoon light fell upon him and his desk, which was piled high with paperwork—always paperwork.

Ross said he would pass the information on to the Chief. Then he smiled, looking too relaxed and unassuming. "I was about to come looking for you, so your timing is perfect. Have a seat," he offered. "How you been?"

Luke eyed him with suspicion. Ross had little time for small talk, and when he did engage, it was often because he wanted something.

"It's been a bit slow the past few months—no homicides." Luke answered with something his boss already knew. "When school's out for the summer, I suppose the kids will keep us busy."

Ross smiled again. "Well, since you and Jimmy are free for now, I have orders straight from Chief Walker. You're to work on some cold cases, and there might a few new wrinkles."

"How so?" asked Hudson, raising an eyebrow.

His boss surmised that what he was about to say would not be greeted with enthusiasm. "Walker wants you to make a temporary lateral move to the Sheriff's Office. Gates has requested that you work with him on backlogged cold cases."

Luke groaned. "Don't they have detectives?"

"Not one as seasoned as you are," Ross said.

"You mean as old," Luke grinned.

"That, too," his Sergeant joshed. "Seriously, Sheriff Gates is young, ambitious, and full of ideas, being in his first term. So he's trying some new things, including developing a few new deputy investigator positions. He's bent on clearing out as many cold cases as possible and Walker thinks you're the right man for the job."

"Sounds like Walker is trying to get rid of me," Luke said, half serious.

Ross answered, "It's just for a while."

Luke didn't feel like protesting. In fact, he questioned Chief Walker's resolve to deal with controversial cases. Maybe the change would be good.

"Okay, let's hear the rest of it," Luke sighed.

The Sergeant continued, "Sheriff Gates wants you to work with one of his deputies."

"Not with Jimmy?" Luke dissented, reluctant to change. On duty the two complemented each other and were dedicated to covering each other's backsides. Kidder was quiet when it was prudent and full of life the rest of the time. Ross's announcement was no plus.

Ross arched his fingers together and put them to his chin. "I'm going to ask Jimmy to work with Maria Santos on a case or two."

Luke didn't appreciate the shake-up. "What's all this about?"

"Nothing, except just once I'd like to see Jimmy work where he's the senior, which he can do with Maria Santos because she's not yet dry behind the ears. I think Jimmy would benefit from leading an investigation. When he works with you, he lets you run with the case, and you know it."

Luke couldn't argue the fact.

His Sergeant went on, "I think it will give Jimmy some experience he needs. Then he'll be back with you when you return."

"I guess that's all right," Luke conceded. "Who will I work with?"

"Deputy Jessica Harte, who graduated from the Sacramento Police Academy with top honors. She's been on duty about two years and fancies taking on one of the new investigator positions. The Sheriff's thinks highly of her, which is why he wants you to show her the ropes."

"There must be more to the story," Luke guessed. "Another wrinkle perhaps?"

"Well, yes," Sergeant Ross proceeded with forethought. "The Sheriff is starting a small core of deputies who can direct his volunteer mounted unit. They'd be used in pursuit, or search and rescue, parades, whatever. Deputy Harte wants to work with that project and Gates thought you could help out."

"You've got to be kidding me!" Luke exclaimed. "The Sheriff has a whole department full of cowboys, why me?"

His boss chuckled, "Because his 'cowboys,' as you put it, say they don't want to ride horses."

"Smart guys," Luke agreed. "I prefer my air-conditioned SUV any day."

"Sheriff Gates thinks you and Harte know horses well enough to get the project rolling and then others will join in."

Luke paused. "Look, I'm not cut out for the riding part of this assignment. I have a bum leg already and I haven't ridden in years."

"So you *have* ridden," the Sergeant noted. "When was that?"

"When I was a kid, I grew up on a ranch in Arizona. But hell, that was thirty years ago."

Ross countered, "Well, I suppose it's like riding a bicycle, once..."

"No, it isn't," Luke interrupted. "Bikes have brakes and they don't have brains. I'm telling you, I don't like the idea at all."

"I thought you liked horses," Ross persisted.

"I do when they're running around the track and I'm watching from the clubhouse. No."

His Sergeant persisted. "At least, give it a shot. Walker owes the Sheriff a few, and Gates wants you to go along with Deputy Harte, who *does* want to go mounted."

"Good," Luke said. "Then she can ride with someone else." Luke was not backing off. "I don't want to get saddled with this kind of work, pun intended."

"The horse you'd ride is older and seasoned, a former LAPD mount."

"Well, then at least we're a matched pair," Luke said with a wry grin. "Hell, I suppose I can try it. But you owe me big time."

"Don't I know," Ross affirmed, "and you're not going to let me forget it, either."

"Keeping score and I'm one up. When do you want me to start and how does it work—pay and all?"

Ross explained, "As I understand it, you'll keep your vehicle and be deputized by the Sheriff's Office for the duration of your stay, so you have authority to work under that jurisdiction. And the two departments have worked out payroll and benefits continuity while you're there. You'll get a briefing and paperwork to sign before you leave."

"I didn't figure I'd dodge the paperwork," Luke grinned.

The Sergeant went on, "Jimmy starts with Maria on Tuesday. You and he can finish the home invasion paperwork here Monday, and then Tuesday you'll report to the Sheriff's Office. That will give you a little time to get used to the idea of a move."

"So you've talked to Jimmy."

"Yeah, he left my office a little bit ago. He seemed okay with it."

"Jimmy rolls with the punches."

Ross added, "I don't think there'll be much horseback riding involved. You'll do most of your scouting from your SUV."

"Good." Luke relaxed a little as he left.

Hudson's real concern was his leg. Since he was wounded with the LAPD, he'd been through the recovery process—unable to walk, then on crutches, and now living with a slight, but permanent limp. On the other hand, being an officer he needed to show he was still physically fit. Though he worked out several times a week, he knew he wasn't what he used to be and the Chief was aware of that, too. Either Walker didn't grasp the ramifications of the Sheriff's horseback assignment, or he didn't care. But Luke was uneasy about it and his hunches often proved correct.

Hudson found Jimmy ready to leave, so they headed for one of their favorites, The Watering Hole. The bar and grill was noisy and buzzing with Friday evening patrons, including cops and firemen.

They asked for seating away from the bar and were directed to a booth beyond the commotion. They ordered beers while Luke told Jimmy about the race commission's rulings. Then he mentioned the lateral move.

"I know. I saw Ross just before you did," he disclosed. "You were probably on the phone with Zayet, so he snagged me first."

"How do you feel about it?"

Jimmy shrugged. "I guess it doesn't matter how I feel about it. It's an order."

Unable to let go, Luke was still gnawing on the unsolved Long Meadows case.

"I keep replaying the racetrack tapes in my head," Luke admitted. "The fact that Jack died of an accidental shot is a bit of a stretch. But I suppose it could have happened the way Kayla said it did."

Jimmy agreed, "It had to be all one movement. The horse hit Monroe while he held the syringe, and that pushed the needle and plunger into him." It seemed logical to the kid.

"I'm still frustrated with Walker."

"Don't say that too loud," Jimmy winced, looking around.

"I'm not," Luke replied, lowering his voice a notch. "It's just that from the beginning, he wanted us to leave Bergman alone."

"Why would he do that?" Jimmy countered.

"The Chief is appointed by the City Council, headed by the Mayor. Real estate is the hottest business in this county, much bigger than farming and racing. I just wonder sometimes how far Bergman's influence and money reaches," Luke murmured with conviction.

"Well, don't go saying that to anyone but me," Jimmy squirmed, "or you'll be out of a job."

"I already am, as far as Walker is concerned." Hudson smiled, "I just can't let go of my detective-minded hunches."

Jimmy grinned, too, and they both looked around, leaving their serious conversation behind. Kidder began reading the menu while Luke noticed a pretty blonde Sheriff's Office deputy in the booth across the aisle from them. Dressed in the dull beige uniform, her hair and face were even more radiant. She tucked a long strand of golden hair behind her ear, exposing her flawless profile. Another deputy sat across the table from her. He was a big African-American with a wide, toothy smile, and a deep baritone voice that carried even though Luke couldn't hear what he was saying. She said something and he let go a hardy laugh, enjoying her company in a comfortable way, like partners. The black deputy answered his cell phone and the blonde looked over at Luke, catching his gaze by surprise. Their eyes locked and she returned a demure smile, reminding him there was much more to life than stewing over police work. He smiled back.

PART II – GONE MISSING

"There can be no keener revelation of a society's soul than the way in which it treats its children."

– Nelson Mandela

CHAPTER 10

Alone and discarded, the small child sat on a large flat rock in the middle of a clearing. A rutted, seldom traveled road wound through the mountain meadow. She tried to understand why they had left her here. Hadn't she done everything they wanted, even when he beat her and locked her in the closet? Even when he slapped her for crying and withheld food and water? Even when he touched her where he shouldn't and her mother ignored her cries? What had she done today to provoke them to abandon her?

Wise beyond her years, she should start school in the fall, if they let her go. In the six short summers of her life, she had learned how to stay alive, but now she wondered if she could survive this. Weren't there bears and wolves and mountain lions in the woods beyond the clearing? How would she find water and food and stay warm during the night? She had cried until there were no more tears, thinking about such things during the hours she sat upon the rock. Perhaps they'd come back, but she doubted it. They never said they would.

Her dress was unraveling at the hem, threadbare and too small. The shoes she wore, she had long outgrown and they pinched her feet. Her flaxen hair had not been brushed or washed in days. The small doll she clutched was her one possession.

The hot summer sun and lack of water were making her light-headed, but she feared retreating to the cool forest because if they returned, they wouldn't see her.

She watched as a large gopher snake slithered across the broken road and into a hole in the tall weeds beyond, but it didn't frighten her. She was much too brave for such trivial fears. Flies buzzed in the stagnant air, and insects crawled in the dry grass. An ant worked its way up her leg and she flicked it to the ground.

The sun was lowering in the sky when she heard the sound of a motor. Maybe they regretted leaving her after all and were returning. She stood and listened intently as the clattering noise came closer, and an old pickup truck entered the field, bouncing down the furrowed road towards her.

The old Dodge slowed even more, as if hesitating. She waved. It was not them, but it was someone...someone.

The truck pulled alongside her and a man sat behind the wheel. His head shaven and face tanned, his dark eyes studied her.

"Are you lost, little girl?" he asked and broke a smile.

"My name is Amber," she said.

"Well, are you lost, Amber?"

She nodded yes, thinking he looked kind enough.

"How long you been here?"

"A long time," she replied, and started to cry.

"Are you hungry?"

"Yes," she sobbed, and looked up at him.

"You come around to the other side and get in. You can go with me. I'm just coming back from the store and I have cookies and milk, if you want 'em."

Smiling through her tears, she walked around the front of the truck, as he leaned over and opened the passenger side door. He reached for her tiny hand and helped her climb inside the cab.

She was never seen again.

CHAPTER 11

When Luke arrived at the Park County Sheriff's Office the next Tuesday morning, the day was warming fast, hotter than usual for the first of June. The two-story brick building wedged between tall trees as if it grew out of the pine grove.

The receptionist behind the bullet-proof Plexiglas window in the waiting area said Deputy Harte would be with him shortly. He wandered around, eyeing photos of past sheriffs going back to pioneer days when they rode horses. Some had moustaches and big white hats, and sat atop silver-trimmed saddles on handsome horses, looking like actors in early black-and-white B westerns. He smiled, reflecting on those days through stories and pictures from his dad.

The office door opened and a tall female advanced, sporting a crisp, khaki deputy's uniform.

"Deputy Jessica Harte," she greeted him, with an outstretched hand. "You must be Detective Luke Hudson?"

"None other, and call me Luke," he said while shaking her hand and noting her firm grasp.

"And you can call me Jess or Jessie. Jessica is way too feminine." She paused to ponder. "You look familiar."

With a smile of recognition, they both grinned and said, "The Watering Hole."

"I was with my partner, Lincoln Lewis. Well, my partner until this assignment," she added.

"Same here," Luke volunteered, giving her a long look. He had expected someone sturdy and hardy or tomboyish. But Jessie was vibrant and attractive, with long, honey blonde hair pulled back in a pony-tail, and a slim, almost model's figure. She held his gaze, as he stared until he felt awkward.

And he was not the detective she had visualized. All the talk about a seasoned veteran of twenty years with the LAPD left her imagining a middle-aged man, getting wrinkled and round. Instead, the man before her was at least six feet tall, wide shouldered, suntanned, and strong. Though his dark hair was graying some at the temples, he appeared younger. He had kind blue eyes and a playful grin.

She broke the moment. "I'll show you around a little before you meet Sheriff Gates."

Jessica turned and walked past him to unlock the reception area door and they entered the inner workings of the Sheriff's Office. They passed a records area on their way to a large room which contained a number of work stations, with desks, and half a dozen deputies at computers.

"This is Detective Luke Hudson, on loan from the BPD. Treat him like anyone else."

"Poor bastard," an older deputy chirped, and she smiled.

"Watch out for Al Carrara," she teased.

Luke nodded at the deputies and followed her down the hall, as she pointed out various rooms for interrogation, conferences, communications, a situation room, and offices for sergeants, lieutenants, and two captains.

"The restrooms," she pointed out, "and here's the all-mighty break room, which is amazingly empty at the moment. The fridge is usually full of leftovers. I suggest you label anything you leave in it. These guys are notorious thieves!"

They both laughed, and she added, "Well, you get the general layout. We should see if the Sheriff is ready for you."

Walking him back towards the front, down still another hall, they passed where the Sheriff's Administrative Assistant worked and came to an open door with the name plate "Sheriff Roger Gates" beside it.

Jessie told Luke she had some paperwork to do and would join them later. Gates was on the phone so they waited until he hung up and motioned for Hudson to enter. Jessie closed the door behind him and left.

Rising from his chair, the Sheriff reached across his desk for a solid handshake to Luke.

"Detective, I'm glad you could join us for a while," Gates said. "I wasn't sure Walker would let go of you."

Luke had seen the Sheriff around, so he recognized him at first glance. Roger Gates was fortyish, with a striking appearance, tall like Luke, only slimmer and more athletic. Flashing a warm smile, he had the confident, relaxed air of a man comfortable in his own skin. He wore his uniform well and his beige Stetson hat was perched on a bookcase behind him. The Sheriff invited Hudson to have a seat in front of his large desk.

In his first two years of office, Gates was gaining a reputation as a reformer and statesman, bridging the gaps among law enforcement, politicians, and the community. Word was that he'd begun reorganizing the Sheriff's Office, making good on election promises. And so far he was favorably regarded.

Gates was eager to get started. "I'm going to give you some background. You're new with us and I want you to understand where we're coming from. I don't believe in keeping personnel guessing. I asked Chief Walker for you for two specific reasons. Well, three, actually. One, I need a veteran detective and your reputation precedes you."

Hudson waited for more.

"Secondly, we're delving into cold cases, some of them serious ones. I vowed two years ago to review those cases, of which there were way too many. You can draw your own conclusions as to why. Personally, I feel that violent crime cases should never be shelved. They're always open in my book."

Hudson liked what he was hearing and nodded his head in agreement.

"Third, I want to reorganize the way some things are done around here. We need what I'll call a Special Victims Unit. It will deal with homicide, missing persons, child and spousal abuse, crimes of a violent nature. Maybe you'll have some thoughts on that later."

"What do you currently have?" Luke inquired.

"Nothing. Sheriff Kelly, who finally retired, believed deputies should do their own investigating. He thought that sharpens every deputy and staves off boredom. And in fairness, there's something to that," Gates conceded. "But the truth is, not every deputy is a good detective, as you can well imagine."

"Not every detective is a good one," Luke grinned, and Gates smiled back.

Hudson was already impressed and knew some background on Gates that he'd picked up during the campaign. Roger Gates was a young detective in the Sacramento County Sheriff's Department before moving to Park County about twelve years ago. He moved here to raise his family and started as a deputy, but soon he was promoted to sergeant. When Kelly retired after some sixteen years as sheriff, Sergeant Gates ran for the office.

Gates continued, "We're long overdue for some changes. I don't mean to speak ill of our former sheriff, but I'm not saying anything that isn't common knowledge."

"That's true," Luke agreed, because he'd heard similar comments. The new Sheriff was both diplomatic and politically astute.

So far Gates hadn't mentioned the mounted posse so Luke was hoping he had forgotten about it.

Sheriff Gates asked Hudson if he had any questions.

"Not at the moment, but I'm sure I will later," he replied.

"I'm going to ask Deputy Harte to join us now," Gates informed him, and sent an intercom message to his administrative assistant.

"Harte wants to be a detective but she's way too inexperienced. I thought she might profit from working with you for a bit. She needs a mentor," Gates acknowledged. "She seems to have plenty of raw talent and enthusiasm."

Presently, she knocked and then bounded through the door and closed it. Gates had her sit beside Hudson.

"Morning, again," he addressed Jessica. "I've been bringing Detective Hudson up to speed and now we can talk about what you two will be doing."

Gates opened a thin folder and gave Luke and Jessie their own copies of the file. "I'd like for you two to start with this cold case, so I'll give you a little of the history."

The name on the file tab was Amber Richards.

"The gist of it is that the six-year-old girl and her guardians lived in an unincorporated suburb of Bidwell from May 'til mid-August about eleven years ago. When she disappeared, she was never reported missing except by one neighbor, Lucy McCormack. A few weeks prior to her disappearance, McCormack reported suspected child abuse, so Child Protective Services and our office got involved. No one saw the child because the mother claimed the girl was with relatives in Reno. CPS asked the mother for a photo and our office tried to follow up on her story, but the names we were given didn't check out. Shortly after our inquiries, her guardians took their personal belongings and left town, taking the girl with them. We found the boyfriend's vehicle abandoned near Reno, so they probably met up with someone who helped them. We think the child was either killed or ditched in this county because traveling with her was a liability."

Jessie and Luke concentrated, jotting a few notes.

Sheriff Gates continued, "If no one is concerned about her missing, you might wonder why we are spending time and resources on the case. Well, I believe there were mistakes made. This child easily slipped through the cracks because no family member reported her missing. Isn't that a bit unusual, Detective Hudson?"

Luke hesitated. "Yes and no. I ran into cases like this one with the LAPD. The child may have been abducted by the people she lived with in Bidwell, so they were not her actual parents."

Gates heeded the new angle, and pondered, "So she might have gone missing in another state and reported there by her biological parents?"

"I've seen that happen," Luke confirmed. "Was she checked against the national database for missing children during or after the case closed? If she was, it should be in the file."

"It isn't, so I assume it wasn't done," Gates admitted.

"Well, that would be a place to start," Luke suggested and opened the folder, which displayed a prominent photo of a light-haired young girl, pretty face, blue eyes, and a slight smile. "Do you have other photos of her?"

"No, just the one," Gates said.

Luke reasoned, "Problem is, Amber Richards might not be her birth name. So an ID may come down to just a photo, which is a tough one. How did the so-called parents check out?"

"The alleged mother, Leona Richards, had a Nevada driver's license. The address was just a post office box, and we couldn't trace her to a physical location. Her live-in boyfriend was Hispanic with no documentation. As soon as our office got that close to them, they skipped town, for obvious reasons. The case went pretty cold after that."

Hudson speculated, "If the child was due to start school, the school would have required documentation that would send up some red flags. If she didn't start school, watchful neighbors would notice that, too. Chances are, the couple wanted to ditch the girl before September."

"Yes, and it was about two weeks from the time McCormack alerted us with suspicions of child abuse, until Amber disappeared and McCormack called us again. By then the couple were gone. Our office tried tracking the adults and discovered they ditched their car in Nevada after they knew they were under surveillance. My guess is that they were heavily into dealing drugs. If the Sheriff's Office had been more on the ball, and CPS had moved faster, they probably could have locked up the couple for any number of things—false IDs, illegal immigration, child abuse, drugs. Who knows? Now it's hard to second guess how things went down."

Luke could see the Sheriff was aware of the importance of closing such a sensitive case. If they were successful, the missing girl's case would fulfil a significant campaign promise and send a message. But Gates had an agenda beyond public image and politics. "This case has stuck with me for a long time. I'm sure you've had ones like that, Detective."

"Absolutely," Luke agreed. "Some cases you carry with you until you've exhausted every angle. The unsolved ones you never forget."

The Sheriff acknowledged the same. "I was a new deputy here when this case broke, and I wasn't assigned to it. I wish I had been, because I thought I was a damned good detective, even if I *was* green. But I was working two other cases and they passed by me on this one. This crime particularly bothered me because I have two young girls and it hit too close to home."

"Do you remember who the lead officer was?" Luke asked.

"Yeah. He's retired since, but his name is Jack Huntsman. He tried, but just couldn't crack it."

"I'd like to talk to him," Luke announced. "Maybe he has some insights that aren't on paper."

"Fine with me," Gates said. "I'll get his contact number for you."

Jessica had remained silent through the two-way conversation, content to just absorb and analyze the facts being thrown around. She and Luke could have their exchanges later.

Moving on, Hudson proposed they get an updated drawing of the missing child. "But not until I talk to Lucy

McCormack and she identifies the girl. The photo could be bogus. Then it will take someone highly experienced to make such a rendition. I recommend one of the top forensic artists who work for the LAPD. Transforming a photo of a six-year-old, that isn't all that good in the first place, into a close facsimile of a 17-year-old, takes skill. It will cost more, but it's worth it."

"You give me the artist's name and I'll take care of it," Gates asserted.

"One other point. Be sure that the artist includes the birthmark on the girl's neck."

The Sheriff looked at the photo as though he hadn't observed it before.

Luke pointed out, "The mark looks like angel wings. That could be a significant factor in identifying the child, since the name in our files is probably assumed."

Gates agreed.

Luke concluded, "So after we verify the photo and get the artist's sketch, then we can go through the national database. Since most crimes take place within the state, or maybe a contiguous state, I would begin here, then Nevada, and if there are no results, branch out into other bordering states, even further if necessary. And while we're waiting on those developments, Deputy Harte and I could begin working the Bidwell neighborhood where the child lived."

"I like the plan," the Sheriff said. "And when you have some down time, I'd like you two to go through our database and prioritize the cold cases. Crimes involving drugs, robberies, sex and vice can go to Sergeant Craig Thomas of the Narcotics Unit. Homicides and potentially violent crimes, including child or spousal abuse, set aside for your own consideration. You'll just have to decide what's what. Frankly, the cold cases are somewhat of an organizational mess."

Gates turned to Hudson. "In time, I'm going to assemble some retired detectives to volunteer on the cold cases. It's worked well in a number of counties and it's very cost effective. Besides, it gives old deputies something to do, since most of them never really want to retire anyway," he grinned.

"I like that idea," Luke responded. "I may be one of them myself someday."

Gates went on. "I figure you'll spend most of this week sorting out cold cases and working on the Richards case. Friday morning, while it's still cool, Deputy Harte can get you acquainted with the mounted posse project. You can go out and meet the horses. Take a ride."

The Sheriff hadn't forgotten the posse.

"I'd rather you just rode in casual wear, no uniforms. Look like the locals. The further out some of these folks live, the more they tend to be suspicious of 'intruders.' You just want to blend, but carry your weapons."

It was all Luke could do to keep from showing his skepticism about the program, but he refrained.

Gates looked at Hudson, "Let me know if I can help in any way. I'll introduce you to more of the staff when I can gather them up. They're a bit like herding cats," he smirked. "Meanwhile, Deputy Harte can fill you in."

First they drove to the park county Assessor's Office and entered the property division. Luke showed his new badge while introducing himself and Jessica. He briefly explained they were working on a case and needed to know through the tax rolls, the people who were living on Mason Street and the street behind it, San Marcos, eleven years ago. And they also would like a current list of residents. Comparing the two lists, they could eliminate the ones who had moved. The desk clerk said she could have the information after twelve, so he and Jessie left to go back to work.

Two boxes of cold-case files awaited Hudson and Harte in a small conference room assigned to them. There were two computers in the room so they could first look at files on-line, do a quick assessment, and determine the crime category. Then they could pull the files and further review the cases. And finally, they would prioritize them according to apparent urgency. They would each make their own lists, so they could compare. There were easily a hundred files.

Around noon, when they left the Sheriff's Office, the temperature felt oven-hot, as heat waves rose from the searing pavement.

Jessie suggested a deli he hadn't been to and they ordered lunch, plus an iced coffee for her and ice tea for him. He ate his sandwich while she nibbled at hers, in between chatting. She was a talker, so he did most of the listening.

"I grew up in the Sonoma wine country," she volunteered. "My folks have thirty acres near Healdsburg. We had Arabian horses that my mom and I showed until I left for college. The land has long been a vineyard, with Zinfandel grape vines."

"Sounds like a good life," he allowed, and took another bite of his Reuben while she continued talking.

"Dad was a pilot for United until he had to retire at sixty-five, about a year ago. He's enjoying the life of a gentleman farmer. My brother, Bruce, followed in his footsteps and is a commercial pilot for Alaska Airlines. He's married, and his wife is a news exec at KGO-TV in San Francisco. Bruce is five years older than I am.

"Are your folks okay with you being a sheriff's deputy?" Luke asked, considering her upbringing in a refined, sheltered world.

"They weren't happy at first, because I have a college degree in wildlife forensics, which Dad thought was a respectable career. I had envisioned investigating poachers and environmentally poisoned salmon, whatever, but at the time I couldn't find a field job without moving to Washington, so I took a lab position and it was boring. Later I went to the police academy in Sacramento and ended up here."

She took a delicate bite of her tuna on rye and asked, "How about you?"

He ignored the question for now and asked about Sheriff Gates's posse program.

"Oh, we have a volunteer mounted group for search and rescue, even pursuit in remote areas. Gates would augment the volunteers with a small group of deputies, maybe four to six, to work alongside them, plus ride in parades, opening day at the racetrack, and so on. Sounds good, huh?" she chirped.

Luke was more cautious. "I don't know. Horses are expensive and take a lot of care for the amount of use they get."

She considered his comment before asking again, "Now, tell me about you."

He wasn't used to talking about his past, but he figured if he didn't tell her now, she'd persist later. "My brother and I grew up on a cattle ranch near Prescott, Arizona. We rode horses, bucked hay, drove tractors, and the like."

"Then you'll fit right in with the mounted posse project," she beamed.

He smiled at her optimism, "That was a long time ago. I'm better suited for wine making now."

She grinned, "What about your brother and parents now?"

"My brother and his family stayed on the family farm in Arizona, and I don't see them often. While I was in college at UC Berkeley, my parents were coming to see me and both were killed by a drunk driver going the wrong way on the freeway. It was a fiery wreck that burned the two cars and all the occupants. That's when I decided to change my major from pre-law to criminal justice and go into law enforcement."

"How awful," she shuddered. "That would be difficult to get over."

"Some things you never get over," he reminded her and himself.

CHAPTER 12

Luke and Jessie went back to the Assessor's Office after lunch and the list was waiting for their pick up. Only three places had the same occupants as eleven years ago. They decided to call ahead and arrange a meeting with Lucy McCormack, because she was the main person they wanted to interview. First, they would cold call the other two residences, and then talk to McCormack last.

As Hudson and Harte drove through the older subdivision, they found Mason Street fairly run down. They passed a place with a "For Rent" sign on a scraggly lawn. A few homes were manicured, but most displayed weedy yards with toys, wading pools, kids, and assorted mutts. Open garages exposed motorcycles and four wheelers. Many of the houses needed repainting. Judging from the tax rolls, the home owner turnover was considerable, and the neighborhood had seen better days.

Two of the three addresses they targeted were on the street where the Richards girl had lived. A woman came to the door of the first place they stopped. She told them that her mother, who had lived in the house fifteen years, now was in the final stages of Alzheimer's and mostly confined to a wheelchair.

"You can come in if you'd like, but she won't be able to help you, and eleven years ago I wasn't here that often."

Luke showed her a photo of the girl at age six, and she looked at it carefully. He reminded her that the Richards' house was two doors down on the same side of the street.

"The only thing I remember is that my mother didn't like the occupants. Thankfully, they weren't here that long, but they were the only neighbors she complained about. She objected to all the people coming and going, some of them on revved up bikes. And they played loud music—the boom-box stuff. The thought crossed my mind that it was a drug house and I considered calling you guys, but my mom was living here alone then and I guess I didn't want to cause trouble that could come back on her."

"Did your mother ever mention the little girl?" Jessie asked.

The daughter weighed the question. "Mother had heard they had a little girl but she never saw her. She said other kids played in their front yards, like now, but not her. I wish I could tell you more," she said, as she handed the photo back.

Luke gave her a Park County Sheriff's Office card with his name written on it and told her, "Please call if you re-member anything else. And if some disturbance happens in the neighborhood again, just call and ask to have a pa-trol car come by. No one needs to know who called in the complaint."

She thanked him and went back inside.

Jessie and he walked past the Richards' former residence. Actually, it was one of the better kept homes on the street and showed some pride of ownership. Right beyond the house was the next home owner they wanted to question. It was a decent dwelling, but neglected. An old man wearing shorts, sandals, and a T-shirt answered the door. His legs were bony and he was almost bald. A TV in the living room had a re-run of "The Andy Griffith Show" on the screen.

As Luke and Jessie made their introductions, it was obvious he wasn't going to ask them in, and he didn't particularly like them standing on his front porch, either. They explained why they had stopped by and showed him the photo. He took a disinterested look and handed it back.

"I wasn't home much then," he said. "The wife would know more, but she passed away two years ago. Those neighbors were a pain in the ass, I can tell you that. Loud music, scumbags in and out, like having the Mexican mafia next door. Never saw the kid. I was glad to see them go."

"Did you complain about them to the Sheriff's Office?" Luke asked.

"Nah, didn't want to get them pissed off when I had to leave the wife here alone. You cops are never around when you need one, you know?" the old man grumbled.

"What do you mean by that?" Jessie asked, starting to get her back up.

"Look at this street! Going to hell in a hand basket, and I don't see you guys out here patrolling around." He glared at Jessie.

Luke gave him his card. "I'll check into whether your street is getting the same coverage as others. Would you like a call back on that?" He knew the old man would say no and he did.

Jessie was more than ready to leave, but Luke persisted. "If you think of something pertaining to the little girl, please give us a call. A young woman's life could be at stake here."

"I'll call if it gets one more pervert off the streets," the old man groused.

Luke thanked him and they left.

"He adds new meaning to grumpy old men," Jessie remarked.

They walked back to the SUV and drove around the block to the house on San Marcos Street, and the resident Luke most wanted to question. The occupant, Lucy McCormack, lived directly behind Amber Richards' house and they shared a common backyard fence. Mrs. McCormack had been the neighbor who reported the missing child to the police. She would undoubtedly have some pertinent observations.

When he and Jessie approached the front door and rang the doorbell, a pleasant elderly woman, probably in her eighties, came to the door. She was spry, with short white hair. Despite her wrinkles she had a youthful sparkle in her eyes. Luke introduced himself and his partner, and showed her his detective badge. He was plain clothed and Jessie wore her badge on her deputy uniform.

"Do come in." Lucy welcomed them into the living room and invited them to sit. The room was a bit too warm, but decorated with a life time of family photographs and memorabilia without looking cluttered.

"My, a detective," she gushed, admiring Luke's presence. "That's about all I read, detective stories, and I watch detective shows on TV, like *Castle* and *Blue Bloods*. Are those shows very realistic?"

"Somewhat," Luke answered, smiling. "However, they solve crimes in an hour and use their guns a lot more often than real officers do."

"I bet that's right," she said, enjoying the interchange. "You probably have some fascinating stories to tell." Then she turned to Jessie, whom she had been ignoring, and said in awe, "And women in law enforcement. If I were young now, I'd be doing just what you are. That was not an option in my day."

Jessie said, "I know. I feel fortunate."

Lucy jumped up. "Well, where are my manners? I must fix you some tea. And I just baked some snicker doodles."

She scurried off to the kitchen, and Jessie remarked, "Isn't she refreshing after Grumpy?"

Luke grinned, finding pleasure indulging the old woman. Shortly, Lucy returned and placed a small platter of cookies on the wooden coffee table in front of them.

"They're still warm," she said, the scent of cinnamon in the air, "and the tea water is on. How can I help you?"

Luke repeated what he had mentioned on the phone, reminding her that they were here to talk about little

Amber Richards. He showed her the girl's photo to refresh her memory, and said, "It's the only one we have. Did you happen to get a snapshot of her?"

Lucy murmured no and took a long time squinting at the enlarged copy of the photo.

Hudson held his breath, concerned it wasn't a match.

Finally, she said, "That's her, all right."

"Are you sure?"

The elderly woman replied, "Yes, I'm sure, Detective. I remember the birthmark, like little angel wings."

Luke breathed a sigh of relief, and Lucy shook her head. "That poor child. I've shed many a tear over her and her memory haunts me to this day. I'm so glad that you are re-investigating her disappearance. I don't think she was ever taken seriously before."

"Law enforcement did what they could, but there was little to go on, and every shred of evidence led to dead ends," Luke explained.

"Is there fresh evidence to reopen the case?"

"Not really," Luke admitted. "But the new Sheriff would like to try one more time to solve it."

Lucy leaned forward in her chair to offer her theory. "You know, I think she's still alive. Her body was never found, and that child was a survivor."

"Tell us what you remember about her," Jessie interjected.

Just then the tea kettle began whistling, and Lucy sprang to her feet. "I won't be long."

She returned with three cups of tea, plus cream and sugar, on a tarnished silver tray. She noticed Luke and Jessie were munching on cookies.

"They're delicious, a real treat," Luke said, and Lucy smiled.

"Thank you, Detective. Let me show you something." She led the two to her back yard. "This common fence was where I spent time with Amber. The high fence kept neighbors from seeing into Amber's back yard, unless you made an effort, like I did. See the knot hole and cracks in the boards? I would sit and talk to her. She was not supposed to talk to neighbors, so I told her to bring her doll to the back of the yard and pretend that she was playing. Then I would read her stories. If her mother or the boyfriend came outside, she would go back to the house and I would resume gardening as though nothing was going on. I think they abused her because I once saw bad bruises on her arm and neck."

Jessica asked, "When you saw she was being abused, did you contact the police or some other authority, like Child Protective Services?"

Lucy choked up when she said, "Yes, I did, but I probably waited too long to say something. I've lived with a lot of guilt over that."

"Who did you notify and what did they do?" Jessie persisted, even though it was a delicate subject.

"CPS, and they called back a few weeks later. Said they had looked into the situation and the girl was out of town with relatives. That's all I heard, but then the next thing I knew, the whole family was gone."

Lucy was uncomfortable talking about it and suggested they go back inside. They sipped their tea in silence, and Luke said, "You were the one who reported her missing. Tell us about that."

"It was mid-August," she began. "You probably have the dates on file. But Amber wasn't in the back yard for the better part of a week, and the adults weren't around either. That was unusual. Amber was outside a lot. I believe she wanted to get away from them when she could, and she liked to have me read her stories. I also noticed that sometimes when I didn't see her, there was loud music playing. I think they locked her in a closet or small room and played music so you wouldn't hear her if she cried out. Though she was so afraid of them, I doubt she caused them many problems."

Lucy stopped, finished her tea, and reluctantly continued her painful story.

"Anyway, when I didn't see her, I called the police. They said to call the Sheriff's Office and I did. They said they were reviewing the case, whatever that means. Some investigator came and asked me questions, but I was sure they were all gone, and the deputy verified as much. It was so heart breaking, because I really feared for that child's life."

"Do you remember the investigator's name?"

She shook her head no.

"Did you see any evidence that Amber was kept indoors for a week or so before she disappeared?"

"I've wondered about that, but I just don't know."

Luke was disturbed listening to her, hearing firsthand what had happened to this innocent child. "What you've told us is pretty much in our reports, but it was good of you to show us around so we could visualize what that child went through. If you think of anything new, please let me know." He handed her his card.

Jessie and Luke thanked Lucy for the tea and cookies, and as they were leaving, Lucy followed them onto the porch.

"Detective," she said, "do you suppose some time I could do a ride-a-along with you?"

"I don't see why not," he said, smiling. "It would be my pleasure."

Lucy beamed at the prospect.

He added, "There's some paperwork required. Could you come in to headquarters to fill it out?"

"Sure, I am still driving," she said with pride.

"Good. I will wait for something special to happen. Maybe pertaining to this case, so it could be several weeks from now. Are you okay with that?" he asked her.

"Of course, whenever you think the situation is right, I'll be ready."

They left with farewells, knowing they would see Lucy McCormack again.

CHAPTER 13

By Thursday, they completed their initial scan of the cold cases on file and found no evidence of another missing girl. It would take a week or more for the artist's interpretation of Amber Richards at age seventeen. Then they could submit Amber's six-year-old photo and the teenage rendition to children's profiles at the National Center for Missing & Exploited Children, NCME. Their report back would take more time. So at this point the case was as cold as when it was closed eleven years ago.

Hudson planned to meet with the former lead officer, quasi-investigator on the case, Jack Huntsman, over lunch at Ruby's Café. Perceptive, Jessie begged off joining him, saying, "You two will probably cover more territory without a third person involved. You can fill me in later."

The noon day was hot and dry when Luke drove to Ruby's. He went inside and glanced around. The hostess said, "If you're Mr. Hudson, I'll show you to your party."

Huntsman was seated in a quiet booth at the back of the dining area. He was already working on a two-olive martini. The retired officer had a snowy head of hair and a white moustache. He wore slacks and a light jacket, no tie, but he fit the image of a detective.

Rising, he shook Luke's hand and they exchanged a few pleasantries before they both sat down and the server asked Hudson what he'd like to drink. He said a club soda with lemon.

Jack Huntsman seemed more than eager to discuss the case, but first Luke got him talking about his life after retirement. Huntsman ate an olive from the cocktail pick and took a measured sip of his drink. Then he answered, "Well, I miss work. It was my life. But fortunately, I still have a wife, two kids, and four grandkids, and they keep me somewhat occupied. And I've taken up golf. My wife was a nurse and saw some of our victims in the E.R. So she knew what we dealt with and understood my work."

"You fared better than I did," Luke conceded. "My wife resented being married to a cop and after almost twenty years we divorced. No kids, either. I just recently made a lateral transfer to the Sheriff's Office. So far I like what I see."

Huntsman said, "Except they need a detective unit and I hear they're working on that."

"Yes, they are." Hudson inquired, "I heard you came from the Fresno PD?"

"I did. I was a patrol officer," Jack said and stopped talking to read the menu. "I'm starved. The wife is trying to keep me slim with granola and fruit for breakfast, salads and lean meat for lunch and dinner, no beef. I think she's fighting an uphill battle, but God love her for trying," he grinned, looking down at his plump paunch.

He ordered a cheeseburger and Luke settled for a chicken salad. While they waited to eat, Huntsman began talking about the Amber Richards case.

"You know, I worked my ass off on that case but it was dead on arrival. Just not enough evidence and no one cared, except the little old lady, who lived behind them. And Leona Richards, who said she was not the girl's mother, but I'll get to that."

Huntsman shook his head and took a hardy swallow of his martini. "I'm glad Sheriff Gates reopened the case. The girl deserves a second chance. Maybe a fresh approach..." his voice trailed off.

A mention of Amber's mother or guardian alerted Hudson. "Tell me what you know about Leona Richards. There's nothing much in the files on her. What happened to her?"

Huntsman answered, "About two weeks into the investigation, I drove to the neighborhood in an unmarked car and parked across the street, a few houses down. I waited until Leona's boyfriend left and then I walked to the Richards house."

"You couldn't be sure who else was at the house," Luke surmised.

"True, but it was quiet, midday, and Leona came to the door. I said I'd like to ask a few questions and she told me to go around the side of the house and she let me in the back yard. The fence was high so no one could see us talking. That concerned me because I didn't know if it was an ambush. But if I called for reinforcements, I figured I'd blow my chances to have a one-on-one with her. She was as nervous as a nun at a penguin shoot."

Luke suppressed a grin.

"She said the child was asleep in the house. This Leona made me promise that what she was about to tell me was off the record. Her boyfriend didn't want any cops around. I don't think she was just being dramatic. She was scared shitless and though she didn't say it, I think she was abused, too."

Nothing about this encounter was in the girl's file, so Huntsman kept his promise.

Their lunch arrived and Jack's burger smelled so good that Luke was wishing he'd ordered the same. Huntsman ate a few hardy bites before going on with his story.

"Leona said the girl was not hers. Amber was the daughter of a topless dancer, drug addict in Vegas who called herself Lady Diana. Leona didn't remember, or else didn't know, Diana's last name. She said they rented an apartment together and took turns caring for Diana's daughter, Amber. They paid cash for the rental and she didn't recall the address. They only lived there a short time and it was two years later by the time I talked to her. Leona worked in the same bar, but she wasn't into heavy drugs."

"What was the name of the place?" Luke asked.

"The Hook-Up Lounge," Jack replied, and took a swig of his martini. "I checked it out. These sleazy places don't like to leave paper trails. They paid their dancers in cash so the girls didn't have to pay the IRS. This Diana was also into prostitution, cash of course. The owner of the lounge conveniently couldn't recall Diana."

Hudson wasn't surprised and let Jack lead on. "Reluctantly, Leona took the kid, who was four at the time, and she and Mauricio Gonzalez moved to California, living a couple of places before coming here. She didn't elaborate. The plan was that Diana would clean up and take her daughter back, but instead, she dropped off the radar screen and didn't even call Leona. So she essentially had a kid who wasn't hers and a boyfriend who, as she put it, was 'bothering' the little girl. She wouldn't go into that, either, but I got the drift."

Jack grimaced and dabbled with his food. "Leona asked when the CPS was going to take Amber away. I said I didn't know for sure. I didn't want to alert them even if I knew, which I didn't."

Luke pushed him, "Did you offer to remove the child right then and there?"

"Course I did," he answered, as if the question were a no-brainer. "But Leona said if the girl left with me, Mauricio would know she tipped off the cops and she would pay dearly. She was really afraid of him. So I told her they could both leave with me and be under witness protection."

Huntsman was troubled telling the story and second guessing his moves that day, but he went on, "Leona sneered at witness protection. She said sooner or later Mauricio would find her and get even. He didn't care about the kid, but his influence was far reaching. She said, no, it would have to be CPS and not the police. It had to look like she had nothing to do with the cops."

Luke listened without judging him. Jack already felt bad enough. "So what happened next?"

"Leona kept looking at her watch and said she couldn't talk any longer and begged me to leave so I did. I'm telling you, this gal was petrified of Gonzalez. As best I could tell, he had big time cartel connections.

"Immediately, I told CPS they had to get right on it and to hell with their procedures. So they did come to the Richards house the next day, mid-morning, but the house was cleaned out of any drugs and personal possessions and they were all gone. They probably got rid of the kid on their way out of the county because traveling with the girl would send up a red flag. My guess is that Mauricio got wind of Leona's talk with me, or she had second thoughts about cooperating and they packed up overnight and cleared out early that morning. That's when we did an APB, and later found that their car was ditched outside Reno. Most likely they were helped by someone else, but they weren't seen again." Huntsman spoke with regret, the outcome still nagging him.

"Was the car checked for fingerprints and DNA evidence, or for that matter, was the house they vacated?"

Huntsman shrugged, as if he hadn't considered that, and took another drink. Luke knew that he would have handled the case in a much different way. Leona had already admitted she thought Mauricio was abusing the child, and McCormack had corroborated the story.

Hudson would have taken Leona in for questioning and removed the child on the spot. They would have stayed in protective custody while the cops moved in on Mauricio and put him away. It seemed rather straight forward as Luke saw it. That was the reason why experienced detectives should be handling serious cases instead of patrol officers. No wonder Sheriff Gates was haunted by the case. He would have likely called the same shots as Luke, but he was not put on the case. Inexperience had led to two missing persons.

"Did you ever talk to Mrs. McCormack, the woman who reported the child abuse?"

Jack thought about it. "No, another officer did that. One who was working with CPS."

"Any theories on what ever happened to Leona?" Luke inquired, grasping for any thread.

Jack sighed, "My best guess is she died near Juarez, Mexico. I figure they drove through Nevada, Arizona, and New Mexico. Then he probably murdered her across the border where no one would ever miss her. According to the *El Paso Times* there've been over 350 deaths around Juarez in the last twenty years and still counting. Some of the women were thought to be victims of serial killers. Many of the cases are unsolved."

Huntsman pulled another swallow from his drink, ate the second olive, and motioned to their server as she passed by that he'd have another martini. Then he said, "It's a shame—Leona and the kid, just gone and forgotten."

"There're too many throw away kids in our society," Luke agreed. "And frankly, this case is still more than dead unless we get a new lead. If you were working it now, what would you do?"

Huntsman contemplated in silence. "You know, I do have something for you," he said with a bit of confidence. "I might be pokin' it in the wrong hole, but if it were me, I'd be scouting out Timber Ridge."

"That's a big forest. Tell me more," Luke encouraged him.

"I got what I considered a good tip after I retired. It was a friend-of-a-friend kind of clue, but I thought it was worth calling in to the Sheriff's Office. Of course, that's when Kelly was sheriff and he was useless as a wig on a warthog, so I'm betting there was never any follow up."

Luke suppressed a smile again, and said, "Well, you've got my attention, so shoot."

"My friend said his buddy was hiking on Timber Ridge about four years ago and came across a man and a young girl, who was seven or so. The man was more or less dragging along a dog on a leash, some black and white mutt that obviously didn't like the guy. Personally, I don't think you can trust someone a dog doesn't trust. Anyway, the little girl seemed frightened.

"This hiker said the man and the girl looked out of place. If they were father and daughter, the little girl was acting like an abused child. Trouble is, my friend's buddy just saw this in passing. He didn't get any names, and didn't even have a good description of the man, except that he was tall and the look in his eyes disturbed him. The girl was blonde, thin, and pretty. She'd been crying."

Luke asked, "Would it be of any use to talk to your friend again, or his friend? Maybe they'd remember something else."

Huntsman answered with a head shake, "No, I've asked him about it several times. He said his friend's story was sketchy at best. There was no car around, so no license plate, and it was one of those things that you see in passing but don't know its significance. My friend only told me about it because he remembered the case I had worked on. He was the one who connected the dots."

Jack added, "The girl wasn't the right age for the missing girl in our case."

Luke noticed he was calling it "our" case, still feeling a connection to his investigation after eleven years.

Huntsman then asserted, "But there might be a link if there's some creep around here abducting little girls. I mean, Timber Ridge is the most remote part of the county if you wanted to get away with something."

"I definitely think it's worth a follow up," Luke agreed. "What if we were to get some cadaver dogs and scout out the area? There's a lot of territory on Timber Ridge, though. Did the friend narrow down where he saw the girl and suspicious guy?"

"Yeah, that's the good part," Huntsman answered, pulling a piece of paper out of his shirt pocket.

Huntsman had been drinking his lunch and seemed to have lost his appetite for the burger. He pushed his plate aside and went over the hand-drawn map he placed on the table, the diagram facing Luke so he could see it easily.

"My friend drew this with the help of his informant, if you want to call him that. Anyway, he said he wanted to remember the location details."

Huntsman pointed to a line that ran to the top of the paper. "This is County Road 5, going east. About two miles past Pine Canyon Trailhead, marked here, is this unnamed dirt road off to the left. He said you stay on the dirt road a couple of miles and it's a rough sonofabitch, totally unmaintained, with 'No Off-Road Vehicles' signs in the area. You pass a meadow with a big rock in the middle that looks out of place. You keep going maybe a mile further and there's a faint dirt road, probably an old fire trail that goes up the mountain a mile or so. He saw the two there." He had placed an X near the end of the fire trail.

Luke was pleased to get the tip and the map. "Can I keep this?"

"Course, that's why I brought it," Jack replied. "I only have one request. Let me know what you find, if anything, okay?"

"Absolutely," Hudson promised. "We'll damn well be celebrating."

FRIDAY MORNING, LUKE AND JESSIE HEADED FOR TIMBER RIDGE. He had briefed her on his visit with Huntsman, and she suggested they use the horses to ride into the remote area, following Huntsman's map. They had apprised the Sheriff of the Timber Ridge tip and he was supportive of them using the horses to peruse the locale. Gates added this was exactly why he wanted horses available.

Luke hoped for a routine scouting expedition, because Sally and Charlie, his retired former partner, were driving up from Los Angeles to spend the weekend. Sally wanted to check out life in a smaller town, as he had suggested, and Charlie never missed an opportunity to be around cops. Luke was eager to see them for the first time in four years.

After checking out, Hudson and Harte left the Sheriff's Office and headed for Timber Stables. The morning was a pleasant break from sorting through cold case files. It was Luke's first visit to the private stable, so Jessie gave directions while Luke drove. At the foothills of Timber Ridge, the stables boarded about twelve horses in a picturesque setting. The barn and turnouts were in a meadow, off a dirt road. A house behind the facility was where the caretaker lived.

The two posse horses were kept together in a large paddock. When Luke and Jessie approached them, the two chestnuts gazed over the fence at them. The horses had finished their morning rations and were contented doing nothing.

Jessie introduced Luke to his horse, retired from the LAPD Mounted Platoon, which was started back in 1987. The horse was a twenty-year-old chestnut gelding, a Missouri Fox Trotter named Pusher. *An odd name for a police horse,* Luke thought. Pusher had a wide blaze and four white stockings that extended well above his knees and hocks on his front and back legs. Jessie's mount was also a chestnut with three white stockings and a narrower blaze. She explained that Gates wanted two matching horses to carry the colors in parades.

"You might know this horse," she told Luke, while putting a halter on him.

"Why's that?" He didn't recognize the big red gelding, clearly the younger of the two.

"This is Bergman's former race horse, Go Laddie Go," she said. "He'd lost about twelve races straight, and no one even wanted to claim him, so Bergman told his trainer to get rid of him. The trainer contacted a Long Meadows track official who helps place unwanted horses, and that led to calling the Sheriff's Office. Gates wants to use rescues whenever possible. I think they just gave Laddie to us, so the price was right. He's pretty mellow, too," she added.

"Well, I'm glad to see he got a good home. A lot of them don't, especially the claimers." Luke gave the retired race horse an extra carrot and another pat on the head.

The horses and tack were loaded into a two-horse trailer, hitched to a sheriff's truck. With Luke in the passenger seat, Jessie jumped behind the wheel and transported them to County Road 5, and then to the area on Huntsman's map. When the road became too rough to go any further, they parked in a mountain meadow covered with dry grass and weeds. The flat-topped rock Jack had mentioned was in the center of the clearing.

Luke held the trailer door open as Jessie unloaded each horse, the thoroughbred first and Pusher last. She tied Laddie, who reared his head and looked around anxiously. Luke was comfortable taking the lead rope of the calm, old gelding, and tying him to a ring on the trailer.

Saddling up, they took drinking water and guns in their saddle bags, and mounted the horses. Luke felt awkward as he swung his right leg—the injured one—over the horse's back, barely clearing Pusher's rump. But he managed and got comfortable in the saddle.

They followed the rugged road out of the parched meadow, and headed towards the pines. Laddie was skittish, shying at shadows and imaginary spooks, but Jess appeared unfazed. "He'll settle down. It's his second home in just a few weeks. Horses don't like change."

"Neither do people," Luke added.

Her gelding had a longer stride and quicker steps than Pusher, who was content to lug along behind. Luke didn't mind. He liked watching Jessie's long golden ponytail sway with each stride, and her hips shift in the saddle, flowing with the rhythm of her horse.

A large hawk circled high overhead, piercing the silence with a shrieking cry. The only other sounds were the horses' hooves striking the hardened ground and the squeaking of leather. Horses had a way of quieting the soul.

Luke couldn't believe he was getting paid to go horseback riding. He remembered rides as a kid with his father. His dad would be smiling to see him now—the sheriff deputy riding along with an "eye-fetchin" sidekick.

He grinned as Jessie looked back at him.

"What are you smiling at?"

"Memories," he replied.

Much to his surprise, Luke found his early years of handling horses coming back to him. His leg might get a little stiff after an hour's ride, but he hadn't ridden in years, so that was to be expected. Jessie, on the other hand, was an accomplished equestrian and at complete ease, quite in her element. Her back was straight and her butt deep in the saddle, well seated if her horse spooked. She pointed to a freshly used bike trail and they followed it further into the pines. It wasn't the fire trail on the map, but the two might intersect. The trail was narrow and cool under the canopy of trees. The horses continued single file, and started to breathe heavier as they climbed the mountain. Pusher began to labor and Luke wondered why go on. The bike trail Jessie had chosen and the fire trail on Huntsman's map were running parallel, unlikely to intersect, and they had been riding more than an hour.

Jessie stopped where there was room for Luke's horse to halt beside her. For some reason, he had a foreboding feeling about this place, as if something had happened here or was going to. Seldom did his premonitions surface, but when they did, he had learned from experience not to discount them.

"I think we should turn back," he said. "I'd like to find the fire trail before it gets too hot and we're not going to get there from here."

Luke needed to stretch his legs, because he wasn't used to riding. Maybe he'd walk and lead Pusher for a ways on the descent.

"Okay, but let's rest the horses for a minute," she said, reaching behind her, into her saddle bag to pull out a bottle of water. Luke did the same. The water was warm but welcome. The horses could go all day without drinking. The forest was silent except for birds chirping and a slight breeze stirring the pines.

A single shot whined overhead, a rifle firing from up the hill. Another shot followed. Jessie was already on the ground, griping Laddie's reins as he danced around. Pusher stood taut, like a statue.

"Get down!" she cried. "You're a sitting duck up there!"

Luke was trying to dismount, but his bum leg was too stiff. He knew if he didn't clear Pusher's back as he swung his right leg over, he would goose the horse's rump and make him bolt.

Jessie saw the problem and ordered, "Get down on the off side!"

"Horses aren't trained for that," he countered.

"Do it anyway," she insisted while tying her horse to a tree.

A third warning shot pinged above them, and Luke hollered out, "We're just horseback riders. Stop shooting!"

Jessie held his horse's reins close to the bridle, as he swung his left leg over the horse's rump, in a clumsy dismount on the right side instead of the left. Pusher was more unnerved by the gunshots than the dismount, but he held his ground. Laddie was pulling and whipping back and forth on his tie rope. The high-strung thoroughbred was ill-prepared for gunfire, but then Luke and Jessie hadn't anticipated it, either.

A fourth shot resonated. "That's it!" she said, pulling her Smith and Wesson with holster out of the saddle bag. "Stay with the horses. I'm going in!"

"Wait," he warned, but she was already running zigzag through the brush.

"Shit!" he muttered and tied Pusher's lead to another pine tree. He was already wearing his gun and handcuffs on his belt, under his untucked shirt.

Still another rifle shot, this time in Jessie's direction, and he ran to the left of her, wanting to give the gunman two targets instead of one.

He reached an opening in the trees and spied a small, weathered, rundown cabin. In front of it was a rough looking unshaven guy pointing a .22 rifle at Jessie, who had her gun on him, in a standoff about 100 feet apart.

Luke had a clear shot at the man, who hadn't spotted him yet.

"Police! Drop the gun!" he shouted.

The surprise of a second person swung the shooter around to Luke, and the gunman pointed his rifle down to avoid being shot. Luke hoped Jessie wouldn't fire.

"Drop it now!" Luke threatened with his Glock.

The offender dropped the .22, but Jessie kept her weapon poised, as did Luke.

"Step back," he demanded, and the man took a couple of steps backwards.

"More, dammit!" Luke yelled, and the guy moved back again, well away from the gun. Jessie ran in to pick up the rifle, while still aiming at the shooter.

Luke had closed the gap as well and commanded, "Face down on the ground!" The guy defiantly didn't drop.

"If you resist, I'll shoot you," he barked, and the man complied reluctantly.

"Hands behind your back," Luke ordered, "and don't move!" He glanced at Jessie. "Keep me covered."

She was only five feet away from the prone man now, with her gun pointed at his head, but she was shaking. Luke holstered his Glock, stepped in, and cuffed the guy's hands behind his back. Jessie lowered her gun while Hudson patted the shooter down for more weapons.

"Son of a bitch, that hurts!" the man cried out, as Luke searched and rolled him on his sides in rocks and dirt.

"You could be dead and it wouldn't hurt at all."

He turned to Jessie. "Do you have cuffs with you?"

"No," she said, ill-equipped.

"Glad I have mine," he said. "Let's get him up."

They lifted him by his shoulders and he stumbled to his feet. Luke walked him to a small, sturdy pine, and told Jessie to keep him covered. He unfastened the cuffs, and recuffed him with arms behind his back, around the tree, leaving little room for him to move.

Now was the first opportunity Hudson had to flash his badge and identify himself as law enforcement. He figured Jessie wouldn't have her badge on her, either, but she instinctively watched the cabin with her weapon in hand.

"Is there anyone else here?" Luke asked, keeping vigilant.

"No," he mumbled.

"We're going to search the cabin."

"You can't do that without a warrant," the guy protested.

"You just gave us cause."

With Luke leading and their handguns drawn, they advanced to the cabin, and cautiously opened the front door. The small one-room cabin had only the one door and a few dirty-paned glass windows. A cot, folding table and chairs, ice chest, clothes, and belongings cluttered the room. There was no electricity, just a kerosene lamp on the table. Through the back window they could see a dilapidated outhouse, a Harley, and a patch of healthy marijuana plants, wire fenced to keep the deer out.

In addition to the marijuana outside, on a low camp table under the window was a small, clear plastic bag containing a powder, probably cocaine, and two hand guns. No wonder the guy was shooting to scare them off. A semi-automatic rifle rested near the table.

"We're lucky he wasn't serious because we were out-gunned," Luke remarked.

They went back outside to check on their guy cuffed to the tree. He was still there, but had managed to squirm himself to the ground in a sitting position. With weapons still drawn they searched around the sides and back of the cabin. Satisfied that the gunman acted alone, they returned to where he sat.

"Do you have your cell?" Luke asked Jessie, and she shook her head no, meaning it was in her saddle bags.

He pulled his iPhone from its belt-clip case and looked at the man. "I don't suppose there's an address here. Does the dirt road have a name?"

"Not that I know of," he answered.

"What's your name and address on your driver's license?"

"Ain't got one."

"A name or a driver's license?" Luke quipped, disgusted. "What's your name, asshole?"

"Rod Chesney," he replied. The guy was maybe mid-thirties and could clean up to be decent looking, though he probably hadn't done that in a while. He appeared high on drugs.

Luke dialed the PCSO and asked for a background check and a 10-78, backup. "Deputy Harte and I are holding a Rod Chesney." Verifying with Chesney, he repeated the full name and correct spelling for Rod Alan Chesney.

"He was shooting at us while we were horseback on a trail off an unmarked road." He then described how to find them. "If you drive to the burn line on Road 5, you've gone too far. We're at an old miner's cabin not used for years. Send a squad car and a couple of motor cops, because there's no road in, only a bike trail. You'll find the trail about a half a mile north beyond where we parked the truck and trailer. The trail winds up towards the burn area on Timber Ridge."

He waited for the check. Rod Chesney had his license revoked for a DUI.

"Deputies are on their way," Luke told Chesney. "For starters, you'll be booked for drugs and firearms possession, plus shooting at police officers."

"I didn't know you were cops!"

"So it's okay to shoot at civilians?" He bristled.

"If I really wanted to shoot you, you'd both be dead and you know it. I wasn't targeting *any*one. I just wanted you to leave. I heard the horses and figured you were a couple of flatlanders."

"You piece of shit. You're squatting in a national forest cabin, shooting at by-passers, growing pot, and in possession of drugs and guns. I don't like your odds."

Jessie was wide-eyed and still shaking. "Go check the horses," he told her. "See if they're still there," he grinned mischievously.

While she was gone, he brought the two folding chairs from the cabin and set them far enough from Chesney that they could watch him but talk in private. Luke estimated a thirty minute wait until sheriff deputies arrived.

Jessie returned leading both the horses and tied them nearby. She brought Luke and herself a bottle of water, and they sat in a shady spot halfway between the shooter and the horses.

It was the first time they could reflect on what had just taken place, and Luke was still frustrated that she took off wildly in the direction of gunfire. He spoke softly so Chesney couldn't hear him.

"You know, charging in alone was just plain reckless," he started. "No partner of mine will pull that more than once."

She blinked to fight back tears welling in her eyes, but he didn't care.

"That's how you get shot. You had no idea whether there was one gunman or two, or what you were getting into. You were unprepared and you left your partner unprotected. It worked out this time because we got lucky. But luck is short lived in police work."

She looked down at the ground, avoiding eye contact. He continued, "I did something that stupid when I got shot. You acted out of inexperience. I acted out of arrogance. Either one will get you killed. I was with my LAPD partner, and if you think I'm being hard on you, I can tell you, Charlie ripped me a new one. We were called out on a convenience store armed robbery in the middle of the night in east L.A. We could have handled it together, but as Charlie held one robber at gunpoint, I went after the fleeing one. That's when I ended up in a vacant lot and got shot in the leg. Meanwhile, my partner had to hold a gun on the other perp until reinforcements came. He was completely vulnerable. The rule is you don't separate unless you absolutely have to. That's why you have a partner, to watch your ass. Didn't they teach you that in academy?"

Jessie nodded contritely, still not facing him. He was beginning to think he'd carried the lesson far enough. She got it. "I just don't want to pick up your bloody body off the ground," he added.

She turned to him. "I won't do it again, ever."

"I know you won't," he said. "You only do it once."

They looked at the horses, who were nodding off, and so was Chesney.

Two motorcycle deputies arrived sooner than Luke calculated, introducing themselves as Deputies Pete Morales and Don Avery. They both stared at Hudson, wondering the procedure for getting the perp off the mountain.

Luke asked, "Is there a patrol car at the horse trailer?"

"Yes, Deputy Lewis is there," Morales said. "He'll do a formal arrest and take him away. I'm supposed to ride out with you."

He motioned over the other deputy who had parked his bike, and approached Hudson saying, "I'm Don Avery. I'll stay here to secure the cabin and collect evidence."

"Is one person enough?" Luke asked, remembering another drug bust gone wrong on Timber Ridge about four years ago.

Morales added, "Sergeant Thomas from Narcotics is coming up, too."

Jessie had removed herself from the scene and stood fiddling with the horses. She said no more than a passing "Hi" to the deputies. They were puzzled by her standoffish attitude.

"I told her to keep the horses calm," Luke explained, covering for her odd behavior.

"The horses have to go back, so Deputy Harte and I will ride out single file with Chesney walking between our two horses," he said to Morales. "If Chesney tries anything, he won't get far. I hate to tie him to a horse in case the horse does something off the wall."

Jessie untied the horses and brought them over to Luke. She was still uncommunicative, except for talking to her horse. They mounted their horses and placed Rod Chesney behind Laddie and ahead of Pusher, as they made their way down the mountain. Morales followed on his bike close behind them. Chesney was given water a couple of times so he wouldn't dehydrate.

It seemed like a long trek by the time they reached the truck and trailer. Officers Lewis and Thomas took over, arresting Chesney and securing him in the back seat cage of a white PCSO's Tahoe SUV, marked with sweeping gold and brown stripes along the sides and bold Sheriff of Park County lettering.

Deputy Lewis made his way over to Sergeant Thomas and Hudson. Jessie had taken the two horses to the trailer and loaded them. Luke kept a partial watch on her, but she handled the task with ease, and he knew she wanted to be alone with them.

Thomas said to Luke, "Good work. Morales will trail Lewis back to headquarters, and I'm going to ride up and assess the situation. Until we know the whole story we'll keep surveillance on the cabin to see if there's any more drug activity coming and going."

The sergeant swung his leg over the bike and started the motor with a single effort. He was tall, tanned, and extremely handsome without the arrogance, just plenty of self-confidence. "I'll let you know how it goes," he said and sped off in a drifting cloud of dust.

Lewis appeared from the passenger seat of the SUV while Morales kept an eye on Chesney. Luke was seeing Lewis up close for the first time since The Watering Hole. He was very dark and tall, likely six foot six. He smiled when he saw Jessie walking toward him, and gave her a comforting hug.

"You okay?" he asked. "You look white as snow," he ribbed her, and she forced a smile. She turned to Luke, making eye contact with him for the first time since the shootout.

"This is Lincoln Lewis," she said, still standing close to her former partner.

Luke stepped forward, and introduced himself, shaking Lewis's strong hand. "I guess you heard we've had a rough day."

"Yes, I did. Glad to see you two are okay," he replied. In the awkward silence that followed, Linc nodded at Jessie and returned to the SUV.

CHAPTER 14

In the early afternoon sun, Jessie drove Luke and the horses back to the stable. She was lost for words, which was far from her usual persona. He worried that she was not cop material. She had a soft side, and in itself that wasn't bad. But could she switch to the hard side that had to be there, too? Somehow he couldn't see her doing what he did today, not even with more experience. Also, she had a quick temper, which ruled her this time. The combination of acting impulsively and then hesitating on the follow through had killed more than one cop. Jimmy could take care of himself from the beginning. With Jessie, he wasn't so sure.

When the horses were watered, brushed, and put away, Luke walked Jessie to the passenger side of his SUV and opened the door for her. He knew she was traumatized and upset with herself besides. As he drove, he spoke first through the hushed lull, "You know, in spite of the fact you rushed in, you handled the situation pretty well."

She stared out the side window.

"Was that your first time under fire?"

"Yes," she whispered.

"Well, you did okay then. You certainly weren't afraid."

"Yes, I was," she admitted. "I was terrified."

"You're supposed to be. A healthy respect for gunfire keeps you alive."

She stayed silent, contemplating.

"You know, you can always talk to me about things, but there's professional support, too."

"You mean a shrink?"

"Don't knock it. In my first encounter with a gunman, I was newly married and in my early twenties, still a kid. It took me a long time to process it. I wasn't offered a shrink or time off. My sarge handed me a bottle of Jack Daniels and said 'Good work, kid. See you at 0800.' My wife didn't understand. How could she? You have to live it."

Jessie looked at him. "Did you shoot the man?"

"Yes. I don't know if it was my bullet or my partner's, but either way the guy was dead. I was hoping we wouldn't have to shoot Chesney today."

He paused awhile. "In war, you don't know who you're killing, but in police work, there's a name to the fallen and a grieving family somewhere."

Silence hovered between them.

Nearing the Sheriff's Office, Luke looked at his watch. Almost three o'clock and time was closing in on Sally and Charlie's arrival around five. What started as a simple morning ride to check out Huntsman's leads, followed by some afternoon paperwork, had turned into a shootout and arrest. Concrete plans were almost impossible in his line of work. That's what compelled Sally to divorce him in the first place. His change in plans would replay old memories for her, but there was nothing he could do about it.

He pulled over to the side of the road, stopped, and fished out his iPhone. He explained to Jessie that his ex-wife and retired partner were going to be in town this weekend and he had to let them know he was running late. He called Charlie and explained briefly what had happened. Charlie said traffic was holding them up, so don't sweat it. Then Luke changed the dinner reservation to seven.

Jessie said nothing, but Luke could see her disappointment that he would be tied up all weekend. He recognized that she might need to talk to him. Only he could understand what she'd just been through, and she probably wasn't going to seek a shrink or clergyman. He would find the time to call or see her tomorrow. And she still had Lewis for support.

THE SHERIFF'S OFFICE WAS ABUZZ with deputies and the press. Chesney had been booked on possession of illegal fire arms and drugs, trespassing, and shooting at officers. They had not substantiated yet whether he was dealing. Chesney was being questioned in the interrogation room when Luke and Jessie walked into headquarters.

The Sheriff himself was waiting for Hudson and Harte. He took the two into his office and closed the door. "We need your statements as to how it came down. Other than that, Sergeant Thomas of Narcotics will take over. You'll be asked to testify in a hearing or arraignment, and you may want to interrogate Chesney."

Gates advised them, "Irving is here from *The Sun*, but we have our own communications department and they can handle her."

Sheriff Gates sat on the edge of his desk. "Take a seat," he offered. "You both look tired."

Curious, he changed the subject and asked Jessie, "How did the patrol horses work out?"

She braced herself and began, "They behaved well. The LAPD mount was good. The thoroughbred needs more training, but he's sensible and eager to learn. As for the efficiency of riding into something like we did today, it's not the best use of mounted patrol. It's dangerous being above the brush line on a horse when you're under fire."

"I can imagine," he confirmed.

"And once you dismount, it's cumbersome to handle the horse and deal with a weapon at the same time. It's nothing like the old west movies," she grinned slightly. "Of course, we couldn't anticipate what happened, but I don't recommend horses if there's a chance of being shot at."

"Makes sense," the Sheriff noted. "I'm just glad you and the horses got out uninjured."

They answered a few more questions and left. Jessie walked out first, but as soon as Luke stepped out of Gates's office, Kate Irving was there, blocking the hall. She was red haired, attractive, and a veteran reporter. Hudson got along with her because he fed her information when he could, but knew when to tell her nothing, and she respected that. Theirs was a cat-and-mouse relationship he rather enjoyed. Kate was not into sensationalism or hand-fed facts, and reminded him of some of the seasoned reporters on the *LA Times*. She was certainly heads above the newbies and neophytes on *The Morning Sun*.

She started without formalities. "Luke, would you care to comment on the shootout and arrest on Timber Ridge today?"

"Kate, you know I can't. The Sheriff's Communications Department will handle releases and I'm not in charge of the case anyway. Right now I don't have any insider information. I haven't even talked to Chesney."

She smiled because she liked him, too. He was a throwback and she admired his investigative approach. "Just thought I'd ask, in case you're in a generous mood," she quipped, well aware that he knew plenty but wouldn't budge.

He grinned and walked past her. "Later, Kate, if I have something worth printing."

While Rod Chesney was being processed, Jessie and Luke waited their turn to interrogate him in the box. A deputy gave them copies of some background they had obtained on the perp and then left them alone with him, and stood watch outside the room. Luke scanned the information while Jessie sat staring at Chesney.

Rod Chesney was thirty-three, last worked as a waiter in Vacaville until he was fired due to repeated absences or not clocking in on time. A high school dropout, with a string of odd jobs, he showed a pattern of being irresponsible and a loser.

Luke turned on the cassette recorder. Many agencies had gone to digital interview monitoring, including a television screen and a sophisticated control panel. But most cops he knew still liked the simplicity of a cassette recording device, which was inexpensive and used countywide. The tapes were easy to transport to superiors and the courts.

He and Jessica sat across from Chesney, who by now appeared stressed.

Luke reintroduced himself and Harte, and asked their arrestee, "Do you want some water?"

Chesney nodded yes and slumped further down in his chair. Jessie went to the door and asked someone to bring three waters.

Luke opened, "You don't have a prior record, other than the driver's license revocation and marijuana possession, so tell me what you were doing at the cabin. It's in national forest, and on the national register, so by living there you were trespassing. When did you settle in?"

"I lost my job about nine months ago. I stayed with a friend through the winter, and then I found the empty cabin and moved in."

"What did you do for money? Sell a little weed?" Jessie asked, goading him.

He didn't answer her, but turned to Luke. "If I level with you, what's in it for me?"

"As much trouble as you're in, you can't afford to jack us around," Luke said. "Answer Deputy Harte. Were you selling marijuana to make ends meet? Or do you have a job we don't know about?"

"I'm living off my savings, as a matter of fact," he answered.

"Likely story," Jessie cracked.

Luke ignored her. "We know better than that. You obviously were selling pot."

Chesney shifted in his chair. "You have no proof. I'm growing it for my own use."

"Which is still illegal," Hudson reminded him. He knew Narcotics would try to pin him with selling weed.

"We found cocaine as well. You want to tell us where you got that?"

"Nope. I'm done talking to you cops. I need an attorney," Chesney announced.

"You could cooperate and save yourself a lot of grief. Your serious offense is shooting at officers. What the hell were you thinking?"

"There was no harm done," Chesney smirked.

"No harm done?" Luke bounced back. "When I first spotted you, you had a .22 aimed at Deputy Harte. You're looking at felony charges. That's the harm done."

Sergeant Thomas would be interrogating him tonight as well. There was little more he and Jessie would accomplish talking to him. He knew when to quit.

"We're through," Luke said firmly. He rose and indicated to the deputy standing outside the box, watching through a window, that he was finished. The deputy entered to sit with Chesney until Thomas had his session with Chesney. Then he would be hauled away to the county jail for three hots and a cot. Chesney looked bewildered, as the drugs had worn off and the reality of his actions was sinking in.

Hudson and Harte walked out and returned to talk in the cubby-hole room he and Jessie referred to as their office. He sat in a chair across the table from her.

"Jess, you're still processing what happened today. I think you should get out of here and go see your family for a few days. I'm taking time off and you should, too. Will you consider it?"

"I've already thought about it," she answered slowly. "I called my folks and they'll be home if I want to come. But I don't want to leave if you need help here."

"I'll be preoccupied with company, so do yourself a favor and go," he said softly. "Take the weekend and two more days. When's the last time you did something like that?"

"It's been a while," she confessed.

They stood and she gave him a fragile smile. "Thanks, and don't worry about me. I'll leave first thing in the morning."

"Good," he said, "and if you encounter any problems taking time off, I'll support you."

She hesitated at the thought of leaving. "Luke, you're a good man. I just hope I can measure up as a partner."

"You will. This is new territory for you," he said and she relaxed her shoulders.

Hudson encouraged Jessie to leave immediately while he completed a summary report. She left, looking back with a tentative smile. She passed by Sergeant Thomas at the door and Luke motioned him in. Thomas closed the door quickly behind him, saying, "Irving is still hanging around. She's been sticking to me like shit on a blanket."

They chuckled and got down to serious talk. Thomas pulled up a chair and sat on it backwards, with his long, muscular arms hanging over the back. "I'll have a go at Chesney now. Did he say anything I need to know first?"

"Not really," Luke answered. "Maybe you'll have better luck with him. I gather he's dealing to make a meager living. Shooting at us was even dumber than growing pot. He's basically just a two-bit punk in over his head."

Thomas nodded agreement. "Unfortunately, they're all too common. We collected what evidence we could while there was sufficient light. We'll widen the trail and take out the marijuana plants, clean up the cabin, and lock it so there will be no future use of it. We won't tear it down because of its historical value."

The Sergeant left and Gates called Hudson back in his office.

"I forgot to ask you if you found the fire trail on Huntsman's map."

"No, we never got that far," Luke confessed. "But I know where we need to go. Do you think we could work that area with the dogs Sunday morning, leaving here around 0800?"

"I don't see why not. I'll get the head of K-9's, Al Carrara, to set it up and he'll call you back to confirm it.

We only have one good cadaver dog, but that should be enough. And I don't want you two up there alone," the Sheriff added. "While Harte's off, I'll put Lewis with you for backup. I'm all too aware of the incident on Timber Ridge four years ago."

He paused. "Let's go home. It's after six."

As usual, Luke had lost track of time and would be late meeting Sally and Charlie.

While driving home, he reflected on the incident that Sheriff Gates mentioned. The new Sheriff had no intentions of repeating the mistake his predecessor had made four years ago.

Luke's first summer with the BPD, two sheriff deputies went scouting in the forest on an anonymous tip that there was a marijuana farm on Timber Ridge. Quite unaware, they walked upon a Mexican cartel operation, and the lookouts, who had been watching them advance, ambushed the deputies before they could even fire back. Both deputies were wounded, one seriously. The dealers disarmed them and beat them savagely, then doused the deputies in gasoline, and set them afire. Most of the marijuana crop had been harvested, so if the forest burned it was no loss to the cartel. Further, the fire would hide much of the evidence and send a bleak message to law enforcement.

That August, winds were fierce, whipping the flames a hundred feet in the air and raising fire temperatures to over 1,500 degrees. At times, the fire burned hundreds of acres in an hour. The first priority was to evacuate campers and hikers in the area. Some homes were vacated, while others were on standby. Hudson worked on evacuation and traffic control, to keep people a safe distance from the burn, and looters from going into abandoned homes.

From his vantage point, he watched tankers soar in front of the fire lines and drop long red clouds of flame retardant on the trees. Helicopters unloaded endless water buckets to extinguish the flames. For the first week, the battle seemed hopeless. Then firefighters and hot shot crews began winning.

News of the deputies' deaths spread like the wildfire their burning bodies started. Their remains were found within 24 hours, but the perpetrators went into hiding and were never brought to justice. Two families mourned the loss of husbands and fathers in a senseless act of violence.

Though Luke didn't know the fallen officers, he grieved with Park County, indeed the whole State, while the inferno on Timber Ridge raged on. Containment took two weeks, and over 14,000 acres of prime forest were charred.

In Southern California, Luke had worked security on numerous wildfires and there was both a commonalty and uniqueness to each blaze. At Timber Ridge, he watched wildlife caught in the inferno—coyotes cried out in fear and anguish, and a deer engulfed in flames collapsed near him on the road. Luke would never return to the burn area without vivid memories of the fire.

CHAPTER 15

When Luke arrived at his duplex, Sally's Subaru Forester was parked outside, and Charlie met him at the door.

"Hey, Buddy!" he greeted Luke with a warm hug. "I didn't have any trouble finding the extra house key, as you can tell."

"It's good to see you!" Luke chimed. "It's been too long. Where's Sally?"

"At the motel, getting ready," Charlie answered, as they both entered the cool living room and closed the door from the fading heat. "We can pick her up on the way to dinner."

The arrangement was for Charlie to stay in Luke's extra bedroom and Sally at the Marriot. It was after 6:30, so Luke suggested Charlie leave now, get Sally, and drive to The Anchor Restaurant in order to be there at seven. He would join them soon after. He gave Charlie the address for the car's GPS, which he knew Charlie wouldn't use, but Sally would.

"I've taken the liberty of inviting my partner, Jimmy, too," Luke announced. "I hope Sally can handle being surrounded by three cops."

"It won't be anything new," Charlie chuckled and headed for the door, while Luke bounded up the stairs to shower and get dressed for dinner.

The Anchor adjoined a city park and was a popular fine dining place. Set among tall pines, with lawns spreading to the river's edge, its patio was an ideal place to relax and enjoy spectacular sunsets over the water. This part of the river had been dredged and dammed just enough to create a large pond that harbored ducks, swans, and an occasional deer along the shore. Outside seating was choice, and Luke had requested a table for four closest to the water.

Jimmy, Charlie, and Sally were seated when he arrived almost thirty minutes late. They had ordered drinks and a few hors d'oeuvres. The guys stood, exchanging hellos, and Luke bent down to kiss Sally on the cheek.

"You look lovely," he whispered, and she did. Her golden red hair caught the late sun and she wore an off-the-shoulder turquoise dress.

"You're looking good, too," she said, smiling. "Age doesn't seem to catch up with you."

"Thanks, but looks can be deceiving," he joked, enjoying her compliment, and taking a chair beside her. The sun was turning crimson, leaving an array of warm colors in the dark blue water. Two swans sent sparking ripples as they passed, and the tensions of the day faded.

"Jimmy tells us you two had a shootout and an arrest today," Sally was saying.

"Actually, Jimmy isn't working with me right now," Luke corrected her.

Their server came to the table with menus and took a drink order from Luke, who asked for a Maker's Mark over ice. As the waiter left, he continued. "I'm on loan to the Sheriff's Office, working on cold cases. The incident today was unrelated. We just happened to be in the wrong place at the wrong time."

Jimmy added, "Luke is temporarily working with a female deputy, and I have a female partner, too. We're investigating a string of auto thefts, same MO."

Luke tried to change the subject. "We don't want to bore you with cop talk."

Sally looked at Luke. "What's your new deputy partner like?"

"She's, uh, in her thirties. Still a rookie, but she has potential."

Sally wouldn't let go. "Is she pretty?'

"I'd say so. She's tall and blonde. Rides a horse lots better than I do."

"You're riding horses?" she quizzed.

"The Sheriff's starting a mounted patrol. We were on horses today, which made the encounter much more unpredictable."

Luke's drink arrived and he welcomed the interruption with a toast, "Here's to good friends and memories."

He took a swallow of the deep amber bourbon, and added, "Dinner's on me tonight, so drink and eat hardy. Charlie can tell Jimmy what it's like to live with a name like Charles Shaw."

"There sure as hell weren't any Trader Joe's around when I was named," Charlie laughed. "I'd like to have a dollar for every time I've been called Two-Buck Chuck."

More laughter ensued, followed by small talk and placing of dinner orders. Luke tried to stay with the conversations, but his mind kept wandering to the ride, the shootout, and Jessie. He hoped she was handling the evening with a clearer head than his.

The conversation had changed to Sally's career, or lack of it, due to budget cuts. "But I have some promising leads for teaching jobs in the L.A. basin," she reassured them and herself, "so something will come up."

Charlie and Jimmy turned back to crime cases and law enforcement. Luke thought Charlie was not aging well. Retirement didn't suit him. Now he was white haired with a white moustache, and though still trim, he was a bit peaked. Charlie had been a tall, good-looking guy in his day, a charmer. He married briefly when he was young, and then remained single. He had had his share of lovers, and Luke had met a few. They were, for the most part, attractive, smart, and adoring. Luke relished hearing Charlie's racy narratives. Some he assumed were grossly exaggerated. And though Charlie had never been shot in the line of duty, he used to joke he was more likely to be popped by an ex-girlfriend.

Sally assumed that if Charlie was running around so was Luke, but she was wrong, except for one woman. He had met someone through Charlie after his divorce and before he got shot—Sonia—but it didn't last long.

He forced his attention back to his table of friends, but he was still removed from the conversations around him. He thought about his current life, how he seldom sat and watched the sun set, or dined in a nice restaurant, or even knew people who weren't cops. How he spent every night alone.

Shadows had lengthened on the water, turning reds to purples. A lone, timid doe approached the river's edge and took watchful, nervous sips of water.

He looked at Sally, also disengaged, and he poured her another glass of red wine.

"Sorry you're surrounded by cop talk," he apologized in a low voice, while Jimmy and Charlie chatted.

"Quite okay. It's what you guys do, right?"

"What do teachers talk about when they get together socially?"

"Students," she laughed, invoking Luke's wry grin that she had grown so fond of over the years.

Dinners were served and talk became sporadic as they ate and commented on how delicious everything tasted. After more wine and toasts, they talked about tomorrow. Charlie had arranged a ride-along with Jimmy and Maria. Luke was taking Sally to breakfast, then they might drive around town past some schools so she could compare. They could have a late lunch at Long Meadows Racetrack and watch a few races, as she liked racing in small doses. In the evening, the three would dine at Bella Rosa's. It was a full day, and Luke could only hope that his work wouldn't interfere.

The yellow orb of a full moon joined a sea of stars in the night sky and shimmered in the dark blue water. Luke took one long, last look before they left.

In the restaurant parking lot, Sally hugged Jimmy good-bye. Luke noted what a good looking kid he was, his dark, short hair, sparkling eyes, and broad smile. He seemed too young to be a cop. Charlie was enjoying the contrast of Jimmy and Luke, probably recalling his long relationship with Luke as a partner years ago. The old veteran, still telling war stories, walked with Jimmy across the parking lot to Kidder's pickup.

Except for their distant voices and the chirping crickets, the lot was silent. Now alone, Luke placed his hand on Sally's bare shoulder and she put her arm around his waist. They gazed at the moonlit water one more time. "Thanks for a perfect evening," she whispered.

His lips brushed her hair with a kiss, and she turned to hold him. The embrace evolved into a long, gentle kiss before she pulled away.

"We had a lot of good times, didn't we, Luke."

"Yes, we did. Maybe we would have made it in a town like this."

She looked at him, deep in thought. "I don't think so. Our worlds are too different."

"I'm close to retirement, you know," he said.

"You'll always be a cop. You'll be like Charlie. It's in your blood," she smiled. "And that's an admirable thing. It just isn't something I can live with, as you know."

He knew all too well. They had tried for years to reconcile their differences. They were good lovers, but not necessarily good companions.

He took her hand and walked her to the car. The spell was broken, with both a sadness and relief. It was time to move on.

After he dropped Sally off at the Marriott and began his drive home, his memories drifted back to Sonia. She was a detective with the Santa Monica Police Department and had met Charlie through some case where their paths crossed. Charlie claimed Sonia was a sharp detective, highly regarded, and he wanted Luke to meet her. Charlie set up a blind date for them, and came along for introductions. Then he ducked out after a round of drinks, announcing he had some prior commitment, and left the two to get acquainted over dinner.

Later, he told Luke, "I would have pursued her myself, but she was too young and too perfect. Hell, I was afraid I'd fall in love."

Sonia was stunning and her mere presence commanded attention, yet she was unaffected by her beauty. She was a tall, shapely brunette with reddish highlights in her long wavy hair. He remembered her deep green eyes and infectious smile. Sonia was about Jessie's age when they met, so she would be forty now.

They had a short-lived, whirlwind affair. Their attraction was so magnetic that they made wild, impassioned love that first night, and several more times in the next few days. Then he got shot and Sally stepped in to help him. He often wondered if Sonia knew he'd been shot. Had she tried to contact him? Or had she stayed away, avoiding complications? Maybe she wasn't that interested in him anyway, beyond a hasty, erotic fling. Or maybe he was describing himself.

While recuperating, he didn't want her to see him—weak, unable to walk, a semi-invalid. Besides, Sally was there. It was convenient to drop Sonia and address his problems first. Later, he regretted treating her like a quick, three-night stand. He soothed his guilty conscience by forgetting about her and blaming their separation on the accident. During his recovery, he rationalized that if she cared why didn't she call? But he hadn't called her either.

Then he moved to Bidwell. His phone number changed and so did his life. He had almost erased her from his memory until tonight. He and Charlie never mentioned her after the shooting and for the first time in four years, he wondered where she was now.

THE NEXT DAY WENT AS PLANNED. Jimmy, and his new temp partner, Maria, arrived in a black-and-white to pick up Charlie at Luke's place. There was a fresh pot of coffee ready, and the four of them sat talking on the back patio. It was Luke's first opportunity to spend time with Maria Santos and he liked what he heard and saw. Maria had a sharp wit and confident poise. Her black, curly hair framed a face graced with high cheekbones, a classic nose, and dark brown eyes that mirrored wisdom beyond her twenty-three years.

Charlie wanted to know how she chose to be a cop.

"I grew up in the barrios of East L.A. with a single mom and two brothers," she started, still carrying a slight

Latino accent. "We were dirt poor. My mom had nothing to give us except her courage. She tried to instill in us the value of an education and of bettering ourselves. My brothers took to gangs and selling drugs, which broke her heart. I finished high school, left home, and began the process of becoming a police officer. It was my best way out, and I haven't regretted it for a moment."

Luke and Charlie sat in silence, sipping coffee, absorbing what her early life must have been.

"Well, the clock is ticking," Jimmy said, rising from his chair, and smiling at Maria. "We need to show Charlie what Bidwell's Finest can do."

They left Luke sitting on his patio, watching birds flitting through the sprinklers on the lawn. Charlie, at seventy-three and loose ends, left Luke determined not to end up like him. He contemplated his own reasons for staying in law enforcement. Having reached twenty years with LAPD when he left, he could have retired four years ago. Yet he was still here. Maybe it was for kids like Maria, one of so many. Or the homicides and cold cases. It was his way of making a difference in a world that increasingly felt foreign to his childhood days on a ranch in Arizona.

In Park County, the officers referred to themselves as "peace makers" and they were. But sometimes the general public viewed them as irritants, writing tickets for inconsequential speeding or one drink too many. People slowed down or had a sense of dread when a cop car came up behind them. The media showcased police brutality and corruption and skimmed over stories about good cops. The public overlooked the fact that without the police, violence and anarchy would prevail.

While couples tucked their children into bed and slept in the safety of their homes, all over the country men and women in uniform were suiting up in bullet proof vests, strapping on guns, stun guns, batons, cuffs, cameras, and central control radios. They often had partners and extra weapons in their cars, but even all that couldn't guarantee they would finish the night alive.

Two cops were shot eating lunch at a pizza restaurant near Las Vegas. Their killers left a swastika and "Don't Tread on Me" flag draped across their lifeless bodies as terrified patrons fled the violence. A Catholic priest was killed in a sanctuary in Phoenix. Twenty-six children and teachers were gunned down at Sandy Hook Elementary. Mass shootings were averaging one a week, yet there was no major outcry to stop the carnage. We needed peace makers more than ever now, but most police departments were facing budget cuts and the prospect of doing more with less.

He rose to go back inside. You couldn't spend too much energy reflecting on the job. You just did it.

LUKE AND SALLY HAD BRUNCH AT RUBY'S CAFÉ. Then he showed her highlights of Bidwell, and the morning brought him back to his usual upbeat self. The racetrack was bustling when they arrived after the first race for a light, late lunch.

They read through the racing form and handicapped some races while they munched on sandwiches. Luke noticed that Shawn Monroe owned a mare running in the fifth race, a $2,500 claimer, and he wanted to stay for the outcome.

When the race was near, Sally jumped up to place a wager on the mare, whose name was White Roses. The gray mare was likely the one Luke had seen in Monroe's stable when he worked the Long Meadows case. Sally gave him a sideways glance. "Do you want me to place a bet for you, too?"

"I'll sit this one out," he replied, deciding to quit while he was a few bucks ahead. "Don't put much on the gray. I know the trainer," he advised.

"Okay, but you know I always bet on a gray for good luck."

Good luck, he thought as she left.

After Sally rejoined him, White Roses was ponied onto the track. Her dappled coat faded with age, but the mare was pretty-headed, with decent conformation and quality breeding, a daughter of Holy Bull. In the post parade, she tossed her head in anxious anticipation and became lathered. The track announcer noted she was "washed out" by the time she entered the starting gate. Not a good sign. She broke clean from the gate and muscled her way to the lead for half of the six furlong distance. Entering the turn, like so many claiming horses that should be retired, her heart was in it, but her legs failed her. The jockey knew she was spent and went light on the whip. The rest of the seven-mare field swept by her in the stretch and White Roses finished last.

Luke and Sally stood and walked closer to watch the after-race ritual. The jockey brought White Roses back in front of the grandstands. There would be no winner's circle for her today, though she had won five times in the past and had lifetime earnings of over a hundred thousand dollars. *When did a racehorse earn retirement?*

Carlos clipped a lead on the mare and patted her neck as the jockey vaulted off her back in a graceful dismount. Shawn Monroe uncinched the girth and pulled the light-weight saddle off, all the while talking to the rider. With a bucket of water, Carlos generously sponged White Rose's face and then splashed the remaining contents over her neck and down her front legs to cool her down. The mare's sides were heaving and she lowered her head, exhausted, as Carlos led her away.

Sally was disappointed with the loss, but she had been warned. They decided to leave.

That evening Luke, Sally, and Charlie went to Bella Rosa's Italian Ristorante. They laughed and talked through a dinner of fine Italian wines, delicate pastas, and gelato desserts. The authentic trattoria atmosphere and strolling musicians kept the mood cheerful, especially when they played "That's *Amore*" and the diners sang along with gusto.

During dinner, Luke announced that he had to work early tomorrow. Sally and Charlie were leaving anyway around ten, but he was cutting their morning visit short.

Sally flashed him the all too familiar look—*what else is new*? His unpredictable work schedule only reaffirmed her long standing resentments.

After leaving Bella Rosa's, they drove to the Marriott to leave off Sally. Charlie stayed in the car, while Luke walked her to her room on the second floor and she unlocked the door.

"Thanks for another lovely evening," she said, giving him a light, parting kiss. "I hope we can still stay in touch and be friends."

"Have a safe trip home," was all he said. They had been "friends" for four years, and he was resolute after this weekend that his life would change.

CHAPTER 16

Sunday morning, Charlie was up and about making coffee when Luke came downstairs, dressed for duty. He wore his protective vest and a khaki sheriff's uniform.

Charlie did a double take. "I've never seen you in any uniform but black or blue, Buddy," he commented.

"It feels a little funny to me, too," Luke admitted, "but today is a work day. We're working on a tip in that missing girl cold case. We'll be scouting out some forest areas with a cadaver dog, so I don't need a suit for that."

"I sure miss work," Charlie said, a twinge of envy in his voice.

Luke told him about the Sheriff's future plan to add a few retired detectives to his force and Charlie's face brightened. He could find similar options in the L.A. area, but maybe he needed a change, too.

"If it comes about, I'll let you know. It might be just what you need."

They drank a quick cup of coffee, said their goodbyes, and both left his house at seven. Charlie planned to pick up Sally for the long drive back to Los Angeles, and Luke was prepared to follow up on Huntsman's map.

When Hudson arrived at the Sheriff's Office at 0800, Deputy Lewis and two K-9 handlers were in the coffee room. Lewis introduced the team—Deputy Al Carrara, who handled the experienced cadaver dog, Rex, an eight-year-old German shepherd; and Deputy Mike Smith, who had a four-year-old Belgian Malinois, training for cadavers and attack.

Lewis had brought enough breakfast burritos for everyone and they ate while planning the day. Hudson told them about Jack Huntsman's tip and the map, which was the focus of their search. He had redrawn and enlarged Huntsman map and passed out copies to each deputy. If the girl or the dog had encountered foul play, this was an opportunity to uncover it. Further, he told them how Huntsman thought the Richards girl might have met her fate on Timber Ridge. He acknowledged the exercise was a stab in the dark, but hopefully it was worth a try, and the men agreed. Hudson had read enough about cadaver dogs to know that a really good, well trained one could work with ninety-five percent accuracy.

Carrara and Smith left to get the dogs out of their two vehicles. Hudson and Lewis followed and waited around, talking and watching, as the handlers gave their canines water and time to stretch their legs, before reloading.

They would go in two heavy-duty four-wheel-drive Tahoe SUVs. The back seats were screened off for the dogs. Linc Lewis would ride with Smith and the Malinois while Hudson rode with Al and Rex. He remembered Carrara as the older guy Jessie had joked with on his first morning at the Sheriff's Office. Al was hefty, jovial, and proud of his K-9 partner sprawled behind the grill like royalty.

As Al drove, he mentioned he knew Huntsman well because they had worked together under Sheriff Kelly. He added, "Jack has never been able to let go of the Richards case, so if we find something, he'll be as happy as a pig in a peach orchard. At least that's what he'd say."

Luke grinned, and looked back at Rex. Their success would hinge on the dog.

Al bragged, "Rex is eight, trained extensively for cadavers. We have very few attack dogs, mostly for SWAT team use. Gates doesn't want the liability of attack dogs. And also they're hard to place in responsible homes when they retire."

Swerving around the mountain curves, Luke wished he were driving, but he tried to relax. Rex settled deeper into the car seat and braced himself.

Al said, "Did you know dogs tested by the University of Alabama found a 30-year-old bone buried a foot deep? And in New York, they found a fresher corpse buried fifteen feet deep. Amazing, huh?"

"Pretty amazing, all right," Luke agreed. "What breeds are best?"

"Well, beagles have good noses but they aren't imposing, neither are Labs. So we use German shepherds and Belgian Malinois. And, of course, a bloodhound is hard to beat on a scent trail. Slobbery bastards, though."

He went on, "They're using dogs now to find drown victims. They can pick up a scent object twenty feet below the water's surface within two feet accuracy. Amazing, huh?"

"Sure is," Luke allowed, not really knowing all that much about K-9s. But he loved animals and anticipated learning and watching them work a tough assignment.

Al slowed the SUV. "Do you think this is where we turn?"

Luke gestured yes and they took the unmarked dirt road, bouncing through the meadow with the large, flat rock, and beyond past where Luke and Jessie had ridden horseback. Luke was following the map while Al drove. The roads were untraveled and rutted, as Huntsman had warned. Rex didn't like being jostled around. First he tried to stand, only to be thrown back in the seat, so he crouched down again and whined softly to convey his disapproval.

They found another dirt road, as faint as a fire trail, and drove east up the mountain, following it to the burn line, where it ended. Behind them were Smith and Lewis. Al parked his SUV and Smith pulled up behind him.

Carrara unloaded Rex. The dog was impressive, muscular and all black, which was somewhat a rare color for the breed, but it made him appear even more formidable. He whined with excitement, ready to go to work.

They established a mental grid to follow. Al and his K-9 led the way while Mike Smith and Duke followed. The Malinois' color was standard, black faced and tan bodied like a traditional German shepherd, only with fewer black markings and no black saddle over his back.

Luke and Lewis walked along behind the handlers and the dogs, as they fanned out and worked their way down the slope.

At first, Rex wandered on a long line, unsure what he should be doing. He would stop to watch Al for directions, but none came, so Rex put his head down and continued sniffing the ground, stopping to survey his surroundings.

Fifteen minutes into the search, Rex planted himself in a taut, protective stance, and sent deep barks echoing through the trees. This week's drug arrest, and the history of Timber Ridge, did not escape the four men as they heightened their vigilance, and stood silent, listening, with guns unclipped in their holsters, ready to draw. The forest was eerily quiet.

They relaxed a little when Rex lowered his head and resumed searching the ground. The shepherd had crisscrossed paths several times, picking up scents that interested him, and then dropping them for whatever reasons. Al knew his dog didn't have a distinct directive, so anything Rex might uncover would be a bonus. Even the dog was aware of his vague mission.

The two dogs had been combing several grids for almost two hours, moving wherever their senses led them. Their handlers had more patience than Hudson and Lewis, who whispered to each other at one point that the venture appeared futile.

Then Rex lowered his head and stopped cold, lifting his right front paw like a pointer, an unusual move for a German shepherd. He sniffed the ground and dug at the dried grass and pine needles. He paused, snuffled the newly exposed top soil, and began flinging more dirt.

Duke joined him, but Rex shouldered him aside, keeping the dig for himself.

There was no doubt the dog was after something. With sharp, excited barks, he pawed a furious pace at the earth, while Duke, equally driven, whined and jumped up and down near him. Then Rex decided to let Duke work with him and the two dogs burrowed together, hollowing the ground at a quickening rate. Al and Mike monitored their dogs in silence, not disrupting their concentration, while Luke and Lewis kept watch on the dogs and the surrounding forest.

Rex growled at Duke again, and Mike praised his dog as he drew him away. With sharp claws, Rex uncovered the first bones.

Al pulled the dog back. "My God," he gasped, "it's a hand."

Luke gazed at the small fingers and wanted to wretch. It was a child's hand.

ONCE THE SHOCK OF THEIR DISCOVERY PASSED, Luke called Sheriff Gates with the news and said they needed the medical examiner.

"I'll be damned," he said, astonished. "At best, it was such a long shot to find a body. Maybe it's the cold case girl, Luke." Hudson hoped not because he wanted to believe she was still alive.

Luke relayed that they were low on water, had not eaten, and would probably be at the location for the rest of the afternoon.

"I'll send Sergeant Thomas. He can bring the stuff you need and you'll have an extra vehicle if someone has to leave," Gates said and signed off.

Luke found it both refreshing and unusual to have a direct line to the top. There were layers of command within the LAPD, and at the BPD he always went through Sergeant Ross. The Sheriff's Office didn't have a Detective Sergeant, and Gates made it clear that Luke would answer to him. Perhaps Gates was measuring him for a future leadership position. Whatever the reasons, Luke welcomed the openness.

He turned to the others and said Sergeant Thomas and the medical examiner were in route.

Lewis volunteered to walk out and meet the ME team. Luke offered to go with him, but Lewis said he'd be fine and needed some alone time.

A half hour passed as the two K-9 handlers and their dogs stayed at the gravesite with Luke. They sat on a log and talked in hushed voices, while the two dogs curled up and went to sleep. In the stillness of the forest, they could hear the medical van lumbering up the road. In time, the crew emerged through the pines. Sergeant Thomas and Deputy Lewis were assisting Ned Jackson and technician Aaron Underwood in carrying cameras, excavation supplies, medical paraphernalia, and their tech gear.

Sergeant Thomas observed the shallow grave and the uncovered hand, and motioned Carrara over to him. Al walked the German shepherd on a "heel" command, and

Rex dutifully sat at his side when he stopped. Thomas said, "Al, your dog did good, makes a believer out of me."

Al smiled like a proud father. "His cadaver training paid off. Once he got the idea, he knew exactly what to do. I just held onto him." There were a few chuckles, and Luke added, "Mike's dog performed really well, too. He's going to be a good one." Smith smiled and patted Duke on the head.

Hudson announced, "I'd say you handlers and your dogs have put in a good day's work. If you want, you can head out."

The two K-9 specialists looked at each other and their tired dogs, now flagged by the heat, and agreed to go. They took some water and sandwiches with them and soon disappeared in the pines. Without a breeze on the early afternoon air, a stifling stillness settled over the forest.

Ned stared at the grim, bony hand of the child and knelt down by the grave. While Jackson and Underwood assessed the gravesite, Luke remarked, "As you know, this is a highly sensitive discovery, so we'll keep the findings here under wraps—no press—until Sheriff Gates gives the clearance."

Aaron and Ned smiled, well aware how reporters liked to descend on the morgue to get the latest.

The process began with Aaron, who took photographs and made sketches, before Ned approached the grave again. Aaron handed out the excavation tools for both himself and Ned, and they began the meticulous job of unearthing soil around the body.

They each took a bottle of water, but said they were eager to get started and would take a break later.

Thomas, Lewis, and Luke sat on a log, ate sandwiches, and talked in muted voices. When the three finished eating, Sergeant Thomas suggested to Luke, "Lewis and I could do a ground search around the gravesite for leftovers if you want."

Thomas meant spreading out in the area to scan for anything left behind, such as cigarette butts, cans, and other manmade items. It was usually overkill on an old gravesite, but a murderer would sometimes return to the location for years. You just never knew. The two left to span out around the gravesite, with evidence gathering materials in hand. Luke would stand guard as the examiner and tech worked.

After more than an hour, Lewis and Sergeant Thomas returned, having covered a wide area around the grave. They found a cigarette butt and two beer cans, which they stored in neatly labeled evidence bags and handed over to Jackson for analysis.

Ned and Aaron took a break and evaluated their progress. They had collected specimens as they worked and had cleared away the dirt, down to the head, neck, and a little of the shoulders. Judging by hair length, the body appeared to be a young girl's. The child laid face up, upper arms at the sides, but forearms were up-stretched, as though the child were reaching skyward, in a deliberate, delicate position. Each arm had to be stabilized by a rod for photographs and documentation, but the rods might have to be removed as the excavation progressed, and then the radius bones would probably collapse. They all agreed that it looked like a premeditated pose.

Sergeant Thomas was antsy and suggested maybe he and Lewis could carry out unneeded items and bring back a stretcher for the body. They left and Luke squatted beside Ned and Aaron as they worked.

Ned offered, "You know, teeth and bones mature at a fairly predictable rate, so we will be able to tell the child's age quite accurately. Permanent teeth start to replace deciduous teeth at about age six."

"What about bones?" Luke asked.

"Length of bone is some indicator, but bones aren't easy to discern until the teen years, thirteen and up. That's when the cartilage epiphyses start uniting to the main bone shafts, and the cartilage growth plates are replaced by bone. This process begins slightly earlier in females than in males."

Ned liked to talk while he worked. Maybe it was his way of not reflecting too much on the human aspect of his subjects. So he told Luke, "With any luck, there will be scraps of clothing, hair follicles, something else to go on. You know, they recently found Richard the Third buried in a parking lot in Leicester, England, and identified him by a DNA match to a living descendent. Out in the open, DNA isn't useful beyond weeks, but buried, DNA can last thousands of years. Fascinating technology."

"Yeah," Luke replied, standing to stretch. "It's changed the face of forensics and made our jobs easier."

The more the body was exposed, the harder it was to watch. As the two worked, they gathered hair and dried skin fragments into evidence bags and Aaron labeled them.

Hudson was first to notice Lewis and Thomas returning with a folding stretcher, body bag, and a few other items Jackson requested.

The forest was still calm, except now a light breeze sifted gently through the pines and tempered the afternoon heat. Thomas and Lewis deposited their items and returned to the log. Luke stood for another stretch, brought them some water, and then went back to the gravesite with water for Ned and Aaron. He squatted again beside Ned.

"Can pelvic structure tell much at a young age?"

"Not really," Ned answered. "That comes at puberty and older, when a female's pelvis becomes more open and broader than a male's, and hip bones more flared. No, that leaves teeth as the determiner."

Luke thought of Jessie, with her wildlife forensics degree, and the lab position she found tedious. Maybe forensics was less challenging in a laboratory setting, but he was fascinated by it, and wondered what she was doing today. So much had happened in two days, that his time with Sally and Charlie seemed far removed, and Tuesday, when Jessie would return, much further.

Ned's glasses had inched down his nose and he pushed them back, saying, "You notice there's no clothing. That would have been helpful to us, but it was clever of the perpetrator. This guy—they're almost always guys—is no amateur. We'll need time on the table to determine cause of death and age of the child, but just guessing at bone structure, I'm thinking female and five to seven. This is sheer speculation."

Hudson had learned to trust Ned's off-the-record, unsupported theories. He was good at his work, very accomplished, and a county this size was fortunate to have his expertise. Vaguely, he recalled that Ned had moved here from a large metro area, San Diego perhaps.

Aaron periodically took photos of each excavation phase. Spelling each other off, he and Ned would stop to stand, stretch their legs, and move around. Ned was so absorbed in the process, that his breaks were short. Luke brought them water, but otherwise felt somewhat useless.

It was nearing five in the afternoon and shadows were lengthening, when the body was ready to remove from the shallow grave. With reverence and respect, the body was placed in the traditional black zip bag, gently lifted onto the stretcher, and carried out by Thomas and Underwood. While they were gone, Lewis and Hudson strung crime scene tape between the trees to help preserve the site, and Ned packed up his equipment.

When the two men returned, everyone picked up whatever they could carry and started their trek back to the familiar white van. The men talked softly as they walked. At the road, the body and equipment were loaded into the ME van. Ned turned it around and left first, destined for the morgue. Sergeant Thomas would drive Hudson and Lewis back to the Sheriff's Office.

Luke took one last look, wondering how a peaceful forest could harbor such evil.

CHAPTER 17

When Hudson returned to the Sheriff's Office, Gates asked him to stick around until they could talk. To pass time, Luke went to the break room. It was almost six, and the coffee in the pot was cold, so he found ice in the freezer compartment of the refrigerator and made iced coffee. Then he added a little sugar and cream, which made him think of Jessie, who liked it that way.

Sergeant Thomas came past the break room and told Hudson that the Sheriff was free now. Luke entered his office and found Gates sitting behind his desk, looking worn. He asked about the excavation.

Luke started, "Jackson assumes the body is that of a five to seven year old girl, but he can't substantiate it yet. With luck, we could get the ME's preliminary report some time tomorrow. Depending on how long the body has been in the ground, we can determine if it's Amber Richards. The killer was probably a male. Again, just a guess, but this is likely a sex crime."

Sheriff Gates frowned, "I guess you've figured by now there were some glaring mistakes made in the Richards case. It's the main reason why I reopened the case with someone who's a seasoned detective leading it. You're demonstrating why we need a detective bureau. It can make all the difference."

Hudson nodded and continued covering the details.

The Sheriff leaned forward in his chair and said, "Where do we go next. I want all my ducks in a row tomorrow morning."

Luke sat down with a sigh, "First, no press."

"Irving is already snooping around."

"I can handle her," Luke assured him. "I'm more worried about TV coverage. If the killer is still in the area and this story gets out, he'll run. Also, I'm thinking we shouldn't have left the crime scene tape up. That just marks the grave. With your okay, I'll go back up there and remove the tape this evening."

Gates shuffled some papers, just to be fiddling while he contemplated. "Do it, but don't go alone. Deputy Lewis is still here. Take him along." The Sheriff buzzed Lewis before he could leave the building. He explained the situation, and gave him the directive to go back to the crime scene with Hudson.

The Sheriff then turned back to Luke, "What else?"

"At some point, I'd sent the dogs and handlers back to the area. Some criminals find a safe place to hide something, or commit a crime, and they'll frequent it again. The girl was buried reaching upwards, which suggests a ritualistic pose. We could be dealing with a serial killer, so we need to know if there is another grave in the vicinity."

The Sheriff said, "I hope not, but it's a good possibility."

He revisited the crime tape issue. "You and Lewis should grab a quick bite to eat before you go and head out as soon as possible so you can get the tape down before dark. The thought of that place gives me the creeps."

Luke waited around about ten minutes for Lewis. As Luke drove, Linc said he was named after President Lincoln, but he wasn't big enough to fit in Lincoln's shoes, so Linc suited him. Lewis was one big deputy. Hudson considered himself tall at six-foot-two, but Lewis's height, at least six foot six, dwarfed him. Linc was eye-catching, muscular and imposing, with a shaven head that accentuated his bulldog neck. He was a good choice for the job at hand, walking around in the forest to a gravesite.

On their way out of town, Luke and Lewis stopped at The Watering Hole, the cops' favorite hangout on the northeast end of town. While they had a beer and a bite to eat, Luke glanced around for Jimmy, hoping to see him, but he wasn't there. He missed the kid.

The sun set over Timber Ridge before they arrived at the trailhead. With still another fifteen minute trek to the crime scene, Luke wished he had heeded Gates's suggestion to get the job done before dark. They should have stopped for fast food instead. Without saying so, both men knew such small miscalculations could spell trouble.

An eerie silence hung in the forest. Even birds were hushed. In the lengthening shadows of twilight, they picked their way without flashlights. The two walked without talking, feeling the oppression of death ahead. Luke tried to dismiss the dread he sensed, but evil followed them. Hudson was open to such omens, but what surprised him was Lewis. The seemingly too-tough-to-care deputy was uneasy, too. As they neared the site, they sensed they were being watched.

Surrounded by murky shadows, they almost stumbled into the grave. The crime scene tape was gone. They drew their weapons and cautiously looked around. Now they were vulnerable. The grave was in the open, too shallow and small to provide cover. They saw no one, but someone could easily see them.

In the bottom of the grave Luke saw something barely perceptible, small and light colored. He whispered to Lewis to cover him, and knelt down to retrieve the object. In a pocket, he habitually carried a plastic evidence collection bag. He carefully opened the bag and with a stick as an aide, he worked the object into the bag. Once it was secured, he lifted the enclosed object into the gloomy dusk. It was a small doll. There could be fingerprints on the plastic arms and legs, but the head was missing. The doll's upstretched arms were a blatant clue.

He showed it to Lewis and murmured, "We're dealing with one sick bastard. Let's get out of here." They retraced their steps, guns cocked and ready, stopping at any sound. One was a rabbit, another a lizard scurrying in the dry grass. They reached the SUV and Luke laid the evidence bag on the back seat before getting in. He started the engine, turned the vehicle around, and they both breathed a sigh of relief.

Lewis spoke first. "That was the damndest crime scene I've ever revisited."

"Me, too," Luke reiterated. "I didn't see any point in staying around, did you?"

Lewis was unnerved. "I couldn't see anyone, but I could feel him there. To find him we'd have to use flash-lights, which would make *us* the targets."

"Exactly," Luke agreed. "The guy was taunting us, waiting for a misstep. Unless he used gloves, his scent will be on the doll. We'll send in the dogs in the morning and get a trail on him."

"Maybe if we'd gotten here earlier..." Linc pondered, with the same guilt feelings as Luke's.

Hudson countered, "We can't second guess. If we'd gone in earlier we'd have been a better target, or disrupted his act of leaving the doll. I think we arrived shortly after him, and that's why we sensed he was still there. Question is, how did he get to the site without a car? There are no houses nearby. It's national forest."

"Motorcycle! Let's go back. You have a spotlight, don't you?" Lewis was pumped.

"Yes, but we're going on speculation. We never really saw anybody. Let him make the next move, and our dogs will sort it out," Luke reasoned, placing more faith in the police dogs than he would have a day ago. Lewis didn't argue.

They stopped further down the road and Hudson put in a call to the Sheriff. Gates rang him back in a few min-utes from his home. Luke could hear the TV and kids in the background. He explained what they'd encountered and expected some coulda-shoulda comments from the Sheriff.

All Gates said was, "It's best you left. As for surveillance tonight, since you didn't see the suspect or a vehicle, we'll wait. The dogs will tell us tomorrow what's up. I'll get the dogs set for 0800, okay?"

"Sure," Luke affirmed, ended the call, and filled Linc in on the conversation. At this point, they called it a day.

LUKE GOT HOME, POURED MAKER'S MARK OVER ICE, and sat down to watch a TiVo recording of the evening news. He left his iPhone on the coffee table and took a sip of bourbon. When the phone rang, he hit pause on the TV remote control.

"Hi," Jessie said, her voice surprising him. "I hear you've had a rough day."

"One of the longest," he admitted. "Who told you?"

"Linc. I called him to see how things were going. I tried your number but no answer."

"I silenced it for a bit of down time." He took another sip and realized he missed her.

"I'm sorry. I just wanted to make sure you were okay."

"No apologies. I'm glad to hear from you," he said, feelings stirring that he hadn't expected.

"Well, Lewis said he couldn't go into today's events, but I gather they were something else when Big Linc reacts," she said lightly, and Luke pictured her smiling.

"I'm coming back tomorrow afternoon," she revealed. "I feel a need to get back on the case before too much passes."

"What's going on is pretty gruesome. Maybe you need another day or two. You're not due back 'til Wednesday morning," he reminded her. She was proposing to return Monday evening, and start working a day early.

"I know," she acknowledged, a twinge of disappointment in her voice. "Would you rather I stayed away longer?"

It was an unfair question. "I want what's right for you. I'm just warning you, the cold case has turned hot. Maybe you need more time. Once you return to this case, it's nonstop."

"I'll be tougher," she resolved.

"You don't have to be tougher, just stronger. I like your soft side." He took another swallow of bourbon, and knew she was getting to him.

Jessie was insistent. "Well, I'm ready to head back. I'll leave early afternoon so I can arrive in Bidwell around five. Then could we get together for a drink and a bite to eat at one of the cop stops? You could bring me up to speed."

"Sure, that will work," he said, eager to see her. "Call me when you get in."

"I will," she promised, "and please be careful. I don't want anything to happen to you."

"Likewise," he returned. "Try to miss the worst of the Valley traffic."

They said goodbyes, and he felt empty after she signed off.

Luke took a gulp of bourbon and returned to the local news. There was nothing about the discovery of a child's grave on Timber Ridge. That would buy them another day.

PART III – FACE OF EVIL

"The world is a dangerous place, not
because of those who do evil, but because
of those who look on and do nothing."

– Albert Einstein

CHAPTER 18

Monday came too soon, and it was time to return to Timber Ridge. The consensus between the Sheriff and Hudson was that since the dogs knew what to look for, and the MO suggested a serial killer, the team should keeping hunting for more graves. Sergeant Thomas would not go along since he was working the Chesney's case. A new addition to the small unit would be deputies Pete Morales and Ben Jessup with the bloodhound, Big Ears, to track the person who was at the gravesite last night.

The team of deputies assembled at the Sheriff's Office, in the break room, to discuss the day's routine before heading out. Luke told the group about last night, how he and Lewis went to the site and found the crime scene tape removed and the headless doll in the grave.

"We dropped off the doll here last night to be checked for evidence. No fingerprints were found, but the technician suggested that we use the doll as a scent for Big Ears. Jessup and Morales, you should go first into the site and follow whatever leads you can find. We know a person of interest was there last evening. Once Ben's team moves on, we'll put the other two dogs to work looking for a possible second grave in new territory. While you're out there, look for the doll's head, in case the POI left it."

Ben Jessup said, "There were half a dozen people there yesterday. How is my dog going to know what to sniff out?"

"True, about the confusing tracks," Luke replied. "But there'll only be one set of tracks leaving the area off our beaten path, and we have the doll for scent. I guess Big Ears will figure it out."

"How smart do you think these dogs are?" Jessup quipped.

"Smarter than their handlers," Al joked and got a few chuckles.

The deputy handlers joined their dogs in the three K-9 SUVs. Ben Jessup took Big Ears in his Tahoe, while Morales followed behind him in another SUV, and they left ahead of the two other teams. Hudson remained partnered with Al Carrara and his K-9, Rex. Linc Lewis would work again with Mike Smith and the Malinois, Duke.

Luke would have preferred the luxury of a day at headquarters. While he was in the field, paperwork was stacking up and special reports remained unordered. He decided when Jessie returned, she could tackle the office workload while he continued with the searches. That would ease her into this grisly scene.

On the ride out, Al was talkative, so Luke prompted him. "What's the Malinois' name? Is it Duke or Dude. I've heard both being tossed around."

Carrara started to chuckle. "There's quite a story on that one. Smith got Duke as a pup and was allowed to name him. He wanted to give the dog a Belgian name. Problem is, every one he came up with, we totally bastardized.

He kept running these names past us because he didn't want us to call his regal dog something stupid or offensive. Smith ran through Pieter, DuPauw, Petit, Van Dyck, and Van Damme, to name the ones I remember. You can imagine how we twisted each one. I think he threw in a few names just to bait us, because they were obvious howlers. Finally, in exasperation he announced he was calling the dog DuPont, thinking it was a lofty name and we couldn't do much to screw it up. We promptly referred to him as DePants. So Smith told us his dog's nickname was Duke, and anyone who screwed with that name would personally answer to him. Boy, he was pissed. We left it at that. Course we called Smith Hot Dog, so he couldn't win."

"You guys are merciless," Luke laughed. "While we're on the subject, what's the story with Straight-Up Thomas?"

Al smiled, then got serious. "That name's got bad connotations, joking aside, so don't ever let Sergeant Thomas hear you say it. Before he came to PCSO he was a lieutenant in Phoenix. Well, he's a good looking guy, and I guess he wasn't thinking above the belt because he got caught in a compromising position in the back of a black and white with a young, pretty officer. Photos sealed his fate, and he was canned, plus his wife divorced him. On the other hand, he was a damned good administrator. So Sheriff Kelly, who preceded Gates, hired him and Gates kept him, with the warning that another such incident and he will boot his ass further than China—his words not mine. Thomas is a good guy, though. Hell, anyone can make a mistake."

Luke agreed, and they sipped their coffees, which were now warm, and speculated about the hours ahead of them. When they arrived at the stop-off point, the Big Ears team was already on the trail to the gravesite. The other K-9 handlers began unloading dogs, giving them water, and gearing up for their own searches.

Morales radioed Luke. They were at the site, and between the scents on the doll and in the shallow grave, Big Ears was hot on a trail. "It appears the suspect was hiding close uphill from you and Linc last night. We're following the scent, heading back towards the road, but northeast of you by a couple hundred yards. We're close to the burn line. Wait a bit longer, maybe ten minutes, and then you can all go to the grave. By then we should be clear of the area. I just don't want you guys walking any place that would disturb Big Ears' tracking."

Luke punched off and waited for an okay from Morales before they left for the gravesite. The forest was alive with bird sounds in the early morning. A deer approached from afar, head alert, tail flicking, in a tense stance. It spun and bounded into the brush when the men and dogs moved. The air was still cool, a good morning to work the crime scene.

The teams reached the grave and Rex showed familiarity with the site. Duke appeared confused, but enthusiastic. And the scents left from Big Ears further bewildered both dogs. They were inclined to follow his trail.

Al Carrara, an expert in the field, quickly recognized the problem. "Let's get the dogs away from here and work down the hill in a grid. Keep Duke a ways back from Rex so neither dog is distracted by the other," he told Smith.

Both dogs were shown a finger bone from the deceased that had fallen off in the move to the morgue. Ned realized it would aid the dogs, so he temporarily rendered it up to the K-9 team.

As they began to work the dogs, Deputy Smith let his Malinois work behind and to the left, uphill from Rex. The enthusiastic dogs seemed unfazed by the tedious work. A sameness set in as the two dogs zig-zagged over the ground, heads down, showing curiosity now and then before going cold. They had worked most of the area in two hours and found nothing worth noting.

Jessup was having better luck. Pete Morales called Luke again. "Eureka! Big Ears took us to where the bike was hidden. It was well off the road and near the burn line. There's a lot of old fire trails up here, so there's any number of ways to ride off and not be detected. This old boy's a good one. I'm talking about the dog," he joked lightheartedly. Luke knew Ben was close and listening to the conversation because he could hear Big Ears panting in the background. Pete added, "And Little Ears is okay, too." Ben chuckled.

Morales continued, "Here's where the trail goes dead as far as the dog is concerned."

"Which way did the bike leave?" Luke asked.

"Down the ridge. I'll order a forensic specialist up here to get tire and footprint castings. We were careful to not contaminate some good specimens, and we marked where they are. How 'bout your operation?"

"Nothing so far, but we're ready to search the north side of the road, unless you'd rather we wait. How far are you from the parking area?"

"We're about twenty minutes away. I'll stick around to work with the forensic experts while they get print evidence, and it would be better if you wait until after they're done."

Luke agreed, knowing they ran the risk of contaminating the north trail the suspect took, or accidently walking across the bike trail. He said they'd hold off and work another grid to the south of where they were now.

The two teams took a half hour snack and water break, with time to rest the dogs. By ten thirty, they resumed the search, working further south of the area they had already canvassed. Linc Lewis acted as their sentinel, though an encounter with drug runners or their person of interest was remote. He wore full protection gear. By contrast, the dog handlers and Luke were garbed in short sleeved khaki shirts and pants, no bulletproof vests, though they all carried their weapons. Linc looked hot and uncomfortable, but he was the only one prepared for anything that went down.

The forest heat rose, but a slight breeze rustled through the pines, cooling the dry air. As usual in June, the fire danger was extreme and the forest a tinderbox, ready to explode from a match, a careless toss of a cigarette, or even a hot cartridge shell from a gun.

Luke dropped to the rear of the search as he fielded a call from Ned back at the morgue. He noted that Lewis was watching and had planted himself between the two teams in order to keep an eye on both.

"Luke? Ned here. We have some results. First of all, the child's body is that of a seven year old, and she's been in the ground maybe twelve years, as best we can determine. Time buried and age don't add up to your cold case. We're assuming a girl because of length of hair. She was dark haired. We're waiting for DNA reports."

With that information, Hudson had mixed emotions. Amber Richards might still be alive.

He told Ned, "That means we either have two unrelated crimes, or worse."

Ned asked if they had discovered anything new.

"You'll be the first to know if we do," Luke assured him, and they disconnected.

Not five minutes after Ned's call, the Belgian Malinois reacted to a spot on the ground, pawing in the dried grass and pine needles. Luke remembered Al telling him that cadaver dogs were trained with dead pig parts because the gasses they emit most closely approximate human remains. Duke had been to such a training session or two recently. Now something grabbed his attention. With his voice, Smith encouraged the Malinois' interest.

Duke whined and then stopped before clawing at the ground again, just as Rex had yesterday. Al and his dog were ahead, so they missed Duke's initial response. Lewis saw what was happening and went to summon Al and Rex to join them.

Duke dug around some, but seemed unsure and had not uncovered any bones.

Al, being more seasoned, asked Mike, "Do you mind if Rex gets involved? Duke's doing good, but maybe he needs a backup."

Mike answered, "Sure, have at it."

Rex sniffed tentatively, too, as though the clues were not as strong as yesterday's. Or, Luke thought, maybe they'd stumbled onto the remains of a poached animal. The ground looked undisturbed, so if something was under the soil, it had been there a long time.

Moving a couple of feet away, Rex found a stronger scent and began to bark and paw. Duke tried to join him, but again Rex was possessive of his find. The Malinois went back to his initial place while the shepherd took over his new discovery, and they coexisted as they dug. First Rex unearthed a child's left hand because it was closest to the topsoil, and Al pulled him away with generous praise. Duke stayed undeterred, and in a few minutes, he exposed the right hand, spread two feet apart from the left one. The dog was taken back from the dig and rewarded with pats and approving words.

The MO was the same, a child, with skeleton hands reaching upward. Perhaps a girl, if this grave mirrored the other one. Luke felt sick to his stomach, but held back the urge to wretch. Serial killers were a detective's nightmare. Not only were they hard to find and bring to justice, the trails they left behind were often ugly and violent.

He made the call he'd hoped to avoid, first to Ned, then to Sheriff Gates, who was out at the time. A message would have to suffice.

Next he rang Deputy Morales and told him what they'd found.

"No shit, Sherlock!" Morales exclaimed loud enough that Luke removed his ear from the phone and the whole team could hear. "Do you want the footprint forensic team at your location?"

"It wouldn't hurt," Luke answered, "especially if the POI was here last night. We'll try not to disturb things any more than we have already. See if Ben and Big Ears can work back this way and find a connection between the two gravesites. Maybe the guy was making his rounds last night."

"Looks like we're dealing with a sonofabitchin' monster," Morales said and signed off.

The team stood around in silence, with the same shroud of gloom hanging over them that they had encountered less than twenty-four hours earlier.

Mike Smith spoke first. "I'm the dad of two little girls, and if someone did this to one of mine..." He stopped, choked with emotion.

Al said, "My daughter is in college, but I can't even imagine what it'd be like to lose her this way."

Lewis volunteered, "I lost a daughter to cancer when she was six, and I can tell you that's not much easier. Death isn't about fairness."

The men went silent again and the dogs lay near the grave as if guarding it, sensing something amiss.

Al commented, "When K-9s worked after nine-eleven, they were overwhelmed by the death around them. The dogs worked in shifts because they got depressed and couldn't take it any better than the firefighters and police."

Luke suggested to Al and Mike, "Why don't you two take your dogs back to the cars. Linc and I will stay and watch the grave. When the ME arrives, one of you could help carry things and bring them to the grave. We don't all need to stand around here."

Al and Mike appeared grateful to leave the gravesite. They left side by side, the veteran trainer and the young father, reaching down to stroke their dogs' heads as they walked, touching something alive and close to their hearts.

CHAPTER 19

By noon the Medical Examiner's team of Ned Jackson and Aaron Underwood made their way to the gravesite, carrying equipment to process the crime scene and excavate. It was a rerun of yesterday. Deputy Smith led them to the site, carrying equipment with him. His dog was at the SUVs with Al.

Luke told them the impression evidence experts had arrived to lift the suspect's footprints and tire tracks, and a patrol car was planted at the main dirt road entrance to keep onlookers and reporters away.

Not long after Ned's arrival, the Sheriff himself walked in with a deputy in tow, who was carrying two coolers filled with sandwiches and water. Gates looked at the unearthing of the child, and went straight to Hudson.

"This is gruesome," he said, more to himself than Luke. "You wonder when it will end..."

"Well, I don't think any time soon," Hudson remarked with a sigh. "Deputy Jessup is working Big Ears through the whole area as we speak, to see if there are tracks to other sites. We're hoping the perp made the mistake of visiting some gravesites yesterday and has left some trails that the bloodhound can follow."

Gates silently watched Ned and his team at work, then turned back to Luke. "This is going to hit the media big time, and soon. I'm trying to figure out how to ratchet it down so the suspect doesn't run."

"I've been thinking the same thing. Let's feed the press what we want the perpetrator to know."

"Such as?"

Luke suggested, "I talk to Irving and tell her we know nothing because this guy is so clever. We're stumped. If he doesn't feel the heat, that buys us more time."

Gates concurred, "I trust you to deal with Irving. Call her soon and fill her in. She's as persistent as a rat terrier." He grinned, and discussed putting a protective barrier along the roads. "I'm considering stringing crime scene tape across the roads and trails into here, and maintaining 24/7 surveillance. That will keep the media and all the curiosity seekers out, for now at least. I just want to catch this SOB, hopefully, within the next twenty-four hours. We're on borrowed time as it is."

The Sheriff winced as he glanced at the gravesite, and said, "I was planning to take Thomas off this case because he's working the Chesney case and couple of others. But this takes precedence, and Thomas has been in on it from the beginning. He has a background in homicide, as well as narcotics, so I think he's a fit. You're in charge, but if you need him, he said he'd like to help."

"That'll be good, plus Harte is coming back today to start work tomorrow."

Gates had no response, and they looked back at the excavation, where the ME team worked in silence.

Luke said, "It's the same MO. Ned says this girl is blondish, probably been buried longer than yesterday's girl, so the dogs had more trouble detecting the body. The age is not determined yet, but he thinks she's six to eight. I hope we don't find that's he's killed one a year."

The Sheriff shook his head. "Wrap it up at a reasonable time today. Even if you find more gravesites I don't want to uncover them today. We have enough work to do at the moment. I'll have fresh officers up here on patrol all night, so you can relax a little. Okay?"

Luke smiled. "Thanks. This is taking its toll, especially on the deputies who are fathers."

"I'm one of them," Gates admitted. "I had to see for myself, so I'd know what you guys are going through."

LUKE STAYED AT THE CRIME SCENE until late afternoon. Meanwhile, he called *The Morning Sun* asking for Kate Irving, but she was out. He said to have her call him back, which she did within twenty minutes.

"Hi, Luke," she said cheerfully. "Thanks for the call. I've been waiting to talk to you, but I figured if I didn't do it on your time frame, you'd just blow me off."

"You're close to right," he admitted, with a slight chuckle, trying to keep the conversation light and flowing.

"I know you have two bodies now," she submitted, "so I have to write something, and my guess is you'd rather give me some facts than let me run with speculations."

"How do you know about the second body," he quizzed.

She laughed, "There are ambulance chasers and then there are ME chasers. I'm the latter. I followed Ned's van to the base of Timber Ridge for a photo op. I could have driven to the site, but I figured you'd throw me out." She laughed again.

"You're right about that," he said. "In fact, the whole area is cordoned off as a crime scene and will be under 24-hour surveillance, so it's off limits to press, bystanders, and anyone not authorized by the Sheriff's Office."

She was silent briefly. Kate was about his age and through subtle body language and hints, he gathered she liked him enough to pursue a relationship if given any encouragement. But he, like most cops, had no interest in reporters. Besides she reminded him too much of Sally.

"This is high profile stuff," she said. "What we reporters long to cover."

"At some point it might be hot news, but so far here's all we have," he started, "and don't say I'm stonewalling you, because I'm not. You're getting the honest-to-God truth as we have it, and you're the only one getting any sort of scoop. And that's only because you're so damned snoopy," he teased her, and she giggled.

"Such a long preamble," she countered. "Where are the facts?"

"You know them. We have two bodies and no clues."

"Not again," she brooded, exasperated. "This is your mantra, Luke. I know you have more."

"I really don't, Kate. I'm as frustrated as you are. Obviously, the girls were murdered. Is there a link between the two? We don't know yet. They were killed about twelve or so years ago. Is the perpetrator still in the area? We don't know, because we don't know who he is, what he looks like, what he drives, or where he lives. He's clever and staying ahead of us in a zone we haven't been able to penetrate. Now, is that frustrating the hell out of us? You bet. But that's where we are, at a stalemate."

"You want me to quote you on that?"

"Those are the facts," he answered. "I wish we had more, believe me."

"Well, do you know if one of the girls is your cold case victim?"

"No, I don't know that, either," he said flatly.

"It's not much to go on," she said, disappointed. "I'll have to resort to photos and fillers."

"Join the club. Listen, Kate, I have to go. Something will break eventually."

He ended her call and fielded another from Sergeant Thomas.

"Luke? If you want, I'm in the area and can come up to help wherever needed."

The detective side of Craig Thomas was taking over. He was eager to get involved, so Luke filled him in and suggested he wait with the K-9s in the parking area until Ben and Big Ears showed up. The K-9 unit was within the Narcotics Unit and under Craig Thomas's command. However, they assisted elsewhere when needed, such as Search and Rescue, or in this situation, with homicide.

"Sounds good," Thomas said. "I could join the Big Ears team and work with them."

Hudson welcomed his expertise, said he could use the help, and Thomas signed off. Luke told Mike he could head back to the SUVs, and that the bloodhound was working a trail and the cadavers could follow. Smith loaded up the items no longer needed and left.

There was little talk as Lewis kept watch on the forest, and Hudson perused the excavation, observing the two experts while they worked.

After another hour, Thomas showed up with Ben Jessup and Big Ears and walked over to Luke.

"Hey, Big Ears led us here," the Sergeant shrugged. "As you suggested, the two cadaver dogs came along behind. They worked the trail that Big Ears laid out and found two spots of interest. We didn't let them dig around, but the locations were marked in such a way that we can find them again. I know there will be surveillance here tonight, but this is a big area to watch. Luke, do you think we should request two patrol cars instead of one?"

"Wouldn't hurt," Luke agreed. "Why don't you request the additional backup? Are the K-9s done for the day?"

"Yeah, the handlers and dogs were exhausted, so I sent them home, except for Ben and the hound dog here.

I needed them to show me where you are, though the trail is pretty clear by now. Hell, I could dog it myself," he said with a playful smirk.

"Sounds good. The plan is to start again at 0800 tomorrow," Luke stated and eyed the big red bloodhound with droopy ears and jowls. Jessup, who was an older deputy and packing around a few extra pounds, looked as tired as his dog. They went with Thomas to sit on a log.

Bloodhounds could follow a scent for days, even across water, so what the hound accomplished today was just typical for him. Thomas made his calls and then passed his water bottle to Ben for Big Ears, who was flagged by the heat. Jessup turned his cap upside down, poured water into it, and offered it to his dog. Big Ears sniffed the cap brim, and then gulped the contents, slobbering all over the sides of Ben's cap. "Dang, this dog drools," Jessup said, half grinning.

Sergeant Thomas and Ben got more water from the cooler, rested briefly, and then loaded up with supplies that could return to the ME van.

By four in the afternoon, shadows stretched across the forest floor as the sun lowered in the western sky. The ME team had finished their excavation. Luke and Ned trekked out with the body bag on a stretcher, another child taken from her troubled resting place. Lewis and Underwood carried out the rest.

Ned told Luke when he was ready to drive away, "I guess we'll be back tomorrow. What time?"

"We're starting at eight with the dogs. Be ready to roll as soon as we find something. We're expecting another full day," Luke said, drained.

Jackson confronted death frequently, but this was different, and it showed on his face and in his voice.

"I just want it to end," he said.

CHAPTER 20

When Jessie called Luke around five-thirty that same evening, she had just arrived in town. Luke was already at The Watering Hole, having a beer with Linc, and invited her to join them.

She sounded recharged. "I sure could use a drink, and I've barely eaten all day. It's a good place to talk."

Fifteen minutes later, Jessie walked in and found the two at a booth in the dining area. The bar and grill was a popular "cop stop" as she put it, not fancy, more a cowboy bar, but the service was good and the food decent.

She joined them and chatted about her trip to Sonoma, while she ordered a Margarita and Linc finished his beer.

Then he announced, "I need to get home. I've been gone a lot lately. Good to have you back, Jess."

"Give my best to Violet," she said, referring to his wife, as he rose and told Luke he'd see him at 0800.

After Linc left, she said, "I'm going to freshen up."

Luke welcomed some alone time with her. They'd only been working together a month, but she was growing on him.

When Jessie returned, she had combed her hair and touched up her makeup, but she was easy on the eyes no matter what she did. She wore a conservative blouse and slacks, probably anticipating their meeting would be noticed.

Her Margarita was waiting. "To partners," they toasted.

She squeezed the juice of the lime wedge into her drink, dropped the wedge in, and licked the droplets from her fingers. "So tell me about the new developments in the case."

"I'd rather talk about something else right now."

Never one to shy from a subject, Jessie changed to, "Okay, how was your visit with your ex?"

"Pleasant, but after being divorced five years, we know it's time to move on," he said, noting a hint of approval in her eyes.

"How long were you married?"

"About twenty years. I guess that's why we were reluctant to let go." He took a deep swallow of beer. "This past weekend just solidified what we'd both been thinking."

"So you've been hanging in limbo for the last four years?" she quizzed.

"You could say that," he grinned.

She ran her fingers through her silky hair and golden strands fell around her face. "Come to think of it, my life's been on the same parallel as yours."

"You've been married and divorced?" he asked, since she was probing his life.

She sipped her Margarita and savored the salt on the rim. "Yes, married for two years, but it was a big mistake. He was a complete asshole."

"That doesn't leave much to the imagination," Luke chuckled. "How bad was he?"

"I met him six years ago, when I turned thirty. We only went together about six months. Not long enough to really know each other. He had the face and body of a Greek god, but he also knew it. He was very possessive and controlling. I found out that he was screwing around on me, but if I even talked to another man, he got jealous. And he was abusive. He hit me once and I told him if he did it again, I'd either leave him or kill him." She smiled, "I left before I had to do the latter."

"What did he do for a living?" Luke wondered. "Not a cop, I hope."

"Yes, with the SFPD. But he wasn't like you. He was in it for all the wrong reasons. He had a lot of pent up anger, and he used his power sadistically at times. He wasn't that way with me before we got married. At least, I didn't see it coming, but my folks never liked him. We haven't talked since the divorce, and I told him if he bothered me I'd get a restraining order on him. I made a big mistake marrying him."

She often gave him more information than he anticipated, but that was just Jessie.

"We all make mistakes," he said, finishing his beer. "At least you got out, instead of letting the relationship damage you. What were you doing at the time?"

"That's when I was working in the forensics lab, but I already told you about that. In spite of him, while we were married I met a lot of good people in law enforcement, so after our divorce I decided I wanted to be a cop. I gradu-ated about three years ago and ended up here."

"How is your family?" he pushed her conversation on.

"We had a good visit, but they're still concerned about me being in law enforcement. If they had their way, I'd be doing almost anything else. They're afraid I'll get shot, so I didn't tell them about the Chesney incident. That would have totally freaked them out."

Jess always laid it out there. She had a way of getting Luke to open up, too, perhaps because she was so unfil-tered. Right now though, he didn't want to go deeper into personal things. He was ready to talk about the case.

In a lowered voice, he told her everything, and she sat stupefied, scarcely saying a word, which was out of char-acter. The more he talked, the more she appeared both-ered. He didn't think too much about her reaction because everyone on the case was troubled.

"It's atrocious. That's what I tried to warn you."

"I can handle it," she said, as if trying to convince her-self as well as him. "I knew it would be rough, just talking to Linc."

She turned silent, taking a drink. "Even *you* look strung out, like the weight of all this is taking a toll."

"It is, on all of us," he agreed. "So I have a plan for how to ease you back into the case and you can fill a huge void at the same time."

"Good," she chirped. "I'm ready for whatever."

"We're way behind on paperwork and ordering reports. If you could work in the office a few days to get that part of the investigation up to speed, it would take a load off me. I'll be in the field again tomorrow. Meanwhile, we also need to do a murder board workup, and you'd be good at that."

"Sure, no problem," she assured him. "Now, let's talk about non-work. I don't suppose you've thought about the horses, but when we get a break, let's take a therapeutic ride."

He smiled and already felt better. They ordered dinner and wine. She was what he needed in a partner, someone positive and vivacious. Jimmy was like that. Luke reminded himself that he should get together with him soon. He glanced around, but again, Jimmy was not there. The place was mostly filled with firefighters. Maybe there had been a brush fire today. He'd been too preoccupied to follow local news except for his own case. Firefighters were a clannish bunch, as joined at the hip as cops. For first responders, it was the constant awareness of death that made them so alive and close knit.

They finished their meals and split the tab, avoiding any impression of this encounter being anything other than business. As they walked to their cars, he said, "I have an unusual request. Don't take it wrong."

Jessie stood at her car and waited to hear him out.

What he was about to say would be awkward, but he wanted to be near her a bit longer. "I'd like to follow you home. Just to make sure you're okay. I know that sounds strange, but I need to know that the people I care about are safe tonight. I guess I'm unnerved by this creep we're dealing with. Does that make any sense?"

"I think so," she said, easing his discomfort. "After all, I do live alone, and I haven't been there for a couple of days. Yeah, that's a nice gesture."

As he drove behind her, he thought about Straight-Up Thomas, and didn't know if he should smile or recoil. Was he letting his feelings for Jessie cloud his judgment? He knew part of his motivation was a sense of vulnerability, of a need to reconnect in a world so disjointed. He wouldn't ask her again.

She turned into her drive and parked in front of the garage while he pulled alongside the curb. When she unlocked the front door, she turned to him. "Come in. You can give me the 'all clear.' " She smiled and he followed her through the door.

He walked around the house and checked the garage. "Everything looks okay," he announced, as she shadowed him. She opened the garage door and parked her car inside.

"How about a nightcap? You're more stressed than I was over Chesney," she quipped.

"I'd like a few days off," he admitted.

She started towards the kitchen and he walked with her. Reaching into a cabinet, she pulled out a rectangular bottle of a rich amber-colored liqueur.

"It's Disaronno," Jessie stated. "Have you had it before?"

"I don't think so," he answered.

"Sorry to say, my ex introduced me to it. It's the one good legacy he left me."

She poured them each a shot.

"It's very good," he said, letting the smoothly blended flavors envelope him.

"It's Italian, and it says here on the bottle 'since 1525'. Leave it to the Italians to improve everything with age."

"Kind of like me," he grinned, and she laughed.

They stood, sipping the Disaronno and looking at each other.

He glanced away, taking in the surroundings. "Nice place," he said.

She showed him around the living room, pointing out family pictures, and a couple of her mother's oil paintings. Her secure upbringing was far removed from the career she had chosen. He wondered if her sheltered childhood had enticed her to marry against her parents' better judgment and then take on a profession they disliked. He'd observed she sometimes vacillated between being conventional and rebellious.

"My mother's very talented. She paints, acts, and sings. It kept her busy when my dad was away. And she used to show horses with me, but I think I told you that."

"Yes, I remember," he said and finished his drink. "I really must be going. I just wanted to see you in."

She took his glass and hers and set them on a lamp table. "Thanks. I was shaken by what you told me, so I feel better now."

Walking him to the door, she gave him a light, friendly hug, which on impulse slipped into a long, intimate embrace. When they stepped apart, they were both flustered.

Slowly, she recovered her composure, breathed deep, and hesitated opening the front door. "I'll see you in the morning."

"It's good to have you back—safe and sound," he said, reluctant to close the door behind him.

CHAPTER 21

On Tuesday, Hudson and Harte were both at headquarters around seven-thirty in their small conference room office. Last night unmentioned, Luke was awaiting the day's orders from Gates, while Jessie prepared to do the paperwork he had suggested. She requested a report from the National Center for Missing & Exploited Children regarding their two new victims, while Luke contacted the Behavioral Analysis Bureau of the FBI. Their Violent Crimes Against Persons (ViCAP) operations would be able to match the killer's MO against others in the national database, searching for a link between known offenders and their case.

They spread out their notes, photos, and materials for a murder board workup. The board would clarify the sequence of events for Jessie. Once Luke had time to tie it all together, he was encouraged by the information their investigation had amassed. The two crimes contained this evidence in common—arms reaching skyward, unclothed girls' bodies, clustered graves, the suspect's return to the sites, and the possibility that both girls died of asphyxiation. Both victims were preteens. The headless doll in the pink satin dress was an additional bonus, a unique clue.

Luke simply took for granted there would be more bodies, based on what the dogs had uncovered late yesterday afternoon.

He had watched the ten o'clock local news last night and the Sheriff's Office kept a lid on TV media stories, releasing few facts. *The Morning Sun*, which he had brought from home to the office, had Kate Irving's front page headliner "Second Body Found in Forest". The story read close to what Luke had discussed with her, including a quote from him and a photo of the ME van and two police cars at the base of Timber Ridge, with a caption stating the area was under heavy surveillance, exactly the message the Sheriff's Office wanted to project.

Turning to the editorial page, a letter to the editor sent chills through him.

WHERE IS JUSTICE?

The bodies found on Timber Ridge raise the question, where is law enforcement on this? Nowhere!
They probably think this is the work of a serial killer. But what if it's the handiwork of someone who sought a safe haven for an abandoned child?
Tell me not, in mournful numbers,
Life is but an empty dream!
For the soul is dead that slumbers,
And things are not what they seem.
Life is real! Life is earnest!

And the grave is not its goal;
Dust thou art, to dust returnest,
Was not spoken of the soul.
   H. W. Long, Bidwell

"Jessie, look at this!" He interrupted her work and handed her the paper.

"What the...this is our killer!" she exclaimed.

"I think so, too. I vaguely recognize the poem."

"It's by an American poet." She googled the "Dust thou art" line on her smart phone. "It's Henry Wadsworth Longfellow, which explains the H. W. Long. It's a fake name. They have to verify these letters, so there must be a Long in town for the address."

She dashed out of the room and came back with a phone book. "There are several Longs. It's a common name, so he could have used any one of the addresses for his own. As for phone number, I bet he used a disposable phone for no traces."

She went back to the poem on her device. "Here's the rest of the poem, *A Psalm of Life*," she said and read it aloud to the end.

They searched for more meaning, but failed to find a line that jumped out as a clue.

"There are lines that you can stretch into something," she conjectured, "like the reference to 'funeral marches to the grave', or 'let the dead Past bury its dead'. But I think we'd be reading too much into it. The real message is that he sees himself as a kind of savior, a hero, an actor above the fray. He's somehow turned his twisted world into one he can justify and this poem reinforces that picture of himself."

Luke was impressed with her deductions, and added, "The reason I know it's him is that he mentions bodies. At the point he submitted this letter, the second body had not been announced, so he slipped up."

Jessie paced around the room as she planned, running with her thoughts. "I'll go to *The Sun* to get the address and phone number he gave them, and see where that leads. It's better if I go. You'll be heading back up Timber Ridge soon and besides, they know you at the paper, so you risk bumping into Irving. We don't want her tying this poem to the case, unless she has already. They don't know me."

"I'd rather we went together, later," he said, "in case we go to the physical address."

Luke was seated as she approached him from the other side of the conference table. She put her hands on the table and leaned towards him.

"I appreciate that you are concerned about me," she started, "but I can handle this. Send me out like you would Jimmy, and let me do my job."

He was taken aback.

Jessie glanced at her watch and it was about eight in the morning. Wearing her badge and gun, she was out the door before he could object.

However, she didn't get far. Sheriff Gates stopped her and asked her to get Hudson and meet him with the team in the situation room. When they arrived, Sergeant Craig Thomas and the Deputy K-9 handlers Ben Jessup, Mike Smith, and Al Carrara were there, along with Deputy Linc Lewis. The dogs were no doubt temporarily housed in the air conditioned kennels.

Sheriff Gates surprised them with his opening statement. "I'm calling off the search today."

Hudson had expected as much, but there were audible mumbles around the room.

"I've been mulling this over all night," he said, looking as if he hadn't slept much. "If we open a couple more graves, there's no putting a lid on it. This will go viral so fast it will be all over the Internet, in the major papers from the *Sacramento Bee* to the *L.A. Times,* and on TV from KGO to KTLA. The killer will go underground so far we'll never find him. He's been under for years and now that he's out, we can't risk him going back. No one really believes he'll stop abusing girls and killing them. If we lose him now, there'll be more graves found years from now, maybe in another county or state. We have a chance to close in on him, and we're going to."

In the hanging silence, Gates added, "Any comments or problems with the decision?"

Hudson waited in the lingering hush for someone else to speak before he said, "Personally, I like the idea. It felt like the crime scenes were unfolding faster than we could fully process them. Judging by the Letter to the Editor today, and the crime scene tape and doll incident, the doer seems to be taunting us. What will help us now is for him to make a bold, stupid move so we can nail his ass."

The Sheriff had seen the Letter to the Editor and passed it amongst the team, then asked them, "Do we do anything with this letter?"

Jessie spoke up, "He used a fake name, playing with the poet's name, Henry Wadsworth Longfellow, and probably used phony contact information, so we won't learn anything by going to the newspaper for specifics and it might alert a reporter like Irving that we're interested in the letter. I say let it ride and wait for his next overt move."

Luke was stunned that her comments were a complete reversal of what she had pushed hard for, and intended to act upon, less than half an hour ago.

Gates nodded agreement with her and went on, "We will continue to keep a tight surveillance on the crime scene 24/7. The only thing I want to stress is that all media inquiries go through our Communications Department so we can keep a handle on the content. And I don't want this case discussed with wives, or girlfriends if you have them..." Chuckles amongst the men ensued as he spoke, "...or with anyone else you know."

He was winding down the meeting. "You K-9 handlers deserve a lot of credit."

There was enthusiastic applause and hoots from the small group and the handlers beamed with pride.

Al said good-naturedly, "The dogs deserve the credit. As Sergeant Thomas puts it, we just hold the leash."

Thomas grinned, "That's before I knew how much training it takes to hold the leash."

More chuckles from the handlers followed.

Gates ended the session. "It's obvious you guys work well together. We'll be sending you back out in the field when the time is right, probably within a week, to finish uncovering graves. I just want to see what might unfold in the meantime. Thomas and Hudson, I need you in my office, not at the same time. Thomas first."

A "woo" went through the deputies, even though they knew the Sheriff's order would be nothing more than briefing and planning. They never missed a cue to make something out of nothing. Luke smiled.

"You're dismissed," the Sheriff said, and took Thomas with him.

Luke followed Jessie back to their makeshift office and closed the door. "That was interesting," he said, but she stopped him before he could go on.

"I know," she admitted. "I changed my mind. Actually, I owe you an apology—again. I went off half-cocked with my run-to-the-newspaper idea. And I wasn't thinking of you as a partner in that decision. I obviously need more coaching in teamwork," she grinned.

"I liked what you said in the meeting," he told her. "As for teamwork, I learned a long time ago that you make fewer mistakes if you bounce things off your partner or someone else you trust."

She was impulsive to a fault and knew it.

Jessie left to get coffee and talk to Al Carrara while Luke called Jack Huntsman and invited him to lunch.

Huntsman met Luke at The Courthouse Cafe around eleven thirty and they found a quiet table where they could discuss the case. Jack ordered the same as before, a martini and a cheeseburger. He hadn't gained noticeable weight, so his wife's efforts to keep him on a diet seemed to be working, whenever she had influence over him. Luke settled for a tuna sandwich and ice tea.

In his usual, colorful manner, Huntsman threw out witty comments and belly laughs. Luke asked him what he'd been doing lately, and he answered, "Well, I wish I could say I've been up to my ass in crocodiles, like when I was a detective, but the truth of the matter is I'm getting tired of golf and honey-do lists. My advice is don't retire unless you're fired."

He continued with a grin, "Hey, I got a little cop humor for you. A policeman pulls a man over for speeding and asks him to get out of the car. After looking the guy over, the cop says, 'Sir, I can't help but notice your eyes are bloodshot. Have you been drinking?' The man gets really indignant and says, 'Officer, I couldn't help but notice your eyes are glazed. Have you been eating doughnuts?' "

They both chuckled as their food arrived and Huntsman ordered another martini. They ate in silence, mixed with a few comments about their food and the hot weather.

When they were more than half done, Hudson began telling Jack about the case. Huntsman turned solemn hearing about the dead girls, and winced at the details, bothered as everyone else on the case.

"I guess that's one good thing about being retired," Jack said at last. "You're removed from some of the pain."

AFTER LUNCH, LUKE RETURNED TO HELP JESSIE with the murder board. They chose a 4- x 6-foot dry erase reversible board on a frame with castors, and rolled it into their crowded conference room office. That afternoon when they were finished, they stood back and reviewed their handiwork. They had arranged the victims in the order of discovery. Richards, still missing, started the chain of events, so they listed her first.

Victim 1 – Amber Richards, 6 years old, fair-haired female, angel wings birthmark on the right side of her neck. Reported missing in August, 11 years ago, by neighbor, Lucy McCormack. Suspected child abuse by the male boyfriend of mother. Photos of the girl at 6, and the artist's rendition at 17, were posted.

Victim 2 – Unidentified girl, discovered June 11, buried 12 years ago at 7 years old, dark-haired female, unclothed, arms reaching up. Possible COD asphyxiation. Gravesite revisited by POI June 11, who removed crime scene tape and left a headless doll, with arms upstretched. *Best clue—satin dressed doll.* Gravesite photos of the girl and the doll were included.

Victim 3 – Unidentified girl, discovered June 12, buried 13 years ago at 8 years old, fair-haired female, unclothed, arms reaching up. Possible COD asphyxiation.

Gravesite revisited by POI June 11. Photos at gravesite were displayed.

Person of Interest – Rides a motorcycle, revisits gravesites, a male sexual predator, possible fixation with dolls and poetry or literature. Copy of Letter to the Editor below. Buries victims with clothes removed and arms reaching up, and prefers girls six to eight years old.

Further investigations into the lives of these girls were on hold, pending DNA, ViCAP, and other reports. But with three victims on the board, all a year apart, Luke tried not to think about the possibility of one victim each of the last 13 years.

CHAPTER 22

The house was empty, except for a child the man had been watching for the past half hour. Her mother had left for work ten minutes ago, her nightly routine. Before she departed, she double checked the locks because she left her child alone all night. Her daughter was a beauty, with golden curls that fell below her shoulders and an angelic face. About six, he surmised. The mother was attractive and also blonde, but mature women didn't interest him. They were worldly and he was attracted to innocence.

He had planned this for several days. After midnight on a Wednesday, the neighborhood street was deadly silent. He hid in shadows, away from inside hall lights that glowed through the living room windows and fell softly across the porch. The stray cat he had taken from its carrier and tied to a front porch rail drew the child's attention. He knew it would. The tabby cat mewed softly at first, and the little girl unlatched the front door to explore the plaintive meows. As he anticipated, the snared cat became frantic when the child approached. The frightened feline hissed and hid under the porch, straining at its tether.

The girl ran back in the house and he listened for the click. She didn't lock the door. He waited a minute or two and peered through a front window pane. He saw her skip down the hall and into her bedroom. Through the open bedroom door, he saw a doll sitting on the floor, leaning against the girl's bright pink bedspread.

He slipped through the door and walked in. The intruder stood in the living room and stared down the hall to her room. The child picked up her doll from the carpet and gently placed it on the bed. Humming a tune, she dressed the doll in a cotton nightgown. He would have her bring the doll along, to comfort and pacify her.

The lovely child glanced down the hall and saw him standing there. She stopped humming and didn't make a sound. She just hugged her doll and walked into the hall, closer to him.

"Who are you?" she asked, bewildered.

"I'm your daddy, Julie," he told her in a whispery voice that took her aback.

"How do you know my name? You're not my daddy."

He guessed she hadn't seen her father in years. This he knew because he had talked to a young boy in the neighborhood, who told him that Julie and her mom lived alone, and he had never seen her father. In fact, the girl never mentioned having a father.

"When is the last time you saw your daddy?" he asked, still murmuring.

"I don't know, but Mommy would have told me if my daddy was coming."

"Not if it's a surprise." A sly, predatory grin crossed his lips. "Your mommy said it would be a nice surprise if I came by and took you out for ice cream. She said you spend too many nights alone. You do like ice cream, don't you?"

"Yes," she answered and dropped the doll from her clutches, just dangling it by one arm. She wore pajamas that looked almost like street clothes, so they could easily leave if she agreed to go. He didn't want to force her and hear her screams.

"Good, we can get you some ice cream, and then I'll bring you home," he promised. "I'll come back in the morning so your mommy and I can talk. Maybe we can be a family again. You'd like that, wouldn't you?"

Unsure, she nodded yes.

A voice echoed from the upstairs loft. "Julie, who are you talking to?"

"A man, Grandma," she answered, still unfazed.

Wearing only a nightgown, the older woman peered over the railing and saw him. He was tall and lanky, with brown hair sheared close to his head, and he wore a T-shirt and jeans. His mouth twisted into a smirk, and his eyes frightened her. They were piercing and stared straight through her.

"Julie, come here at once," she demanded, and the child, bewildered, started towards the stairs.

The woman shouted down, "You get out!" He was striding towards the front door.

She rushed down the stairs, bounding two steps at a time, and brushed past Julie. Before she peered out the window, she dead-bolted the front door, and then watched until she caught glimpse of an unfamiliar old gray truck go by, leaving the quiet cul-de-sac. Then she ran to phone 911.

The central dispatcher was a woman. The grandmother identified herself as Loretta Rushing, explained briefly what had happened, and described the old truck she thought he was driving.

"Ms. Rushing, were you or your granddaughter harmed?" the dispatcher asked.

"No, other than scared to death. He just walked right in. Invaded our home."

"We'll send the police as soon as possible. Keep your doors locked until the officers arrive, and stay away from the windows," the dispatcher advised.

The grandmother was savvy. "I'm not going to touch the doorknob. He wasn't gloved, so maybe he left fingerprints. The way he was eyeing my granddaughter, I know he's a predator."

"We should have a patrol car there in a few minutes," the dispatcher reassured her. "Would you like to stay on the line until the police arrive?"

"No, I think we're okay," she replied in a shaky voice and hung up.

Her granddaughter cringed in the stairwell and Loretta went to her.

"It's all right, my darling," she said, holding her tight. "You didn't know what to do..."

CHAPTER 23

Before one a.m. Wednesday morning, Hudson's phone began ringing, jolting him from a deep sleep. He rolled over, picked up the receiver, and mumbled, "Detective Hudson..."

"Ross here," the sergeant said. Luke, still groggy, wondered why his former boss from the Bidwell Police Department would call in the middle of the night.

"Hudson, a dispatch just came in that you might want to follow up on. A woman outside Bidwell just called 911 saying that a man was trying to lure her granddaughter out of the house."

"Hell, yes. Thanks for letting me know," he said, suddenly awake. "I'll contact dispatch right now."

"This pervert just might be the one in your case," Ross said and hung up. Luke had never met a cop who didn't hate child molesters, the lowest of predators.

He dialed central dispatch and a female gave him the details. She had sent a police car to the address. He told her he was the lead detective on a child molestation case and there was a possible connection between tonight's incident and his case.

"Oh, you mean the Satin Doll?" she asked, and he wondered if there was anyone in county law enforcement who didn't know the case and the nickname, dubbed after the satin-dressed doll discovered in the first grave.

"Yes, we believe the perpetrator lives at the base of Timber Ridge. Have you been notified of any further action to stop this guy, like roadblocks leading into that area?"

She said, "Not yet, but other calls are coming in."

He thanked the dispatcher and hung up to answer a call-waiting from the Sheriff's Office.

"Detective Hudson, this is Lieutenant Bailey," a woman in a deep, poised voice announced. "I've ordered full coverage of the Timber Ridge area as we speak. We're to keep a low profile, like we're checking for DUIs. Too many cop cars and the perp will run in another direction. The roadblocks will be manned by officers in or close to the area, so no flashing lights or sirens until the blocks are up. We have a description of the guy, and we want everyone stopped in case the pickup was not the perp's vehicle. Are you on your way?"

"Yes, Lieutenant, this is what we've been waiting for. Thanks for the call."

Before he signed off, the Lieutenant said to report back to her. He thought about Bailey as he bounced out of bed. Lieutenant Nala Bailey was about his age and a good superior, but tough. He'd spent little time around her, but she was his superior when Gates was unavailable. Vaguely, he recalled someone telling him that Lieutenant Bailey was born in Africa and a former homicide sergeant with the LAPD before coming to the Park County Sheriff's Office.

In subtle ways, Gates was building his chain of command for changes in the Sheriff's Office. Utilizing Bailey was one of them, and a good choice as far as he was concerned.

He considered phoning Jessie. She was, after all, his partner, and she would be upset if left out. Instead, he got dressed with the clothes he'd been wearing, put on his bulletproof vest, strapped on his gun, and called her from his SUV.

She said she was ready. "I got a heads up from Lewis after Lieutenant Bailey called him. Swing by and pick me up, okay?"

Luke chose the northbound Green Springs Highway as he and Jessie left Bidwell. The road wound north and turned east towards the Sierras. It seemed the logical, most direct route from where the incident took place and Timber Ridge. County Road 5 was to the south, and these were the two main roads leading to the forests, except for the main highway. Traffic was sparse this time of night and Jessie sat in silence, envisioning a chase.

Without warning, they encountered the first roadblock around a bend in a 45 mph zone. The stop was positioned so a driver wouldn't see it coming up until it was too late to turn around. Hudson slowed to a crawl and stopped. A sheriff's deputy recognized his car as an unmarked police SUV, and leaned down to talk to him. "They think they've spotted him about five miles ahead, and he's supposedly doubling back."

Luke told the officers he wanted through and they waved him on.

He passed a large country subdivision called Mountain Oaks and continued driving east. His police radio broke in with Linc Lewis's broadcast call: *POI stopped on Green Springs at marker 9, 11-99.* Officer needs help. Hudson answered the call with a *10-4*, meaning received and understood. He drove towards the distress area and soon approached a sheriff's Tahoe SUV that had skidded to a halt a short distance in front of an older gray Dodge pickup. Tire marks behind the truck revealed it probably slid to a stop when edged off the right side of the road by the sheriff's SUV. On both parked vehicles, headlights glared and car doors were open wide, as the suspect ran and at least one officer followed in pursuit.

Luke screeched to a stop in front of the SUV, which was probably Linc's. He looked over at Jessie and said he was going in and she should stay with the vehicle. He radioed to Lewis that he was coming, and Linc replied with a vague description of his location.

Though the night was dark and cloudy, the police lights and headlights illuminated the trees and underbrush in the area for a hundred feet or so before gloom set in. In the shadows, Luke couldn't see in front of him and had to feel his way with each step, hoping not to rouse a rattlesnake or stumble and crash in the brush.

After another hundred yards, Luke heard Linc's lowered voice only feet away, "Shit, Luke, don't bump into me."

"I didn't see you."

"It helps to be black," Linc whispered. "I've been waiting for backup. It's too damned dark to go it alone. Stay right behind me."

The two advanced with cautious steps, treading lightly on the dry twigs under foot. The perpetrator was less careful and they could hear him stomping about. Though they couldn't spot him yet, he grunted and snapped branches somewhere in front of them.

A brief break in the clouds opened the sky to moonlight. They glimpsed the suspect running through a clearing and chased after him, sprinting forward with guns drawn. Linc, with his long strides, was gaining on the perp, who tripped and tumbled to the ground. Lewis caught him as he staggered to his feet and shoved him back into the dead grass.

With Maglite in one hand and his Glock in the other, Luke overtook the two of them. Lewis yanked a handgun from the guy's belt and threw it aside, while Luke kept him covered. Linc holstered his gun and rolled the trapped suspect onto his stomach, straddling him as he cuffed the man's hands behind his back. Luke lowered his gun, and along with Lewis, they raised the shaken suspect to his feet, and checked him for other weapons. He was clean.

The cloud cover returned, blocking the moon, but the high-powered flashlight led them. They picked their way through brush to the roadside with the perpetrator staggering in front. The suspect bled from a few superficial scratches, and both he and Linc appeared disheveled from the scuffle. Lewis marched the defeated offender to his SUV.

"What's your name?" Luke asked.

Nothing.

Lewis barked, "Give us your damned name and your driver's license."

The man fumbled around a hip pocket with his right cuffed hand, and Hudson reached in to help retrieve the man's wallet. Luke opened it and announced, "James Calvin Perry."

Calmly, Lewis told him he was being arrested for eluding police at a roadblock and read the suspect his Miranda Rights. Then his large hand covered and ducked the perp's head as he scrunched into the back seat of Linc's vehicle. Lewis closed the door, and locked the back so the suspect was isolated behind the grill.

Jessie, looking relieved, walked over to Lewis' Tahoe, and Luke assured her they were okay.

Leaving them, Lewis strolled over to the California Highway Patrol car that had pulled in behind Perry's pickup. The CHP officer said he had left the roadblock to assist Lewis's call for backup, but two Chips were still in place. The officer explained that when he arrived, Hudson was already in pursuit so he stayed with Harte, waiting for another distress call.

Linc told them, "We think we have our suspect, but until you get orders otherwise, I guess the roadblock is still up. Could you stay with the pickup until it's hauled in?"

He thanked him and returned to Luke and Jessie. After two in the morning, the road was devoid of cars, as

Luke rode with Lewis and the suspect, while Jessie drove behind in Luke's black SUV.

James Perry stared ahead, and Luke made eye contact with him through the rear view mirror. He asked, "Where were you earlier tonight?"

"Out and about. At a bar and I can prove it."

"Why did you run?" Luke queried.

"Cops scare the shit out of me," he smirked. "I just did something stupid. No law against stupid is there? If there was, half the country would be locked up."

"You're a real smartass, aren't you," Linc cracked. "Maybe you'll come down a notch at headquarters."

Linc was tired but elated and talkative, "I was staked out with the CHP block when we saw Perry's truck turn around. We just knew it was him. I took off after him and I think the CHP waited to see if he was going to turn back again. The roads are quiet tonight, so I was able to pass him, and slow him down. At that point, he slammed on his brakes and skidded to a stop, jumped out and ran. Of course, by the time I slowed to a stop and went after him, he was in the woods. "

"It was risky going in alone," Luke told him, saying the obvious.

"Sometimes you have to chance it, you know that. I didn't know if he was armed, but I figured he couldn't see me any better than I could see him."

Linc Lewis was neither careless nor impulsive, but he was fearless. Maybe losing a daughter to cancer made him less concerned about his own mortality. Whatever drove him, he was a good, reliable deputy to have on your team, and Luke surmised he was overdue for a promotion.

Luke looked in the rearview mirror at the suspect again. Perry could overhear the account of his own arrest, but he acted indifferent to the conversation and gazed out the window into the opaque night.

Linc suggested, "When we get to the SO, why don't you and Harte go home. Separately, of course," he added with a knowing grin that made Luke uneasy at his cop sense of humor.

"I'd prefer to stay until he's put away," Luke told him. He planned to question the arrestee tonight, before lawyers got ahold of him.

WHEN THEY ARRIVED AT THE SHERIFF'S OFFICE, Luke and Jessie stayed with Lewis as the three of them escorted the suspect through a back entrance and down a hall into a holding cell area. The arrested individual, James Calvin Perry, was 41, Caucasian, and employed part time as an auto mechanic at Barry's Automotive on Taft Street. Because he lived in a rural area with no named streets, his driver's license only had a post office box address. Perry said he was not revealing his physical location until he talked to a lawyer or unless the officers had a warrant to search his house. Deputy Lewis ran a check for priors and found several minor citations for speeding tickets years ago.

Lewis ordered Perry into a chair near the cell and he was tested for sobriety with a Breathalyzer. The move was well justified on Perry's admission that he'd been hanging out in bars and avoided the roadblock. His blood alcohol was under the .08 threshold.

Then Luke sat eye level to Perry and took a crack at interrogating him. Jessie started to join him but Perry stared her down. Hudson was uneasy with Perry's reaction to her, so he asked her to help process the arrest report. She decided not to question his order and stayed with Lewis, who was standing guard.

Hudson's first question was, "Since your record is clean and you weren't drunk, why did you dodge the roadblock?"

Unflustered, Perry answered, "I'd had a few and I didn't know what my blood level was... sir," he emphasized with a hint of sarcasm.

Luke ignored him. "Where have you been this evening? And be specific."

Perry leaned back, "A couple of bars."

"Can you name them?" Luke pressed.

"No, I can't, and I'm not saying another word without legal representation, period. I'm done talking to you."

Luke rose from his chair. He was tall, but so was Perry, with long legs stretched nonchalantly out in front of him. Perry was digging in for a prolonged battle, probably something he had strategized well before tonight.

"It's your call," Luke said. "I guess you're ready for a tour of the county jail."

Two more officers arrived and prepared to transport the suspect to the Park County Jail.

Hudson put a call into Lieutenant Bailey and told her, "We believe we have the guy we wanted. Lewis and I caught him. Hopefully, he ties into the Satin Doll, but so far he's said little and wants an attorney."

"Good, then I can call off the roadblocks," she answered and asked, "anyone hurt?"

"No, not even the suspect," Luke answered. "We got lucky."

"We deserve a little luck once in a while," she said.

He informed her that their suspect was being hauled off to jail, and she said, "Then I'm going back to bed. You guys wrap up and do the same."

With questioning over, Hudson felt comfortable leaving. He and Jessie got in his black SUV for the ride back to her place. He was in no mood for what he anticipated would be a lecture about how he excluded her from the questioning. But she surprised him, as she often did.

"I think I know why you asked me to leave. Did you see the creepy look he gave me?"

"Yes," he answered tersely. "I didn't want to indulge him."

She turned silent.

Finally, he said, "You're awfully quiet. You, okay?"

"Yes, I've just been thinking," she answered, pensive.

"Does this bring back memories of the Chesney arrest?" he probed, knowing something was eating at her.

"No, Perry's different than Chesney, who was sort of a young smart ass, full of himself. This man is an evil predator. I can feel it, and yet it's kind of sad."

"How so?" He tried to figure where she was going with her rational.

"Well, he was once someone's baby boy. Serial killers and child molesters are not born. Something or someone turns them into the monsters they become." She turned to Luke as she continued, "Is that weird reasoning?"

"No." He collected his thoughts. "It's good to feel some empathy. That keeps you from becoming cynical. But don't read too much into this guy until you spend some time around him. Serial killers are the most complex criminals I've ever met. They run a full range of emotions, from remorseful to vengeful in minutes. Most of them don't understand what makes them tick, so neither do we."

He drove her home and walked her to the door. "Thanks," she said, appearing drained, and closed the door behind her.

GETTING HOME AFTER THREE A.M. and up at seven, Luke had slept little, before he showered and dressed for work. When he arrived at the Sheriff's Office, Gates was in the building and the two men sat and talked in Hudson's make-shift office. He gave Luke two copies of the Perry report, as Jessie joined them.

Gates said they had 48 hours to find reasonable cause to keep James Perry longer on a specific, more serious charge than running a roadblock. He had carried a handgun, but he did not threaten officers with it, nor did he violently resist arrest, so at this point the charges were

S RESLER NELSON

minor. They had to prove he was the man who walked into Rushing's home last night and tried to lure her granddaughter away.

Luke told Gates, "I want to bring in the Rushing woman and see if she IDs Perry as the person in her home, so we can nail down whether he's the invader. If he is, it would be timely to go back to Timber Ridge with the K-9s and check for more graves. But that's your call."

The Sheriff was in an awkward position until the Unit was formed. Working this case accentuated the necessity for a better chain of command. How the former sheriff worked with this haphazard organization was beyond him, and he realized all the more why he needed to clean up the mess Kelly left.

Luke said, "I think we'd better get Rushing in here this morning, if possible."

Gates looked around the cramped room that Hudson and Harte occupied. Four metal frame, wooden seat chairs, the murder board, a file cabinet, and a conference table filled the room. The Sheriff stood and stretched his long arms. "I've got a real office for you two. You can move right away. The case is getting more complicated and you need a decent place to work."

CHAPTER 24

Later Wednesday morning, Loretta Rushing sat across a conference table from Hudson. In her fifties, shapely and blonde, age had been kind to her. She was flanked on one side by her daughter, a young mother in her early thirties, accompanied by a smiling, wide-eyed granddaughter. All three were blonde in varying shades and bore close resemblances to each other.

Loretta spoke first, turning to her daughter, "This is my daughter, Caroline Rushing, who works nights as an ER nurse. She's kept her maiden name," Loretta explained.

Smiling at her granddaughter, who clutched a flaxen haired doll, she said, "This is my sweet Julie, who is six and starting school this fall. She is the one who encountered the intruder first, but before he fled I got a good look at him, too. If I can positively identify him, I'd rather leave Julie out of this."

Luke clarified, "The traditional line-up isn't used much anymore. We use photos instead. I'll show you six different mug shots and you identify him from that, if he's the one."

"Oh," she said, surprised. "Well, in that case, it wouldn't hurt for her to look. She did spend several minutes with him."

He added, "I probably don't need to tell you this, but when she looks, there should be no coaching of any kind. Kids will often ask questions and be uncertain what their role is. Are you comfortable with me handling that?"

"Sure," Loretta said, "whatever it takes."

"Do you all three live in the same house?"

"No," the grandmother answered. "I live near Sacramento, but after this incident, I'll be moving here so I can help watch over Julie."

Her daughter, Caroline, interjected, "I've been putting Julie to bed and double checking the locks in the house before I leave, ever since I lost a sitter about a month ago. I knew it was a bit risky, but this has really convinced me."

Luke wondered how a parent could justify leaving a six-year-old unattended in a house all night. He glanced at Jessie, who rolled her eyes, directed at him, but the grandmother caught the look.

"We thought it was a very safe neighborhood," Loretta said defensively.

Luke countered, "You can't be too careful. Unsavory things happen, as you now know."

"Yes," Loretta agreed. "Can we just get on with it? I've already given an account to a deputy."

Hudson took a not-so-fast approach. "Why was the front door unlocked? You have three locks—the regular door lock, a dead-bolt, and a security chain."

"Yes, I know," Caroline replied. "I always lock them all and check the back door, which has the same locking system, and then I go out through the garage. I didn't think

Julie could unlock the chain and dead-bolt. She was supposed to be in bed, but she must have gone outside. She's never done something like that before. She says she went on the front porch because she heard a kitty and wanted to see it. When she came back inside, she didn't lock anything and the man just walked right in. It terrifies me to think what would have happened if my mother hadn't been there."

"Exactly," Jessie emphasized. "Just for future reference, you can be cited for leaving a child home alone if the age poses a risk. Six is very young. Child Protective Services would not consider that a safe age to be home alone overnight. Obviously, you know the consequences now."

Both adults sat contritely while the child played with her doll, "walking" it across the table in front of her.

Dramatically, Loretta said, "It won't happen again, I assure you. Are the photos ready to be viewed?"

Luke asked Caroline if she would go with Deputy Harte and take Julie outside the room. They left with the doll tucked under Julie's arm.

In front of Loretta, Hudson placed six mug shots similar in appearance, known in law enforcement slang as a six-pack. As soon as she saw Perry, she said, "That's him, all right. I'd never forget those penetrating eyes."

"Are you sure?" Hudson asked. "Take your time."

She studied the photo a bit longer, and then stared at another photo, before turning back to Perry. "Yes, I think that's him. I took a hard look at him when he was talking to my granddaughter, because I thought maybe he was a friend of Caroline's since he was in the house. He spoke softly, but I heard something about 'ice cream and bringing her home.' Also, he talked about 'being a family' and I knew he wasn't anyone I'd ever seen before."

Luke questioned, "You said 'I *think* that's him.' You have to be sure." He knew the grandmother had only viewed the suspect from an upstairs loft.

Sensing his doubts, she said, "I'm pretty confident about his identity, but just to cinch it, let's have Julie look at the photos, too. I want this bastard locked up with no glitches later."

Motioning to Jessica through the window, Luke had Julie and her mother brought back into the room.

Hudson had Julie stand so she could have a higher vantage point and better view as she peered at the photos. Then he asked the child, "Have you ever seen any of these men?"

She gazed at each photo with curiosity, then placed a finger on Perry's photo, and said, "That's the man who said he was my daddy. He wanted to take me for some ice cream. Why is his picture here, Grandma?"

Luke thanked them for coming in and assured them they had been most helpful. The conversations had been recorded and the witnesses' observations officially added as evidence. James Perry had indeed entered their home unlawfully. The Sheriff's Office could now go forward with his arrest for trespassing and luring a child. In the afternoon they would question Perry and a search of his home could follow.

It was eleven-thirty in the morning and the June summer day was turning hot outside. Luke and Jessie, with some help, had moved into their new office. The walls were bare, and they still had plenty of arranging to do, but Luke had a desk with drawers and a swivel office chair. Jessie had a table with a few wooden shelves and an office chair, much the same arrangement he and Jimmy had at the BPD. There was a window that faced two pines and scattered shrubs.

"It's good to have a place to work. Let's catch an early lunch," Luke suggested to his partner.

They strolled a few blocks to a nearby deli called The Courthouse. The Sheriff's main office building was in downtown Bidwell, walking distance from the BPD headquarters. They were both within a few blocks of the Courthouse Square. Only the county jail was a drive south out of town, in a rural setting, because when it was constructed nobody wanted it in their back yard.

When Hudson and Harte walked into the deli, Jimmy waved them to the table where he and Maria were seated. Jimmy stood and gave Luke a warm hug. Jessie and Maria did not know each other that well, but exchanged introductions and pleasantries.

After Luke and Jessie were seated, Jimmy said, "Hey, the talk is you snagged a big one."

"We'll see," Luke remained reserved. "We haven't interrogated him yet."

They stayed off cop talk and delved into other things, from the weather to politics to K-9s and horses. Jimmy admitted he hadn't been to the racetrack in months and the racing season was half over.

Luke said wistfully, "I hope things slow down soon. I'm taking some time off when this case is over. Then we can go fishing and to the track."

Jimmy smiled, his eyes shining with the prospect. He agreed, "We both need a break. Not to mention that you gals do, too."

Halfway through lunch the Sheriff called Luke.

"We have a situation with our suspect," he started. "Perry wants to talk, but on his terms, and he will only talk to the lead detective—you. And he says he's ready to talk now. He's demanding it's now or nothing."

"No problem," Luke responded. "We'll wrap up lunch and get back to the office. Can he be brought to the main office? We can use the old lineup room so there's the one-way window and sound. That way Harte can watch and listen from outside the room for the one-on-one."

"You got it," Gates said and hung up.

WHEN THEY ARRIVED AT THE SHERIFF'S OFFICE, the fingerprint results were in. The two prints lifted from the Rushing doorknob were smeared so they did not have a conclusive match to Perry's. Hudson shared the report with Jessie and then told her the protocols he would follow during questioning.

"I'm taking the approach that's he's a pedophile, and most of them you handle differently from other criminals," he began, trying to read her body language. "I've requested the old line up room, so you can be in the observation area."

Luke paused, expecting Jessie to blurt out 'you're protecting me again', but she waited for him to continue, exhibiting a more analytical attitude.

"You're perfectly capable of questioning him," he said, "but he preyed on a little girl, and for all we know he seeks older ones, too. You're attractive and he may find you a distraction, someone to play with verbally."

Jessie interposed, "Why not let me start out with you? And if you don't like his demeanor, you can give me a nod and I'll leave. I get what you're saying, but maybe we should test him a little. Then at least we'd know how he reacts to a mature woman."

He accepted her plan, "But feel free to leave if *you* sense bad vibes I don't pick up on. And if you do go outside, I want you to take note of anything you question or detect. We can talk later. I'm not taking notes because it might distract or intimidate him."

"Seems you'd want to intimidate him."

"That's not necessarily a good idea with serial killers and pedophiles. In some cases it's better to win their trust and not appear judgmental. I'll be a good listener. I know it sounds crazy, but he has been rejected all his life. If I want to open him up, I have to create an atmosphere where he can let his guard down. I've walked this line before, and it usually works."

"Okay," she said, knowing he was the expert. "I'll go along with whatever you say. I might learn something," she grinned.

THE INTERROGATION ROOM WAS ARRANGED the way Hudson wanted it staged when James Perry arrived. Luke and Jessie were seated when he sauntered in with a corrections officer. Handcuffed in front, Perry did a double take at seeing Deputy Harte at the table.

"Only the lead detective," he reiterated his demand. "Not her," he said with disdain, and then gave her a leering stare.

Jessie rose and left the room without looking back.

Hudson stood and introduced himself, and then he asked the officer to uncuff Perry. After doing so, the officer stood guard outside the room during the interrogation, where he could watch through a window, but not so close as to hover. Luke had removed anything from his person that could be used as a weapon. He wore a white shirt, no tie, no pen in the shirt pocket and nothing on his belt but his ID shield.

Perry was in his orange jail clothes, but he looked refreshed, as if he had showered, washed his short cut brown hair, and eaten lunch. His first words caught Luke off guard. "She's beautiful."

"Excuse me?" Luke said.

"The deputy or whoever the hell she is. Don't tell me you've never noticed."

Luke was uneasy. "Let's stick to your concerns."

Perry leaned back in his chair and with a knowing smirk and piercing eyes, he further tried to disarm the detective.

Hudson thought, *he's good, a manipulative pro.* Aloud, he pushed back a little, "So what did you want to talk about?"

"I heard the cops are going to search my house later today."

"Not necessarily. We're waiting for a warrant," Luke replied. "What's the problem?"

"My daughter, Annie, lives there and I don't want you bastards scaring the crap out of her." His eyes flashed anger, then calmed. "Detective, can you go along? Make sure she's treated okay?"

"Sure, I'll look out for her. Though our deputies are very professional," he assured Perry.

"That wasn't my impression last night," Perry quipped.

Luke didn't respond to the remark. "How old is she?"

"Annie's barely seventeen. I've protected her a lot, so you guys storming through the house will terrorize her."

"It would be a quiet search. We don't storm through houses." Luke tried to lighten the tension, but James Perry steeled himself.

Then Hudson asked, "Does she know you've been arrested?"

"Yeah, my one call went to her. She's distraught. I'm all she has." Perry leaned forward, the smirk off his face. "What will happen to her now?"

Measuring his response, Luke answered, "She can't be left alone, so I'm glad you told me about her. Temporarily at least, she'll go to Child Protective Services."

"Shit," he muttered. "CPS is a laugh. They're famous for letting kids fall through the cracks."

"Are you speaking from experience?"

"No, but I read a lot. I know what happens to unwanted kids," Perry divulged.

Hudson was taking mental notes. Annie was the age Amber would be. Perry was highly suspicious of governmental authorities and adamant about discarded children. He was calculating and probably well read.

Luke decided to cut to the chase. "Since you have a daughter, why were you trying to lure away another girl last night?"

"Is that what you think?" Perry started to rise. "Is that what you think?" he shouted.

"Please, sit down," Luke advised, calm and unfazed. "If I'm wrong, enlighten me."

Seeing the guard advancing towards the door, Perry lowered into his chair.

"I have an appointed attorney now, so I don't have to tell you anything. The truth is, you don't have a scintilla of evidence against me, and a judge will rule in my favor," he sneered with confidence.

Unruffled, Hudson said, "You're right. I haven't heard your side. I'm just curious how you ended up in someone else's house last night."

"I was driving through the neighborhood because I heard at work that there was an old, antique truck for sale parked on that street. I like old trucks, so I drove by but didn't see it. What I did find was a little girl alone on a lit front porch after midnight. It didn't look right, so I went back to check. I mean, what kind of parent lets a little kid out unattended that hour of the night?"

Perry sniffed, scratched his nose, and continued, "I parked and saw the girl going inside so I followed her in, to talk to her parent, guardian, whoever. I asked about her daddy and her family. She mentioned something about ice cream, as if she wanted some. Who knows what she was thinking. She's a little kid. Anyway, I thought she was alone and I was thinking about reporting it when a woman appeared from upstairs and freaked out, so I left. I knew what I did would be hard to explain, but I'd do it again. Honestly, I thought the kid was alone and in danger. See what I'm saying?" Perry waited for the detective to digest his version.

Luke wasn't impressed. He wasn't buying it, and a judge probably wouldn't either. But a jury might, if his case went that far.

He asked, "Why didn't you just stand watch outside and call the police? Let them sort it out."

Perry didn't answer.

"You took a risk," Luke acknowledged, wanting to keep him talking.

"I know. I think it was Einstein who said 'The world's a dangerous place, not because of people who do evil, but because of those who look on and do nothing.' I saw a wrong and tried to right it."

James Perry was quoting Einstein and someone else he'd heard. The man was a clever work of art and had conjured up an explanation he perceived as believable.

The Rushing girl had alluded to a "kitty" on the front porch, her reason for going outside the house. But the cat's leash had been cut, and a partial thin leather lead, with cat hair on it, was all that remained when the police arrived.

Luke used that to throw Perry off.

"What about the cat tied on the porch?"

"I didn't see a cat. What are you taking about?" Perry showed indifference to the question.

Hudson tried to keep him going. "I know you don't have to answer me, but why were you driving around so late at night? You could see the truck better in daylight. And what about your own daughter at home?"

This time Perry recognized his mistake of overreacting, so he toned down. "I'd been out for a few beers. Annie's old enough to leave home alone. In fact, because I'd had a few, that's why I turned around when I saw the checkpoint. I didn't know if I was legal and didn't want to chance a DUI. I didn't run a roadblock, I simply avoided it. I doubt that what I did was against the law. Frankly, you and the black dude overplayed your hand. You know what I'm saying?"

Perry had covered himself with halfway plausible answers for all the major arrest points. Unless there was something at his residence to discredit him, Luke figured

Perry was going to walk with minor charges. Forty percent of homicides remain unsolved in the country, so his case could end up being just one more statistic.

Still, they could buy more time if James Perry could be held on PC602, Criminal Trespassing, punishable by a maximum of six months in jail and a thousand dollar fine. But a good attorney could get the penalty reduced or even dismissed. Luring the child was an ambiguous charge which more or less would turn into a he-said, she-said argument. And often, a six year old child's testimony carried little weight, considering the seriousness of the offense. Avoiding the traffic stop was technically not illegal. His attorney could raise suspicion there was even just cause to pursue him in the first place, so their suspect might be exonerated.

Luke surmised this was not the right moment to drag on an interrogation. He wanted more facts and a clearer strategy before he faced Perry again. Once they brought in the daughter, if indeed Annie was his daughter, perhaps she could provide some insights into the real James Perry. Somehow things didn't add up, but he couldn't finger it yet.

Perry must have sensed they were through because he rose slowly. The man had angular features, taut thin lips, and haunting eyes. His demeanor could change in an instant from arrogance to reticence. He'd been through years of hard knocks and his face showed it.

Luke didn't want his suspect deciding when the interview was over, so he claimed, "Just a few more questions, to help me understand."

Perry sat down again.

"You seem like a man who is educated and has had other jobs besides a mechanic. Do you mind telling me a little about your past?"

People like talking about themselves, especially when the topics are positive, so Perry began. "I only have a GED which took determination to get, but I'm an avid reader, and I got some training in the Army. I was in the Middle East in 1998 during Clinton's Operation Desert Fox and bombing of Iraq. Remember that? I served as a helicopter mechanic, and I liked it. But I couldn't wait to get out of the service after that stint."

"Why's that?"

"Once you see the casualties of war... We said hundreds of Iraqis died, the Iraqis said thousands. One is one too many. Only the dead have seen the end of war. As far as I know, we didn't suffer any losses, at least not in body count. Head count is something else."

Luke knew he was referring to war's mental toll on soldiers. This Perry was absorbed with being philosophical, throwing out lofty quotes and concepts. He was a complex man, complicated enough to either be gifted or a serial killer or both.

Hudson asked, "Why didn't you remain a chopper mechanic? They make good money."

"Most of them work on military bases. I'd had enough. I'm fine working on cars. Never happier than when I have grease on my hands," he grinned, glancing at the detective's unlabored hands.

"So when did you move to this area?"

Perry hesitated, pondering if it was a trick question, one to nail him down. "Uh...I don't remember exactly. In my twenties."

That would place him in the county when Amber Richards disappeared.

"How old were you when you left the Army?" Luke asked casually.

"Obviously, in my twenties."

Hudson knew he was walking a fine line but he asked anyway, "Your daughter is seventeen, so you were around twenty-four when she was born? And in the Army?"

Perry was taken aback, unprepared for the question. He didn't answer, so Luke figured he was going to shut down, but he finally said, "Yeah, something like that. I got a girl pregnant and later she didn't want the kid or me, so I raised my daughter."

Waiting for a reaction and getting none, Perry said, "Are we done now?"

Luke sensed that their suspect was reaching the end of his patience, so he took a stab at one last inquiry. "Where is your daughter going to school?"

The question threw Perry. "Uh...she's home schooled. We live too far out for busses, and I work. She's a smart girl."

With that, Hudson stood and thanked Perry, who also rose from his chair.

"We'll be talking again," Luke said. "And I'll see that your daughter is treated right. She will probably be brought into CPS so she won't be unsupervised, unless you have a relative who would be suitable for her to stay with temporarily."

"I really don't," he answered, which indicated he was a loner, no family, or at least no one he could rely on.

"Do you want to see her?"

"Of course," he retorted.

James Perry walked out with the corrections officer. He had less spring in his step as the realities of his situation were setting in.

As soon as Perry was gone, Luke cut the recorder and Jessie hurried into the room. Luke sat down again as she took the chair beside him.

"That was a trip, huh?" she remarked with a slight grin.

"Yes, it was," Luke agreed. "What did you take away?"

"I want to see his military records. By his account he was in the service when his daughter was born. And the girl's name is Annie, as in Little Orphan Annie."

"Good deduction," he smiled, "but you're too young to remember Orphan Annie."

"Yes, but I saw the musical *Annie*." She ran on, "The comments he made about me were provoking. But, hey, could that man quote. You know, people who love to quote do it because it makes them look smart and well educated. Also, the quotes they memorize have special meaning for them. That's why they bother to memorize them. I bet he's the Longfellow letter writer. He quoted Einstein, and then listen to this, because I think the Kennedy quote reveals how Perry sees himself."

Jessie read from her smart phone, "Teddy Kennedy in his eulogy to Bobby said, 'to be remembered simply as a good and decent man, who saw wrong and tried to right it, saw suffering and tried to heal it, saw war and tried to stop it.' Sound familiar? Perry fancies himself a decent man who tried to right a wrong in Julie Rushing's situation. He says he feels the suffering of abandoned children and he's anti-war."

"They're interesting connections," Luke conceded. "His self-image fits with a serial killer's profile. We tend to think of criminals in terms of good and evil, black and white, but I think it's the gray areas that confuse them and us the most."

"I've never thought of it that way," she admitted, and took time to digest his words before concluding, "His quote about 'only the dead have seen the end of war' is from Plato. Interesting, huh? He's probably brilliant."

"Or he spends a lot of time in front of a computer," Hudson quipped.

"Another thing, I know what he did was wrong going into the Rushing house, but he may not be our serial killer. That's an assumption we've made, totally unfounded at this point," Jessie argued.

Luke was tired of sitting, so he rose. "You're right. We have lots of work to do. I want you in on the search this afternoon."

Jessie stood facing him and smiled, "Did you think I would miss it?"

CHAPTER 25

The Perry house was modest and rustic, with no address, on an unnamed dirt road in the foothills of Timber Ridge, nearly a mile from national forest. It was about five miles from where the graves were found. No landscaping existed, but the entire house was fenced with five-foot chain link.

Luke's SUV and a car driven by a Child Protective Services case worker pulled up in front. The CPS representative was Michael Rhodes, in his late thirties, with a boyish air about him, but a professional attitude. Carrying a briefcase, Rhodes followed Hudson and Harte to the garage. Perry told them how to enter. His garage opener taken by the police from his truck would get them into the garage. With the keys Perry had at the time of his arrest, they were to unlock the door that went from the garage into the kitchen. Perry had demanded they not force their way in and scare his daughter. Luke promised that wouldn't happen.

They gained entrance into the garage and rapped on the kitchen door before Luke called out to the girl.

"Annie? Your dad sent us here. We're deputies and Child Protective Services."

She hollered back, "Go away! I don't need your help."

"I think you do," he countered. "You're locked in, and when you run out of food, you're out of luck."

"I'll wait 'til then," she argued.

"You really don't have a choice," he said back to her. "Once we unlock the door, we're in. I just didn't want to frighten you. Your dad is worried about that."

"I'm already scared. Now leave me alone," she cried.

"We can't do that," Jessie said, hoping a female voice would calm her. "We're coming in and then we can all talk, okay?"

There was no response from the other side of the door.

They waited and then unlocked the padlock and opened the door a crack. Luke had asked Perry if there were guns in the house and he said yes, but the girl couldn't get to them. He hoped Perry told the truth. Rhodes stayed outside in the garage as Luke and Jessie entered into the kitchen with guns drawn, just in case. Annie peeked through a narrow gap in a hallway door and screamed when she saw them.

"Step into the hall," he said, "and keep your hands up."

The girl was terrified and he wished there was another way to approach her. She appeared unarmed and they lowered their weapons. He and Jessie stepped from the kitchen into the darkness of the living room, keeping a keen watch on the girl, who remained in the shadows of the hallway beyond.

The living room décor was Spartan. Old curtains and drapes hung unevenly from the windows and the furniture was well worn. The room could use some cleaning, but overall it was not cluttered and contained just the bare necessities. Numerous books were stacked on boards supported by concrete blocks, creating homemade book shelves. Luke noticed an old set of the Harvard Classics because he had grown up with a similar collection.

He asked Annie to come down the hall. She inched towards them with hands still above her head.

Harte met her halfway and frisked her, saying to Luke that the girl was no threat.

"We're so sorry to frighten you," Jessie said. "You can relax now."

"Relax!" Annie cried. "Are you crazy?"

"We had to enter armed," Luke said in a softer voice, "just to be safe. Officers get shot by kids a lot younger than you."

He smiled, but she didn't think it was funny.

Luke showed her his badge. "I'm Detective Hudson and I've brought my partner, Deputy Harte, and Mr. Rhodes, from Child Protective Services." Rhodes had entered the house by now, closing the garage-to-kitchen door behind him, and stood in the entry to the living room.

"You must be Annie," Luke said and she nodded yes. He was unsure how much information he should give her, especially about the CPS presence, until she calmed down. Her frightened eyes told him that one misstep and she would scream again.

"I talked to your dad earlier today. He wanted us to come here and make sure you're okay."

"That sounds like my dad," she said, with slow delivery.

To cancel the dreary living room light, Jessie pushed back the curtains and the bright sunlight caused Annie to blink and rub her eyes. Luke noted the windows were double-paned with black iron security bars on the outside. From what they had seen so far, the house was a fortified prison.

He moved closer to Annie and she flinched. There was a scar on the right side of the girl's neck, where Amber's birthmark would have been. Closer, he observed the crude burn that marred her smooth skin and erased the birthmark. She was a pretty girl, aside from the blemish. Her hair was dishwater blonde, a dark gold with flecks of brown. She had blue eyes, fine features, and a medium height frame sporting jeans and an oversized man's T-shirt. She wasn't wearing a bra.

He introduced Michael Rhodes but did not mention CPS. He had given Rhodes the background on Perry and his reaction to the agency. They thought it best to avoid the reference as long as they could. Anyway, Michael was there more as an observer at this point. Rhodes said hello and awkwardly stood around, waiting for his cue to do something. Hudson asked Annie if she would show them around.

"I'd rather not," she said with reticence, but Luke gestured for her to lead them down the narrow hall, and she did, hesitating with each step. Off the hall were four doors for three bedrooms and a bathroom. The door on the left, which was probably the master bedroom, was padlocked. On the right side of the hall was a padlocked bathroom, and two bedrooms separated by the bath. Both those rooms were unlocked. The one closest to the living room was Annie's and faced the back yard.

Luke and Michael sensed she wanted little to do with them, so they stood at Annie's bedroom door while Jessie walked into the room with Annie and the girl didn't object.

The first thing the men examined was the locking system on the outside of Annie's bedroom door and the barred window inside. She could be locked in her room with access to the bathroom and held there, making her a prisoner in her own room. She had a laptop computer, no doubt blocked from internet access. There was a single bed, a TV, and a small collection of books. The closet originally spread across the interior bedroom wall next to the bathroom, but it was cut open near the middle of the closet to provide for a crudely framed, narrow doorway that led to the bathroom. The bathroom could be accessed from the main hall, but it was padlocked on the outside, giving her a private bath.

Perry had removed the closets doors and instead built makeshift shelves and a limited space to hang clothes. Annie's clothes were basic casual wear and dresses that were more like costumes than something a teen would choose to own. The other half of the closet had shelves where Annie kept books, bedding and towels, underwear, and personal items.

He asked, "Do you have a phone?"

She shook her head no.

"Why the bars on the window and padlock setup on the door?"

"It's for ou...my protection. So if someone broke into the house while my dad's away, I would be safe in my room."

"But if you're locked in a barred room and a fire breaks out, you'd die," Luke told her.

She said nothing and glared up at him.

Jessie gave Luke "the look" and involved Annie in talking about things in her room, which relaxed and distracted her. The two men knew they had best leave.

They continued down the hall, passing the padlocked bathroom. Michael gave Luke a wary glance. At this point, Luke didn't have a search warrant, only the authority to remove the minor from Perry's house, so he was limited in what he could do. But Michael whispered the girl was being held against her will, and Hudson, in a muted voice, said that unlawful restraint of a minor is a criminal offence, punishable by several years in prison, and a warrant would be forthcoming now.

They moved on to the next bedroom and the door was open, though a padlock setup on the door was in place and a lock hung on the unsecured hasp. The window had bars and looked out onto a high, wooden fenced, back yard. Michael had noticed this back yard from the living room. The high privacy fence surrounded a small patio off the living room and the two men now assumed that the high privacy fence ran the length of the two back bedrooms and was an area where Annie could be allowed outside when Perry was home. But she still couldn't go beyond the back yard because two strands of barbed wire extended above the six-foot tall planks, like a prison yard. *How long had the girl lived like this?*

The second bedroom was stripped of everything and cleaned until it had a perceptible antiseptic odor. Luke entered the room alone, only about half way to look around, but not touch anything. He was mindful of contamination and anticipated a future, thorough search soon.

The room mirrored Annie's bedroom. Again the closet had been altered to make two storage areas, with a door to the bathroom in the middle. It could be padlocked to prevent Annie from coming through the bathroom into this room and then having access to the house, but it was not locked at the present. The door to the bathroom was narrower, probably because the toilet would have prevented cutting a larger doorway. The closet and shelves were spotless and bare. Luke detected a plastered patch in the back wall that was about the size of a medium doggie door, and speculated at one point Annie might have had a dog that had access to the back yard.

With the empty bedroom unlocked, the area had already been contaminated. He left the room and joined Michael. The bedroom across from it was no doubt Perry's, with probably a master bath. It faced the frontal dirt road. Of course, it was padlocked on the outside so no one could enter. No telling what they would find in Perry's room. Michael wrote more notes and said softly to Luke, "The locks alone are enough to remove the girl and place her with CPS. And Perry is facing a lot of legal grief over this."

They returned to the doorway of Annie's room, where she and Jessie were talking. Annie became silent when the men appeared.

Luke asked Annie about the empty room.

She froze and then replied, "It's just a spare room."

He didn't believe her and Jessie didn't know what he was talking about.

"Did anyone else live here besides you and your dad?" he persisted.

"No!" she exclaimed, tensions rising.

"Did you have a dog?"

Annie stared at the two men in anger. "No! Okay? Leave me alone!"

By now Jessie was exasperated and brushed Luke off. "Don't you two have work to do?"

Michael wanted to document any other locks in the house, so they left and continued their walk through the house. The front and back doors had sliding bolt latches that were padlocked from the inside so no one could leave the house. Perry obviously left through the garage and then had an outside padlock to keep anyone inside the house from leaving once he was gone. It was hardly a conductive environment for raising a child.

Jessie had brought Annie into the kitchen and they were seated side by side at the table, talking, when Luke and Michael joined them. The men sat across the kitchen table and Annie became increasingly anxious.

Luke told Annie, "With your dad in jail, we need to talk about your immediate future."

He turned to Michael, who proceeded, "You'll have to come with us and stay with Child Protective Services..."

"No!" she shrieked. "Let me stay here! You can lock me in my room and keep a cop car out front. Obviously, I can't run away."

"We can't do that. We'd be treating you like a prisoner."

"I'd rather be here than in a CPS prison," she cried, echoing Perry's opinions. "My whole life is locked up in a prison, anyway," she sobbed. Hudson didn't know if she was referring to her own life or to Perry's incarceration.

She was spiraling out of control. Luke had to calm her if he could, but he only made matters worse. "You are a minor under eighteen so you can't stay here alone."

Annie moaned and rocked, borderline hysterical.

Jessie stepped in, speaking softly, and the girl listened. "Annie, it is only temporary, until things are sorted out for your dad. You may have the impression that CPS is bad, but they have changed a lot. You'll be pleasantly surprised, I think. Mr. Rhodes will take you there and..."

"No!" Annie cried. "I'm not getting in a car with him—ever!"

The extent to which Annie was terrified of strangers, especially men, said volumes about what she had experienced in her short life.

Jessie glanced at the two men and suggested, "Why don't you two go somewhere for a few minutes?"

As they were leaving, she ventured to tell Annie, "You will meet some girls your own age and be well cared for. I will *personally* see to that. I know you can handle it for a little while, and it would put your dad at ease. He doesn't like CPS either, but he also doesn't want you to be left here alone, and there's no family member to send you to. Please give it a try for your dad's sake."

Annie settled down a notch or two.

Jessie offered, "If you want, I can help you pack a few things."

Luke and Michael stood in the living room, and both sighed with relief when Jessie led Annie to her room.

Hudson felt that if Annie were left to her own devices, she was a flight risk, even if it meant living on the streets. CPS was the only alternative, but she had the potential to harden under CPS custody and end up in juvenile confinement. He hoped Jessie could guide her through the process. Further, he wanted Lucy McCormack to see her. He and Michael discussed the options, considering Annie's blatant mistrust and anger towards men and protective custody.

Rhodes said, "Luke, I don't need to tell you, this girl needs a lot of counseling. The first thing I will do is put her with a female case worker. One she can relate to. Anything short of that will be disastrous. I'd be willing to bet she's been abused by men, repeatedly.

"You and Jessie should take Annie in to the Sheriff's Office while I find my replacement. That will take a few hours."

Luke had additional plans. While Jessie was with Annie, he phoned Lucy McCormack.

"Oh, I knew you'd call one of these days," she beamed.

"How about a ride along this afternoon? It's short notice but I have a surprise for you."

"Well, how long do I have to get ready?" she asked anxiously.

"About an hour," he told her.

"I'll look forward to it then."

At the sheriff's office, luke took jessie aside while Annie Perry was seated in a waiting area. He explained that Michael Rhodes would find a suitable female CPS case worker and Jessie was relieved.

"Thanks for saving my ass," he grinned, and told her he wanted to bring in Lucy Cormack late this afternoon to see if she recognized Annie as Amber Richards.

"You're asking a lot of this girl," she objected.

"I know, but we need to build a solid case against Perry, as soon as we can. For now, why don't you get her something to eat and let her see her dad. Do that and you might shore up your relationship with Perry," he smiled mischievously.

"Lots of luck," she smirked.

"You can introduce Annie to a McDonalds or Starbucks drive-through on the way to the jail."

"I'm not sure it's a good idea for her to see Perry today," Jessie ventured.

"I disagree. She needs a reality check, to see for herself that her dad is locked up. Take a female deputy with you. Have Annie sit in back and lock the back doors. I think she's a flight risk," Luke said in a serious vein. "Then bring her back here after she sees Perry. Use my car and I'll take a patrol car. I'd rather not have Annie in a cop car and Lucy McCormack will love it."

Jessie assured him it would all go smoothly, as she left to join Annie.

Meanwhile, he dialed Sergeant Thomas to get a report about Perry's place of employment, Barry's Automotive.

Thomas was on top of it. "According to the owner, Perry has a bike. Usually drives it to work. It's in the shop, so we can compare tire tread with what we got on Timber Ridge. Things are looking up, Hudson," he said lightheartedly for the first time in days.

CHAPTER 26

Lucy was given a tour of the Sheriff's Office by Gates's administrative assistant while Luke checked in with Jessie. She had spent almost two hours with Annie and felt she was gaining the girl's confidence. She said at the moment, Annie was sitting with the female deputy who accompanied her to see Perry.

Jessie added, "I've contacted CPS and she'll be in an all-female dorm-type living arrangement until they can place her in a foster home or sort out where she should go. CPS has a replacement for Rhodes. The new case worker is one they think can handle her phobias. She's an older, experienced employee, Ellen Stone. When we finish here, I'm going to go with Annie to meet Ellen and stay awhile to help her adjust."

Luke told her, "Lucy is here and it would be helpful if they at least meet, to see if they recognize each other. Then Lucy, or both of them, could see the doll. And I'd like to get DNA from Annie. We have Perry's DNA sample, but with her, the swab would have to be consensual..."

Jessie interrupted him, "No, you're throwing a lot at her. She's only a child, and a very screwed up one at that." Jessie was being the child's advocate and Luke knew she was prepared to dig in.

"You're probably right. At least I'd like her to see Lucy and the doll. Is that asking too much?"

She detected a hint of sarcasm in his question and summed it up to his being a control freak, used to calling the shots. Further, she guessed his mood was the same as hers—tired, emotionally drained, and eager to wind down the day, while tied to time constraints and hours more work that couldn't wait. It was four in the afternoon.

"Okay," she conceded, "let Lucy see Annie from the side room of the old lineup room. If she doesn't recognize her at all, there's no use putting Annie through it. If she has an inkling, we can let them meet. And then maybe the doll can come into play. Agreed?"

He nodded, impressed that Jessie was asserting herself and telling him what to do. He knew he tended to be a heavy handed regulator.

"I'll get Lucy now. She won't know why she's looking in on you and Annie. That would be leading the witness," he grinned slightly.

"Good," Jessie said with authority, and turned to go back to Annie. The two must have developed a bond that he could never muster.

Lucy entered the side room with him and he explained this is a room they use to view a person of interest. She recognized Jessie immediately and then studied the girl facing her.

"Can she see or hear me?" Lucy asked.

"No, you can say what you want."

"Well, the girl looks familiar. She looks like the girl in your photo update of Amber. I mean she has a mark where her birthmark was, and she's about the right age, and something about her facial features. But I can't be sure. That was eleven years ago," she reminisced. "Is she Amber?"

"I can't answer that. You tell me."

Lucy strained her eyes and peered closer to the glass. "I wish I could be sure. I know that's important, to be accurate."

Hudson asked, "Would it help if you met with her?"

"Yes, I think so," she answered in a measured tone.

"There're no tricks here," he assured her. "We don't know if she is Amber or not. I can't tell you any more than that about her. When you meet her, let the girl—her name is Annie—lead you. She's very fragile at this point, so we don't want to throw things at her that she can't handle, if you know what I mean."

"Yes...I think I do," Lucy said. "I'll take my cues from you, Detective."

"You're a good partner," he said grinning, and she smiled back. Her frame hunched slightly, with weary, unsteady steps as she walked with him. He steadied her on his arm and they entered the room with Annie and Jessica.

Annie's immediate reaction was to study Lucy, as if trying to place a face from the past. She and Lucy stared at one another, neither speaking.

Luke broke the silence. "I was showing my friend around the Sheriff's headquarters. She saw you and thought maybe she recognized you. Lucy, this is Annie Perry."

Lucy smiled and said, "You've grown into a pretty young lady."

Annie was still entranced, searching for answers. Her long hair fell to her shoulders, and she wore the clothes Jessie had her change into before she left Perry's house. Stress showed on her face, even though she finally smiled. Luke understood Jessie's concerns about overtaxing her.

The teenage girl spoke. "You look familiar, too. But it would have been a long time ago, when I was very young."

"Yes, it was," Lucy agreed, and looked at Luke as if wondering how far to proceed. Jessie suggested Luke and Lucy take a seat.

Hudson led with a probing question. "Do you two remember where you might have met before?"

Lucy took his verbal prod to open the past. "Well, speaking for myself, I think it was maybe eleven years ago. Annie looks like a little girl I knew when she was six. I used to read stories to the child, through a wooden fence, because the little girl and I were back yard neighbors."

Jessie noticed Annie becoming tense, fidgeting, and jiggling her crossed leg. She asked, "Is this making you uncomfortable, Annie?"

She shook her head no, wanting to continue. "There's just so much I don't know any more," she murmured.

Luke and Lucy remained quiet and Jessie reassured her. "Annie, maybe you've had enough for one day."

Annie remained strong. "I'm starting to want answers," she said, resolute. "Then maybe it will all be over and I can go home with my dad."

Luke froze. He had forgotten to tell Lucy the "dad" connection. Lucy looked at him and read his concern because she said nothing. Jessie caught Luke's eye and mimed "the doll" and he took the signal.

He said with care, "Annie, anything we talk about or do here has to be with your approval. I have a doll to show you, and that might jog your memory or mean something to you. But I won't do that if you'd rather not see it."

She sighed, "Go ahead. I want this to end, so help me."

Hudson rose and came back shortly with the doll in an evidence bag. He placed it on the table and Annie focused on the satin dressed, headless doll. He looked at Lucy and put a finger to his lips, cueing her not to talk. She understood and just watched.

"It's my doll," Annie whispered, tears welling in her eyes. "Why is its head missing?"

"We don't know," Jessie said.

Annie wiped a tear from her cheek. "I haven't seen it for a while. Where did you find it?"

Luke answered, "We've had it for a week or so. I found it in the woods." He did not want to talk about finding it in a grave. "Just the way you see it now. The head was nowhere around. Sorry."

"I can't keep it, can I?" she looked up at him, her eyes red and glistening with tears.

"Not now," he said. "It's evidence."

"Against my dad?"

"We don't know. I think we should leave it at that. You've had a rough day. But thank you for sharing what you know. I know it wasn't easy."

He gave her a weak smile and rose with Lucy in tow. He sensed the elder was on the verge of talking and he wanted her out of the room. He nodded to Jessie and ushered Lucy out.

They stepped away from the room and Lucy could hold back no longer. "I know the doll. You notice the dress is faded. She played with that doll like it was a little sister. That was the doll she often brought out of the house with her. Head or no head, it's her doll. And that girl is Amber."

"Maybe so," he said as he led her to the break room and offered her a soda. "You did a wonderful job. Would you be willing to sign a sworn statement about the doll?"

"You bet," she said. "Anything to help. Will I be a witness in court?"

"You're jumping ahead. One step at a time," he told her. "For now, I need to get your identification of the doll and then I'll take you home."

They went through the ID process and Luke helped her out of the building. He brought the Sheriff's patrol car around for her. She took his arm and he guided her into the passenger seat.

"This has been one of the most memorable days of my life," she said, looking up at him, a sparkle in her eyes. "I hope we get to the bottom of that poor child's case."

"Don't we all," he said, closing the door carefully.

She had no idea how successful she had been in breaking the case wide open. No idea and he couldn't even tell her.

It had been a long day. Luke was leaving after six when Jessie called and wanted to talk.

"Can it wait until tomorrow?" He knew her to be tenacious when she had her mind set.

"I'd rather not. I'd like to fill you in on Annie. We need a quiet place to talk, not a cop stop."

"What do you propose?" he resigned.

"I'll pick up Chinese food and bring it to my place. You can meet me there. It's sort of on your way home," she still had energy left; he didn't.

"I don't really like Chinese," he groused.

"How about pizza and a salad?" she offered.

"That works. What time?"

"In a half hour?" she suggested, tightly wound.

He agreed and signed off. Maybe food and drink would give him a needed boost so he could keep up with her.

When he arrived at her house, she had "freshened up," as she called it, and gone casual as well, in jeans and a sporty top. Almost her first words were "What do you want to drink?" She had a glass of red wine in her hand.

"Do you have beer?" he asked.

Jessie brought him a Sierra Nevada Pale Ale, and he took an easy chair as she sat on the sofa, her legs crossed.

She commented, "Long day, huh? You weren't exaggerating about this case being non-stop. Thanks for humoring me by coming. You'd probably rather be home."

"No, this is good," he said, feeling better already. She had a way of disarming him.

"About Annie," she started. "Does Lucy think she's Amber Richards? I sure do, but I didn't go there. I wasn't sure how to approach it. I'd rather get DNA to prove she's not Perry's daughter and then perhaps she'll talk about it. She must have some memory of being six."

Obviously, Jessie was charged and talkative, her usual demeanor.

Luke took a couple of swallows of the ale. "Well, Lucy emphatically believes the girl is Amber. She says the child played with that doll a lot and head or no, she's certain. I got a statement from her to that effect, so that's our first solid evidence."

"That's worth celebrating," Jessie said.

"I'm withholding judgement until we get the DNA, but there's no doubt about Perry's unlawful restraint of a minor. And we can probably add child abuse and rape to that, so it will be a long time before he sees the outside of a prison."

Jessie continued, "I hope so. Annie was terribly upset after seeing Perry. At first, she was relieved that he was okay, but maybe it was the way he looked at her. He was trying to intimidate and control her. I was in the room so he couldn't tell her what he wanted to, but he lipped something and I caught the last words. I think he conveyed,

'You know nothing.' At that point she became agitated. I asked if she was ready to leave and she didn't object, so I got her out of there. We took her to CPS, which distressed her to some extent, but Ellen worked wonders. She is going to connect with Annie and that's just what needs to happen."

She grew pensive and sipped her wine. "That kid gets to me. I can't even begin to image the hell she's lived in. I promised her I would be her advocate, be right beside her through this process. I said I'd ensure that she is safe and well cared for, whether it's a foster home or a temporary arrangement. That calmed her down some. And then as she spent time with Ellen, she was more reassured."

They finished their drinks and Jessie said, "Let's eat."

She served the warm Pizza King combo and a pre-packaged Caesar salad. A vase of cut flowers were the centerpiece on a small dining room table set for two. The meal was inviting as she gave him another beer and poured herself a second glass of wine.

They discussed plans for tomorrow as they ate, specifically their upcoming testimony in the Chesney case. Then Jessie revealed another insight into Annie's life. "I think there are other victims. That's what the empty room in Perry's house was for. I wouldn't be surprised if he was planning to kill Annie. The Rushing girl was to be her replacement, and if he could have successfully abducted Julie, Annie would have been history. It fits his pattern. He likes them young and innocent, so I'm surprised he let Annie live as long as he did. Maybe it was because she truly believed he was her father, or maybe she played along with that to stay alive. But she was becoming baggage."

That thought had crossed Luke's mind, too, but Jessie said it with such conviction that she convinced him.

"I shudder to think what would have happened if we had not intervened," he said.

"Now you know why I'm so protective of her. I doubt she's ever had someone who really cared." Jessie went silent, holding back tears. This case was hitting her harder than it did anyone else working it, and he liked that in her. Intellectually, he knew you weren't supposed to get emotionally involved in your victim's circumstances. But on a personal level it sometimes became impossible to avoid.

"To hell with it," he said, to himself but aloud.

"What?"

"I was just thinking. I'm glad you care so much, even if it probably isn't protocol."

Jessie smiled for the first time since he'd arrived, as if a weight had lifted. She stood and proposed they return to the living room. She sat on the sofa, one leg crossed over the other, and leaned against the armrest. She motioned for him to sit beside her, and when he did, she curved her body to look him in the eye.

"There's one more thing," she began, not sure how to proceed. "I shouldn't be your partner."

She caught him off guard, not for the first time.

"Why? What brought this on?" he asked, confused and offended.

She knew it had come out wrong.

"What I'm getting at, is I don't want to be your partner after this case."

She took a deep breath, trying to measure her words so she wouldn't do more damage. "I have a problem being your partner because I'm too fond of you. To work with you, I mean," she confessed. "And maybe you feel the same way, but you don't have to say anything. Just think on it."

"Is that all," he grinned mischievously. "I have the same problem."

"I'm serious."

"So am I," he assured her.

"At least we know where we stand," she sighed with relief.

He knew it was time to leave. They both rose and looked at each other. The same gaze they had exchanged when they first met, which seemed so distant now, yet was only a month ago.

Then they kissed, holding nothing back. Reluctant, he took the initiative to stop.

"We have to get through this case," he whispered, still holding her. "There's too much at stake, and I want you with me."

"I know," she said, pulling away.

PART IV – LOST AND FOUND

"All things truly wicked start from innocence."

– Ernest Hemingway

CHAPTER 27

On Thursday, Sheriff Gates ordered the canine team back to Timber Ridge. He had basically taken ownership of the case and was leaving nothing to chance. He needed a satisfactory outcome, not only for the Sheriff's Office, but for his own peace of mind. If more bodies were to be uncovered, the time was now, with their suspect, James Perry, behind bars, and charges mounting against him. The plan was to have Deputy Lewis go with the K-9 handlers. Sergeant Thomas and detectives Hudson and Harte were scheduled to be in court with the Rod Chesney case through the morning. They would join the K-9 team when they finished the hearing. Meanwhile, Annie Perry had spent her first night with Child Protective Services and Ellen Stone reported to Harte that the girl managed fairly well.

The State verses Rodney Alan Chesney had gone through arraignment a week ago. Chesney pleaded guilty to a misdemeanor rather than a felony in hopes of avoiding a trial, which would risk a harsher judgment. Further, Chesney's dad worked for the State of California and wanted to avoid the publicity a trial would garner and was pushing to settle the case as soon as possible.

The morning proceedings involved law enforcement statements and attorneys presenting their arguments, keeping in mind that a plea bargain was on the table. When the court recessed at noon, Sergeant Thomas left for Timber Ridge. Hudson and Harte remained near the courthouse to await the outcome. At two in the afternoon, the court reconvened.

Judge Wooden handed down her verdict. "Shooting at officers and resisting arrest at gunpoint amount to assault with a firearm, which is a felony. Maximum penalties are a ten thousand dollar fine and four years in prison."

Chesney's attorney remained stoic, waiting for her lower the charges.

"On the other hand, you are a young man with no serious priors and a felony would follow you a lifetime. Therefore, this one time only, the Court will expunge the felony from the records and drop the charges to a misdemeanor. You could be sentenced to a year in prison, which is the maximum for this misdemeanor, and a thousand dollar fine. The fine would be restitution for living on federal property, destroying evidence, and having possession of both illegal drugs and guns. You personally will be expected to pay the restitution within a year of leaving prison."

Rod Chesney was only slightly relieved, still expecting a year in prison.

"There is more," she said. "Since you cooperated with the investigation, the Court will lower your jail sentence to six months. That term could be shortened if you continue to demonstrate good behavior. However, when you are released, you will be on probation for a full year. During that time you are expected to be gainfully employed so you can pay back your thousand-dollar fine. Further condition of parole is no possession of any illegal drug or firearm. Violation of your parole will put you back in prison for at least a year."

Wooden leveled the gavel. "Court adjourned. I'll see you in my chambers."

There would be follow-up discussions and papers to sign. Of course, the decision could be appealed, but not likely, Hudson surmised. It was lenient enough that it wasn't worth fighting.

When they left the courtroom, Jessie found a quiet corner in the courthouse and called CPS to inquire about Annie. She was able to get through to her case worker, Ellen, who explained they were trying desperately to find an appropriate place for Annie to stay, likely a group home where there would be easy access to counseling and she could be closely monitored. Meanwhile, Annie was checked into the Bidwell Medical Center to be examined both physically and mentally.

"How long will she be in the hospital?" Jessie asked, knowing it was the psych ward.

"It depends," Ellen said. "While she's there we will run gynecological tests to determine any damage Perry may have done, and we will also get bloodwork results, DNA, and more. As far as psychological, we need to assess whether she is a flight risk, a suicide risk, or even a risk to others."

Jessie understood these were all necessary evaluations. To ease her mind, she asked Ellen, "Can I spend some time with Annie today?"

"I don't see why not. There may be times you can't be with her, but other times she might respond well to you being around."

Jessie told Ellen she would leave shortly for the hospital.

Luke checked his watch and said, "Let's see what's happening on Timber Ridge."

"You'll have to go it alone," she told him. "I need to be at the hospital with Annie."

He had overheard snippets of her conversation and she supplied him the rest. Luke agreed with her decision. She left while he called Sergeant Thomas, who had just joined the K-9 team on Timber Ridge, which fell under his supervision, as head of Narcotics.

First, Hudson briefed him about the verdict in the Chesney case.

Then Thomas said, "If you're wondering what's going on up here, try nothing, *nada*."

"The places marked off didn't produce results?" Luke queried.

"Nope, and it's hotter than hell. If something sparks, it's going to make the first fire on Timber Ridge look like a practice fire drill."

"Any point in me coming up?" Luke pressed.

"Not unless you want to see a dead dog," Thomas replied.

"What do you mean?"

"Not one of ours," Thomas remarked. "One of the two promising sites turned out to be the burial ground for a dog. It either died of natural causes or was killed and buried by someone. I was going to call in the ME but nothing else materialized after we snooped around the site a bit."

Hudson was not satisfied with Thomas's assessment. "I'm coming up," he announced. "Maybe Lewis could meet me where the cars are parked to take me to the site." Luke knew only the general location.

On his way, he stopped at a grocery store and stocked up on water and sandwiches for the team. He arrived after three in the afternoon. The forest was sweltering with a dry heat that sucked the moisture from the pines and undergrowth, leaving the ground parched and hungry for rain.

Linc Lewis was waiting, sitting in his car with all the doors open and he was still sweating. He was grateful for a sandwich and water.

"We ran out of water about an hour ago," the deputy announced, taking big swigs of water until the bottle was empty.

"Mind if I have another," he asked.

"I brought a case," Luke said. "What's with the dog?" He trusted Lewis's instincts.

"Personally, I'd call in technicians," he answered and gulped water, some dribbling down his chin. "The dog could be Perry's doings. Or maybe there's a body under the dog. No telling. I'd just want to know more."

Because the sun was lengthening, Hudson didn't wait to see the grave before calling Ned. Based on Lewis's assessment, he called Sergeant Thomas to tell him the ME was on his way. If that didn't sit well with Thomas, the Sergeant said nothing.

Luke and Lewis waited until the white van arrived. Then the two, along with Ned and his technician, Aaron Underwood, gathered up equipment, food, and water and began their trek through the pines, motionless in the stifling air.

They trudged to the dog's gravesite and greeted Sergeant Thomas, along with the K-9 team. Luke told Thomas, "If you want, I can fill in now and you can head out."

"Sure, have at it," Thomas said, flagged and indifferent. "I don't think you'll find anything, but fresh eyes won't hurt. I could stay..."

"We're good. We have plenty of help," Luke said, not wanting Thomas there in case the Sergeant was wrong in his decision to stop the search.

The site was just as Luke envisioned—a shallow grave, shaded by pines. He recognized the dog as a blue heeler cross breed because he'd seen them on farms in Arizona. The mostly white dog had random black spotting on his body. A male dog, he was medium sized, with prick ears, and a black patch over one eye. His lips curled back in a grimace, bearing the teeth, and there was no collar.

Ned and Aaron went to work, brushing away the dry soil, and protecting the integrity of the dog's carcass for evidence.

Jackson said, "It would be something if the dog is micro-chipped. If he is, we can hopefully trace the owner.

Since the dog is a cross breed, if it came from the Humane Society, it would have been chipped there."

Hudson admired Ned's wide range of expertise. Whether the grave contents were human or animal, Jackson was in control. Hudson knelt down beside Ned and Aaron, observing more intently. "So you think this dog may tie into our Satin Doll case?"

"It could. It's in the same general area as the other graves," Jackson answered, becoming increasingly somber as he further uncovered the dog. "This dog met a violent end. I'd say beaten to death. He appears to have a broken neck and caved-in ribs. It's sickening."

"Aaron, I want some photos," he said, rising and stepping back, as Luke did the same.

While Aaron photographed the dog, Ned explained, "Good thing the dog wasn't a nondescript mutt. With such unique markings, he will be easy to identify when the right person sees the photos. Judging by the decomposition, I'd say the dog was buried this winter when the ground was softened by rain and easy to dig, say within the last six months. Then the killer carefully covered the grave to leave no trace. A lot of work to bury an unwanted dog."

When Ned and Aaron resumed excavating, it bothered the handlers and their K-9s to be in proximity of the dead dog, so they moved away. The three men sat on a fallen tree trunk, with their dogs near them, as they talked softly and drank water. Shortly, Luke joined them and told the three deputies they could take their dogs and leave. He watched as the men left through the forest, leading them dogs, and carrying out items no longer needed, then Luke wandered back to the grave.

"Sonofabitch," Ned muttered and caught Luke's attention because the medical examiner rarely swore. "You'd better come and look."

Beneath the dog's body, touching its fur, was the partially decayed hand of a child.

THE EXCAVATION REVEALED YET ANOTHER girl's body and the nightmare began again for the medical examiner's team. But this discovery was even more gut wrenching, with the two buried together, and the child's upturned hands touching the black and white dog.

Ned called his office and requested another technician, Rita Lopez, to join them for the exhumation. And she should bring, among other items, high beam lights because they would be working into the night.

Hudson rang Sheriff Gates with the discovery. There was a long pause on the end of the line before Gates said, "That's the last news I wanted to hear, but at least maybe with this body we can nail the bastard. I'll send backup to stay through the process and protect the area after you guys leave. We don't want contamination of the site."

Luke agreed and described the new dead girl. "She is fair-haired, about ten or eleven, and unclothed. The body has been in the ground about six months, so there's a tremendous amount of evidence to work with. And we're hoping the dog is micro-chipped, which may open more doors."

"It makes you wonder how many more graves are out there in other locations," Gates pondered.

Luke avoided the implication and stayed focused. "What I need by morning is a warrant, as permissive as we can get it, to search Perry's house for hair, photographs, computers, clothing, any evidence to advance the case."

"You got it, and whatever else you need, I'll arrange it. I want answers ASAP," Gates said and signed off.

Next, Luke called Jessie and told her about the new grave on Timber Ridge. She was silent and pensive, then offered, "Should I come up to the grave site?"

"No, I'd rather have you arrange for Annie to see us first thing tomorrow so she can view photos of the dog and girl. It won't be pretty," he warned.

CHAPTER 28

Friday morning, Annie Perry sat uneasy in the Sheriff's Office interview room, where she had been questioned two days earlier. CPS case worker Ellen Stone had arranged for Annie to be discharged from the hospital, and later in the day she would be admitted to a girl's group home until she was placed in a foster home.

Earlier, Jessica went with Ellen for the pickup. They felt the change in surrounding and the drive over would help Annie's mood, as would a stop for coffee and a pastry at Starbucks drive-through. They kept the conversation light and Ellen told Annie they had lined up a tutor for her. The girl was receptive to the idea.

"I'm beginning to see how much I have to learn," Annie said, as she emerged from Ellen's car at the Sheriff's Office. "It's a big world."

"One day at a time," Ellen told her, "and it will eventually all come together."

Annie released a rare smile.

The plan was for Hudson to be in the room, but only if his presence did not upset the girl.

Stone sat next to Annie, while Jessie was directly across from her. Luke was a bit to the side, near the door and not in Annie's straight line of vision, since the

335

teenager appeared uneasy around men in general. That anxiety would be a major hurdle to overcome in incremental steps.

Ellen Stone began. "Detective Hudson is here because he was the one present when the little girl and her dog were found in a grave."

Annie tensed and looked down at the table.

"We don't know if you have any idea who the child is, but we have to ask, for the girl's sake. It's a mystery to us now, and you might be a great help, or not. We'll see."

"Show me the photos," Annie said evenly, and Luke pushed the folder over to Ellen.

Two photos of the black and white heeler mix were on the first page, showing both sides of the dog. Annie gasped and then began to cry silently, tears slowly streaming down her cheeks.

"It's Pepper," she moaned. "He was Emma's dog."

Frantically, she shuffled through the pictures and stopped at a facial photo of the dead girl. She touched the photograph, the long blonde hair and the grizzled face, as if trying to still connect with her.

"This is Emma," she whispered. "I've been lied to again and again."

Annie lost control and her body racked with sobs. "Only one person could have done this, and I hate him for it."

Dead silence filled in the room, except for Annie's painful weeping. Ellen pulled her close and she continued to cry until she was left with only spasmodic sobs. Still no one spoke. Ellen reached for a box of tissues and Annie began to dry her tears and blow her nose.

The girl took a deep breath and sighed. "I will tell you everything I know. Emma is not going to die without him paying for it. And neither is Pepper."

Ellen asked, "Who did this?"

"Who do you think?" she shot back in anger. "James Perry. The man I thought in the beginning was my father because he rescued me. And when I got older and started to question things, I had no way to fight back. The only way I could survive was to agree and go along with him, no matter what he said."

Jessie leaned towards Annie and inquired softly, "Do you want to start at the beginning? Or talk about Emma?"

"I'll tell it all, from the first day, because I never want Perry to hurt someone again," she said bitterly.

Luke, who was closest to the door, rose and left the room. He thought the time alone with just the three women would reduce the tension. He got a drink of water and brought back three waters for the others. Annie thanked him, and even made eye contact, perhaps a step forward. She wiped her nose again, and gulped some water. Drained of tears, her involuntary sobbing had subsided.

Jessie measured the girl's pain and said, "When you're ready to talk, we'll record it, Annie."

"Don't call me Annie again! From now on I'm Amber." Her sudden demand stunned everyone. No one had mentioned Amber Richards to her for fear of leading a witness, but obviously she was no stranger to the name.

She added, "That's probably not my real name, either, but I never want to be Annie Perry again. I'm not sure what my real last name is. My early years were confusing."

She stared down at Emma's photos and closed the folder on memories too agonizing.

They all remained silent. Ellen knew the parameters, how to ask open-ended questions and not to suggest or lead. The three had discussed such a scenario as this. Luke and Jessie deferred to her, knowing she had the best rapport with the girl.

Amber collected her thoughts and then started to explain how she had been abused and left on a dirt road in the forest when she was six. She knew her age because she was looking forward to going to school.

"I remember being Amber, but when he found me, he insisted I change my name because now I would have a new life. He let me chose it." She avoided saying Perry's name.

"I thought he was my father because my mother would say 'someday your father will come along and you will be safe again.' I'm not sure the woman who said that was really my mother. I vaguely remember having two mothers."

"Do you remember any names?" Ellen asked.

Amber searched her memory in silence. "Yes, I remember a man the most. I know *he* wasn't my father. He was too mean to be anyone's father. His name was Mauri and he called my mother Lee or Leona. She was kind and tried to protect me, but I think she was afraid of him, too.

I'll never forget him. He hurt me, locked me up, and did things no man should do to a child. Perry did bad things to me, too. But by then I assumed it was normal. Something *all* men do."

She glared at Luke, but saw his anguished face, and softened. "Maybe not all men," she whispered.

She was willing to use James Perry's name again. She waited and then said, "At least Perry wasn't mean. He fed me well, read to me, gave me a TV, played games with me, and wanted me to call him dad. I said I wanted to go to school, but he said he would teach me. So he bought books, lots of them. He brought home workbooks and taught me how to read and write and do math. I think he actually liked doing it. We would play school in the evenings, after he came home from work. And I was supposed to study during the day."

She paused and reminisced, deep in thought. The three adults said nothing to prompt her, letting Amber follow her own course.

"But it wasn't enough. After years of being alone, I wanted a friend. So about five years ago—I was maybe twelve—he brought home Emma and her dog. Maybe because of me, she is dead."

Amber started to cry again, and Ellen put her arm around her. "No, please don't think that way. There was nothing you could do."

Bewildered, Amber thought about that and stopped crying. Slowly, she resumed, "Emma was six, the same age I had been when he found me. He said he found her wandering, and no one really cared about her. But that wasn't her story."

Amber stopped talking and began wringing her hands. "Emma cried a lot and said she wanted to go home to her mommy and daddy. She told me her name was Emma Miller."

Now they had the name of the latest victim and could start searching databases. But they stayed expressionless, waiting for Amber to continue.

"Perry left her alone at first and didn't take her into his bedroom. He told me to keep her happy, and he said it as a threat. It was the first time he frightened me."

Again, Amber became silent and stared at her hands, which were calmer now. The hush lengthened, and Ellen asked, "Are you okay? Do you need a break?"

"I'd like to use the bathroom," she murmured.

Ellen ushered her out of the room, leaving Jessie and Luke alone. They had time to talk, but said nothing, drained of words and filled with emotions.

When the two returned, Amber settled into her chair again, and continued, "Our bedrooms connected through the bathroom and Perry put a doggie door in Emma's room. He measured our shoulders to make sure we couldn't fit through the door. At least Pepper could come and go."

"Did Emma eventually accept her new life?" Jessie asked.

"No, never. She liked me a lot, but whenever Perry would take her to his room, she would return crying and saying he was a bad man. I hate myself for it now, but I told her she would have to try to like him, to get along. She said she couldn't stand him. She'd rather be dead. Her words scared me, and I tried to get her mind on other things, reading to her or playing with Pepper, but I could see she was never going to adjust. I told Perry she just needed time, and finally she did give in, sorta."

Amber sat quietly before saying more. "There was some peace for several years, and then Emma became agitated again on a regular basis, no matter what I tried to tell her. By now, Perry mostly left her alone, but I could tell he was through with her. I imagined ways we could escape but there were none. People didn't come by the place and we were locked in our rooms when Perry was gone. And we were padlocked in the house when he was there. Once I found his cell phone but I didn't know how to use it. He told me if I did that again he'd give me a lashing I would never forget."

She drew in a deep breath and exhaled slowly. "He didn't like the dog and told me he was going to kill him. I told him if he did that, he might as well kill Emma, too, because Pepper was all she had left. He let it go for a while. Then one day last fall, he took her and the dog and drove off. I thought he was probably going to kill them, but an hour or so later they returned, and I was so happy to see them again. Maybe he just took her away to threaten her, but in the end, that's what he did anyway, huh?" That brought on more tears.

Luke had not interacted with Amber the whole time, and felt it was best to stay silent. The two women seemed to keep her communicating.

Ellen said, "Can you tell us what happened the last day you saw Emma?"

Amber hesitated and then steeled herself. "Yes, Perry said he was taking her home and she should bring Pepper with her. Emma was so happy that she hugged me and cried and thanked me. Perry just stood there, looking bothered, which made me question him, but I couldn't be sure what it all meant."

Again, Amber broke down and took a long, painful minute to recover. "Emma and I hugged again and laughed and I told Pepper goodbye. He was jumping up and down with joy because we were happy. Then they were gone."

Amber was visibly distraught and the three wondered how much longer she would be willing to talk.

Jessie asked softly, "How did Perry act when he returned?"

"He said she was in her forever home now, and so was her dog. That's all he said. His words seemed a little odd to me, but I didn't question him. Of course, now we know what he means by a 'forever home.' "

Sighing, Jessie reluctantly pressed her, "Did he ever mention other girls to you?"

"No. As far as I know there was only Emma," she answered, and looked around. "Do you suppose we can quit now? I'm so tired."

"Of course," Ellen said. "You have been tremendously helpful. Now you need to rest."

"Are you mad that I didn't tell you this earlier?" Amber's lips trembled with emotion.

"No, we understand. You've gone through so much. It takes time to sort things out," Ellen assured her.

"Once I saw Emma and Pepper, I wanted you to know everything. Before that, I kept hoping it was all a bad dream, and somehow I would go home again. Now I know it was no home at all," Amber murmured, fighting back tears. "I'm lucky he didn't kill me, too..."

Ellen put her hand on Amber's shoulder and asked Jessie, "Could you take Amber to the break room? I'll join you in a minute."

As Luke had suspected from the beginning, Amber exhibited the Stockholm Syndrome. She had bonded with her captor for survival, defending Perry when they found her, refusing to see the intervention as a rescue. Over time, as the facts unfolded, she began questioning things. The syndrome had been around long before the term was coined in 1973, after a hostage incident in Sweden. The behavior engulfs a wide range of victims, from prisoners of war to abused wives who refuse to press charges against their husbands. The subjugated are controlled by everything from acts of kindness to threats and violence.

After Jessie and Amber left, Luke turned to Ellen and mentioned it. She agreed and added, "There's one more thing that Amber didn't say."

Luke raised an eyebrow, waiting for yet another unsettling disclosure.

"You can get the information from her medical examination report, but I didn't want you to miss it. During her exam, Amber admitted to a female gynecologist that she was pregnant once, about a year ago."

"Good Lord," Luke stammered, and paused. "Did she say what happened to the baby?"

"Apparently, she miscarried. She wouldn't talk about how far along she was in the pregnancy or the sex of the child, only that Perry took the baby away. It was a boy and God knows what he did with him, but I hope you can get some answers out of Perry."

BY FRIDAY AFTERNOON, A CORRECTIONS OFFICER had transported James Perry to the Sheriff's Office for questioning. Luke and Jessie had strategized before and over lunch how they would handle his interrogation. Luke wanted her to sit in just long enough to see how he would react to her. If it was negative, she was to leave, and follow the proceedings through the viewing window.

While Perry's correction officer waited and watched outside, Perry sauntered into the room and sat down with an arrogant air about him that pissed off Hudson from the start.

"Wipe that shit-eating grin off your face," Luke barked. "When I'm through with you, you'll have nothing to smile about."

"Whoa, relax, Detective," Perry smirked, throwing up his hands is if warding off a vampire. "What's got your jockeys in a twist? Maybe this little beauty sitting next to you?"

Luke started to rise and thought better of it. Instead, he said, "Cut the crap, you sick bastard."

Jessie's eyes were wide. She'd never seen Luke lose his cool so quickly, and knew Perry was baiting him, reveling in the moment.

"I'll bet she's delicious in bed," Perry taunted, licking his lips. "I'm sure you've tried her."

It was Jessie who jumped up and grabbed his orange jail shirt before Luke could respond. "You sonofabitch. I'm a police officer, and if you say something smartass like that to me again, I'll kick your balls until you can't stand. You get my drift?"

Perry calmly removed her grasping hand from his shirt. "I get it, and I hope you get out. You're bothering me," he grinned, eyeing her with a salacious leer.

"Don't worry. I'm not your type," she glared back. "You like young, defenseless little girls. I can't stand the sight of you," she stormed out, slamming the door as she left.

Luke tried not to smile. Instead, he rose and scowled at Perry, "One more chicken-shit remark out of you and I'll have you in solitary confinement."

"I'd welcome that," Perry said comfortably, leaning back in his chair and crossing his arms over his chest. "A little solitude would appeal to me about now. You ever been in jail?" He answered himself, "Of course not. It's noisy. Always somebody whining about something. I don't recommend it."

"Get used to it," Luke remarked, "because it's your new home."

"You're very confident," Perry quipped. "Problem is, you have very little on me."

"Wrong," Luke said, pushing photographs of Emma and her dog in front of him. "We uncovered her grave and she's been positively identified as a child you molested and disposed of."

Perry was speechless. All haughtiness drained from his face. He stammered, "Did Annie talk to you? A couple of photos don't mean a thing."

"They do when the dog was micro-chipped and the owners were contacted. And it was their six-year-old daughter's dog. And both Emma and the dog were abducted from a suburb of Reno five years ago. And the FBI is now on the case, since the child was brought across state lines. And we are conducting DNA tests from two other graves on Timber Ridge. We have enough hard evidence to put you away for life and beyond," he promised, watching Perry squirm.

Luke didn't let up, "There're at least three dead girls, not counting the girl you just tried to abduct. And the baby Annie miscarried. How did that happen?"

Perry had regained his composure. "Surely you know how babies are made," he sneered, and paused, digesting the accusations. "I don't know what you're talking about."

Luke had had it. "Yes, you do, and we have medical records plus sworn statements to prove it. How did she lose the baby and where did you dispose of it?"

Perry leaned back, a smug smile on his face again. "She just slipped it. Too bad, because I was planning on raising it."

Hudson's anger peaked and Perry smirked, enjoying the interchange while he taunted the detective.

"Where's the baby's body?" Luke bellowed.

"Easy, big boy," Perry grinned. "Keep that up at your age and you'll give yourself a heart attack. You know what I'm sayin'?"

"Where's the body?" Luke repeated through clinched teeth, as he rose, scraping back his chair.

"That's for me to know and you to dig up," Perry jeered. "Isn't that a detective's job?"

Luke was reaching for Perry when Deputy Lewis opened the door and interrupted his move.

"Hold it, Luke," he said in a muffled voice. "Let's both go at him."

Hudson cooled off enough to sit down beside Lewis, who reckoned that Luke was losing his effectiveness along with his temper.

Perry gave Lewis a disdainful smirk. "A token black on the force, I see," he said, trying to get a rise out of Linc, as well, but Lewis ignored him.

Unflinching, he told Perry, "Actually, you don't need to say another word. Hudson here hasn't gotten the latest news. Seems you buried the baby, a little boy, under Emma.

The medical examiner's team found a package in the grave and took it back for analysis. That's when they unwrapped the baby's body. So that's number four and counting."

Perry's cocky attitude weakened and he stared at the table.

Linc persisted, "There's evidence that the baby was frozen and then buried when you dug the grave for Emma and her dog. No jury is going to cut you any slack after they hear that."

Pausing, Lewis let Perry digest what he'd said.

Luke was sickened by the news and grateful for Linc's intervention. He seldom lost control during an interrogation. But his empathy for Amber had affected his professional demeanor. At least for now, Linc seemed able to hide his disgust.

"There's just one thing we want to know. We'd like to understand why you did what you did to those girls." Lewis asked in a compassionate, non-threatening voice. "What happened in *your* past? If you don't tell us, we'll never be able to help someone else like you. And believe me, there's plenty more."

Perry stared at the darkened one-way window, probably wondering who all were listening and watching, besides Jessie. "I could use a drink of water," he said, almost whispering.

Luke played water-boy and came back with cold water for all of three of them. While he was gone, he doubted Perry had said a word. He was lost in thought, even a hint of remorse.

Linc was a powerful man, but his eyes were kind, and he was showing a tender side that Luke hadn't seen since that afternoon on Timber Ridge.

"I lost my six-year-old daughter to cancer," Linc said softly. "So I know what it's like when things are completely out of your control. To be helpless and wonder why it's happening to you."

Somehow, Linc's words struck a chord with Perry and he slumped in his chair, resigned to opening up. He took a long drink of water, and began, "I was molested by my stepfather and my mother was too weak to do anything about it. I hated the bitch for that, and from then on, I hated women in general, I suppose." He fell silent again, and Linc waited.

Perry went on, "God knows, I never meant to hurt anyone." He quoted from Saint Matthew, "The spirit is willing but the flesh is weak."

James Perry was a tormented soul, and both deputies saw it in his face. He continued, not speaking to anyone in particular. "I'm sorry the most for Annie. She sure didn't deserve what I put her through. Neither did the others, I guess."

"Tell me about the others," Linc suggested, hoping Perry would talk about them, but he just sat there. His silence ended the session.

Luke stepped outside to talk to the corrections officer, and advised him, "James Perry is depressed. I think he could use some counseling, if he'll accept it. At the very least, keep a close watch on him, so he doesn't try to harm himself."

The officer acknowledged he'd look into it, then he retrieved Perry and they left.

Lewis was still sitting in the interrogation room when Hudson reentered and sat down across from him.

Shrugging, Linc said, "I turned off the recorder, if you want to talk about anything."

"Thanks for saving my ass. I guess I was pretty worked up. I let him push my buttons and I know better," Luke admitted. "This case is so emotionally charged that it's hard to stay objective."

"I know," Lewis said. "Hey, we all lose it some time. Today was your turn; tomorrow may be mine." Then he flashed a big smile. "Were you blowin' smoke out your ass about the FBI and contacting Emma's parents?"

"I've been known to do that," Luke grinned, "but not this time. We *could* call in the FBI. I don't know that we will. And we *did* contact Emma's parents following Amber's testimony."

Luke wondered where Jessie was, and supposed she saw them talking and decided to leave them alone. She was much better at reading him than she used to be. Now he had to work on reading her.

He looked at Lewis. "What do you say when we get done with paperwork, we have Jessie join us for a drink and maybe a bite to eat?"

"Sounds like a plan," he said. "I have a feeling this case is not going to be resolved any time soon."

CHAPTER 29

On Saturday morning, Luke was off until noon, so he took the luxury of sleeping in and lazing on his patio until his phone rang around eight. Abe Zayet had something he wanted to discuss.

"Detective Hudson, I hope I am not disrupting things, but I have something I'd like to show you. Perhaps, when you are free, you can drive out to Long Meadows?"

"Sure," Luke responded. "What's it about?"

"Well, it is rather a sensitive matter, so I would just prefer to see you in person."

Luke's interest piqued. "I can be there in about two hours."

"Very good," Zayet said. "And you can bring your friend, Detective Kidder, along if you'd like."

He signed off and Luke called Jimmy, who said he had the day off, too, and was game to tag along.

Around nine, Luke picked up Jimmy. The days were long now, in late June. The drive to the track passed through outlying subdivisions with names that had no meaning—Quail Run, where quail no longer nested; Deer Meadows, consumed by a hundred houses; and Bidwell Ranch, where homes were squeezed onto cramped lots. Luke focused on the mountains, looming in the east. The air was cooler than usual, with even a few clouds forming over the Sierras.

Being a Saturday, the track pre-race crowds were lively, a jazz band played, and children enjoyed free cotton candy. Business was good, as a security officer showed the two detectives into Zayet's office on the third level and left. The track owner was more comfortable and welcoming than he had been the first time they had met.

"Thanks for coming," he said, and wasted no time. "I want to show you two something of significance. Or at least we think it is."

Zayet pointed to a stack of files on his desk. "We found a box of files that my accountant believes are a second set of track financial records, dating back to when Long Meadows was owned by Trackon. The interesting thing is that these sums are noted as cash flow in from various sources but no names appear on where the cash goes out or who receives it—a hundred here or a thousand there, until over the years the transactions amounted to around a five million. Only David Bergman's name appears a couple of time for cash out, but not in huge amounts."

Hudson and Kidder stared at the files as if they were a treasure trove.

"They were on the take?" Kidder asked, wide-eyed.

"It appears that way. We believe one or more persons, plus Trackon's financial director, were cooking the books, keeping two sets of records, so they could siphon off funds."

"But why would they leave incriminating files behind when the track closed?" Luke asked.

"I don't think they meant to. The box was found in the back of a little alcove that had been dry-walled over. It was an unsightly, useless little space so our maintenance men removed a small door and closed up the wall. Only they got sloppy and didn't clear out the trash in the space. We had a pipe leak in that area a few weeks ago and opened it up again. That's when we found the box of files in the back." Zayet seemed proud of his discovery as he looked up at the two taller detectives.

"The implications are huge," Luke said the obvious. "Where do you go from here?"

Scooting around his desk, Zayet sat down. "Have a seat, detectives."

Luke and Jimmy sat across the desk from him, still staring at the volatile evidence.

Abe Zayet fiddled with a pen and answered, "I've been in touch with Trackon's CEO, Gerald Harkin, who was the track manager. It seems Bergman was a silent partner, one of five owners when the track was operated by them. The corporation is very interested in seeing these files."

"Where do we come in?" Luke asked.

Zayet leaned back. "Ah, good question. I'm taking these files to the Trackon headquarters in Las Vegas tomorrow and I'd like one of you to fly with me. It will give more weight to the discovery if a law official is along. At least that's my thinking."

Luke didn't disagree about that, but the discovery raised numerous questions. "Do you think it's wise to give Harkin the records? Especially when he could be one of those on the take?"

"Ah, we've thought of that. Harkin will only get some of the records and they are copies. We'll keep the originals. They could be evidence in an indictment for embezzlement. We wouldn't be the plaintiffs, but some Trackon investors might get 'hopping mad' as you say," Zayet grinned, "if they hear about this. As for now, there are still many unanswered questions. That's why I thought detectives should be involved."

The information unfolding went along with Hudson's theories about corruption at the track under its previous ownership. He relished the thought of investigating the new developments, but he was dedicated to the Perry case and couldn't lose focus. He looked at Zayet and asked a question, knowing the answer he was after, but wanting to test Zayet's perceptions.

"What do you figure Harkin will do with the files?"

Zayet answered with foresight. "Ah, if he does nothing, he has something to hide. If he wants to indict, he is not the player and Mr. Bergman or another owner might be the culprit."

"You're quite a detective yourself," Luke grinned, and Zayet beamed at the compliment.

With reluctance, Luke explained, "As much as I'd like to be a part of this, my participation might have to wait a while. I'm heavily involved in a high profile case with the

Sheriff's Office. And I'll have to get clearance to go with you tomorrow because I'm technically not off.

"No problem," Zayet assured him. "I like working with you two and you're both familiar with the background. This situation has been around for years, so a few more weeks won't hurt. Besides, it will take time to see what Harkin plans to do with the files."

Luke sighed with relief. "I think you know how badly I'd like to uncover the mystery of the track's closure."

"Yes, I do," Zayet smiled. "I will fly to Las Vegas tomorrow, and if you can manage it, I hope you can accompany me. The real mystery will come later."

ON THEIR WAY BACK TO BIDWELL, Hudson and Kidder debated their options. Jimmy thought Luke should go, and added, "I'd like to get involved, but I don't suppose Chief Walker will want me in the mix."

"I'd just as soon he doesn't know about it. Let me talk to Sheriff Gates and see if he'll give me an okay. Walker has no stomach for going after Bergman or reopening the case, so we'll cut him out," Luke noted, still harboring resentment over the Police Chief's handling of Long Meadows.

He didn't expect to find Sheriff Gates at work, not on a Saturday, so he rang him on his cell phone. Gates was out with his family and said he'd call back.

The two detectives decided to have lunch and found a diner downtown called The Lone Star, and Luke thought of Jessie. Oddly, he missed her, even though it felt good to be spending time with his former partner.

They requested a corner booth and read through the laminated menu. Jimmy ordered a jalapeno cheeseburger, fries, and a beer—the works, but he was young and muscled like a fire fighter. Luke knew better and chose a chicken Caesar salad and a Maker's Mark on the rocks.

Jimmy smiled.

"What are you smiling at?" Luke asked, with eyebrow cocked.

"I'm just noticing you're staying in shape. Trying to keep up with your new partner?" he grinned.

"Maybe. But I'm also trying not to overload my ticker with cholesterol. You'll deal with it someday, so enjoy while you can."

Gates returned his call. The restaurant was noisy, so Luke felt comfortable discussing work. A couple of times the Sheriff asked him to repeat something because of the background din. Without using last names, Luke told him what Abe had discovered and that it might involve a high level person in the county. Gates was filling in between the lines.

"If we don't pursue it, when it does break, the Vegas authorities will completely bypass us and we'll be sitting around here with our heads in the sand."

Gates agreed, so Luke asked, "Do we have track jurisdiction?"

"Anywhere in the county, if we deem it necessary, so I'd say this applies. Besides, Zayet expanded his track operation by buying some county property, remember that?"

Luke knew that at one point but had forgotten about it.

"Why don't you go with him tomorrow and deal with this new issue when you find the time. I wanted to talk with you anyway. The FBI will be coming here from San Francisco Monday to work on the Perry case," Gates announced, "and I'd like you and Harte prepared for their visit. You can do that Monday morning."

Gates talked freely on the phone. "As you know, they come in a wide range of competencies, from those standing around with their dicks in their hands to those who are actually pretty sharp. Hopefully, we'll get a couple of good ones."

Luke listened, comfortable with the feds through his years in the LAPD. "At the very least, we'll have quick access to their databases and that won't hurt."

The Sheriff added, "The agents are Jason Lowe and his trainee, Angel Amaro. I told Harte and she didn't seem very comfortable with it. Maybe she hasn't been exposed to feds."

Hudson said with assurance, "She'll get used to it. She's adaptable."

"We can talk some more Monday morning about their visit. The suits don't arrive until around noon, the drive and all."

"You mean they're not flying in a government jet?" Luke joked.

"Money's tight, even for the feds," the Sheriff jibed and signed off.

More cop talk ensued in quiet voices between the two detectives, still avoiding last names.

"You really like him, don't you?" Jimmy asked.

"Very much," Luke admitted. "He's a straight-shooting guy, pun intended, who's not afraid to take on controversial issues. The only people he has to please are the voters and they like going after the big boys."

Jimmy pondered, "Maybe I should become a deputy."

ON SUNDAY, HUDSON MET ABE ZAYET at the Bidwell Municipal Airport and flew to Las Vegas in Zayet's corporate jet. While in the air they talked about the files and the possibility of opening a new case with the Sheriff's Office. Luke dodged talk about Chief Walker's role, or lack of it, and Zayet quickly picked up on that. He was satisfied as long as he had the cooperation of one of the two law enforcement agencies. Zayet had nothing to gain by dogging the closure issues except that he was a man of principle.

Flying over Las Vegas was like soaring above an expansive movie set, with a pyramid, ocean bays, a volcano, New York, Italy, and Paris all in a line. They landed smoothly and took a taxi to Trackon's headquarters. Located in old town, it was a modest workplace, no comparison to Bergman Enterprises' well-appointed offices. By contrast, Trackon appeared struggling and underfunded. Whether the collapse of the racetrack took its toll, or they were always short of capital was hard to say.

When they reached the entrance intercom and Zayet gave his name, Trackon's owner buzzed them in. His office was closed and he had made special arrangements to meet with them. Gerald Harkin introduced himself and ushered Zayet and Hudson the short distance from the reception area to his office, which peered out over gray, sun-bleached buildings. A gold name plaque on his desk titled him as CEO. *Of what?* Luke wondered.

Harkin had a limp, uneasy handshake and was casually dressed in jeans. He was overweight and his belly tugged at his polo shirt. The skin around his eyes wrinkled and sagged.

Luke was overdressed in a sharp, dark blue suit and tie, but he believed detectives should look as professional as the feds for that air of competence and authority. Abe Zayet always dressed impeccably.

The room reeked of smoke, with an ashtray on Harkin's desk filled with cigarette butts and a partial cigarette burning. A ceiling fan jiggled and clicked as it turned overhead, stirring the tepid air.

Luke thought about removing his suit jacket but didn't. Zayet's face was turning red. Harkin offered them seats on overstuffed, over-worn, vinyl-covered chairs. The two sat down, before Harkin planted himself behind his desk and picked up his half-smoked cigarette to inhale and blow out a long puff. The smoke dissipated into the gray haze. He offered them coffee or water and they chose water, which was straight from the tap, with a chemical taste and tepid.

The door opened and a spindly gentleman entered, carrying a briefcase. Older than Harkin and jittery, he twitched like someone who never fully relaxed. Harkin introduced him as his accountant, and then went directly to the heart of their visit. "I'm anxious to see your discovery. A couple of seasons into Long Meadows we suspected something was up, but we couldn't prove it. We were losing more money than we should."

Harkin blew smoke to the side, away from his guests, and stared out the window before his eyes came back to them. "There's so damn much cash floating around a track that it would be easy to siphon off money and it wouldn't be traceable. Kinda like drug money."

Zayet knew what he was getting at, and glanced at the plastic file box near his feet, that he had carried in. "It's all here," he said. "My financial advisor analyzed the files for several days and came to the conclusion that they were created by your financial director, a Patricia Woods. Why she kept separate records on the money, we can only conjecture. Perhaps we can ask her."

Harkin took a last pull on his cigarette before crushing it in the ashtray. "We don't know where she is, and believe me, we've tried finding her," he offered, matter-of-factly.

Hudson stiffened in his chair. "Who is 'we'?"

"The Clark County Sheriff's Department, mostly. The logical explanation is that she absconded with what she could of the money."

"How long ago was that?" Luke asked.

"Right after Long Meadows folded. The theory was that she anticipated being charged with embezzlement and left the country. She's probably living comfortably in

Mexico. Guess we'll never know," Harkin shrugged and stayed silent. The accountant sat frowning, eyeing the file box.

Luke broke the lull, "She couldn't have acted alone. You'd need at least two people to pull off taking that much money. Someone had to be complicit."

Harkin squirmed a little and lit another cigarette, then replied, "Not necessarily. Admittedly, we didn't provide enough oversight and not enough auditing. We were all new at this, sort of the blind leading the blind. It wouldn't take a genius to figure out how to hide incoming cash."

Hudson had a string of questions, but zeroed in on the investors. "Did you suspect any of the partners? And where are they now?"

"Well, the other three took their losses and bitterly went on their way. They were wealthy, so they could withstand it financially. Probably got nice tax write-offs," Harkin commented too lightly for Luke's comfort.

"What about you? It doesn't look like you appreciated the hit," Luke bantered.

"No, I didn't. It's been a struggle, so you can see I didn't gain much, other than a job that went belly up."

"Who do you think helped her?" Luke persisted, determined to get answers, no matter how long he had to dig.

"Well, that's for you to uncover, but personally, I've always suspected Bergman. He lived right there in Bidwell, while the rest of us were based in Vegas. He had the easiest access. Plus he recommended Woods for financial director and even audited her books, if you could call it that. It wouldn't surprise me. Bergman being a silent partner and so secretive about his involvement in the first place," Harkin speculated, puffing smoke into the air, his new cigarette half spent.

Luke jumped on the comment. "If that's your line of reasoning, no one was at the track more than you were as the manager."

"Hold on, big fella!" Harkin objected too loudly. "I'd be the first one they'd suspect. I'm not that stupid. Give me some credit here."

Zayet sat quietly, content to follow their exchanges, moving his eyes from Luke to Harkin as their discussion ping-ponged back and forth.

Turning to Zayet, Harkin went on, "You say you found possibly thousands missing per year? We will go over the files with a fine-toothed comb. If we find what we think we will, your Mr. Bergman will be arrested."

"He's not *my* Mr. Bergman," Zayet shot back. "I have my own grievances with him surrounding illegal use of drugs on his horses. He's no friend of mine."

"Then we have a meeting of the minds," Harkin said. "Is it okay?" he nodded at the files. His accountant was waiting to swoop in like a hawk eyeing a field mouse.

"Of course, but we would like to know your findings. I brought Detective Hudson along because if there is a cooking of the books, our law enforcement will get involved."

Luke concurred, "The embezzlement, if that's what's going on, occurred in Park County, so we could file charges there. Depending on who's to blame, it still might involve extradition across state lines, which is time consuming with lots of hoops to jump through, unless we involve the feds."

Harkin frowned at that and raised an eyebrow. "Whatever it takes," he said half-heartedly, removing a cigarette stub dangling from his lips and stuffing it in the overflowing ashtray. He stood and offered a reticent, final handshake to Zayet and Hudson.

"Gentlemen, I appreciate this more than you'll ever know. I promise to stay in touch."

As Zayet and Hudson left, their last image of the two Trackon men was Harkin lifting his hand in a half wave, a freshly lit cigarette between his lips, and the accountant clutching the file box to his chest.

The flight home left the two engulfed in their own thoughts. They gazed out the windows at the endless miles of nothingness except dirt roads to shabby houses or trailers with broken-down cars and lean-tos. A few corrals penned solitary horses baking in the hot sun. The land was parched and vegetation sparse in the dirt and sand. The western foothills of the Sierras were a welcome sight, as the plane descended over the mountain forests into Park County.

THAT EVENING LUKE WASTED NO TIME contacting Jimmy to suggest they get together to talk about what transpired in Las Vegas. "This is one time when what happens in Vegas is not going to stay there," he joked. They decided to meet at Luke's duplex so they could talk freely. Jimmy would pick up deli sandwiches. Luke felt an inkling of guilt not inviting Jessie, but this was his and Jimmy's case as he saw it. He knew he was being territorial, but it is not unusual for officers to guard their work, sharing only with their partners until the case cracks wide open. It was no different than his desire to build the Perry case exclusively with Jessie. In fact, deep down, he resented the feds coming Monday.

The evening sky was hazy with smoke from a wildfire to the south. Though it was hundreds of miles away, it still affected the atmosphere. A slight breeze kept the temperature on his patio pleasant. They ate and drank beer while Luke relayed the events from Las Vegas and Jimmy listened intently, interspersing questions here and there.

Luke moved on to what he really wanted to run by his partner, Harkin's accusation that Patricia Woods embezzled the funds. After Jimmy mulled it over in his mind, he was ready to espouse some theories of his own, and that was what he and Hudson did best.

"Well...she would have a hard time getting away with it unless someone looked the other way," he said with a slow start.

"Exactly," Luke replied.

Jimmy observed, "You really want to investigate this, don't you?"

"I'd love to, and hopefully we can pin it down."

The partners relished playing the "whys and what ifs" as Jimmy said, "The big question is why she kept separate records in the first place. I mean, if they were siphoning cash, why leave a paper trail?"

"Maybe the files were her security blanket. If Bergman or someone else tried to rat on her or threaten her, she had incriminating evidence to keep them at bay," Luke guessed.

"Then why didn't she take the evidence with her when the track closed?"

"That piece doesn't fit yet," Luke agreed. "And I'm having a hard time believing in her disappearance without a trace. How about her family and friends? We need their take on all this. Someone has to know where she is. The first thing is to submit a missing person's inquiry."

"But then what if she was having an affair with a co-conspirator in the company?" Jimmy conjectured. "What if she was setting Bergman up by creating those files while she and someone else were on the take?"

"Possible," Luke allowed. "See why I'm intrigued? There are several scenarios. And I didn't like the way Harkin talked about her disappearance, as if it was no big deal."

"Maybe he's trying to throw us off. What if he's the reason she's missing?" Jimmy loved being the devil's advocate.

They bantered back and forth until they ran out of ideas and it was getting dark. Luke finally asked about Maria.

"She's a good partner, learning all the time. How about Jessie?"

"Same thing, working out okay," Luke downplayed his true feelings.

Jimmy goaded him a bit. "Well, if I become a deputy, are we going to be partners again?"

"You've got to learn to ride a horse first," Luke teased back.

CHAPTER 30

Monday morning Hudson briefed the Sheriff on the Vegas trip, but Gates was more interested in discussing the Perry case. They talked in Luke's office where he and Jessie would be interviewing the parents of Emma Miller in an hour. Amber's testimony had identified Emma and her dog. Then the buried child was positively linked through DNA to Perry, while her micro-chipped dog led to the girl's family, who lived near Reno, Nevada.

Jessie entered the room and took a seat beside Luke, across the conference table from the Sheriff. "Sorry, I just went to get coffee," she said, holding the hot Styrofoam cup carefully.

For Harte's benefit, the Sheriff announced, "Besides the Miller girl, we think the first two unidentified girls also came from out of state, probably Nevada. The feds will work with Ned Jackson to order up some new DNA tests and database searches. Hopefully, we'll pinpoint the victims' names and backgrounds, and see if they link to James Perry."

Gates continued, pumped up. "The feds will only be here through Wednesday unless we need them longer. And just so you know where I stand, the Perry case was yours first. The feds are here to help, but if they get too pushy, push back. On an interrogation level, you know more about Perry and how to handle him than they do."

Pleased to have a savvy and supportive boss, Luke grinned, "Thanks, we may need your backing."

On Sunday, while Luke was in Vegas, Jessie had prepped for the Miller's visit, and busied herself updating the murder board for the FBI's benefit on Monday. The number of victims had grown to six, and with the three newest entries, the board looked crowded. Jessie wrote a synopsis of the board's contents, including photographs of each, whether living or dead.

Victim 1 – Amber Richards, **abducted when 6** years old, and by Amber's testimony, she was sexually abused by Mauricio, the Hispanic boyfriend of guardian Leona Richards. Unverified whether Leona was the biological or surrogate mother, both are unaccounted for. In June, Amber was discovered locked in suspect James Perry's home. According to her testimony, he sexually abused her. Now 17, she is in CPS custody, evaluated, and awaiting foster home.

Victim 2 – Unidentified girl, discovered June 11, **buried 12 years ago at 7** years old, dark-haired female, unclothed, arms reaching up. COD was possible asphyxiation. Gravesite revisited by POI June 11, who removed crime scene tape and left a headless doll, with arms upstretched. Amber Richards recognized the doll as hers.

Victim 3 – Unidentified girl, discovered June 12, **buried 13 years ago at 8** years old, fair-haired female, unclothed, arms reaching up. COD was possible asphyxiation. Gravesite revisited by POI June 11.

Victim 4 – Julie Rushing, 6-year-old, unharmed victim of alleged **home invasion June 14** by James Perry. Adult witness is grandmother, Loretta Rushing. Julie's mother is Caroline Rushing.

Victim 5 – Emma Miller, discovered June 15 and buried 6 months. She was abducted July 12, 5 years ago, at 6 years of age. COD was asphyxiation, at age 11. Light haired, buried below her dog, Pepper, black and white heeler mix, microchipped, identified by Amber Richards. Parents, Doug and Leslie Miller, Reno, Nevada, identified their daughter and dog.

Victim 6 – Amber's child, miscarried 1 year ago, a boy, frozen after birth, and later buried under Victim 5. DNA verified parents as James Perry and Amber Richards.

Suspect in custody – James Perry, rides Harley motorcycle, drives 1979 Dodge gray pickup, and lives on Timber Ridge, where he kept two girls in captivity. Currently under psychological analysis, he is charged by PCSO for crimes against victims 1, 4, 5, and 6. Victims 2 and 3 are still awaiting verification of DNA, COD, and ID.

THE MILLERS ARRIVED EARLY at the Sheriff's Office and were escorted in to talk with Luke and Jessie. The murder board, with Emma's cold statistics, had been removed from the room. The photos and autopsy reports were grim enough without more reminders of the heinous crime against their daughter.

The couple was in their mid-thirties and distraught, their faces wracked with grief. The wife, Leslie Miller, was fair-haired and slim. She wore a modest blue dress and carried a tissue to dab her tearful, red eyes. Her husband, Doug, was heavier, not overweight, just stocky. Dressed in slacks and a short-sleeved white shirt, he took a seat beside his wife. At first, they both avoided eye contact, and their pain was palpable.

The four soon went beyond light introductions and were faced with the excruciating task of discussing Emma's abduction and captivity that led to her gruesome death.

Leslie began with an outpouring of emotions. "I can't tell you how much we've anguished over Emma's disappearance and the guilt we've carried. We've relived that day over and over..."

She began to sob, and when she regained some composure, Luke asked her husband, "Maybe you can start from the beginning."

He deferred to his wife. "Actually, I was in a meeting, so Leslie will be more accurate."

They waited until Leslie steeled herself. "We lived on a five acre parcel outside Reno. We bought country property so Emma could have a horse when she got a little older. Emma loved animals. That's why we got her Pepper from the Humane Society."

Leslie paused. "I'll never forget the day she went missing. It was July 12, five years ago. It was a hot, but beautiful afternoon, and Emma wanted to take Pepper for a walk. I told her I had to see our neighbor first and we could go a little later when it cooled down. That maybe Daddy would be home by then and we all three could go. But when I came home, the front gate was open, which frightened me because we were careful about closing gates so Pepper couldn't get out. He liked to chase cars."

Sighing, Leslie took a deep breath. "Of course, I started looking for Emma and Pepper. When I didn't find either one, I became frantic."

Her husband continued, "Leslie called me and I told her to call 911 and report Emma missing. Washoe County Sheriff deputies came out right away and got photos and lots of information about our daughter and Pepper. The APB's went out quickly, but the kidnapper probably drove across the border back into California and hid her, because she was never found."

"That's very possible," Luke confirmed.

"I blame myself for leaving her alone, even if only for a half hour or so," Leslie moaned. "When I was a girl, my parents didn't have to worry about such things. Not when they were nearby. We didn't even lock our doors. I thought we lived in a safe place, but I don't know what's safe anymore."

Doug put his arm around his wife's shoulder and let her cry.

Hudson asked the husband, "Did you ever notice a strange vehicle in the area before the abduction?"

"We knew most of the cars that went down our street because it dead ended. I did see a gray pickup truck a day or two before. It was parked near our house and pulled away when I stepped outside. I didn't think anything of it at the time."

"Did you tell the deputies about it?" Luke inquired.

"Yes, but I didn't have a license plate number, or even notice if it was out of state, so it wasn't much to go on. Just one of those things you see and don't realize it's important at the time. You know?"

Luke persisted, "Mrs. Miller, did you see anything different in the neighborhood before Emma went missing?"

"I never paid much attention to the cars, but I think I saw the pickup one other time. I just can't be sure. I've always wondered whether Emma took Pepper for a little walk and was picked up, or whether she was taken from the fenced yard. Our house set off the street about 200 feet, so she had to be outside at the time. I don't think anyone would risk walking up to the house, and there were no open doors or evidence of that."

"What did the police think happened?" Jessie asked.

"They wouldn't speculate on it, but there was no sign of any scuffle, and Pepper's lead was missing, so it must have been on him, which tells me she willingly left the yard with the dog."

Jessie offered, "Did they bring in a police dog to track Emma and see if she left the property for a walk?"

"No, but I don't see what that would prove," the husband replied.

"It would establish whether she went walking and encountered a stranger driving down the road who picked her up. Or whether she was taken from the yard and put directly into a vehicle," Jessie asserted. "Taking her from her yard is a more overt action than picking up a child randomly on the road." Jessie thought about Perry trying to lure Julie from her house and wished they could establish a pattern.

The couple acknowledged that her supposition made sense. Jessie and Luke had read all the reports and it was obvious the couple had little new information to disclose, so Luke thanked them and said they would be apprised of any new developments.

Jessie ushered the Millers out of the room and when she returned, Luke turned their focus on the FBI's arrival in a few hours.

"Jessie, is there anything you want to discuss about the feds before they get here?"

She hesitated, "Well, yes. I've been ignoring the subject, but there is something you need to know about Agent Jason Lowe."

He frowned and looked at her quizzically, as he often did when trying to judge where she was coming from.

In a faint voice, she said, "He's my ex-husband."

FBI AGENTS JASON LOWE AND ANGEL AMARO arrived after lunch. They met with Sheriff Gates before he introduced the agents to Hudson and Harte. Gates left the four to get acquainted and plan their interrogation of James Perry, who was being transferred to the Sheriff's Office from the county jail.

Taller than six feet, Agent Lowe's presence commanded attention. He was more than handsome in a rugged sort of way—square jaw, strong chiseled features, short dark hair, sharp blue eyes, and fortyish. Agent Amaro shadowed him and their ages contrasted by ten or more years. The younger agent was also striking—shorter, with a tan complexion, and warm brown eyes. Jason flashed a broad smile at Jessie but she avoided his stare.

She turned to Hudson and Amaro and said, "I'd like to have a word with Agent Lowe before we get started. Would you two mind leaving us for a few minutes?"

Luke raised an eyebrow and Angel was close to saying something, but he didn't. Agent Jason Lowe strolled over to her and Jessica found it difficult to hide her distaste. She and Lowe went into the interrogation room and closed the door.

Angel left for the break room and Luke stayed nearby hoping the sound from the interrogation room to the observation room was on. It wasn't, so he watched body language.

"What are you doing here?" Jessie snapped at Jason.

"My job. What's your problem?"

"Of all the agents in the state, you just happen to be assigned to this case? Bullshit! You asked to come here. I was hoping to never see you again."

"I've changed," he smiled, his eyes roving her body.

"I doubt it. A tiger can't change its stripes," she bounced back.

"It seems you haven't changed, either, but now that I'm here, let's be professional about it." He smirked and leaned towards her. His long arm reached out to the wall and his hand braced his body as he looked down at her. She felt trapped by him and cornered against the wall.

"It's good to see you again," he said, turning on his charm.

She ignored his comment. "I'm requesting to talk to Perry first. I have a few issues to cover and I want to do it before he starts backing away, listening to you."

Lowe remained in her space, which made Hudson uncomfortable, but he waited to see Lowe's next move.

"Is that his usual response? To retreat?"

"It is if he feels threatened. Go easy or you'll lose him," she warned.

"Do you feel threatened?" he whispered.

"Go to hell, you bastard," she snapped.

Lowe shoved away from the wall. "Okay, you can go first. But take Angel with you. He needs the experience."

"I will," she said tersely, thinking it was going to get interesting with Jason and Luke side by side in the observation room. Luke wouldn't like him. For starters, her ex was arrogant and condescending. She wondered how long he would last in the FBI.

When Jason opened the door, Luke and Angel stood outside the box, sipping coffee. Lowe asked Amaro to join Harte, explaining they would go first. Close by, Perry lingered in his bright orange jumpsuit, waiting with a correction's officer and his court-appointed lawyer.

Jason and Luke disappeared in the side room to watch and listen, while Angel walked into the box and took a seat beside Jessie. Perry and his lawyer entered and went through introductions. The attorney was Will Wilson, an older gray-haired man probably in his late sixties, short and round.

Briefly, Jessie told Perry she wouldn't be long, only a few questions. Then FBI Agent Jason Lowe would take over. She noticed Perry's resignation. His haughty, contemptuous expressions were missing. Now maybe they could have a dialogue.

"Mr. Perry, you like quotations, so I have one for you," she started, while he remained stoic, listening.

"It's by Dostoyevsky, who said 'Nothing is easier than to denounce the evildoer; nothing is more difficult than to understand him'."

Wilson drummed his fingers on the table and said, "And your point?"

"I'm coming to that," she said too defensively, and looked directly across the table at Perry. "I want to understand a couple of things that are unanswered so far. Maybe you can help."

Still no response from James Perry.

She persisted, "For example, two of the girls we uncovered were buried with their arms reaching upwards. What do you think that means?"

His attorney objected, "You have nothing tying my client to those girls." He warned Perry, "Don't answer."

Jessie shrugged, "I know. We're just supposing."

Perry couldn't resist the opportunity to engage. "If we're just supposing, I'd say they were reaching for heaven, their forever home."

The last two words clicked. The exact words Amber used to describe what Perry told her when he took Emma to her "forever home".

Wilson frowned, displeased by Perry's disclosure.

Softening her voice even more, Jessie said, "Thank you. That makes sense." She offered another assumption. "Those first two girls we found, who had been buried 12 years or so, are still nameless."

"My client knows nothing about them," Wilson insisted, and again reminded Perry not to talk.

"I'm not asking for specifics. It's just frustrating that no one has come forward to claim them. It's as if they were throwaways." Jessie remarked, connecting with Perry's eyes.

Perry shot back, "They were. There're a lot of girls out there like that, you know what I'm sayin'?"

Wilson rolled his eyes and drummed his fingers again.

"Not really," Jessie answered, playing dumb so he could enlighten her. He liked supposing.

"They're the kids of drug addicts, low-lifers, and abusers who should never have had kids in the first place, because they don't deserve them." Perry's anger rose quickly.

Completely irritated, Wilson sneered, "What the hell are we doing here? My client is through with this ridiculous line of questioning."

She rose and gathered her papers. "I just wanted some insights into Mr. Perry."

"Good luck," Perry said. "Hell, if I knew what makes me tick, I wouldn't be here." Then he grinned, not a smirk, but a genuine grin.

"Thanks for talking with me," she smiled back. "Now the 'professionals' will begin."

Jessie left and passed Jason on his way in to the interrogation room. He was on a mission and she was well aware that his heavy-handedness would turn off Perry. She headed for the break room and brought back coffee for Luke and herself, and homemade cookies someone had left on a tray. Quietly, she sat beside him, wondering what Luke's first comment would be. The sound was one-way, so no one could hear them.

Luke patted her on the shoulder. "Good job. You got him to admit why the bodies were buried with their arms up and that they were throwaways. My guess is he picked up the two girls around Reno, likely in or near casinos while their guardians were preoccupied. Or maybe it was more sordid than that."

"Did Jason say anything while he was with you?"

"No, he just sat here with his shit-eating grin, shaking his head in disapproval. You know how he is," Luke joshed.

"Only too well," she sighed, and finished a chocolate-chip cookie while they listened. Jason did all the interrogating while Angel squirmed in his chair, uncomfortable even being in the same room with him.

"I bet you, Jay and Angel won't last long as a team. Angel's too smart and too low key to tolerate him," she offered. "He'll make it in the FBI. But if Jay keeps it up, no one's going to want to work with him."

Luke nodded, offering nothing, and ate his second cookie, comfort food for the moment at hand.

"His nickname on the force was Jay-Lo and he hated it, because of J Lo, the singer," Jessie disclosed with a mischievous grin. "But I didn't dare call him that."

Immediately, Jason started demanding where Perry found the two girls, asking a stream of questions. Wilson tapped his fingers and objected to the probes, one after another.

Lowe hammered, "The FBI has enough to put your client away for life, whether he talks or not."

"We don't know that and neither do you. That's for a jury to decide," Wilson asserted. "Mr. Perry doesn't have to sit here and be browbeaten. This session is over," Wilson declared and crossed his arms over his portly chest, while his client sulked in silence. Perry hadn't said one word to Lowe.

Threatening another round tomorrow, without any "touchy-feely stuff," Jason fumed out of the room and down the hall. Angel gathered his papers and nodded with respect to Perry and his lawyer before he left. Then he ducked into the side room where Jessie and Luke were preparing to leave, too.

"So much for that," Angel said, shrugging his shoulders, and addressing Jessica. "You were right. The guy shuts down if he's intimidated. I know Jason. Anything you can say to help him change his approach would be helpful. He doesn't listen to me."

"Don't look at me," Jessie said. "I've known the guy for years and he's never listened."

Angel opened his mouth to ask something.

"Don't even go there," she smiled.

CHAPTER 31

After two o'clock that night, a phone call awoke Hudson. Calls in the middle of the night were becoming routine, and they were never anything you wanted to hear.

Sheriff Gates himself delivered the message. "James Perry was found dead in his cell about ten minutes ago. I thought you'd want to know, even at this ungodly hour."

Luke bolted upright and shook his head, processing the news. He threw back the sheets and swung around, his feet hitting the carpet. "How did it happen?"

"For openers, he made a big ruckus last evening during dinner. So they put him in solitary confinement. Looking back, that's probably what he wanted."

Luke offered, "I knew he was depressed and told his guard a couple of days ago to get him some counseling and keep an eye on him."

"That's what I wanted to hear," Gates said. "Since the feds were the last to talk to him, they will try to pass the buck as to who agitated him or what put him over the edge."

"No doubt, but we're in the clear," Luke assured the Sheriff. "I watched the entire interrogation. Harte went easy on him. In fact, Agent Lowe called her questioning 'touchy-feely'."

"That asshole," Gates grumbled, and Luke suppressed a chuckle. "I wanted to get your impressions before the media feeding frenzy begins."

"I can tell you, Harte's questioning was low key and she managed to get two important clues out of Perry. She warned Lowe to go easy. That's what experience taught us about him when I got heavy-handed.

Gates listened and Luke continued, "I didn't talk to Perry at all and deferred to the agents. Lowe pushed hard and Perry clammed up, saying nothing. Lowe said they had enough to put Perry away for life. That's when his lawyer stopped the interrogation and they left. Agent Amaro didn't get a word in edgewise. Lowe left Perry with the threat they would be back at it again today."

Gates asked the sensitive question. "Did you see a need to intervene?"

"Definitely, I would have, if his attorney hadn't been present. But Wilson had it under control as much as I could have, so I saw no reason to interfere."

"That's all I wanted to know," Gates promised him. "I've got your backside. Don't worry about the feds."

"Good," Luke said. "I appreciate your confidence. But how did Perry do it, anyway?"

"Strangulation. He made a crude garrote with a nylon shoestring. He tied it as tight as he could around his neck. Then he used a pencil as a tourniquet to wrap it even tighter and pressed his neck into a pillow and laid on it, so it couldn't release. He was found in bed, facing the wall and covered, so a guard wouldn't have noticed anything for hours. They think Perry did it right after their one o'clock routine check."

Gates paused in silence. "Any death is hard to take. He's at the morgue, and Jackson will be examining him to verify time and cause of death."

Another lull. "He left a note," Gates added. "It's not specific, but it says a lot. You can read it when you come in."

"Should I come in now?" Luke inquired. Going back to sleep would be impossible.

"There's nothing you can do right at the moment, except we haven't notified Harte. Do you want to, or should we tell her?" Gates asked.

"I'll do it," Luke volunteered, knowing how sensitive she was. He added, "Amber Richard's caseworker should be notified, too, so she isn't caught off-guard with the morning news. And she can tell Amber, so the kid doesn't find out some other way."

"I hadn't thought of that, but it should be done. Thanks, Hudson," Gates said and ended the call.

In a stupor, Luke sat on the edge of the bed, considering his call to Jessie, who might prefer to call CPS. Death was so final and never easy.

HALF-HEARTEDLY, LUKE REPORTED TO THE SHERIFF'S OFFICE around eight. Jessie had just arrived, too, but she told him she was in no mood to deal with Jason and promptly disappeared.

A half hour later, Jason Lowe ambled into Luke's office, with Agent Amaro in tow, and announced, "I've just talked with the Sheriff and told him we're going to pack up and leave. It's all over now. Don't worry about anything negative in my report about Perry's death. As I see it, the suicide was coming regardless of anything we could have said or done."

Luke somewhat agreed, but if anyone rattled Perry, it was Jason. Angel listened while Lowe spouted on, in detached, clinical terms. "The Sheriff showed me Perry suicide note. The guy chose his last words carefully, words he'd thought about for a long time. And he picked an inconspicuous way to do himself in. One pretty much guaranteed for success. He was a suicide candidate sooner or later."

Lowe dropped some files on Luke's desk and continued, "Here are the missing persons' reports on the two girls, plus one on a Patricia Woods. Of course, even with DNA from the two girls' teeth, it doesn't do any good if we have nothing to match it with, and we don't."

Jason quizzed, "Who's Patricia Woods?"

"A woman missing from another case we've just re-opened," Luke answered.

"That's a strange one, too," Jason remarked. "No one has reported her missing, either. Where are the families in all these crimes?"

Luke grimaced, "Beats me. They're more than dead. They're forgotten."

"Well, you have your work cut out for you, Detective." Jason flashed a sly grin. "Take good care of Jessica for me," he winked. Hudson did his best to appear undaunted by the asinine comment.

Jason motioned for Angel to follow and headed out the door without looking back, taking arrogant strides down the hall.

The younger agent held back. "If you need another fed sometime, give me a call. I'd like to work with you again. And I'll come alone," he smiled.

"We just might, and I'll keep you in mind, as long as your sidekick stays home."

"He's not *my* choice, either, but the pairing was decided by someone above my pay grade," Angel grinned playfully.

They shook hands, and Angel left, walking towards Jason, who stood at the end of the hall, hands on his hips, waiting with an impatient glare. Luke anticipated working with Amaro again, if the Long Meadows case evolved into an across-state-lines investigation.

BEFORE TEN IN THE MORNING, KATE IRVING was standing at Luke's office door. Jessie took the hint and left, while Kate invited herself in, took a seat, and posed with a tablet in hand.

"I was good, don't you think?" she started with a smile, her skirt hiked above her crossed knees. "I held off bothering you while the feds were here, but now I'm hoping you have some inside information regarding James Perry's suicide."

Luke was tired and frazzled. Kate only added to that, so he sighed and said, "You know the routine at the Sheriff's Office. You want to know something, go to communications."

She frowned and complained, "I miss being a real reporter, going to the sources instead of being hand fed. I'll just write what I can get my hands on and not worry about the consequences. These days it's easier to apologize than ask for permission."

Hudson identified with her resolve to uncover the facts.

"Actually, I do have a scoop for you, only it's about another case," he announced, soothing her frustrations. "And it's fresh news that I haven't mentioned to anyone else."

She grinned, "Now you have my attention."

Planting information that he hoped would further the Long Meadows case, he informed her the Sheriff's Office was re-opening the case. "Furthermore," he added, "the case has completely changed. While Trackon Corporation owned the track, large amounts of money were unaccounted for, and the track's former financial director, Patricia Woods, is missing."

Her eyes were wide. "Who do you think took the money?"

"That's what we're investigating. If Woods would come forward, she could be instrumental in clarifying a number of unanswered questions. We'll get there on our own, but it just takes longer. If she fears retribution, we can safe-guard her with the Witness Protection Program."

"Wow, this is potentially another big one," she noted.

"You bet it is," he assured her, building the case larger. "The ramifications are far reaching. But one thing is clear, the Zayet Corporation is in no way implicated, and owner, Abe Zayet, has been extremely accommodating."

He answered a few more questions before Kate rose and promised, "You'll see this in tomorrow's *Sun*. It was worth the wait. Thanks..."

"Just don't name your source," he requested, and she nodded okay.

Luke hadn't cleared it with the Sheriff, but he planned to tell him. He trusted Gates would agree with his reasons for the "leak." If he didn't, it was too late.

CHAPTER 32

A week later, on a Friday, James Perry, age 41, was laid to rest in the Bidwell Cemetery. Calls to the Mayor's Office and County Supervisors poured in criticizing his burial place, until the Sheriff's Office issued a statement saying this is where his mother wanted him buried, and everyone deserves to rest in peace. That put an end to the controversy.

The graveside service was heavily guarded by police, keeping the press and malcontents away. Luke chose to stand alongside a sheriff's deputy at a close distance from the proceedings. Since his parents' funeral, he had avoided attending another. He was mostly there for Jessie, who came to support Amber. The Richards girl chose to appear, explaining to Jessie and Ellen that she just wanted to see for herself "that he was gone for good." Perhaps it was closure for the young victim. Amber promised that she would "not say anything or make a scene." They trusted her word.

Robert Perry, the father, had led a grim existence. The man served time for molesting young boys and when released, he died on the streets of San Francisco from a drug overdose.

Janet Perry struggled with waitressing jobs. Earlier in her marriage to Robert, she filed a complaint against him for wife and child abuse when James was pre-school age. A preliminary hearing judge dismissed the charge on lack of evidence and she never filed again, probably fearing her husband's retribution. The scenario was all too familiar. At least, it proved that at some point, James Perry's mother tried to protect him and the system failed her.

The Reverend Andrew Turner, from All Saints Episcopal Church, had agreed to officiate and stood at the head of the grave. Perry's mother stood near him. She resembled her son—tall, lean, and solemn. Her gray hair pulled back in a bun, reddened eyes fixed on the casket, she avoided looking at others and said little, except a quiet, "Thank you for being here." She carried a lifetime of sorrow in her fragile frame.

A plain pine box perched on poles above the shadowy hole, with dirt piled on the far side. A spray of flowers spread over the middle of the coffin. Four women were positioned alongside—Perry's mother, at the head, Ellen and Amber in the middle, and Jessica near the feet. Luke decided to join them and stood next to Jessie at the end of the line. No others gathered beside the open grave.

The location was at the far end of the cemetery, not adjoining any other graves. In time, when the publicity died down, someone would buy the plot next to James Perry on one side. His mother had purchased one on the other side.

Sun filtered through the tall evergreens, leaving a lacy patchwork over the lawn around them. Father Turner, dressed in black, with his traditional white collar, held the Bible and began by reading passages from the letter of Paul to the Romans 7:15-25: "I do not understand my own actions. For I do not do what I want, but I do the very thing I hate...For I know that nothing good dwells within me...I can will what is right, but I cannot do it...I find it to be a law that when I want to do what is good, evil lies close at hand...Wretched man that I am. Who will rescue me from this body of Death?"

Father Turner paused in silence. "These were James Perry's last words, hand written on a note found beside his body. I do not read them in judgment, because only God can judge. I repeated them because with those words he was reaching out, trying to understand his own actions... to the very end.

"We are gathered here for very different reasons, but I believe the one thing we all seek is peace, within ourselves, with God, and with a prayer that James Perry is now at peace.

"We conclude with Psalm 23:4: 'Yea, though I walk through the valley of the shadow of death, I will fear no evil, for Thou art with me; Thy rod and Thy staff, they comfort me. Amen."

Perry's mother broke down and the priest put his arm around her, comforting her as best he could.

Faltering, Amber walked away from the grave with Ellen beside her, and they made their way through the morning sunlight to a CPS car.

Jessie and Luke stepped away as well, each silent in their own thoughts.

"Thanks for joining me," she told him.

"It was the least I could do," he murmured. "As you once said, regardless of all his heinous acts, he was a victim, too."

JESSIE AND LUKE RETURNED TO THE OFFICE but they sat in silence, emotionally drained. They accepted the fact that two of Perry's victims would likely never be identified and claimed by loved ones. Even their killer had a mother who cared enough to bury him.

Time passed interminably slow.

Gates had promised Luke and Jessie the afternoon off, following a short talk with Luke. The Sheriff rang when he was ready, and Hudson went to his office, closing the door behind him.

"Please, have a seat," Gates offered. "And relax, this isn't about Perry. We're moving on."

Relieved, Luke breathed easier.

Settling behind his desk, Gates began, "Now that the Perry case is closing, are you thinking about returning to the Police Department?"

"Not really, I like working here," Luke replied, comfortable with his decision.

"Good, then there's some future plans I want to discuss with you," Gates returned with a smile. He leaned forward, resting an elbow on his desk. "I'd like you to organize the Special Victims Unit. Your title would be Detective Sergeant, under the command of Lieutenant Bailey. I don't visualize it as a large department because we don't have a lot of serious crimes in Park County, as a rule. This summer has been an exception."

Luke nodded agreement.

"As I've mentioned before, the SVU will include homicides, cold cases, and crimes of a violent nature. Getting the unit set up will involve more time with administrative work and less in the field, but I hope we can minimize that some. I know you like detective work."

"I thrive on it, maybe to my own detriment," he grinned.

"How well I know. I still miss investigating," the Sheriff conceded, and paused. "I'm pleased you're staying. It's lonely at the top, and I like bouncing ideas off you."

Luke responded, "Well, at the risk of overdoing it, I admire your leadership style."

The Sheriff posed a question to ferret out if Hudson had given the new position much thought. "Do you have some preliminary ideas on how the SVU should shape up?"

"I think Deputy Lewis would be a good candidate for second in command, and if we get retired detectives working on cold cases, we would free up our full time detectives for the hot ones. Jack Huntsman is a possible and so is my old partner, Charles Shaw."

"That's a hard name to live with," Gates grinned. "I like your suggestions. Run with them."

An easy silence fell between them as they both weighed options.

Gates spoke first. "On the heels of Perry's death, maybe this conversation is untimely, but it sort of fits with seeking closures. I'm figuring you would like to continue investigating the Long Meadows case. I know it's important to you."

"Yes, it's a case I'm itching to solve."

"I believe you will. Any leads from the *Sun* story?"

"Not yet, but it's early."

The Sheriff leaned back in his chair, as he often did when he was distancing himself in thought. He pressed his hands together and brought his fingertips to his lips. He let out a barely audible breath and went on. "Now for two more subjects, both a little touchy."

Luke held his breath.

"First, I'm going to chuck my idea of keeping horses on the Sheriff's Office expenditures. I'm learning something that I think you knew all along. Horses are expensive and hard to justify. We still have a volunteer mounted unit and that's enough."

"What will happen to the two we have?" Luke questioned with apprehension.

"I'll pay any expenses they've accrued to this point out of my own pocket. That way no one can say I spent budget money foolishly or for my personal recreation."

Luke regarded Gates's political savvy, but that wasn't the answer he sought. "I mean, where will they go now?"

"Oh, that. No worries. I need to find a good home for Pusher, and my daughter wants Go Laddie Go. She's horse crazy, and he has potential for jumping and dressage, which are her new passions. She's begging me for a younger, second horse that I can ride and she can show.

She's been shopping at Long Meadows, looking at their rescues, and likes one called White Roses."

"I've seen her race," Luke said, remembering when he and Sally went to the track and watched the mare run for Shawn Monroe. "She's nice."

Gates spoke with enthusiasm Luke hadn't heard before, which left him both envious and pleased. "I want to spend as much quality time as possible with my two girls. Niki is wild about sports, while Jordan lives and breathes horses, so I'm going to take time to ride with her and encourage her to show. I guess this Perry ordeal with the neglected girls changed my priorities."

"Good decision," Luke approved, but still pondered Pusher's fate.

The Sheriff picked up on that. "Would you be interested in Pusher? I'd keep him myself, but Jordan thinks I need something more high powered, like White Roses. Frankly, I think she's over estimating my horsemanship," he laughed.

Luke didn't hesitate, "Pusher is about my speed, so I'll buy him...sure." He expanded on his horse talk. "You've been good to share the horse with me, so please feel free to use Pusher when you want. He's supposedly bomb-proof for parades."

"I'll take you up on that," Gates promised.

Then he leaned forward. "One last thing," he suggested gingerly. "Since your job is changing, you won't need a partner *per se*."

Uneasy, Luke shifted in his chair.

"I gather you'll be working with different deputies, depending on various situations," Gates clarified.

"What's in store for Harte?"

"She's indicated that she'd like to work with Sergeant Thomas in the Narcotics Unit."

Hudson felt possessive and jealous. Gates's information caught him off-guard, and he resented that Jessie hadn't mentioned this move to him first.

Gates sensed his discomfort. "Maybe I wasn't supposed to say anything yet, but she approached me yesterday with the idea. I assumed you knew. She's thinking ahead, I guess."

"It's probably a good move for her," Luke granted. "She's usually one jump ahead of me."

WHEN LUKE LEFT SHERIFF GATES, he wandered back to his office, where Jessie sat, staring out the window. She turned to him and smiled. "I was thinking we should go to lunch and talk. You look like you have lots on your mind. And then we could go horseback riding. It's a beautiful day and we need a break."

He ignored her suggestion and frowned.

"Something's up, isn't it. What did Gates say?"

"You should know."

"Know what?" She sensed him getting riled.

"Why didn't you tell me you were switching to Thomas?"

"Oh, that." She drifted into an awkward silence.

"Yes, *that*. I have a hard time reading you, or even following you."

Now she was the one who bristled. "If I have to explain it to you..."

He stopped her midsentence, "You don't *have* to, but you might *want* to?"

She shrugged, "I was going to tell you, but I didn't want to be presumptuous."

Luke started to interrupt, but she cut him off.

"Let me finish. We both know Gates has been priming you for a leadership position. And I thought some day we might have something more between us." Jessie glanced around as if checking the privacy of their exchange. No one was outside the windows, or waiting at the door.

"So Thomas had an opening and I told him I was interested in taking it." She smiled mischievously, "By now you've either connected the dots and approve, or I misread you."

"I'll get over it," he grinned wryly. "You just caught me by surprise, that's all."

"Well, I was going to talk to you about it, but things got crazy. Anyway, I told you some time ago that maybe we shouldn't be partners."

She worded her thoughts with care. "At least now you won't be my partner or my boss, so we're freer to be who we really are."

"Which is..." he prompted.

"Don't overthink it," she smiled and he chuckled.

Any other thoughts he left dangling, not even sure why. Except this wasn't the time or place to talk. He dropped the subject and told her about the change in the Sheriff's horse program.

"Why didn't he tell me this yesterday when we talked?"

"Maybe he wanted to choose a better time. It's been a rough week for all of us."

Disappointment fell across Jessie's face, and he attempted to cheer her. "You can still ride Pusher. Now, let's get out of here and go to Long Meadows."

BEFORE THEY LEFT THE SHERIFF'S OFFICE, they both went to their locker rooms and changed into casual, cooler tops. He donned a polo shirt and carried his jacket. She put on a sleeveless top and wore it under her sheriff's shirt when they left in his SUV. She tossed her shirt in the back and turned to watch him as he drove and they talked. He glanced at her, admiring the scooped-neck white top she wore, and how well she filled it out. Her mood had brightened already.

The afternoon was perfect track weather, a bit too warm, but a light breeze tempered that, along with slow moving clouds that partially blocked the sun. Timber Ridge loomed on the horizon, rich with dense forest, except where a large section of black, like an enormous scar, marred the mountainside.

The land bordering the track to the east and stretching to the base of Timber Ridge was a golden carpet in the summer sun, grassland that had died and gone to seed, awaiting fall and winter rains. Sprawling subdivisions, a few strip malls, and scattered country properties spread out on three sides of the track's land, occupying much of what once had been countryside.

Despite the encroaching developments, Luke savored the drive to Long Meadows, which stirred memories of family outings at Turf Paradise racetrack in Phoenix. And he enjoyed being around the horses.

After lunch in the clubhouse, he and Jessie followed several races. Jessie was familiar with the racing form and handicapping, so they discussed various entries. More surprising to her was Luke's knowledge of racing and horses, and she liked that about him.

For the fourth race, a three-year-old miler for colts, Luke and Jessie stood along the rail near the finish line so they could be as close as possible. The horses loaded into the starting gate, one or two at a time, with the gate crew urging them into the close quarters. One colt, a black, refused to load. Once in, he tossed around, banging the padded sides. His rowdiness excited the horse next to him and they both fussed and bounced. The jockey on the black bailed off and remounted when the horse settled down. The colt reminded Luke of Dark Saint, who was fractious and full of himself like this one. He checked the program and the colt was O.K. Corral.

The starting gate clanged open and eight horses charged out, except for the black colt. He stumbled out the gate and trailed as the others thundered away. They went into the first turn, a blur of bright jockey silks and shiny-coated horses, with the black still trailing.

On the backstretch, O.K. Corral began to gain ground, sixth, then fourth, and into the home turn he was fighting for second position. The jockey urged him on with his whip, his arms, and his voice. The black surged alongside the leading colt, a dappled gray. The two—black and white—outdistanced the rest of the field. They pounded across the finish line, nose to nose, in a photo finish as the crowd roared and cheered. The two colts ran on, side by side, slowing down while their jockeys stood in the stirrups and finessed them down to a trot. The two riders turned and headed back to the winner's circle, patting their horses.

Luke looked at Jessie and smiled, "Quite a race, huh? I was pulling for O.K. Corral, Arizona and all..."

She smiled back, "I put money on Greyson. Who won, anyway?"

The announcer said to hold all tickets until the photos were made official. After a brief pause, he announced the winner, Greyson by a nose.

"I just won fifty bucks!" Jessie beamed. "Thanks for bringing me here." She reached over and squeezed his hand. "I needed this."

She let go and they walked in silence a few steps. "This morning seems so far away."

"Every day has been like that," Luke observed, "like slow motion."

They made their way to the ticket window and she cashed in her winning ticket.

"You didn't bet?" she asked.

"I seldom do," he admitted. "But this time I should have. I really like the O.K. colt."

"They were both special."

The two made their way to the clubhouse.

"Drinks on me," Jessie invited him, smiling.

They passed a table where a trainer Luke recognized sat alone. He was Frazier Chandler, at least eighty, gray-haired, but tan and robust, with an easy smile. He invited them to join him. Luke introduced Jessie to him and they sat down.

Frazier grinned, "Some race, wadn't it. A humdinger the way those two ding-donged to the wire. I should have had an exacta on 'em. It paid big."

"Jessie won fifty on a ten dollar win ticket," Luke bragged on her.

"Nice goin' young lady," he said.

Jessie smiled and ordered drinks. Frazier passed, saying he had to leave in a few minutes. He looked at Luke and asked, "You're the detective working the track case, aren't you?"

Luke nodded, and the trainer downed some of his tepid coffee and Crown Royal. "I've been around here since Long Meadows opened years ago. There's always been something fishy about the first owners. The scuttle-butt is that money was being taken on the side, but no one ever proved it. I hope you figure it out. That closure was so sudden it cost us horsemen a lot of heartache and money. We had to relocate our stables at the last minute and scramble for stalls anywhere we could get 'em. Well, you probably know the whole story."

"I wish I did," Luke acknowledged, "but someday I will. I think it was Buddha who said, 'Three things cannot be hidden: the sun, the moon, and the truth'."

"Ain't that the truth," Frazier smiled and raised his cup to truth.

As LUKE AND JESSIE LEFT THE TRACK, she guided the conversation back to work. "Don't worry about my new assignment," she announced. "Narcotics will be a new experience and I'm looking forward to the challenge. I'll miss working with you, though."

"Same here. So what do you think of Sergeant Thomas?" He wanted her take on him.

"He's good. I know about his past indiscretions. Like who doesn't? But he's darned good at what he does. He's going to work me into undercover work. And if we're out on K-9 patrol, I'll work with Al Carrara."

Luke didn't like that idea, because statistically one of the most dangerous things a cop could do, other than domestic violence calls, was a routine traffic stop. But he said nothing.

Jessica had made the right move in spite of him. Now they would be under less scrutiny when together. He suggested an out-of-town dinner tomorrow night, but she stopped him.

"Thanks, but I have other plans, like spending time with my brother tomorrow. Bruce and his wife are going to be in Sacramento and I'm driving down to meet them. Want to come along?"

"Maybe another time. I'd like to meet them, but something tells me you need some space."

"I do, just to clear my head."

Luke stopped in front of Jessie's house. "Maybe we can have dinner Sunday night?"

"I'll call you if I get back in time, but I doubt I will," she said and jumped out of the SUV.

Just as he envisioned more closeness, she seemed to be pulling away.

CHAPTER 33

A week passed while Hudson began shaping his new department. He deserted the plain clothes and dressed in a deputy uniform decorated with his badge and three inverted chevrons of a sergeant, trying to get used to the idea of being in charge. The days were uneventful, just paperwork, meetings, and planning, including a proposal to Linc for joining the Special Victims Unit as Corporal, and second in command of the SVU. Lewis accepted without hesitation. Officially now, Luke reported to Lieutenant Bailey, though unofficially, he maintained close ties with Sheriff Gates, and they still went horseback riding almost weekly.

Since Jessie moved to the Narcotics Unit, Luke saw little of her, and just as well. His defense mechanisms were in place again, leaving him reluctant to make the first move. And he questioned the wisdom of getting involved with her even if the opportunity arose. Affairs in law enforcement departments were deadly, because personal attachments clouded judgment in life and death decisions. Jessie was better forgotten. He lied.

When the workday ended the next Monday, Hudson didn't linger. Tired and bored, he drove home, had a drink and left-overs while watching the news, and fell asleep on the couch. Around ten o'clock, he was awakened by his cell phone ringing. He answered, groggy and half awake. It was a central dispatcher who said, "I have an urgent call for you from a Patricia Woods. Do you want to talk to her?"

"What?"

"Patric..."

"I know," he said. "Please put her through."

The line sounded dead.

"Hello?" he searched. "Hello?"

"Oh, hello," a female's voice emerged on the line. "Are you the detective on the Long Meadows case?"

"Yes. I'm Detective Hudson."

"I'm the infamous Patricia Woods, according to the papers."

He scarcely could believe it. "I'd like to talk to you, at length. Where are you?"

"I'm on my way to Bidwell, about twenty minutes from Long Meadows. I want to talk to you, too, but I have to know something first."

"Sure, anything."

"I need your assurance of witness protection. Can you promise me safety?"

"We'll do everything we can."

"Good, because I think I'm being followed," her voice was losing strength.

"Right now?"

"Yes, I shouldn't have come, especially at night," she said, fear rising in her voice.

"Stay with me." He strapped on his gun, scooped up his badge from the coffee table, and bolted to the garage.

"You still there?" He could hear her frantic breathing. "Describe your car."

"I don't know. It's a rental."

He backed out onto the quiet dead-end street.

"Try. What's the make and color?"

"It's white. A Honda, I think."

"License?"

"Nevada, ends with NTE. I just turned off the highway onto Long Meadows Road and he's still behind me."

"Go straight to the track's backside gate. There's always a guard on duty and you'll be safe. I'll find you there. I'm calling for help. Just don't hang up."

He sought to reassure her as he radioed a Code 3, ramping the alert to an emergency and giving dispatch her location. Then he sped towards the track, his red-and-blues flashing.

"Don't speed up," he warned her. "Just drive like you don't know he's back there."

Her voice again, "He's alongside me, trying to run me off the road! What do I do?"

"If he does, stay in the car."

She dropped the phone somewhere on the seat because the sounds were distant, guttural noises.

He hollered into his cell, hoping she could hear, "Put on your flashers and lay on the horn." He heard the blare of her car horn that blocked all other sounds.

He was back on his radio, pushing the urgency of the call.

A sheriff's patrol answered, "We see two cars off the road ahead. The front car is pulling out. A dark truck, Nevada plates, headed towards the track. The other car, white, has flashers on."

"Stay with the woman in the white car. I'll alert dispatch for more backup."

The officer responded 10-4 and signed off.

Luke breathed a little easier and sent dispatch the message for officers to follow the offender. As he turned onto Long Meadows Road, he fully expected to encounter the fleeing suspect coming towards him, unless the guy took a side road. Hudson's siren blared. They had to apprehend him before he ducked into a subdivision, or endangered drivers on the road in a high speed chase.

He passed the entrance to the racetrack and kept driving. The terrain was now more rural. No cop cars were behind him when he spotted the perpetrator's pickup hurtling towards him on the two lane road. Seeing Luke's car and the flashing lights, he swerved onto a side road. Hudson knew that lane led to a large private ranch that raised Angus cattle and Thoroughbreds. The driveway was gated and dead ended at the house.

Slowing down, Luke radioed his position and a 10-78, backup. Pete Morales came on the radio and announced he was near the ranch road. Luke knew him from the Chesney case. He looked in his rearview mirror and saw

Morales tuck in behind him as they headed down the lane to the ranch entrance.

A heavy wrought-iron gate loomed ahead. The suspect swerved left to miss the gate and rammed the field fencing instead, taking at least three posts and a thirty-foot section of fence with him. The trailing fence clung to his truck's undercarriage like heavy netting behind a small boat, and his vehicle ground to a halt.

The man threw open his door and ran, taking several wild shots at the SUVs as he zig-zagged across the pasture. Headlights illuminated the field. Three horses stood like statues, staring at the streaming lights before they snorted, whirled, and galloped into darkness.

Hudson and Morales stopped at the black wrought iron gate and blasted their sirens. Automatically, the sound of emergency alarms triggered the opener, and the huge Rocking R gate swung wide. Cutting the sirens, the two SUVs rolled through. Luke asked Morales to continue on to the ranch house and alert the residents, saying he would go after the suspect.

Following the deputy, Luke looked for a side gate so he could drive into the field. He found a metal gate, opened and closed it, and got back into his SUV. Switching on a side-mounted spotlight, he drove into the field, but couldn't find the guy. He unholstered his Glock, fully expecting the perp to shoot at him from a hidden location. The field was mostly flat, with sparse vegetation, and grass grazed close to the ground. A single barbed-wire strand above the field fencing would deter the man from climbing over and out.

In the spotlight, two horses caught Luke's attention. They stared, snorting at a depression in the ground, then looked up at the lights and trotted away, heads and tails held high. The horses alerted him to the suspect hiding in the irrigation ditch.

His SUV approached the trench and Luke swirled the spotlight into the dry trough. The light beams caught the guy as he scrambled to his feet and ran, taking pop-shots that went astray.

Luke stopped and sprang from his vehicle. Using the door for protection, he shouted, "Police! Stop or I'll shoot!"

But the man kept running wildly. A second set of headlights shone, as Morales joined the scene and kept the suspect well lit. Luke fired a warning shot and the perp fired back, hitting his windshield. Then Hudson aimed low, targeting his legs, but the second shot missed. He dropped the guy with the third bullet.

The man writhed on the ground, rolling in pain.

"Keep your hands up where we can see them or we'll shoot again," Luke hollered, and the man obeyed, moaning in agony.

Pete held his Brite-Lite and weapon on the suspect while Hudson approached him. The fallen guy reached up, hands higher. Luke swept in on the perpetrator's weapon that lay near him and kicked it aside. The man was unshaven, burly, and short, with black hair. He lay on his back while Luke checked him for more weapons, then cuffed him in front, careful not to move him. Bone protruded through the skin, his fibula broken. His leg was bleeding but he would not bleed out.

"I'll call an ambulance," Morales told Hudson and returned to his SUV.

The man became quiet, only his occasional gasps and grunts interrupting the night. Luke chose not to talk to him. Instead, he took in the eerie silence. The stars shone brightly with the waxing moon. Beyond the void, Bidwell's city lights sparkled on the horizon. Four distant horses relaxed and lowered their head to graze. He and Morales waited until the ambulance's far away wail broke the calm.

WHEN THE PARAMEDICS TOOK OVER, Luke asked Pete if he would follow the ambulance to the hospital. He explained that he needed to check on Patricia Woods, the woman the perp had threatened, and that he would join him at the hospital later.

Luke called dispatch and discovered Woods had arrived at the track and was waiting in the clubhouse with Detective Jimmy Kidder. He wondered how in the hell Kidder got to her first, but he was relieved.

Morales left behind the ambulance, and Luke trailed. Outside the entrance gate, Luke stopped and assessed the broken down fence. His ranch upbringing kept him from driving away, leaving mangled fencing on the ground and horses in the field vulnerable. He turned on his lights, figuring his vehicle's pulsating reds and blues would keep any curious horses at bay.

The ranch owner arrived with a hired hand. He thanked Luke for hanging around and together they viewed the damage. Hudson told them the Sheriff's Office would impound the truck and haul it away in the morning. Meanwhile, the owner decided to stretch some new fence and cordon off the area. He said it was too dark to round up the field of horses, and they were riled up already.

Satisfied that the horses were safe, Luke headed to the track. Nearing midnight, it seemed an ungodly hour to question a witness, but apparently she was ready to talk now and he was more than ready to hear her.

Hudson stopped at the Long Meadows main entrance gate and the guard on duty spoke as though they were expecting him.

"Detective Hudson? Miss Woods is with a police officer in the clubhouse," he announced.

Luke parked and went through more security, before he entered the main building which housed the grandstands, the restaurants now closed, and various administrative offices. He took the elevator to the third floor. Sporting his uniform, no questions were asked and still another guard pointed to a table where Jimmy sat talking to Patricia Woods. The lights were dimmed and easy on the eye.

Luke approached them, and smiled, "What the hell are you doing here, Kidder?"

He took a seat before releasing a long sigh.

"Have a drink, Sergeant," Jimmy grinned, pouring brandy and sliding it over to him. "You look like you could use one."

Luke took a sip and Kidder joshed, "I have friends in high places, namely Sergeant Ross, who told me what was happening. When I met up with Miss Woods here, at security, I told her I worked with you on the case. So we've been marking time ever since."

Jimmy was decked out in dark slacks and matching lightweight suit jacket over a white shirt. He commented he wasn't on official duty, and Luke said he didn't know whether he was officially on or off. Kidder smiled.

Patricia Woods was very attractive in a special way, with shoulder length brown hair and eyes that sparkled even through her weariness. She wore casual slacks and a sleeveless top. Her shoulders sagged slightly from the weight of the ordeal.

She looked at Hudson. "I'm okay now, but what a night."

He nodded. "Where have you been for the past three years?"

"I've been in hiding, outside Reno with a friend. I helped out with rent and worked keeping books for a law firm. Ironic, huh?" A faraway smile crossed her lips. "I'm tired of living on the fringe."

Luke leveled his eyes at her.

She glanced away to the track. "I spent over ten years of my life here. So much has changed. For the better, I see." She sipped her brandy and held back. "Now that we're here, I might as well show you where I hid some files that were duplicates. They verify how much was taken."

"The new owner found the files already," he informed her.

"Oh...that's just as well." She stared out the window at the dark track again. "I suppose you think I took the money."

"I don't know what to think," Luke answered. "You tell me."

Jimmy stayed quiet. Obviously, he had worked to calm her down and engaged in small talk about her years at the track. He had left the heavy questioning for Luke.

Hudson glimpsed at the guard who stood discreetly by the clubhouse entrance, far enough away to not over-hear their conversation. Then he returned his eyes to Patricia's. Her hair was wavy with reddish highlights and she gently pushed some strands off her forehead, away from her hazel eyes. She was twenty-eight, but looked older and wiser. She raised the brandy to her mouth, took a delicate sip and then licked her lips. Woods carefully placed the glass in front of her. Luke had not touched his again.

"Before I say anything more, I want to cut a deal," she disclosed. "I took a big risk to come out of hiding. By the way, I assume you got your man?"

She flashed a slight smile and her alluring eyes captured his. He measured how easily a man could be swept in by her. She had a flirtatious way about her that came across as natural and innocent, not provocative.

He tried to concentrate. "Yes, we did. He wasn't very professional or he'd have done a lot more damage to you and me. It was more an attempt to intimidate. He was shot in the leg and is at the hospital by now. Under arrest, so you can sleep easier tonight."

"I guess that's good." She breathed out and said, "So let's make a deal."

"What do you want?" He glimpsed at Jimmy, who tossed back a swallow and shrugged.

"I want immunity." She didn't flinch. "In return, I'll be State's witness and tell all."

Luke let out a labored breath. "It's not that easy. You need legal counsel to work out the details. I'm in no position to bargain. That's done through the District Attorney."

"If I'm arrested, it will ruin my career in finance."

"I can't guarantee you won't be, especially since I haven't heard your story."

Patricia stared out the window again, as if gathering her thoughts before they scattered like wild horses on a windy day.

"I guess I'll have to trust you and the system. I don't have many choices, do I?"

"No, you don't, but you don't have to talk now. You can wait until you have an attorney, and then talk to the D.A.'s office. Whatever you decide, I'll do what I can to make the process as painless as possible."

Letting out a sigh, she reached under her hair and massaged the back of her neck. "I just want to get this behind me, so I can start living a normal life again. I have to start somewhere, and you seem like someone I can trust."

"You don't have much to base that on," he grinned, "except my track record."

She smiled slightly and began, "Then, I'll give you the short version. I have a B.A. in finance, so David Bergman hired me fresh out of college to work for him and his financial advisor. I did that for about a year. Then Long Meadows opened and he thought I could handle being the track's financial director as long as I consulted with his advisor. I suppose the way it went down, Bergman could have been fingered for skimming because he had access to the track's books, and his advisor audited them the first year for us, until Harkin asked him to stop. David Bergman did nothing wrong."

She'd lost interest in the brandy and pushed her half-empty glass aside. Luke took a swig of his. Her disclosure that Bergman was blameless surprised him. He had been so sure that the real estate developer was culpable. Obviously, Bergman's involvement in the drug case prejudiced his judgement on this one, and that bothered him, but he kept quiet and listened.

"Gerald Harkin—Jerry, I called him—became the track manager by the second year. He supposedly had lots of experience with Churchill Downs, but it turned out that he didn't. This track was struggling and he seemed like a logical fit. He demanded a hefty six-figure salary, and the shareholders didn't object."

Patricia Woods stopped, as if pondering why she was disclosing all this. The two detectives didn't rush her, and unpressured, she decided to go on.

"Jerry wasn't handsome, but he was a smooth talker, flattering, and flirtatious."

Luke thought Harkin must have changed a lot in those years, but he said nothing, and Woods continued.

"I was young and impressionable, so I fell for him. He whisked me around Vegas as he gambled and called me his good luck charm. I got caught up in the glamour of dating a racetrack owner and high roller at the tables. He always hopped from casino to casino so he didn't get a reputation as a big-time gambler, and no one knew how much he won or lost...mostly lost."

She gained a second wind and the words flowed easier, so Luke and Jimmy just followed.

"Taking money began as cash bonuses for 'working so hard.' But his gambling habits got the better of him. He saw how easy it was to siphon cash as long as I covered for him, so he increased his demands on me *and* the track's finances.

"Even I could see that the track would collapse under its own weight. A half million a year was cutting into already meager profits. Harkin really couldn't manage well, even if he had been honest. So I confronted Jerry and told him I was through concealing financial evidence of his skimming. First, he tried sweet talking me. You know, the 'but I love you' stuff. When that didn't work, he began to threaten me."

Remembering pained her, but she persevered.

"Finally, Bidwell got a new police chief, and Bergman, already suspicious, went to Chief Walker. Sometime later, David told me about his visit to Walker, cursing the Chief for being so 'chicken shit' as he put it."

Luke suppressed a grin at exactly his own sentiments.

Again her voice lapsed into still air. "I guess you know the rest."

"Not completely," Luke countered. "How was he taking funds without someone getting wise?"

"He took all he could in cash. He really couldn't take from the betting windows because that's well regulated. But he phonied up track maintenance bills, showing larger amounts for track footing, repairs, building materials, any expenses that looked legit that he could pad."

She stopped and went back to her brandy. "Sadly, he did this not only at the expense of the investors, but also the horses and horsemen. I'm not proud of that."

Woods glanced out the large windows at the shadowy track. "He even went so far as to set up a Thoroughbred retirement fund, and then he kept the money while horses went to slaughter. For me, that was the last straw."

Tears welled in her eyes and she inhaled a deep breath.

"What did you get out of it, financially?"

"Nothing. Makes me look pretty stupid, huh?"

Luke caught her eyes, "No, it makes you look pretty smart for not getting in deeper."

He deliberated before saying, "I think your story and evidence will be credible to the D.A.'s office."

She visibly relaxed and let out a soft sigh. She glanced at Jimmy, but Luke spoke. "What did Harkin do with the money? Five million is a lot to hide."

Woods was decisive, a bitterness in her voice. "He hid cash in the walls of his house. But probably half of it he frittered away. He bought a nice car and took me with him on some trips to the Caribbean, but mostly he gambled it. What a waste..."

Luke sensed she was at the end of her testimony. She was tired and so was he, and she had divulged most of what he needed to hear. Her statement would come next, then a warrant for Harkin's arrest on charges of embezzlement, threats, and endangerment.

Hudson asked one last question. "We have copies of your records revealing how much was embezzled. We need you to look through them and prepare to use them as evidence in court. Will you do that?"

"Of course."

He regretted he and Zayet had taken duplicates to Harkin, but it was done. He didn't want to go into that with her tonight. Harkin's defense would have a head start, but with her testimony, it wouldn't save him from prosecution.

The night would be long. He needed to deal with the perpetrator at the hospital. And he would have to arrange a secure place for Woods to stay. Harkin was still a threat until he was in custody. Even then, they would have to remain vigilant until Harkin received strict restraining orders. He explained some of that to her, but her mind was drifting.

Luke called for a patrol car to drive her and he would follow. Jimmy wasn't on duty and though he was still personally involved in the case, he was professionally removed. Kidder said he might as well go home and they'd talk tomorrow.

Hudson had drunk little and it appeared Woods had gone easy, too. He asked Jimmy about the bottle of brandy. Kidder said he requested it and the security guard brought it over. On their way out, Luke recognized the guard from his visits with Zayet. He asked him what they owed and the guard said, "Nothing. It's on the house."

As Hudson followed the deputy's car carrying Woods, he considered the coming days. The perpetrator would be charged, as would Gerald Harkin. He planned to ask for Angel Amaro to go with him to Las Vegas. The FBI presence would give weight to the arrest and make extradition easier. Harkin would be tried in Park County since his crimes were committed here. The entire process might take months.

He passed through the suburbs and entered Bidwell. The streets were all but empty, the night air warm and balmy. He fielded a cell phone call from Jessie.

"Are you okay?"

"Yeah. You're still up at one in the morning?"

"I am when Linc calls to tell me you've been in a shootout."

"It wasn't quite that dramatic," Luke replied.

"Well, he said to tell you that he's at the hospital with the perp, who confessed he was hired by Harkin to scare Woods."

"Good. What else?"

"He said for you to call him, but he thinks you should go home. He can handle whatever else needs to be done tonight."

Luke welcomed the offer. Now that the adrenaline rush had dissipated, he was hitting a low. He'd call Linc and have him arrange security for Patricia Woods.

"Linc's a good man," he said. "Anything else?"

"Yes. Would you stay here tonight?" She paused. "I don't like the idea of you going home to an empty house."

"I'd like that," he said.

CHAPTER 34

Seven months later, into March of a new year, Detective Sergeant Luke Hudson was preparing to leave for a month long vacation. He had taken little time off in the past year, not since he began investigating Jack Monroe's death at Long Meadows Racetrack. Now that he had completed the formation of the Sheriff's Special Victims Unit, it was an opportune time to leave. Linc Lewis was now a Corporal and sported two inverted chevrons on his uniform. He was directly under Luke's command, and would fill in for Hudson the month he was away. Gates thought Hudson needed some serious time off, and that would allow Corporal Lewis to gain more leadership experience.

A cold case division was created within the SVU, staffed with retired detective volunteers. Luke's old partner, Charlie Shaw declined, reluctant to leave his Los Angeles base. Jack Huntsman had signed on and was determined to get more information on the two unidentified victims in the Satin Doll case.

Jimmy Kidder had submitted an application to join the Sheriff's Office as a detective and would work for Hudson. He would likely come on board while Luke was away. Since he and Luke were former partners, the election would be unbiased with Luke removed from the process.

On Tuesday, as Luke worked on tying up loose ends, he recalled the final outcome of the Long Meadows case. After his arrest, Gerald Harkin accepted a plea bargain with the court on three major counts. Charges were dropped against Harkin for recklessly endangering Patricia Woods, with the stipulation that he would not have contact with her in any way. He was warned that any attempt to harm her again could lead to felony charges. Harkin got the picture.

Under California law Gerald Harkin was charged with felony grand theft embezzlement, punishable by three or more years in prison. With Patricia Woods's testimony and financial records to back her, he couldn't finagle his way out, so he pleaded guilty to the charges. He and his attorney wrangled with the court over a restitution payout of $5 million dollars to be divided among his three business partners. In the end, he and his lawyer settled with the judge on one-point-five million each, shaving a half million dollars off his debt. Luke doubted the guy would manage to pay back that much in a lifetime, considering his marginal Trackon Corporation, but the court worked out a lien structure based on his ability to pay. In exchange, Harkin avoided incarceration, as long as he lived up to the terms of his plea bargain.

Even though Patricia Woods had turned State's witness, Hudson fought to keep her from being cited as Harkin's accomplice. He argued without her cooperation, they would have no case. An accountant corroborated that, stating that the second set of books, on which Harkin's conviction was based, would mean little without her testimony. The fact that she covered for Harkin but did not take money saved her from formal charges. Hudson found some consolation in the settlement. At least Harkin was held responsible for most of his criminal misconduct.

Patricia Woods remained in the area, working for Bergman Enterprises. Luke speculated that recently she and Jimmy Kidder had become close. How close he didn't know, didn't ask, and Jimmy didn't say. She was about his age but certainly worldlier. Whatever their relationship, Kidder was removed from her professionally because he was never officially part of the Harkin case.

The same was not true for Luke. The last thing he wanted was another flawed relationship, so he had distanced himself from Jessie. She found the stalemate frustrating and eventually became withdrawn. He accepted it, sometimes wondering if his work was a convenient excuse.

Feeling restless, Luke stood, put on a coat, and left his office. He poured a cup of coffee in the break room and stepped out into a small courtyard where officers gathered to smoke or talk and eat. This morning it was empty, too chilly, even though the sun shone through an opening in the clouds. He took a seat on a cold concrete bench and let his mind drift back to the balmy summer night when he apprehended Patricia Woods's assailant.

THE LAST TIME HE AND JESSIE WERE ALONE together was that same night, seven months ago. She had invited him to stay at her place after the incident, so he wouldn't go "home to an empty house."

"I'd like that," he had said, but he had second thoughts as he pulled into her driveway.

Jessie peeked from behind the door when she unlatched the chain and let him in. She wore shorts and a loose-hanging, sleeveless satin top that was both elegant and seductive, especially with nothing under it.

She closed the door and greeted him with a warm embrace, leaving little to his imagination as she dissolved into him and her inviting, fragrant body pressed against him. She was tantalizing, but he was reticent.

Jessie stepped back and holding his hands, she smiled. "Would you like a drink?"

"Go ahead," he said. "But I'd just like to talk. I almost fell asleep driving here."

"Of course," she said and slipped off to the kitchen. She returned with a Disaronno for both of them.

"Just in case you change your mind," she demurred, and left his glass on the coffee table in front of him. Then she came around the table, took a sip of her drink, and sat down on the sofa beside him, tucking her willowy legs under her so she could face him. Her golden hair, which she usually wore back, fell on bare shoulders.

Even when he was tired, she loved looking at him—the strong features, his deep, intense blue eyes, a wry smile, hints of gray in his dark hair—and anticipating the feel of his body.

She rested her hand on his thigh and leaned into him with a light, delicate kiss, but he knew where this was going and it seemed out of sync. Maybe it was because she hadn't been there tonight, hadn't experienced what he'd just been through. Maybe she felt uninhibited because he was no longer her boss. How had she put it? *We're freer to be who we really are.* But he didn't feel any freer. He felt more pressured than ever by new responsibilities and Gates's high expectations of him.

Uneasy, he pulled away. As much as he wanted her, if he spent the night, their encounter would be short-lived, a repeat of Sonia.

"Jessie, I should leave," he murmured, noting rejection in her eyes. "I'm exhausted and need to go home. To sleep on what happened tonight. I know you understand."

She nodded, but disappointment was still on her face.

"You are beautiful and caring and exciting. And I'm very fond of you," he added. "But I don't think we should see each other like this."

"Out of uniform?" she teased, releasing some of their tension.

"Yes," he grinned back at her. "Even if I *am* as tempted as Adam was to Eve."

Deep down, she knew he was right. "Okay," she acquiesced. "Please don't think less of me."

"Of course not," he reassured her. "I think more of you...for understanding."

She relaxed her shoulders and sighed. "Linc can fill me in tomorrow. I agree. You do need to go home."

He kissed her on the forehead. "I'll show myself out," he said, and rose to leave.

"Drive carefully," she replied, "and call me when you get home, so I know you're safe."

"I will," he promised, and looked back with a wistful smile.

ENOUGH REMINISCING ABOUT THE PAST, Luke shivered, dropped his empty Styrofoam cup in the trash bin, and went back inside the warm building. When he reached his office, his phone was ringing, with Abe Zayet on the line.

"Detective Hudson," he said in his customary proper manner. "If you have time this week, I'd like to meet with you here at the racetrack. I have something to discuss with you."

There was silence on Luke's end of the line.

Zayet laughed, "Don't worry. It's not a new case or a continuation of the old one."

Luke suggested, "I can meet with you at five-thirty today, if that works for you."

"Yes, and bring Detective Kidder if you'd like." Zayet hung up, leaving Luke guessing.

Luke and Jimmy left for Long Meadows after five. The afternoon threatened rain in the unpredictable March air. After they cleared commuter traffic, Luke finagled Patricia Woods into the conversation. "I hear she's working for Bergman. Any truth to that?" he asked, knowing the answer.

"Yeah, it was pretty decent of him to hire her because it will reestablish her credibility."

Finding the perfect moment to prod the kid, Luke flashed a bemused grin. "What's with you and Woods, anyway? Personally, I mean."

"We're just friends. It's a little awkward, me being with the PD and all."

Kidder bounced the question back, "While we're on the subject, what's with you and Harte?"

"I wish I knew," Luke pondered. "We're just friends, too, but I see less and less of her. We used to ride horses together, but lately she's been running back and forth to Sonoma County. My guess is that her folks found a suitor for her. They were leery of cops after she married and divorced Jason Lowe."

"Well, whoever, there's someone out there for you. I can just feel it."

"You're always saying that," Luke grinned, and pulled into the Long Meadows parking lot.

Tuesday was a dark day, no racing. The track was dim in the fading gray dusk. They took the elevator to the third floor and Zayet waved them to his clubhouse table. Abe stood, shook hands, and invited them to sit. Luke did a double-take at the drink in front of Abe, which appeared to be a shot of bourbon or whiskey.

"I drink on special occasions," Abe said, noticing Luke's stare. He confessed, "I'm not Muslim. I'm a Coptic Christian. I go to the Greek Orthodox Church here in town."

"It's none of my business, really," Luke smiled. "Detectives are always trying to put two and two together, even when it's unwarranted. It's an occupational hazard."

Abe laughed, "No problem. Won't you join me in a drink? I'm the bartender."

The two detectives said they'd have what he was having and he brought over a bottle of Hennessy's Cognac and two more glasses from the bar.

Zayet looked at Luke and forged ahead with his reason for the meeting. "I'm considering hiring a law enforcement liaison person, and since you've been our contact with the Sheriff's Office, I thought you might have some thoughts on that. I want someone with an extensive law enforcement background who knows how to bridge whatever happens here with the right people in the Police Department or Sheriff's Office. What do you think?"

"It makes sense. Sounds like you want someone who can quickly decide if an issue here can be handled internally or needs the attention of outside law enforcement."

"Ah, exactly," Zayet concurred. "I think Monroe's death and then the embezzlement case showed me the necessity for such leadership at the top. Most of my security officers come from private security and have a limited police background."

"Yes, I see," Luke agreed. "Do you have anyone in mind?"

Zayet paused, "I'm looking for someone like you, though I know you're not available. I want a person with lots of experience, could even be retired from law enforcement. The job would be part time, though it might evolve into more."

The track owner hesitated. "I've taken the liberty of writing up a job description, if you would be so kind as to look over it and give me some feedback."

"Sure, I'd be glad to," Luke responded.

"Very good, and both of you might think of someone you could recommend." "We'll give it some serious thought," Luke promised. He paused before adding, "You know, since the job isn't full time, you might want someone with a private investigator's license. The investigator could advise you when needed, but would be an independent agent otherwise."

"Ah, that's even better," Zayet beamed. "We have empty space here, near my offices, where the person could set up such an operation. Let me show you."

They left the table and Zayet led them past his suite of offices, further down the hall to a suite of rooms—a reception area, three offices, an open space for a break room or conferencing, and a private restroom. The walls were painted light, neutral colors, and the windows opened to the east, onto a view of the track's backside, making an overall pleasant place to work. This suite and Zayet's offices were cordoned off from the clubhouse with a separate hall and entrance, so staff and clientele could take the elevator and enter the suites without coming through the public areas on the third floor.

Zayet smiled. "This arrangement could be beneficial for me and the investigator. The rooms have been vacant since we opened. I've been waiting for the right tenants, because this smaller suite is near my offices. An investigator seems a good fit. However, where would you find one?"

Luke didn't have anyone in mind, but said he'd check around after he returned from vacation. Zayet was visibly pleased, as they returned to their table. The track had darkened with the sky, and the three of them were alone, except for a security guard.

"One more thing," Abe Zayet ventured after they sat to finish their drinks. "Mr. Bergman is working back into my good graces, though I will keep an eye on him when he races here again."

"What's he doing," Luke queried, raising an eyebrow.

"He is donating all of his monies from the Harkin settlement to our rescue program. And he is paying it forward, putting one-and-a-half million in our fund now rather than piecemeal, so we can plan ahead."

"That's very generous of him," Luke admitted.

Zayet looked at Hudson and changed the subject. "Do you still ride?"

"Yes, I go riding about once a week with the Sheriff. We just enjoy the trails and talk. Sometimes his daughter joins us on another track rescue. But I'm still trying to get Jimmy on a horse."

Luke looked at Jimmy, who quipped, "Riding's easy. Falling's the hard part."

They laughed and said their goodbyes.

JESSIE DROPPED BY LUKE'S OFFICE ON THURSDAY. Dressed in uniform, she closed the door behind her. Her hair sparkled with raindrops and her cheeks blushed from being outside in the cold wind.

"I wanted to say goodbye before you leave on vacation," she announced. "I won't be here tomorrow, when you leave."

"Are you going out of town?" he asked, curious.

"Yeah, back to Healdsburg. You may have heard, but my folks introduced me to a lawyer. He's about forty, a friend of Bruce's. My parents were so afraid I'd fall in love with another officer." With a tinge of melancholy, she added, "And I almost did."

An awkward silence fell between them before she found the words to continue. "Oh...I have news about Amber Richards."

"Good, I've wondered about her." Luke welcomed moving on.

The last he heard, Amber's case worker had approved Emma's parents, Doug and Leslie Miller, to foster the girl. The fact that they lived out of state involved extra hoops, time, and paperwork. Amber left after the start of the school year, so she'd been in her new home about six months. Since Doug was a high school counselor and Leslie, a teacher, CPS reasoned that they would be well qualified guardians.

Jessie smiled, "Amber is doing well. Leslie Miller called me a few days ago and filled me in. She said they hired a private tutor, a great gal who is home schooling Amber, as well as taking her places to expand her social life. Things like swimming lessons at the Y, an art class, a book club, and so on. Amber had adjustment problems at first, as to be expected, so the Millers were afraid to throw her into public education."

"I should think a big high school would have been overwhelming," Luke contributed.

"Exactly. If she passes the entrance exams, they will ease her into a community college in the Reno area. If not, they'll continue her home schooling. They seem to be making a lot of right decisions for the girl, and they think the world of her."

"How well does Amber get along with Doug Miller?" he asked.

"Apparently, okay. Leslie said she is learning what a real family is like, which will be invaluable when she starts dating, and eventually gets married and has kids of her own. Leslie says Amber is determined not to make the mistakes that were made in her childhood. Isn't that good news?" Jessie beamed.

"Yes, very good."

"And one more thing. She has legally changed her name to Amber Miller. Leslie was happy about that."

Another pause and Jessie fidgeted in her chair. "This isn't for publication yet, but I'm planning to leave the Sheriff's Office."

Luke frowned and leaned forward in anticipation of yet another of her unforeseen surprises.

"I'm moving back to the Sonoma area," she revealed. "I've mentioned it to Linc, and I'll turn in my resignation to Sergeant Thomas Monday. So I won't be here when you get back."

"Are you going into police work in Sonoma County?"

"No," she confided. "I'm going to work with Child Protective Services. Who would have guessed?"

"I would have," Luke answered. "I always thought law enforcement wasn't your heart's calling."

"You were right. In fact, you were right about so many things. I learned a lot from you and I'll never forget you." Her eyes turned misty. "You're a good man, Luke, and someone will come your way. Someone much better suited for you than I was...though I sure was infatuated with you."

She let him think on that and he smiled, remembering their last time together.

"We learned from each other," he said.

THE AFTERNOON WORE ON TOWARDS FIVE O'CLOCK. He fielded a couple of calls and conferred with Lewis about some outstanding cases. Linc's readiness for a month in charge was palpable. Corporal Lewis was a good choice for second in command.

Luke sighed and watched the wall clock ticking the minutes away. He contemplated the weeks ahead. First he'd visit his brother and wife, and their two teenage sons, near Prescott, Arizona. He hadn't seen them in well over a year. Driving through Williamson Valley, past rugged Granite Mountain, he'd arrive at the old cattle ranch homestead where he was raised. March was vibrant in Prescott, a mixture of sunshine and unpredictable storms, much like Bidwell. The rolling grassy hills, dotted with junipers, would be greening before the summer heat.

At the most, he would stay a week with his brother. *Then what?* Luke detested vacationing alone and Jimmy would be working. He'd have to think of something new to occupy the other three weeks. Maybe a month away was too long.

It was nearing time to leave, and he thought about going to the stables, not to ride, just to be around the horses. But it was rainy and approaching nightfall. A bitter wind blustered outside his window, swaying the pine branches. A smaller, lone pine swirled like a whirling dervish.

In a downer, restless mood, he opted not to be with anyone, even Jimmy. Instead, he decided to stop at a deli for takeout clam chowder and a salad, and eat at home.

When he parked in his garage and entered the house, the rooms were dark and cold. He flicked on a light switch, turned up the thermostat, and carried the food into the kitchen. What he really wanted was a drink.

Pensive, he took the Maker's Mark from the liquor shelf and stared at the signature red wax top. He had read that each glass bottle was filled with Kentucky bourbon, capped off, and the top several inches was hand-dipped into a hot, red wax. Then turned upright, the wax flowed freely down the upper third of the bottle, until it cooled and set like a lava flow gone cold. It was a reflection of his personal life—the flow had stopped, waiting for someone to break open the seal.

He smiled at his foolish analogy—something a writer or some poet would dream up. Pouring a shot over ice, he sauntered into the living room and turned on the gas fireplace. Music, TV news, not even a book appealed to him. He took off his coat, removed his gun and badge, and sat down, sinking into the leather sofa.

Then he noticed the blinking red light on his landline. He was not particularly in the mood to talk to anyone, but he listened to the message anyway. A woman's voice, sultry and self-assured, filled his ear. "Hi, Luke. Please give me a call when it's convenient." She repeated her phone number.

Sally perhaps? But it didn't sound quite like her, and the area code was different. Maybe she had moved. Curiosity got the better of him.

He hesitated, tossed back a swallow of bourbon, and dialed the number. He was about to hang up when the same cool voice came on the line. "Hello?"

"This is Luke Hudson returning your call."

"Luke...this is Sonia. Sonia Lantz."

He was speechless, so he took a gulp of bourbon in the hanging silence.

"Sorry I didn't identify myself in the message, but I was afraid you wouldn't return my call. I hope you don't mind," she said, waiting for some reassurance.

"No...of course not," he replied. "It's good to hear from you. I was just thinking about you, not that long ago."

"I've thought of you often, I must admit," she said in the stubborn lull.

"What are you doing these days?" he asked to fill the gap.

"I'm still with the Santa Monica PD, but I just finished my twentieth year, so I can leave with full retirement. I ran into Charlie for the first time in a couple of years and he gave me your card, said you were a Detective Sergeant now and head a Special Victims Unit. He thought you were looking for another detective or two, and I'm contemplating a move." Her voice stayed confident and strong.

He said nothing, engulfed in thought.

She grappled with the charged, silent moments. "I'm sorry. I shouldn't have called. This is awkward for both of us."

"No, please," he rushed. "You just caught me off guard."

"I know, and I didn't mean to. I guess I didn't think it through."

"No apologies necessary." He took a sip of his drink and stared into the amber liquor.

"Let's come back to work later," he suggested, buying time. "How's your personal life? Are you married?"

"No, I'm still single," she said. "It seems to suit me."

Memories stirred of his last passionate night with her and he fought to refocus on her question.

"And you...are you married?"

"No, only to my work," he conceded, and became reflective again.

"Look, I've blind-sided you..." She stopped midsentence. "What if we both stand back. You think about it, and if you're interested in hiring me, or you know of some other opening, we could talk next week. I could come to Bidwell and meet with you about a position. How does that sound?"

Her visit would cut into his vacation plans with his brother, but he'd work it out.

"It's the best proposal I've had in a long time," he said and they laughed together, easing the tension.

He turned serious again and his voice softened. "I'm glad you called. I was never comfortable with the way our relationship ended."

"I know. It was difficult for both of us, but let's not revisit the past. You might not even like me now, other than professionally," she added. "If I must say so, I racked up some pretty impressive commendations through the years."

"I'm sure you did."

Charlie had told him Sonia was highly regarded, with outstanding credentials.

"Just give me a minute," he said, turning local detective opportunities over in his mind. He knew there would be an opening at the Bidwell Police Department if Kidder took a detective position in the Sheriff's Office, but the BPD might prefer to promote someone from within their ranks.

And there might be a position in Narcotics, with Jessica leaving, but Sonia was stirring too many old feelings and desires, and he didn't want another Harte situation. Then he remembered Zayet's proposal.

"Does it have to be a detective position?" he asked.

"No, I'm open to other ideas."

"Good, I know of an excellent possibility for you." He told her about Zayet's search for a liaison with local law enforcement agencies.

"That sounds promising. I'd like regular hours and something more low key. I've been shot at enough times." She laughed again and he caught himself smiling.

Luke continued, "You'll like Abe Zayet. He's very pleasant, and he thinks the position will expand. Meanwhile, you might consider a P.I. license to augment the part time position."

"That would open a lot of doors," she agreed, and he felt her spark of enthusiasm.

"Before you meet with Zayet, I could show you around and introduce you to the law enforcement agencies here. Give you a tour of Long Meadows, so you get a feel for the place."

A peace drifted between them and Sonia spoke first.

"I'd like to pursue this, Luke. I could fly into Sacramento next week and drive to Bidwell, so I can see the countryside." Her words warmed him.

He had forgotten how much he relished her rich voice and their easy exchanges. Something still endured between them. Otherwise, why would she call him or even consider Bidwell?

His feelings flowed, "The change might be just what you're looking for, Sonia. And I'd like to see you again."

She thanked him, and when the line went dead, he realized he was no longer lonely or cold.

ABOUT THE AUTHOR

S Resler Nelson has been writing throughout her life, producing travel journals, short stories and award winning poetry. **More Than Dead** is her first mystery novel in the Luke Hudson Mystery Series, and Sandy is currently working on the second book, **More Than Gone**. A former high school English and art teacher in Oregon, she has traveled in seven African countries, plus Australia, New Zealand, Turkey, Jordan, Ecuador, parts of Europe and Southeast Asia. Other than writing, her passions include oil painting, singing, and horses, spending years raising and showing Arabians and miniature horses. She grew up in Northern California and lives in Arizona with her husband and two spoiled Shelties.